ARGENT

Argent is a work of fiction.
Many of the characters and events in this book are invented.
Some other characters are real, and also dead, leaving little room for complaints.

Argent copyright 2016
Cover art copyright J Caleb Design 2016
Story & Copy editing by Two Birds Ink
ISBN 978-0-9968957-1-2

Follow Baird Wells on Facebook
Join the official Baird Wells mailing list at http://www.bairdwells.com
You can follow Baird on Twitter: @BairdWells

First Printing: April 2016

To Wes, and all the trips we've taken together around the sun

CHAPTER ONE

Broadmoore, North of London – May 2nd, 1814

Spencer Reed searched the ballroom's churning ocean of color, sorting its noisy crush. More specifically, he sorted the *female* half.

He had come to his friend John's masquerade with one aim: to avoid London. The city's noise and its obligatory social schedule chaffed after months in the field. Not that a ball sounded much more appealing; he'd rather be locked away in solitude.

And yet, all such hopes had been dashed in the first thirty minutes his feet had been back on British soil. A crowd which had gathered in front of his Mayfair townhouse warned of peering and prying which was to follow for days. London's populace was eager for a glimpse of their newly-minted hero, and patriotism and good manners demanded he afford it to them so long as he remained in town. There would be no peace, no anonymity in London; the invitation to John's country estate could not have come at a better time.

There was no riding without stopping every block to make conversation, no walking to the Exchange without arriving wrist-cramped from lifting his hat again and again. Five minutes alone in the study was a rare blessing; Lord Reed being 'not at home' didn't stem well-meaning efforts. There was not true peace to be had; for now, moving masked and unrecognized between the violins and laughter would have to be sufficient.

It *was* sufficient, so much so that he'd warmed to the evening and now pursued a very different aim: company.

Spencer picked now through his choices; both the married and the young ladies were out. He was too old for a midnight tryst *and* a dawn appointment. Women he recognized – there were one or two – were out, as well. His mask afforded him anonymity and he found, despite his earlier reserve, that it was to his liking. He observed the dancers and the men and women seated in ivory silk chairs at the edge of the floor, the quartet's cellist dabbing sweat from his temple at a rest; he observed *them* and kept inconspicuous in a shadow near the terrace doors.

She caught his eye by coincidence, a crimson rose on her black velvet mask flashing when she turned her head and laughed. There was a softness to her cheek which spoke of maturity when it filled out against a smile. A swirling crowd of bandits, devils, and kings vying for her attention hinted, perhaps, at the absence of a husband.

A harlequin, he realized, as he shouldered through the crowd and drifted between islands of revelers. She was turned almost facing him now, and he could see her costume better. Her gown, like her mask, was one half white satin and the other plush black velvet, tailored by someone who'd grasped what her body was capable of. Dark curls swept her crown like a raven's wing and framed her face. Inside his glove, Spencer's fingers twitched at the smooth skin of her bare shoulder. She was made up of textures meant for exploration by a man's hand.

He took the long way through the crowd, jabbed by elbows and whacked by ribbon batons but hardly noticing, his eyes never leaving her. It had been pleasure enough to study her. Now he hungered for more.

Pushing through a rowdy collection of her friends and admirers, he paused behind her and brushed his glove over the warm skin of that tempting bare shoulder. She gasped, spun around, and wide blue eyes behind her mask settled the matter of whether she'd come unescorted. Clearly, she had not expected anyone to touch her.

Bowing low, he held out a hand. He liked her smile, hesitant but warm, full lips turning up at one corner. She opened her mouth to speak but he bridged it with a finger and shook his head.

2

Shoulders relaxing, her smile blossomed and she nodded. She'd grasped his game.

He wrapped her gloved with his and guided her toward the other dancers with an insistent pressure. A low groan of disappointment from her ring of admirers trailed them and he indulged in a small smile. His heart beat with something beyond simple anticipation, something like pleasure. He'd been a *very* young man the last time he'd enjoyed an engagement as much as he was now. Maybe it was her willingness to play along, the confident way she returned his grasp. Her perfume, a musky floral scent, enveloped him each time they paused. He longed to lean in, trace the curve of her neck and catch the scent on her skin.

He pulled her up short as they reached the edge of the dance and turned to face her. Eyes, wide and curious, followed his movements as he removed his gloves. He ran a finger along the band of her white satin one, traced its black embroidery, and hooked it. Tugging slowly to the wrist as he would her gown, her shift, he stripped each of her fingers in turn and undressed her hand. He considered her slender fingers against his stouter, rougher ones, heart pounding a pace faster at the thought of slipping them together.

Folding up her glove, he tucked its bundle into his pocket with a wink. If she wanted it back, it would cost her a waltz.

She was watching him, her head cocked and eyes half lidded behind her mask, where a question played out. Whatever she struggled with, he knew she'd answered it when she reached for him.

Spencer fit his naked hand over hers, calloused palm pressing her smooth one and creating an electric current which sang through his body. They stood there a moment, a charged tension humming between them, their eyes locked. He pressed her back, she arched, and they were off.

Two steps back and they swirled in with the others. Velvet at her waist clung to his hand, whispering the heat of her body against his palm. At first, she only rested fingers at his shoulder, a hesitant fluttering through his sleeve. When he led her through the first turn she gripped tighter, an intimate pressure which didn't relinquish.

3

Spencer drank her in, from a surprisingly modest neckline to the crown of her head. She was older; he had been correct. She was more beautiful than he'd appreciated at a distance, with a mischievous smile which lit the depths of her cornflower eyes.

He smiled in reply, inhaling sharply with something like joy. He wasn't sure what had come over him, and he wondered at the last time he'd pursued a woman this way. Before Portugal, maybe longer; never with such enthusiasm from his quarry. It had been three years, at least, since something other than a functional arrangement had satisfied his needs. Perhaps it was turning forty, or a musket ball that had been a hair too low to finish him at Toulouse, making him predatory tonight. He wanted to chase, and to win her.

The quartet's last warbling strains found them in amber light at a far corner of the ball room under a welcome cool breath from open terrace doors. Her hand relaxed against his now that their dance had ended, but Spencer had no intention of letting go unless she protested.

He laced fingers tighter between hers and turned. He loped through laughing, pressing bodies, overjoyed when she matched his pace. They passed through the doors out into a moonless spring night. Honeysuckle and early roses mingled with her perfume, and a chill which promised morning dew cooled sweat at his temple. They dashed down the steps and along a dirt path, skirting a tangled hedge. Her footsteps padded gently behind as they ran, matching the pulse hammering in his throat.

When they rounded a corner of the orangerie's wall, jerked her to him, and trapped her between his body and the greenhouse's coarse stone. She gasped, caught her balance with hands pressed to his chest, and sighed. He shivered and leaned into her warmth against a breeze, surprised and thrilled that she had followed him this far. How had he gotten so lucky?

Her arms circled his neck, slender fingers twining in his hair as her lips brushed his in a sweet invitation. Something tightened low in his gut; he may have led the waltz, but his lady was making clear that they were on equal footing now.

4

He rallied, responding with aggressive pressure, catching a tantalizing hint of almond in her mouth. Fingernails raked through hair at the back of his collar, a distinctly feminine assault which tore free a groan. He nipped the hollow beneath her ear in retaliation, the perfume filling his nose as intoxicating as he'd imagined. His reward was a gasp and she arched. Pressure from the contact was his body's undoing.

Grabbing her waist, he hauled her atop a low brick wall bordering the side yard. Rucking up a fistful of her skirts, he jerked them to her hip and chuckled when she pushed at his hand. She was sweet, playful, and he brushed her lips again in response. On his second attempt with her skirts, however, her grasp was trembling and earnest and her hand refused him any farther.

He groaned and surrendered the fabric to bury his face in her curls. He'd made an error somewhere; she had a husband or a lover. Perhaps he'd been too aggressive, or mistaken her enjoyment of the party for more.

He was set to pull away and apologize when something stopped him; her foot brushed his calf, head cradled on his shoulder, and she held him tight. Intrigued, he kissed her under the ear, and she shivered. She seemed perfectly content, judging by her soft panting, to let him continue tracing her neck with his tongue.

Her tentative hand slipped inside his coat, smoothed his chest and darted away, brushing his side through the linen of his shirt. Not, in his experience, the act of an unwilling partner. Her fingers teased the ribbon of his mask and she cradled his cheek and urged his head back. He dared lips against hers, one last kiss before they parted ways.

Her tongue brushed his, shocked him and lit a fuse. Spencer grasped her skirts again in spite of himself; a reflex, in answer to her breasts crushed against him. This time she fell back until her palms caught the wall's edge, not interfering when his trembling fingers traced the top of her stocking. He was nerves and breathless aching; when had anticipation ever affected him so?

Now. His body demanded it. They had crossed some tipping point, his self-control frayed to threads. Stumbling fingers worked over each button of his breeches. Her fists strangled his coat and used it for leverage to fit their mouths together, her soft groans humming against his lips.

"Alexandra!" a man's voice called.

Spencer realized he had caught it faintly, moments earlier and further away, but animal hunger had told him to ignore it. Now, they were nearly caught.

He didn't care. A masquerade, a garden; what was transpiring should hardly surprise anyone. It was tame by comparison to wilder London parties. But the lady was up now, frozen and clinging to the wall's lip.

"Alexandra?" *Halfway down the path.*

Panting, she pressed him back with a hand. She looked to him a moment in silent apology before sliding down, turning and disappearing at a run behind the hedge's screen. Her racing footsteps faded into the darkness, shadow into shadow, and she was gone.

From the opposite direction, a dark figure rounded the corner and coalesced into a familiar shape. "Alix, are you there? Oh, Reed!" John glanced around, turning in a wide, drunken circle. "What are you doing out here?" *A chuckle.* "You out here with a lady?"

Spencer did a poor job of hiding hands inside his coat, stuffing his shirt tail and wrestling with the fall-front of his breeches. He was fourteen all over again. "Amusing. We've been friends, what, near ten years now? Have you ever known me to indulge in garden assignations?" He would not admit to John, even though they were best friends, what he'd been up to; he hated questions.

John crossed his arms. "I've never known you to get foxed and piss in my garden either, but your trousers are only half done up."

"I'll have a word with my tailor about the matter."

John held long arms wide. "Thought I'd do you a kindness, Reed, and assume it was owing to your being with a lady."

"No, Hastings," he admitted, "I am not, as you can well see. And don't use my name." He adjusted his mask, pulled askew by fingers he already missed. "Spoils the mystery."

6

John's head bobbed out of time, under the influence of good wine. "So it does." He planted a fist to his hip. "And just so, I'll thank you not to use *my* name!"

Spencer wondered if John appreciated the irony of his mask hanging around his neck, then shook his head. "I stepped out for some peace, some air. Why've you come?"

"Looking for my cousin, Mrs. Rowan. The Jerseys have arrived and I'd like to make an introduction."

John's cousin, Chas Paton, and his wife Paulina, along with his Chas's sister, Mrs. Rowan, had come from New York to take in a London spring. That detail, and that Paulina had offended John's wife on multiple counts, was all he knew or cared to know. Anyone who greeted Laurel Hastings' hospitality with rudeness was hardly worth his notice.

"You have time to find Mrs. Rowan," Spencer drawled. "Once the Jerseys arrive, it's impossible to get rid of them." The Jerseys, George and Sarah Villiers, made any party a success, and they enjoyed that influence and admiration as much as others enjoyed paying it to them.

Laughing and clucking his tongue, John's long face was disapproval at his brows and amusement on his lips. "Villiers is an old name; high in the heel, Reed. And they're tolerant of Americans, God bless them. Lord and Lady Jersey are good people to rub elbows with."

Exhaling, Spencer rested arms atop the wall, unwilling to have the argument with John about Sarah Villiers' brand of influence. Her snobbishness, her lovers. John and Laurel were looking to move up the social ladder, and there was no arguing that the Jerseys were a necessary rung.

He wouldn't argue over it, not tonight. Tense, frustrated, he was not in a mood for their usual banter. He wanted a silent moment to relish lips on his, perfume which still clung to his shirt.

Perceptive for being so foxed, John didn't press the matter and instead backed up a few steps, weaving on long legs. "If you see her, send her to me directly?"

"How's that, now?"

John shook his head. "My cousin, Mrs. Rowan?"

"Masquerade?" Spencer held out his hands and glanced around. Unlike John, most guests were following the rules.

"Right. Dammit. Um..." John made a shape with his hands that could have been mistaken for water boiling. It was nothing he recognized as descriptive of a woman. "About so tall. Black and white affair and a winged sort of mask. Has a flower on it, if I recall."

Spencer froze. His *body* froze. His lungs stopped and he turned his head without meaning to, his eyes boring into the darkness where his lady had disappeared.

John, mistaking his silence for dismissal, backed a few steps further away. "Enjoy yourself, Reed. See you back inside."

He raised a hand in half salute, still peering into the darkness. *John's cousin.* Guilt, shame, dismissal; he waited for each in turn, but they didn't come.

Alone again, he pulled the glove from his pocket and buried his face in its cool satin, inhaling her scent. "Mrs. Rowan," he whispered into the darkness. A voice whispered back, for him to put her away, to leave it alone. It insisted that their moment was over, its fleeting magic something he couldn't recapture.

A pointless argument. She was a mystery now, a puzzle to be solved. Spencer knew himself too well to believe they were truly done.

CHAPTER TWO

Oakvale, the Reed Estate

Two days later found him less convinced of going out into company in order to find her. There were no masks for protection at Oakvale, and the calling cards were never-ending. In the bustle of activity from waking to sleeping, Spencer began to convince himself that perhaps his garden encounter could never be more than a memory.

Few admirers were deterred by the twenty-five-mile journey from London to Oakvale. He'd muddled through tea with Lady Frances Webster, endured supper with the Duke of Cumberland, and ground away back teeth tolerating Lady Jemma's roving hands and stifling perfume with his virtue intact. The social calls showed no sign of stopping, and nowhere seemed far enough away to escape.

When had he become such a solitary creature? His frustration was compounded by a doubt which at first had tinged the edges of his confidence, but then had taken root, convincing him that the whole Mrs. Rowan affair was a fool's errand.

Against his better judgement, he'd retreated to his study under a black cloud, secure in the knowledge that his brother Bennet would not leave him unmolested for long. He could confess himself to someone who would offer no quarter.

Finishing his tale, he settled deeper into a leather wing-back chair and rested his boot on the clean white hearth, scowling at his brother's obnoxious grin. "It isn't amusing, Bennet."

"It is, actually." Bennet leaned forward, bottle in hand, and replaced the whiskey in Spencer's abandoned glass. "Poor

Reed. Famous in two countries, hounded by beautiful women. What a struggle."

"It's not amusing," he repeated, scrubbing hands over his face. "I nearly plowed my best friend's kin. In his garden."

"But you'd have taken her without reservation, had she been a stranger? Hair splitting." Bennet's handsome features bent into a scowl, a perfect imitation of their father's, and he waved a hand. "I know you enjoy torturing yourself over everything, but it sounds as though you had some help."

He had. Her hands inside his coat, that look in her eyes haunting him for days now. Spencer groaned, sinking deeper in the chair. "You're muddying the water."

"Stop being such a baby," snapped Bennet, draining his tumbler. "Just go and speak with her."

"About what? Waking up in a sweat, or the poor fit of my breeches when she comes to mind? Which is more appropriate conversation?"

It was a genuine question. John had sent an invitation every day, and he was running out of reasons to decline. What would he say to her? Had she puzzled him out? Could they sit stiff-backed across the table from one another and make mindless conversation?

Bennet shrugged, propping up his boots and folding his hands, a posture that signaled return fire. "How true and straight your infantry marches. How many medals you have." He winked. "The size of your *artillery*."

"Stop speaking, Bennet."

Bennet shook his fist. "Just go to John's, see her. This is beyond ridiculous. See what happens, what she says. So you'll have to press some hands and suffer adulation." He snorted and took a long draw from the bottle. "You'll manage."

Spencer admitted that, despite fifteen years between them, his younger brother was sometimes very wise. Admitted it *silently*, of course. Draining his own glass, he crossed his arms. "Fine. I shall go. But not because you've convinced me. I lent John a saddle and I'd like to retrieve it."

Bennet's grin was victorious. "That's more like it. Stick to the stables, and stay clear of the garden."

*　　*　　*

Alix stretched beneath her favorite ivory quilt, raking a fingernail over its red and coral roses, blinking up at the canopy. It was something from home to make her comfortable in England, though she wasn't exactly eaten up with homesickness just now.

She pressed fingers to her lips, smiling, and stretched farther. Her handsome stranger had occupied every waking moment since the ball. At first, she thought he must be an acquaintance, someone to whom John had already introduced her. Surely no *stranger* would touch another with such familiarity, would be so bold. How wrong she'd been. She wasn't well connected to many people in England, certainly none so tall, so quick with a heart-stopping grin, with dark hair as thick and crisp as it looked. Not any man she could call to mind.

She closed her eyes and drew him up in her mind. His eyes might have been green or gray; in the ballroom she'd had no question of their color, but garden shadows and his mask's border had muddied her recollection and made them a shade deeper. Artists hands, or a sculptor; his long fingers had learned her rather than simple touching, explored with a roughness that had made her wonder at a gentleman with a laborer's hands.

It had been on her lips more than once, to question John and try to discover the man's identity, but she had resisted. Sighing, Alix wriggled against her pillows. She didn't *want* to know, not really. That would spoil the mystery, and mystery was all she had now.

So, what if they met again? That question had plagued her too, and she knew the answer. There would be no carrying on as they had at the masquerade. It had been a single moment, magical and impulsive, and *over*. She beat a dimple into her hapless pillow and wriggled onto her side.

Damn John for interrupting.

Making love with a rogue in a garden's inky depths. It only existed in the horrid novels ladies hid beneath the cushions until they were alone. It had been unlike anything she'd done before, and she had been thrilled to come so close, the most fun she'd had in thirty-two years. After, she had expected shame to

11

intrude, some embarrassment at what she'd been willing to do. It never came; her only remorse was over being interrupted.

She yawned. *John, you bastard.*

No matter how much she worked up her nerve, something always spoiled the fun. The horse race from Parson's Green to the bridge, or the time she'd smuggled French brandy into the house, or even the simple act of engaging the native women on a scouting trip back in America. Some prying eye, some wagging tongue, or some crease-faced goodwife was always there to clear their throat or whisper damning gossip to Paulina.

She recalled the sailing trip and shifted uncomfortably against the mattress, pulling her quilt to her chin. *Just to see the fleet come in,* she had lied to Paulina, with her scant savings sewn into the lining of her dress. Had her sister-in-law already known she intended to elope with Edward? It wouldn't have surprised her to find that Paulina's father, Silas, had had her followed by his men, had been watching and digging.

Her face burned at the memory of being escorted through the crowd at the docks, Edward shouting behind her that he loved her, and that she did not have to go. Alix rubbed a fist, smearing tears over tired eyes. She should have stayed on the ship with Edward, should have found the spine to fight Silas's and Paulina's threats. It was simple to blame tattling neighbors or a disapproving parson, but was she really the one at fault? When had she ever had the courage to run and keep running until she outpaced them?

Shifting to get comfortable, Alix decided that she was too tired and too resigned to answer the question.

She should count her luck. It was only their first week in England. She had already laid money on an investment and made a very lasting memory. With a whole spring and then summer ahead, who knew what else could happen?

CHAPTER THREE

Broadmoore, The Hastings Estate

Spencer hadn't appreciated how much he hated John's house until his last deployment through Europe. As ruins went, the house would be an excellent place to visit: a wide lawn, a long pool framed by the boughs of newly green oaks. But it wasn't a ruin, unfortunately. It was a functioning house and grounds, despite having fallen into disrepair a century before. Broadmoore Abbey's crumbling skeleton was a fine landmark but a derelict residence. The house was drafty, dripping, and generally uncomfortable. Its cavernous fireplaces and furnishings would have been in vogue for the last Tudor king. The whole mess had been saddled to John by a father set on keeping tight reins on his heir, the same man who had reputedly sent his own sister running for the colonies, never to return.

In an accident of agreeable circumstances, that sister's children, Chas Paton and his sister Alexandra, were eager to see their homeland. John was anxious for the financial opportunity they offered, happy to make his kin welcome. Chas Paton had managed his family's shipping business to a peak of success and had money – coin John could use to dig himself out from under Broadmoore. In turn, John had connections that the Patons were eager to make use of.

Spencer sighed and stretched his legs farther into the carriage's foot well, longing to be home. Whatever good the army had brought him, it had also meant long nights in wind and rain with thin blankets and worse rations. He was done with all that; he wanted a roaring fire, a sturdy chair, and the nearly endless parade of good food from his own Oakvale kitchens.

13

John was a friend, though, and he would tolerate Broadmoore for the company. Intriguing company now, he amended. Mrs. Rowan would be there, too. After Bennet's prodding, he'd found renewed courage, so why was he struggling now with seeing her?

Because he didn't want to meet her, to know her. The *real* her. He wanted to preserve quite possibly his only impulsive decision outside of a battlefield. Her voice wouldn't be as deep and rich as he'd imagined. There would be a whining point to the sound of her words. She would be too well read to be talked to or so vacuous as to be limited to parasols and ribbons.

Spencer laughed at himself, looking out the window at his waiting hosts. Age had made him impatient, rigid. Bored. Something in Mrs. Rowan's eyes, a clever playfulness when he had taken her hand, scolded that he was wrong to worry. Spencer rejected his fear and brushed away a disappointment which promised that reality could never equal his imagination.

The carriage lurched to a stop. Spencer bounded down, planted his hat back on his head and raised a hand to John and Laurel where they waited at the yard's edge.

He started forward, girding himself. *Once more into the breach.*

*   *   *

Seated before a frightened little desk in the small parlor, Alix hunched and braced elbows as she wrote, and tried ignoring an aching back and jostling surface in equal measure. The desk's joints creaked in protest each time she dipped her quill. It was impossible to give her correspondence the attention it deserved while not panicking under the belief her work surface would collapse and summon the very people she'd been avoiding. The last thing she needed was Paulina catching on to her scheme.

Second to last was Chas. At the thought of his name she stabbed the quill and tapped it with violence, earning a cry from the ancient furniture. Her brother. Her own brother, the traitor. It was enough to swallow, that he'd married into a family bearing them so much ill will, allowed his wife and father-in-law dominion over his person and business. Subjecting her to it…

14

She paused, drew a breath and held it, quill suspended long enough that a drop of ink fell onto her letter. She didn't bother blotting up the stain, determined for the first time in years to follow her thoughts on Chas. There were no memories of him during their father's final years; why had she expected more afterward? Because she had told herself then, as much as before and a long while after, that he would grow up. Without Father to take the lead, Chas would become a man, set Paulina in her place, and break Silas's grip.

Evidence to the contrary had begun with a small thing; Chas's promise to hold her money from the sale of their family home. Just, he had promised, until she and Mister Meacham could settle what to do with it.

Emily Aldridge's body had been found washed up on the river bank just a few weeks later. Alix recalled it well, the tragedy coming so close on the heels of her own father's death. The pretty young thing of eighteen had gone missing on a walk back from town, and groups of men had gone out each day from sun up to sunset looking for her. It was agreed that an animal must have gotten her, a wolf or coyote.

Alix shivered and drew her shawl tighter. Doctor McCraddock's examination had said otherwise. Poor Emily had been beaten, clubbed to death. Though the town agreed that no one inside its borders could be capable of such a heinous crime, doors were bolted at night and no lady walked anywhere alone. Some families didn't allow their daughters out of doors. Alix recalled how close in age she'd been to Emily, three or four years, and how she had wondered to Chas through his newspaper that she'd walked to town often, even at dusk, and never worried.

And then it had all become a horrible memory, until months later when she had asked Chas to have her money transferred to Mister Meacham. Weak agreement had escalated to refusal and then an eruption concluding with Chas's admission that he'd been forced to give her three thousand dollars to Silas Van der Verre.

Why? Why had he given *that man* money which was rightly hers? Alix rested her quill in the inkwell and massaged a drumming temple. She'd been so naïve in those days. A wide bruise had marked the length of Chas's jaw, running a spectrum

15

from plum to rust and finally to a slow-fading yellow, a shape remarkably like those found on Emily. Scratches: he had tried to conceal them by the height of an over-starched cravat. She had accepted his story of a dull razor. Screaming matches had rattled her door from Chas's bedchamber at night, Paulina reaching an octave so piercing that it had torn them in half and left her brother in a separate bedroom for good.

Silas's hasty replacement of a once-favorite walking stick.

Emily's bloated belly, filled more with child than river water.

If she had known, had allowed herself to believe, she would have been too afraid to ever defy one of Silas's edicts. She had been bright and colorful, brave in those days; Alix resolved once more that her taste of freedom would be Silas's downfall, not her own. She had tasted a life without fear.

She would have it again.

Determined, Alix claimed the only weapon available: her quill. Tapping it off and willing the sad desk to be as strong as she was, she signed yet another offer for shares of Van der Vere Shipping, an offer at a price too high to be ignored.

CHAPTER FOUR

Broadmoore's drawing room boasted more people than he would have liked, but not as many as he'd expected. In a revelation, Spencer realized it wasn't *company* that he minded. Bennet had throngs of loud, obnoxious young bucks in for cards and drink nearly every night outside of the Season, and it hardly figured on his daily existence. He had guests of his own and no qualms being a guest elsewhere as long as the lodgings and company were good.

No, it wasn't the company, it was the *questions*. Eager and bright eyed, desperately patriotic and painfully misguided, men and women hounded him at tea, at dinner. *Tell us about your infantry charge. How many French did you kill during the siege? How many times were you wounded? What did the Prince Regent serve you for dinner?*

Bland enough, and he didn't fault them for their curiosity, just for the memories that it stirred. There was no recalling an allegedly brilliant charge without also remembering the dead and mangled, their frozen screams and wide blank stares. Explaining that the siege had cost him Leighton Powell and nearly John, his two closest friends. He'd mourned in a foot of mud and shite, grief dulled by whiskey and a stomach full of moldy biscuits, certain of bleeding to death from a musket hole in his side.

It would be impolitic to say that the prince was a pompous bore, rumpled and a bit undignified, with a mind nearly as scrambled as his father's. No one wanted to hear the bloody or the embarrassing details, and he was a saner man for not having to recount them.

Spencer claimed a lone ribbon-back mahogany chair by the fireplace, watchful for anyone who recognized him with the

17

telltale gleam of an unanswered question in their eyes. As he sat, he winced at a lack of stuffing in its fine blue silk cushion, and without warning felt *old*. Old and tired and cantankerous. Knees which had led the uphill charge at Toulouse protested an hour of standing in London company. In winter or poor weather, the wounds which had made him famous throbbed with the price of victory. His hearing, which had somehow survived the best efforts of his riflemen and heavy artillery, was grated on by the drone of gossiping voices. No, fame was not for him. Glory hoarding was for the younger, more brash among the army. *For Bennet.*

John appeared, handing him a glass of port without asking and without needing to. "Knock it back quick," warned John, "before the ladies take notice."

"Here's to the rules," whispered Spencer, briefly raising his drink in salute to a social convention they'd broken on more than one occasion. Imbibing in the company of ladies was only bad form if you were *caught*; he and John had shaken hands on it.

Down went the port, warm and sweet, coating his throat like pungent honey. John snatched the glass almost before it was clear of his lips, hurrying back to the cabinet to conceal their evidence. Spencer fought a smile, leaning into the chair's sturdy frame to survey the room, letting the wine go to work.

John's lovely wife Laurel, small and willowy with a mound of auburn hair, flitted along the horseshoe arrangement of her guests. Chas Paton, seated near the center, held a decent resemblance to his cousin John, with the same shade of blond to his hair and same upturned nose, neither of them particularly tall but both fit and with a lot of bearing. Chas's wife, Paulina held court beside him, narrowed gaze weighing those around her. Taller than her husband by a finger or two, her ashen locks and dark eyes might have been exotic, framed by the sharp and invading European angles of her face and limbs. A sniff when she found his eyes on her and something withheld in their flat brown depths heightened his distaste for the woman.

Mrs. Paton had already managed to make a poor impression on Laurel, and that had made a poor impression on *him*. Laurel was a mutual responsibility of sorts, and his own responsibility should his friend be killed. She filled the role of hostess at his estate now and then, saw to his domestic staff, and nattered about his health, his exercise, and his love life with equal concern. Someone had to, he supposed, and bless her for it. She was altogether lovely and Spencer treasured her almost as much as John. Anyone who treated her poorly was suspect, as far as he was concerned.

Finishing a study of the room, he frowned. His raven was nowhere in sight, a revelation which was more disappointing than he had expected. At least a good look at her, with no mask and in daylight, would assure him that she was not as tempting as he remembered. This thought occupied him while John muttered introductions, most of which were not necessary, and everyone casually took each other's measure.

"Mrs. Rowan." Spencer had thought the words, but didn't realize he had spoken them aloud until several sets of eyes snapped his way.

John leaned in. "What's that, Reed?"

He met their gazes, swallowing to recover. "Mrs. Rowan. Is she not also visiting today?"

"She's in the small parlor," offered Laurel with a meaningful glance at Mrs. Paton. "Writing a letter. Would you like me to introduce you?"

"Here I am. Forgive my tardiness."

The voice startled him. He sat up quick enough to bounce the chair legs and turned in his seat.

For a long moment he stared, nearly certain she could not be the same woman from the garden. She was taller than he remembered, and older. Thirty at least, though it was her carriage rather than looks which gave her age away. A modestly cut pale mint gown hugged long arms and draped longer legs, still managing to hide a body he *thought* he remembered well. Her hair was the right shade of silky ink, but its mass was harnessed into a tight knot at her crown. She was not dowdy or plain. She was lovely, in fact, but entirely different from his recollection.

He relaxed against the chair, deflating with relief. Then, he stood up, bowing to Mrs. Rowan at John's introduction. "Alexandra, this is Major-General Lord Spencer Reed." John waved a hand. "Reed, this is my cousin, Mrs. Alexandra Rowan."

Alexandra dared closer, eyeing him, and for a breath Spencer was certain she had recognized him. Then she curtsied, a small gesture that brushed him with a hint of her perfume. That was the same; he knew it and his *body* certainly knew it. Without thinking, he pressed a hand over her glove tucked inside his pocket.

"Lord Reed. It's very kind of you to make some time to visit here with us. As John explains it, you have a great many obligations." Her *r*'s were firm, syllables full on an American tongue, voice rich and sweet. That part at least was meeting his expectations. He wished she would say more, give him more than polite asides.

"Not as busy as I'd like," he muttered, awkward. "Or as much as is good for everyone else."

Easy, a spring breeze; her laughter came naturally at his jest, checking his breath for a beat.

Then he waited for the questions, the stilted adulation.

Instead, she cocked her head and smiled. "We've all been warned, then."

His heart skipped. Spencer struggled to follow his comment, to keep her there, but silence broke the thread between them and Alexandra moved off.

She folded onto a hulking floral brocade sofa beneath the window, slipped a book from the ledge, and seemed to forget that she was not alone. Absorbed as he was in studying her, he didn't miss Paulina's sour frown at her sister-in-law.

"Hastings, what's our order of the day?" asked Chas, a strange contrast of desperate affability against his scowling wife.

"Well." John glanced to Laurel, who smiled over a hard swallow. "Well," she began, then faltered. Spencer didn't have to guess why; John had grumbled over their struggle for weeks now. John's army pay was in arrears, going back to well before the Battle of Paris. He'd dumped a small fortune into Broadmoore just to make it livable and then the Crown had left him out to dry. Now John had a baby on the way and an unexpected house full of guests to entertain. "Well," she

20

repeated, "John has arranged us a lovely picnic today out on the heath –"

"The weather is cold," sniffed Paulina.

"The weather is *English*," retorted Alexandra, piercing the other woman with a glance over her book. A silent, pointed exchange hung between the women for long enough that Spencer anticipated more barbs. Finally, Alexandra dropped her gaze, cutting the tension.

Laurel's shoulders relaxed a measure at being defended. "And tomorrow, we'll –"

He sat forward, interjecting himself into the group. "Tomorrow you will all come over to Oakvale. I have entertainments planned for Saturday and Sunday so that Lady Hastings may have a respite to enjoy your company."

Laurel's smile was absolute gratitude, and John nodded.

John needed his cousins, and Laurel could not risk alienating them by saying what truly ought to be said to Paulina Paton. But he would, and could. Let her cut a swath with her tongue under his roof and see how she fared.

"That is very kind of you, Lord Reed." Alexandra was watching him without blinking, book forgotten in her lap.

His intent in bringing the group to Oakvale was to do Laurel a favor. Now it occurred to him that he would be under the same roof with Mrs. Rowan, in her company as much as he wished. A thrill shivered up his back, his eyes holding a moment too long on her mouth.

He returned her stare a moment and something hung between them, something tantalizing, for just a moment.

Then Laurel cut the thread, scooting her chair until it separated their respective perches. "Mrs. Rowan, your brother mentioned that you paint. Do you instruct, also?"

There was a hopeful note in Laurel's voice that Spencer imagined only he would recognize, but Alexandra seemed to pick it out, too. "I have not a bit of formal instruction, but I'm happy to share what I know. I don't do portraits, ever. But the natural world..." she nodded slowly. "Perhaps I could show you a thing or two."

"Oakvale has some noteworthy landscapes," he offered, eager for Alexandra's notice.

"It's true!" Laurel clasped her hands. "Oh, Mrs. Rowan, you have never seen anything quite like it. More of the Highlands than here, full of stone cliffs and low peaks. And, at the same time, green and rolling. A natural lake below the lawn catches the sunrise. It's breathtaking."

Laurel's praise warmed him, but it was Alexandra's reaction which interested him.

"Breathtaking. That's high praise. I can hardly wait," agreed Alexandra, meeting his eyes and then glancing away. "I saw humbling country some years ago, when we trekked west as far as the Missouri. Chas sent some men to take stock of an outpost, for a fur venture. The country, the people..." Her smile was radiant. "I struggle imagining its equal anywhere on earth."

Spencer looked her over, mind aching at her growing enigma. "You went west, just the three of you?"

Alexandra's blue eyes narrowed. "I traveled with Chas's foreman Mister Mattingly, his sons and his wife. Chas was *occupied* and Paulina does not travel *au provincial*." She spat the accusations half under her breath, dodging Paulina's cocked ear. "Three scouts, two white guides and our native guide. Some of his people traveled with us, coming and going. At harvest time, there is a great deal of trading and communicating between the tribes."

"Goodness," breathed Laurel. "Were you not overwhelmed the whole time? I have heard the frontier can be very savage."

Shrugging, Alexandra chewed her lip. "Anywhere can be, it seems. But those are often the places to find adventure."

Spencer shifted in his chair, frustration growing by the moment. It was her. Alexandra was the same woman he had taken to the garden, playful and willing, adventurous. He had kissed the lips smiling at him now. The pieces just didn't fit. The woman before him was soft spoken if frank, a little demure and perfectly sweet to their hostess with not a hint of passion. He stared at her, puzzled.

Lost in his confusion, he drifted away, only catching himself when her brows lifted in question. "Something troubles you, Lord Reed?"

"It does."

Her brows rose higher, and for just a breath Spencer swore something spilled into her gaze, something she'd kept bottled up, more which lurked just below the surface. Just as quickly as it came, the cork was stuck back in and Alexandra claimed her forgotten book, not a ripple to her expression.

Looking from her to the others, he caught Paulina's narrowed eye, first on Alexandra and then on him. Understanding dawned at last. His lady from the garden was in there somewhere, hidden as much from her family as from him. What hold did Paulina have over her sister-in-law?

In the end, it didn't matter a fig. She was in there, and he would draw her out.

CHAPTER FIVE

Alix stuffed her trunk until it strained, its lid creaking at an excess of eyelet and lace. She would pack a single trunk and save herself trouble. Paulina would demand three, even four, for a weekend. Limiting her own accessories, Alexandra could spare herself a speech from her sister-in-law about the woman's deprivation without shawls, petticoats, muslin and silk gowns. Rooms too hot or too cold could spell Paulina's death, of course, and only the most callous would deny the woman a necessity. Nine pairs of slippers and twelve silks in nearly the same color; who had the right to pass judgment on what Paulina required to survive?

Not much longer, Alix smiled to herself, latching her trunk. Chas might be saddled with Paulina and that was a sad pit of his own making. But she was not, and soon their mutual tolerance would be at an end. She would take the same leap she had made years earlier getting on that ship, and this time she would not get off for any number of Silas's threats. She'd pinched what little money Chas had deposited on her shares to a miserly degree, eking out one meager return at a time. Cheated from the sale of their family house in Malton, hers in accordance with Father's will, progress had been glacial. Now and then she had made an investment, a small one with its return guaranteed. Each exchange moved her one step closer to her coup: to buy up any and every share of Paton & Son Shipping, enough that Silas would be forced to reckon with her at the bargaining table. Chas might live inside Silas's grasp, but she was too old and too fed up to endure him any longer. He would *not* demolish what her family had worked so hard to build.

Coming to England and meeting the Hastings was not the family reunion Chas had claimed to John. Mother had detested her father and eldest brother, the former Lord Hastings, and there was no love lost at the estrangement. Silas was convinced that England offered opportunity, and had sent Chas and Paulina to harvest it for him, exploiting family ties his idea from the start. Underhanded, but his scheme had offered Alix a convenient opportunity, too. Private shippers made top coin in contested waters, making England just the place to fatten her bankroll out from under at least one set of prying eyes.

A handsome stranger, plentiful investments, and now the intriguing Lord Reed. Alix hefted up her trunk, reveling in a bit of smugness. For a trip she hadn't been thrilled to make, a lot of good things were happening.

Trunk packed, a footman appeared on silent cue to drag it away, and Alix locked the door behind him. Settling in front of a deep oak vanity, she fished a tattered list from her apron pocket and rested it back against the mirror. She reached into the foot well, recovering the writing case she'd hidden there. She had pinched it from the small parlor, convinced that neither her nerves nor the frail desk could withstand another round of correspondence.

Over the next hour, she penned the same brief letter to the last six names on her list; an offer to buy out their shares of Paton & Son at a generous price. At the foot of each she added the details of her father's attorney, signed them 'Alex Rowan' and blew sand across the ink.

When they were sealed, she crept out into the hallway and wound down the back staircase until she encountered a servant going up. Alix held out the bundle. "I have letters of introduction from Lady Hastings. Please see that they're posted this afternoon." Catching voices farther downstairs, from out in the main hall, she backed up a step. "If you encounter any trouble, you're to come to me directly. Mrs. Paton is in an ill humor and is not to be bothered. Understood?"

At Paulina's name the young maid swallowed, green eyes wide with an obvious if unspoken question: Why had her mistress given letters to a guest, to be given to a servant? She worried her kerchief with anxious fingers, studying the bundle of post with the same trepidation as a live snake.

Had Paulina already bullied the girl into the position of unwilling ally? Domestic staff could lose their place over the smallest complaint, and no one prodded with veiled threats as skillfully as Paulina. Alexandra's nerves erupted in response to the maid, and she snatched the letters back and jammed them deep inside her pocket.

"Never you mind. Do not trouble yourself." She dug beneath the letters for a coin and pressed it into the maid's limp hand. "No need mentioning this; I can settle the matter myself."

She didn't wait for an answer or even a nod as the voices grew louder, their owners moving up the main staircase. One of them was distinctly Chas, and Alix wondered if the maid would rush her, reveal their exchange to him in a fearful confession. Turning, she raised her skirts and raced back up the way she'd come, relieved when no steps followed behind. Chas and Paulina were just coming into sight when she reached the landing.

"You're making something out of nothing," her brother whispered, glancing behind them.

"It's only nothing until it occurs," Paulina hissed back, her thick Dutch weighting each word into a blow against her husband. "Can you imagine if she does catch the eye of some rutting Englishman? Think of the scandal when people start asking who she is, where she comes from!"

"Let them ask. What matter is it to us?"

Here Paulina ground to a halt, swirled on Chas and stabbed his breast with a sharp finger. "What matter is it to my father!"

In a rare fit of bravery, Chas slapped down the offending hand but gained no reprieve from her proximity.

"My father has made his wishes, his *expectations* known to you." She deflated just a breath, folding her hands. "And his consequences."

"Alexandra will be kept at heel," he murmured, head hanging.

And so will you. Alix shook her head. Being used to being discussed and enjoying it were two different things. She crossed her arms and cleared her throat, snapping around both their heads.

"Alexandra," muttered Chas, not meeting her eyes. "What are you doing out here?"

"Last I was informed, I am free to come and go." She narrowed eyes at Paulina, who stared past her. "Or has that changed?"

Unlike Chas, Paulina showed not a hint of discomfort at being overheard. "Not so long as you keep from shaming us." Judgment in her accusation hit like a slap.

Alix raised on tip toes, putting them eye to eye, forcing the woman to look at her. "The day may come, very soon, when you'll choke on your own wickedness." She immediately regretted the words. It was foolish, letting Paulina get the better of her and giving away even a hint that she could get the upper hand. It could be dangerous information later.

Paulina's step back, a dimming to the malice in her eyes, eclipsed all worry. Alix tasted a small but delicious bit of triumph. She turned her back on the pair, Paulina's abuse and Chas's cowardice, filled with satisfaction.

CHAPTER SIX

Oakvale, the Reed estate – May 16th, 1814

Laurel had not exaggerated Oakvale's beauty. She *had* failed to mention its size. It was more than just a house and grounds, Alix discovered, as they bounced over dusty, hard-packed roads. Fields, bronze and pale green, hugged low hills, and then a village rose from the horizon. Neat gold thatch and a gray stone church tower dominated its charming ramble. Then the road curved away and up a low rise, gaining the cliffs Laurel had mentioned. A wide serpentine lake filled the valley below, green and silver beneath an afternoon sun.

Whether by design or on a whim, Lord Reed had insisted on her and Laurel riding with him, asserting that the ladies would be bored with John's talk of business. Alix pressed a smile behind her fingers, noting that he had excluded Paulina from his concerns.

"Something amuses you, Mrs. Rowan?"

She wished he wouldn't call her that, wished no one called her that. Alix shook her head. "Just delighted. Lady Hastings has described your home perfectly."

Reed was silent, something which occurred any time she was eager for him to say more. "Is your family in London?" she ventured, the best way she could manage to ask, without asking, if he had a wife.

Reed continued staring out the window, the line of his brows pulled down into a vee of concentration. "My brother Bennet resides with me on occasion. Keeps the house when I am away with the army." Firm lips turned up into a hint of a smile. "London leaves him too deep in the pockets for land of his own."

28

"You'll adore Bennet," Laurel promised. "It is simply impossible to not enjoy one's self in his company."

"Oh no," countered Reed. "It is really very possible. If he seems unmanageable at home, I challenge you to command him on the field."

The information surprised her. "Both in the army? In the same regiment?"

"No longer, saints be praised. We're well separated, when he's not out adventuring or playing pirate." Reed snorted. "Smarter uniforms."

"Ignore our host, Mrs. Rowan. Bennet has acquitted himself well."

"So he has," admitted Spencer. "He'll come out all right, yet."

She watched him while he wasn't looking, sun catching a hint of bronzed stubble kissing his cheeks. Gray eyes absorbed the scenery, shaded beneath the brim of his polished beaver hat. Chestnut sideburns, shaved neatly at his ears, framed a firm jaw. He was forty, John had said, though she struggled to believe it. A few winged creases at the corners of his eyes, a pleasant line on either side of his mouth betrayed it, but she found him no less handsome for his age.

Handsome but less satisfying, unequal to her stranger. Not a fault of his own; any man would be. Much as she had convinced herself of maintaining a perfect fantasy, the garden affair plagued her waking and sleeping. She had fought it for days, but resolve crumbled faster and faster. Soon, very soon she would give in and quiz John and Laurel about her stranger.

"You stare very frankly, Mrs. Rowan." Spencer was looking at her now, eyes dancing, having caught the full force of her pointed study.

"I do," she admitted, earning a giggle from Laurel. Thank God for sweet Laurel, a bright spot in her family circle. And a heap of shame on Paulina for being such a harridan to their hostess.

Laurel groaned and pressed a hand to her stomach, closing her eyes while her head lolled back against the chocolate leather squabs. "I should have eaten more at breakfast. Or less. Reed, will you open your window?"

He grunted, complying while she took in Laurel's appearance. Tired shadows across her face, stomach complaints; the realization struck like lightning. "Laurel, are you with child?"

One green eye cracked in her direction. "Not as far as anyone but John and Reed are concerned."

"Oh." Alexandra swatted at a pang of jealousy. Unmarried and very much un-pursued at thirty-two, she had resigned herself to a life without children. "Well, here," she fished her reticule from between them, locating a tin and popping off its lid. "Mint and soda ash. Starch. I keep them for dry air, but I've heard they can ease stomach complaints." She dropped a candy into Laurel's palm. "And your secret is my secret."

"Thank you," Laurel murmured, laying the mint on her tongue. "After losing the last one… We'd just rather not say anything for a bit longer."

She squeezed Laurel's fingers. "I understand."

Spencer was watching them with a tight expression she couldn't interpret. She smiled, and he looked away. Why were they always out of tune?

Laurel made a noise, and grimaced. "Not a taste I'd choose to have in my mouth, but I admit to feeling better. Are these also for your cough?"

"What?" She'd heard the questions; now she stalled for time to construct a reasonable explanation.

"Chas shared with us that you have lung complaints, coughing fits." Laurel's mouth pulled into a sympathetic frown. "The clean air here will make that better, I think."

Alix bit her cheek against a smile. She did not have a lung complaint. She had a Paulina complaint, and a clever excuse to avoid going just about anywhere with her brother's wife. Her only embarrassment was that it had taken so many years to concoct a remedy. Hot peppers from the East, a little soot from the grate, and like magic she'd contracted a debilitating chest ailment. Who would notice that it was aggravated anytime she was forced to share company with the horrible woman? "Oh," she murmured, studying her glove and trying to sound frail, "I'm not certain that it will."

*   *   *

Over the years, Laurel had taught him a thing or two about being a good host, and now had seemed the perfect time to put her lessons to use. Having never been married, never having had a woman to manage the gentler aspects of his estate, he'd often relied on her to make the house presentable for guests.

Laurel had teased him about his companions now and then, insisting that he could entertain a lady just fine without her help. He'd been provoked, after much harassment by John, into explaining that *his* sort of entertaining was not suitable for London company. The women who had passed through his life didn't cross stitch or pour tea.

Some years ago, upon noticing his lack of domestic ability, Laurel had taken it upon herself to impart her wisdom, educating him on comforts and niceties which impressed visitors. From where the chairs should be arranged on a cold day for guests to be warm but not soot-covered, how to arrange the table so that disagreeable pairings were avoided without creating hard feelings, Laurel had mastered all the rules. Having sent his groom ahead to Oakvale to have tea and refreshments ready for their arrival, he was proud that some of her lessons had sunk in.

Almost upon arrival, Chas and Paulina had stomped upstairs under complaints of fatigue from a poor carriage ride. Now, standing in the hall and watching John usher a green-about-the-gills Laurel out into the garden for air, Spencer felt cheated of his moment.

He turned to Alexandra and held his breath, waiting for her to make an excuse and take her leave, as the others had. Instead, she smiled and shrugged. "More for me, then. *I* am famished." He dared a hesitant smile of his own and opened his mouth, only to be cut off by a warning of footsteps, boots striking marble at the top of the staircase. He turned, disappointed at the thought of Chas returning and was greeted by the sight of his brother. A smart blue riding jacket and buckskins announced that Bennet was on his way out.

"Reed." Bennet took the stairs in a military double-time, scowling and hooking a thumb over his shoulder. "Who in bloody hell were those two dowdies? I swear that woman gave me a look to plain freeze my –" He skidded to a stop and craned

31

his head, grinning. "Oh. *Hello.*" He painted Alexandra in a quick once-over, and he met Spencer's eyes with a nod of approval.

Spencer sighed and gave Bennet quelling shake of his head.

"Hello." Alexandra stepped forward and pursed a smile, ducking her head and charming him.

Bennet strode forward, eyes on her all the while. "I don't believe we've met, and shame on my brother for it." He kicked back a leg and bowed for all his worth, as though they were at court.

Always showing off to the ladies. Spencer supposed to an extent it ran in the family. His history was marked with a few acts shamelessly aimed at grabbing attention from the fairer sex. He stepped aside and raised a hand to Alexandra. "This is Mrs. Rowan. Mrs. Rowan, this, unfortunately, is my brother, the *honorable* Bennet Reed."

Alexandra curtsied to Bennet. "And you have just had the pleasure of meeting *my* brother, Mister Paton, and his wife Paulina." Bennet had the decency to look stricken, until Alexandra threw him a sly look. "And what a *pleasure* it was, I'm sure," she said.

Now Bennet looked to him, head and lips cocked, and raised a brow at her wit.

Spencer raised a brow of his own and communicated as best he could with only his eyes that Bennet had better not even consider it. Alexandra Rowan was not on the market, as far as he was concerned.

"My brother has told me a *great* deal about you," Bennet was toeing a line to get in his dig; Spencer resisted an urge to wring his neck. "And it seems it was all true."

Alexandra brightened. "That's very kind. We're all grateful to be invited." She paused and glanced up the stairs, then shrugged. "I am very grateful to be invited."

He had been ready to shoo his brother away and seize an opportunity for a moment alone with Alexandra, but now reconsidered. As they traded quips, he watched her engage Bennet now in a way he had not observed in all their time together since the garden. Bennet always had an easy charm which drew people out and gained their confidence, and Spencer appreciated that there might be an advantage to keeping his brother at hand today. "We were just going in for luncheon," he said.

Bennet nodded. "I was headed to the stables."

"You should have something to eat before you exert yourself."

"I'm not particularly hungry," Bennet said, puzzled.

"You always say so," ground out Spencer, "and then you feel unwell after. I really believe," he said, stressing each word with eyes wide, "that you ought to come in with us and have a little something."

"I – oh! Oh." Looking back and forth between his brother and Alexandra, understanding dawned on Bennet's face. "I should. You are correct." In a coup, he pushed past and took Alexandra's arm before Spencer could say another word.

They settled at the breakfast table around a tempting spread. Its crisp white cloth and centerpiece of molded sugar paste fruit renewed a pang of disappointment that a majority of his guests had missed the brilliant efforts of his cook, Mrs. Tate. It passed a breath later when Alexandra *ooh'd* and *ahh'd* enough for three people.

"You're right to be impressed, Mrs. Rowan," said Bennet, snatching a tiny pink cake from its tray without waiting for her to go first. "When it is just the two of us, Reed makes us sit on the floor at the kitchen fire and eat from wooden trenchers."

"That was my plan for today as well," he teased, watching Alexandra for a reaction. "But Mrs. Tate must have missed my instructions."

"Ogre," she said without looking up from her plate. She didn't have to; her expression had softened, and he caught some of the warmth which had first drawn him to her. A shiver of concern intruded, and Spencer wondered again at the looks which had passed between Alexandra and Paulina at the Hastings'.

"How are you finding England?" Bennet managed, finishing a bite.

"I hardly have words," she said. "We arrived in London first, and that was one sort of beauty. There is a strange pleasure

33

to be had in its clockwork busyness. It all seems like chaos, the crowds and parties, but there is a rhythm to it that you notice when you really examine the city."

He had never thought of London as anything other than the crush she had first described, but upon reflection, Spencer appreciated that she was right; he may not enjoy being a part of the mechanism, but London was not the bedlam he had accused.

Her opinion had surprised Bennet too, who was nodding slowly and trying to formulate a reply.

Alexandra's interference saved them both. "Anyhow, the north is spectacular in its own way and these lands in particular…" She shook her head, eyes half closed. "As Laurel promised, they really are breathtaking."

"It is kind of you to say," Spencer muttered. Pride welled in his chest at her praise of his home, further igniting his attraction. He pretended an examination of his plate, stealing glances at her until Bennet caught her in conversation. Then he dared a more blatant study.

She was easy with Bennet, as she had been with Laurel in the carriage. When she smiled at a part of his outlandish story, her cheek filled out and lent her face the same delicate softness which had charmed him at the masquerade. His eyes paused indecently long on her mouth, thrilling at the memory of her lips on his. Her hands on his face, her fingers in his hair…

It was a long moment before he grasped that the conversation had stopped, and that Alexandra was staring at him. He met her eyes, which were filled with mischief.

"You stare very frankly, Lord Reed," she said, and Spencer nodded in recognition of his earlier words to her.

"I do." His admission hardly changed her expression, but he didn't miss a hint of pink which flushed her face.

"That is not staring," interjected Bennet, oblivious. "Reed is an intellectual sort. He prefers the term 'contemplative'."

Alexandra clutched her belly and giggled, a beautiful sound which set his heart to pounding. When she tossed him a fetching look, warm and unreserved, he was undone completely.

He decided that Bennet had been right in ordering him to Broadmoore to see Alexandra, and absolutely capital for agreeing to tea.

Stiff-backed in her chair, Alix read the same page for a third time, bound up by a cord of silence strung between Chas and Paulina, whose eyes had been fixed on her for the better part of an hour. Now and then something stuck in the woman's craw, something Alix said or did. There would be no end until Paulina had her say, but Alix would read the same page fifty times rather than make it easier.

A sigh.

Alix braced and turned the page.

Chas cleared his throat. "Alexandra."

She glanced up, not at Chas but Paulina, who perched at the edge of her chair, pulling Chas's strings with a nudge or a clearing of her throat.

Closing her book, Alix didn't bother marking her place. She gripped it edge and spine and strangled the poor little tome in effigy.

"Our cousins travel with a certain set," he pressed. "You need to be mindful of your conduct."

Alix recalled the conversation she'd caught on the stairs between her brother and Paulina and realized she hadn't won, only delayed punishment. "I should be uncivil? Make no conversation, engender no good will?"

"I am surprised at you," cut Paulina, clearly not trusting her husband to get the job done. "For all your claims of loyalty to our family, our trade, your glib attitude does neither one credit."

A simmering anger, always beneath the surface, began to boil. "Glib? Just the opposite. I am mindful each day of being beholden to Mr. and Mrs. Paton. To our benefactor and patriarch Silas Van der Verre!"

A flash of ivory muslin was scored by a chair toppling against the hearth. Alix raised her book in preparation, but a hair too late, and Paulina's slap caught her jaw and shot sparks behind her eyes. "Unthinkable, my father wasting his affection on a *hoer*."

Cradling her stinging face, Alix looked past Paulina to Chas, who sat staring at his hands folded in his lap.

35

"The only thing your father is wasting," she returned through gritted teeth, "is the effort he spends to get control of my shares."

"A letter!" threatened Paulina, drawing up. It was her warning of punishment, spanning most of their forced existence together. A detailed account of her transgressions would be given to Silas for a future reckoning. "He will have a letter at once!"

"I may get my blows," said Alix, smug firmness hiding her fear, "but not until we return to America."

Paulina's bony fingers gripped her bun and canted her head back. Lips next to her ear spat words in a low growl. "Father may be closer than you think."

The information sent a chill along her spine. It was a terrifying thought, no matter its truth. He couldn't have followed them, could he? In a flash, her mind ran through a decade of Silas's dominion, and she answered the question with a hard swallow.

The tearing in her scalp subsided. Paulina withdrew her talons and blew past, her exit announced by a door shuddering in its jamb.

Alix massaged her head and returned her attention to Chas, spearing him with a glare and willing him to look up. When his sudden bout of immobility persisted, she pressed him. "One day, Charles, it will be me shutting the door between us."

He snorted at her idle threat, certain of its impossibility. Until a few months ago, he would have been correct. With Silas's fists around her inheritance, no revenue from shares, not even a home to call her own, it was an unspoken punchline that she had no place to run and no means of getting there. Her abandoned tryst with Edward Mills had proved it, Silas already waiting when their ship put in at Charleston. The reach of his lacquered black walking stick had reinforced, blow after blow, that she would never be beyond his grip. She closed her eyes against the memory, still throbbing from long-healed bruises.

Recovered, she sat forward and tried a different tack, giving him a desperate stare and sure that her effort was fruitless, as always. "Father broke his back to build what we have. How can you bear losing the company?"

36

His arms flailed. "We're not losing it! Where does this madness come from? Silas is rolling everything into Paton & Son. We're more solvent than ever, nothing but growth."

Paulina's words, no doubt. There wasn't enough belief in Chas's tone for him to have concocted the lie himself.

Chas had never been the one with a head for business; that much had been apparent on countless occasions. It was apparent by his not wondering at Silas desperately farming new customers for an already successful venture. Even a child could puzzle out which company was absorbing the other.

It would be a defeating prospect except she'd found a way to fight back. She'd made excellent progress consolidating Paton's shares and even some from Van der Verre, behind Silas's back. Her father's solicitor Mister Meacham wasn't able to do much, but he deserved sainthood for what he'd managed already. At least *someone* was still loyal to their father. She snorted her disgust at Chas, slouched and pale in his seat.

"Why do you do it?" she asked.

A blink, a stare.

"Is it truly a simpler thing, suffering? Watching me suffer, letting them own your pride rather than just saying no?"

Chas came half out of his chair, face etched with more emotion than she had witnessed in years. He beat a fist against his breast. "Pride?" he sobbed. "He owns my *soul*, Alexandra!"

"And your bollocks, too? You certainly haven't enough to fight back!" She found her feet, mirroring his posture while tears stung her eyes. "And I am added compensation to your deal with the devil!"

He deflated back into the chair, eyes shuttered once more. "Don't —"

"*Make trouble, Alexandra.* I know." She did, by heart.

"And don't cross Paulina. For both our sakes."

She huffed. "Your wife is brainwashed enough to die for Silas's approval. You're a matched pair." Alix moved behind her chair, putting it between them as insurance against Chas's occasional instability. "But I am not like you."

"Don't make trouble," he muttered again, scrubbing hands over his face. "You lack the ammunition to do battle with him. And I won't help you." His voice hitched, and for a moment she thought there was something there, something below the surface. "I *cannot* help you."

Her fingers twitched for want of circling his throat. Her nail beds ached with a need to claw his face, to provoke something besides cowardice. Instead she drew a breath, the slow effort fading rage into a red tint edging her thoughts.

"I will remember that you said so. And when the time comes," she backed up, a pace at a time until she reached the door, heart hammering in her chest, "*you* remember that you said so, too."

CHAPTER SEVEN

Spencer was determined not to let Paulina spoil his reconnaissance of Alexandra, but it wasn't easy. Alix was not conversational by any stretch when under Paulina's gaze. There were pursed lips, sideways glances, and many a clearing of the throat. Paulina was a harridan whose reason for existence appeared to be ruining everyone else's sport, with the bulk of her ire directed at Alexandra.

For Alexandra's part, it wasn't intimidation he saw in her downturned expressions, but a quiet resignation. The attitudes were one and the same as far as he was concerned. He wanted a moment unchaperoned to flush out the woman in the garden rather than the woman who sat silently in his drawing room. Wanting and getting were desires keenly separated at the moment by the snooping nose of Paulina Paton.

"Mrs. Rowan." He stopped behind her, close as he dared, leaning on the mantle and watching her. They'd been listening in silence to Laurel's mastery of the pianoforte.

"Lady Hastings plays beautifully." Alexandra's words were an awkward bridge strung between them. They were stilted, obligated, and Spencer sensed he was a victim of politeness.

"Lady Hastings boasts all manner of accomplishments." He dared a half step closer, breathing her in. "She has taken Broadmoore in hand. Arranged a very fine garden with some exotic specimens. I wonder if you had an opportunity to see it during the ball last week."

Holding his breath, he pierced her, searching for any reaction – a flinch, a blink.

Alexandra exhaled at a forlorn pace, nearly a sigh. "It was dark."

There was something cryptic hidden in her words, he would swear it, but it was not a hint for his benefit. She showed no sign of being his paramour from the masquerade. Once more, he was at a loss.

A few notes trailed between their silence, and then she sighed in earnest. Turning, she curtsied in a half-hearted dip before moving away. He watched her, down the hall and to the stairs, a whisper of dove gray silk over marble filling the growing distance.

Despite their exchange in the garden, and whatever her feelings, Alexandra was giving him nothing but sand to grab. He watched until she slipped from view above the staircase, resolving for now to let her go.

"...Reed can take us all up to the promontory for a basket lunch." Laurel had stopped playing, addressing the little gathering.

"There is no grasping the English fascination with dining out of doors. Eating on the ground like savages." Paulina shuddered.

"The savages don't eat off the ground," said Chas.

"Don't contradict."

Silence filled the room wall to wall, Laurel dusting at her music stand, John picking an imaginary thread at his sleeve. Spencer hardly noticed. He was too busy wondering what kept any man married to Paulina from taking his own life. Or hers.

Finally, he cleared his throat. "I have matters that require my attention. As Lady Hastings knows and loves her little spot, I shall promote her and place her in command of your party." He raised a hand, cutting protests and tongue clucking. "A diversion Saturday night. You have my word."

"I am fatigued," announced Paulina, as though he hadn't been speaking.

"We do not walk to the promontory," offered Laurel, "We ride. Your husband accounts you a fine horsewoman; you would appreciate the terrain."

A sniff. "My skill is rarely tested. I suppose we'll see if the course is all you claim."

Silently thanking the Lord, Spencer exhaled, not realizing he had been holding his breath. He flushed with the same near-death sensation he'd had on the battlefield; the prospect of being alone in the house an entire day with Paulina Paton sounded like his definition of hell.

*   *   *

Damn Paulina, the hateful old battle ax.

Alix planted her slipper against a claw foot, tottering a chair and pacing while she fought for a hold on her temper.

Her failed tryst in the garden had likely been the closest she would come to living out from under Paulina's prying gaze, at least until she could leave the harpy behind for good. Curse John and his good-natured obliviousness for spoiling it. Curse Lord Reed and his mention of the garden, so much salt grinding at her wound.

He was being civil, graciously making conversation with no idea of the trouble he was causing. His attention had stirred up a hive of suspicion in Paulina, making it almost impossible to enjoy his company. She had more than once contemplated engaging him just to spite her sister-in-law, indulge a bit of defiance. Only twice had she dared to defy them. Not heeding Silas's pompous edicts the first time, Alix recalled how painful it had been learning her lesson the second time, with Edward.

She should have kept going when the ship reached Carolina and never allowed Silas to bully her onto land. She should have been more careful, cleverer about leaving. Silas had used her absence to get control of her shares while Paulina had invented a bizarre tale to explain her absence. Married quickly, Paulina had hinted to their neighbors, and widowed just as quickly. The woman's story had painted Alix in just enough gray to make her an object of disapproval without shaming Paulina or her dear father. It had also guaranteed that Alexandra could entertain no suitors for a year during her imaginary mourning. Meanwhile, she'd been forced to march to the beat of Silas Van der Verre's drum, too fearful of what he might do to Chas or Paton & Son, what he might do to *her*, to step out of line.

Not fearful enough to marry the bastard. He hadn't managed to compel her, not yet. Alexandra knew better than to think he'd given up. She shuddered against memories of his attempts at courtship, not having to wonder how far he would press her.

Too agitated to sleep, Alix took her candle and slipped out into the darkened hall. The flame spilled light through the scrolled iron railing, casting shadowed vines onto the wall as she padded down the staircase. Gilt frames winked and flickered when she cupped a hand to shield the wick, and ancient brush-stroke eyes followed her progress to the main hall where a single lamp bathed the white marble tiles in amber. Roses overflowed their blue china bowl on a nearby table, a sweet perfume drifting past her. Their presence might have surprised her, out of place in the home of a bachelor, except that she'd noted similar touches throughout the house all day. Flowers, a fine cashmere throw, good chocolate set out in the parlor; it seemed Lord Reed was attentive to his female guests. Alix turned him over in her mind once again, wondering at what lay beneath his brusque exterior.

She had miscounted the doors along the hall, and realized once inside that she'd missed the library. This was Lord Reed's private study, she guessed. A desk commanded one corner of the room, its domain framed in by the rectangle of a thick Persian rug and set at an angle to a high fireplace.

Good manners demanded she turn back. Private rooms were just that: private. Curiosity whispered for her to dare a step further, creep to the window and see the view as Lord Reed did each day. It urged her to study the bric-a-brac atop his desk and mantle, search for clues to puzzle the man out. Her candle's light caught the glass front of a floor-to-ceiling case on the far wall, silhouetting its murky contents. With a glance off her shoulder, Alix invaded the study by inches.

When she reached the case, she raised her candle and tipped its light inside. She'd expected to find medals, mementos of Lord Reed's military exploits. Instead she was greeted first by an acorn-shaped idol, teeth bared across his pitted stone face. A gold scarab glinted back, mounted on crimson velvet inside a dark wood frame, the pattern of his thumb-sized carapace carved with ancient craftsmanship. A silver case the size of a shoebox occupied the lower shelf, religious figures stamped in relief on each side. Its lid was propped half open to display the wealth contained inside: silver bands embracing milky emeralds, hand-minted gold coins, and a fairytale diadem set with almond-sized rubies. A scrap of brocade was framed beside the chest. Red, blue, and gold silk strands held a trace of their original luster, woven into a splendid garment, a royal gown or tunic, hundreds of years before.

Alix held her breath, illuminating each treasure in turn. Cathedral stones, tattered flags, lacy tarnished keys; she wondered at the story of each, lost in the past.

"Mrs. Rowan."

She'd been so lost that she'd forgotten her trespass, forgotten to be on guard for footsteps in the hall. Alix gasped and pivoted on one foot, eyes fixed to the floor. She couldn't meet his eyes, had no excuse.

"I saw the light and thought someone had forgotten to extinguish a candle." Rather than accusing, Spencer's words were curious, and something else she couldn't identify.

It was ingrained in her to hide the truth, but where Spencer was concerned, it was impossible to lie. "Lord Reed, I apologize. My aim was the library, but when I saw the case..." She turned back and waved a hand across it, "I was drawn in. That's no excuse for my intrusion."

He was behind her. Warmth filled the scant space between their bodies. She caught the spice of his cologne, a familiar scent she didn't recall noticing before. He reached past her, a sturdy shoulder pressing her back, and ran a hand along one side of the display. "I would argue there is no better excuse." His words brushed her ear. Eyes closing, she swallowed and fought an urge to lean into him.

"You've curated an impressive collection," she stammered, wishing she was more glib in moments like these.

Spencer chuckled and moved beside her, setting distance between them. "This is all Bennet's work, actually."

"Not to offend, but your brother doesn't strike me as a collector."

"Bennet doesn't collect." Spencer said. "He ... *acquires*."

She frowned. "I don't understand."

Spencer tapped the glass. "That statuette? Recovered from a cave in Brazil. Natives chased him back to his ship at spear point and nearly skewered him." She followed the path of his finger until it rested before the fabric she'd admired. "A scrap of canopy from the bed in which Elizabeth of York was conceived. Bennet and his crew discovered the chest in a crypt, taken from England during the civil unrest. It was tucked away by Spanish looters beneath an abandoned cathedral in Portugal."

She blew a breath between pursed lips. "You were serious when you called him an adventurer."

He was staring now, watching her. She caught a glint of his eyes in the candle's glow while keeping her own fixed on the artifacts. A chill ran up her back, helped along by cool skin where his heat had left her moments before, and Alix realized she was frightened. Not of Spencer's intentions, not of being alone with him. She was frightened of herself any time he was near. He stoked embers inside she'd banked long ago, flames she couldn't risk kindling now, when she was so close to realizing a victory over Paulina and Silas. What frightened her most was how delicious it felt each time she gave in to temptation, teased him or returned a glance, igniting the same impulsive passion she'd enjoyed with her stranger.

Her stranger. She shivered again at the memory of rough fingers grasping her naked thigh. He'd been a risk, and yet so much safer than Lord Reed. A few minutes of passion, a brief, anonymous respite from her rigid existence; she could dare that much. The way Spencer watched her now, in the flickering light...it was too dangerous.

Spencer cleared his throat and broke their silent exchange. "I imagine you and Bennet would have a great deal to discuss."

Now she dared to meet his eyes. "Why is that?"

He rested a hip against the case and laced arms over his chest, threatening in his ease. "You are both adventurers, by my estimation."

"You're teasing me." She relaxed and smoothed a hand over the cabinet door, mind drifting to better days. "I suppose I was an adventurer, once."

Leaning in, he peered at her until she laughed and moved a step away.

"But no longer?" he prodded.

"Not at the moment. A temporary state," she promised.

44

"Mm. Cryptic. But I think I take your meaning." He claimed her candle from the side table and swept a hand toward the door. "In that case, I look forward to witnessing your renaissance."

At the heat of his palm ushering her, pressed against her back, she wished dearly that he could.

CHAPTER EIGHT

If Laurel hadn't told him that the sound from upstairs was a person, Spencer would have believed his hounds had gotten inside the house. Another round of barking drew Laurel up beside him as they shuffled upstairs. Chas, coming down, paused and shook his head. "Not the worst attack I've ever seen, but she's not fit to go out."

"Should we send for a physician or..." Laurel held out her hands.

"Nothing to be done. Rest, hot tea, an open window." Chas shrugged. "Eventually it passes. Just wish I knew what brought it on in the first place."

A flat drone to Chas's concern pricked at Spencer, who narrowed his eyes and studied the other man. For what, he couldn't quite say.

"I should stay in with her," insisted Laurel, gathering her skirts.

Seeing his first opportunity for solitary reconnaissance, Spencer had no intention of relinquishing it. He caught Laurel's arm. "It will do you no good, as Mister Paton has said. The fit must run its course." He pressed her shoulder. "Go; I'm already obliged to stay in. Someone will be at home, should Mrs. Rowan need anything. Ill as she is, she can hardly want company."

If she was ill. He was growing less convinced by the day that Alexandra was as frail as everyone claimed, despite the ragged hacking upstairs. Her cryptic remark in his carriage tickled at a suspicion, stoking a desire to unravel the mystery that was Alexandra Rowan.

Tension melted from Laurel's shoulders and Chas, for his part, kept the same weary expression as they went down together.

Spencer stationed himself in the front hall long enough that he was useful to Laurel, and to see everyone packed up and bustled out. After, he stood in the quiet shadows a moment, appreciating the complete silence. He couldn't help but notice an end to the coughing above, and wondered that it coincided so perfectly with everyone's leaving.

For now, he would listen and wait. Nothing in his study required immediate attention, despite what he'd told the others. He passed it by, opting instead for his favorite room, the library. Settling into a deep brown leather chair, Spencer tucked himself into a corner between two high windows where he closed his eyes and soaked in mid-morning sun.

He missed the army, the sharp sounds of drill, the synchronized volley of musket fire. He longed, sometimes, for the cheers and shouts of his men around their tents in the evening. The cacophony of London traffic with its stiff clothes and stiffer manners was hardly a substitute, and he made do instead with comfortable silence.

A creaking door figured briefly into his quiet moment. Household staff came and went throughout the day, not an event to break his respite.

When a feminine sigh reached his ear, he bothered cracking an eye. Alexandra, swathed in a flattering yardage of sky blue silk, raked book spines with a knuckle. She perused the shelves across the room in silence, oblivious to his presence.

She looked hale and whole for a woman bedridden an hour ago. Slouching deeper in his seat, Spencer rested a cheek to his fist and watched her. She was softer today, her hair piled in a mound that was calculated to tempt a man's hand. Light silk fell from a high-cut bodice, catching the fullness of her hips swaying with each step. Slender fingers, fingers whose touch he'd recalled in private moments, pulled down a book, cradled and inspected it, then traded it for another. He drank in her movements until she paused for a narrow red canvas tome that met her approval.

She slid it atop a long oak table dividing the shelves from the rest of the library and tossed a crisp white apron down beside it. She snapped the chair forward, bumping the table in her eagerness, and pried back the cover.

Reaching the peak of self-torment, Spencer cleared his throat.

Her chair rocked, pages fanned and she gasped. Certain she'd go straight over backwards, he started up to catch her.

Recovering before he could close the distance, she pressed a hand to her chest, panting.

"Mrs. Rowan."

Her eyes narrowed. "Were you going to say anything?"

He chuckled, caught. "Were you?"

She fixed him with a stare that he was only too happy returning. For a breath, there was something familiar deep in her gaze, a glimmer of the challenge she'd given him at the masquerade. Then it banked, cooling the blue of her gaze even as he willed it to stay.

Alexandra ducked her head, studying the tabletop. "I thought everyone had gone out," she muttered.

Everyone, including him. Spencer took her point, hating a sting in his chest. "Everyone who wished to, has. I stayed behind because I have business to attend to, and because Lady Hastings was concerned about your *health*." His last word hung between them in the library's silence.

Shifting in her chair, she looked away and then got up. "I should be upstairs resting."

She snatched her apron, flinging something from its pocket which pelted against the floor. It struck with a sharp tinkling of glass and rolled to him over polished wood as though drawn by his curiosity.

She rushed him, but he'd already pinched up a long glass vial half filled with rust tinted powder. He shook its contents, squinting to identify the tiny grains. Holding it up to her wide eyes, he waved the bottle. "What is this?"

She swallowed, eyes fixed on her lost property, and kept silent.

"Hm." Spencer pulled the chipped cork from its neck and waved the vial under his nose. An itch, first along the roof of his

48

mouth and then in his throat. Burning followed, high in his nose. Coughs wracked his chest and Spencer plugged the bottle before more could escape. Burying his face in his sleeve, he dodged her snatching fingers, tucking the prize into his pocket. He patted his aching breast.

"You could have warned me when I removed the cork," he panted.

She smiled, and for a moment he recognized her. It was a genuine smile, unguarded, and he decided it had been worth damaging his lungs.

"I *could* have," she admitted, unrepentant.

He rallied, not willing to give her the upper hand. "Coughing fits? Seems your affliction is more *culinary* than chronic."

She exhaled, a sound resigned to being caught. "Paulina gave me the idea, if you can believe it. Not directly, of course, but she's always fiddling with her herbs and tonics."

"Hm." He could *not* believe it, struggled believing Mrs. Paton had time for anything beyond feasting upon her husband's sanity.

"Are you going to tell anyone?" Her eyes narrowed; he was being reconnoitered.

He tried sounding severe. "Lady Hastings was *very* worried about you."

She stiffened. "You're enough acquainted with my brother and his wife by now to grasp why I'd resort to subterfuge for a moment's peace."

Manufacturing a seemingly genuine illness was not a moment's peace in his book. It was, however, an awful lot of trouble to go through for a few hours alone. "You are not of an age where you can demand it?"

She flushed. "I am not in a position to demand it." She didn't elaborate, and he didn't press her. Instead, he added one more question to his ever-growing list.

Alix looked him over again, worrying her lower lip. "Will you keep my secret or no?"

She had given him fantastic leverage and he seized the opportunity. "On one condition."

Her eyes widened.

Gathering his courage, he blurted, "Spend the afternoon with me."

A long glance over her shoulder was telling as any words. She wanted to say yes despite a hunted look. He was certain she would agree if he could promise her the peace she sought.

"An hour out, an hour back. Time to appreciate the view and grow weary of your brother's wife. They won't return until three, at least."

An ounce of tension drained from Alexandra. He caught the slightest drop to her shoulders. "Blackmail, then?" Her smile was hesitant, teasing, skipping his heart. "If that's your game, then I suppose I have no choice but to play along."

He was closing the distance between them before he realized it, eager for every minute in her company. "What do you do for enjoyment?"

She shrugged, backing away a step. "Read."

He rolled his eyes. "What do you do for enjoyment when *Mrs. Paton* is absent?"

She laughed. "*Read*. Walk the pasture. I'm fair enough at the piano."

After, he could not say why he'd done it. Insanity, perhaps. He'd been a mess of frayed nerves for days. At the prospect of an afternoon with Alexandra, he was lost. Fumbling inside his coat, he grasped the familiar length of satin and held up the glove for her disbelieving eyes. "What *else* do you enjoy?"

He'd rehearsed this moment a hundred times, and the drawn expression on her face was not what he'd imagined. He had been overeager, lacking finesse ahead of an awkward segue; he appreciated it too late.

She blanched and backed away in earnest, stumbling against the table. "I ... I misunderstood your offer." She swallowed and fumbled a retreat. "And I think you've misunderstood me. That night was –"

"Wait!" He grabbed her wrist and halted her escape. "Just your company today. I did not mean to imply more. Only that I'm certain you amuse yourself with something besides reading." He held out the glove for her anxious fingers.

50

She searched him with a tight expression, and Spencer had the sense of being weighed.

Finally, she tucked the glove into her apron without meeting his eyes. "I'm a fair opponent at cards. I play billiards, though I'm not much of a challenge. I ride but not in company. Side saddle on a horse is like hanging under a carriage to get somewhere; no enjoyment. I like good brandy, good chocolate." She shrugged. Her shoulders were tense, eyes guarded, but she wasn't leaving and for now that was enough.

He clapped hands together, rubbing eagerly at the progress they were making and then swept an arm toward the door. "Let's begin with cards and follow with brandy." He held his breath and waited for her protest.

Instead she perked up, and pressed an exaggerated hand to her mouth. "Lord Reed, it's barely noon."

He nodded, heart thrumming faster. "Already halfway through the day. We have some catching up to do."

*   *   *

Alexandra couldn't bring herself to look directly at Spencer, who was setting out their tumblers on a sideboard. All along *he* had been her masked stranger. And *he'd* known it. A burn in her cheeks doubled while the realization sank in. She still couldn't reconcile that the broad fingers unstoppering the brandy had also tangled in her hair, brushed her waist. Lips cocked up now in a small smile had kissed her own. More than embarrassment, she suffered another sharp pang of disappointment at John's poor timing.

Spencer set the glasses between them atop a round card table easily meant for three times as many players. Its nicked, scuffed, tawny wood said it frequently saw such a crowd. She claimed her brandy, swirled it and inhaled. It's warm, sweet aroma filled her nose, adding to her thrill at being admitted to Spencer's inner sanctum. The room was obviously intended for himself and masculine company; it was bold and tasteful, shadowed by navy velvet drapes. Tan leather and dark wood carried the theme. A billiard table imposing enough that the room might have been built around it occupied the room's far

51

side. Alix could practically feel heat from a white marble firebox, hear raucous laughter of gathered men, their camaraderie scented with sweet tobacco and citrus gin. Her heart beat a pace faster.

Spencer settled across from her, palmed their deck of cards, and held it out.

"No," she laughed, splaying her hands. "My fingers are too short. You'll end up with creased cards and a mess." Grace and dexterity had never figured among her better qualities.

"Fair enough." He nodded and began to deal. She watched him while he was absorbed in the process, his stern left brow furrowed to mimic the concentrated lift of his mouth.

"Do you know," he asked, still counting out their hands, "that I am always aware of your watching me?"

She snapped her gaze to the tabletop, winning a lusty chuckle.

Spencer hadn't shown himself to be anything but a gentleman during their time together, but they were crossing lines now at full sail. His expectations for how their day would conclude might not be as innocent as she'd envisioned. Gathering her cards, she cleared her throat. "Lord Reed, what happened in the garden –"

He stopped arranging his hand and gave her his full attention. "You do not have to explain yourself, make an excuse."

She took a breath, pressing on. "I'm not. I had a wonderful time with you." It was true. Uncomfortable to admit, but she was not ashamed.

"Help me understand the enigma that is Mrs. Rowan." Spencer leaned in, squinting, staring into her eyes until his gaze drew her close. Then he leaned back, looking satisfied. "She's in there, my lady from the garden. Where does she hide?"

He was still a stranger, and John's friend. She would tread carefully. Mistaken trust could spell her end, now when she was so close to freedom. "My brother and Lord Hastings are both relying on this partnership," she offered weakly. "I don't wish to make a poor impression."

"Bollocks." Spencer leaned further back in his chair, feet bumping hers beneath the table, and crossed his arms.

"Really," she chastised, face aching with a smile at his swear.

Fanning his cards, Spencer shook his head. "I do not believe for a moment that you're a woman who holds her tongue to skirt a little bickering."

Thanks to a long draw on her brandy, she found her nerve. "Paulina's father, Silas Van der Verre, owns a majority of Paton Shipping. A majority of my brother." She shrugged, picking up her hand. "And me." A safe, if oversimplified explanation.

He sat quiet a moment, the look on his face contemplative. "Seems that should be more your brother's complication than yours."

It should have been. Another woman would have married and moved away, left Chas and Paton Shipping to their fate. Any woman not as invested as she was hunted. "My father built Paton & Son with his blood and sweat, no exaggeration. My mother's pedigree opened a few doors for us, but she came to America with nothing. Silas would shred our family's business for profit as much as to make a point. He is shredding it. His success would gut me."

"You could marry. It offers some protection," he argued.

No dowry, no means, and not a waking moment to herself; hardly a recipe for finding a husband. There was no space to breathe out from under Silas's bullying, his threats. It was more tangled than Spencer could possibly comprehend and too shameful for her to explain.

She slapped down a card, knocked to end her turn and sat back. "I'd like to discuss something else." She braced for more digging, resistance.

Spencer ducked his head. "As the lady wishes. Name your subject, then."

She slid a card on top of his. "Why are you hiding here?" She had watched the way he arranged his days to avoid company, hustling from one place to another always ahead of or behind the crowd. And, of course, she had gleaned all that she could from Laurel.

"Hiding?" He shifted in his chair, eyes focused on cards he must have memorized by now. "I am not hiding."

"Laurel says that you are."

He studied her above his cards, brow arched. "I am a regular topic of conversation between the two of you, then?"

A second mouthful of brandy on an empty stomach made her bold. "As often as possible."

It was true. Laurel was an encyclopedia where Spencer was concerned, handy with some detail or anecdote in nearly every conversation. Alix was eager for each and every one.

"Spies in my camp," he grumbled, trumping her play with a smug flick of his ace. "Anyhow, I am *not* hiding. I go to London when I must and occasionally for some diversion. Generally, I prefer to stay away. A regiment of men for months on end offers no peace and little privacy. I'm inclined to have both, when able."

She understood perfectly. A single moment off Paulina's lead was a breath of fresh air. Half an hour alone to write an uncensored letter, a godsend. "Yet here we are," she finished, studying Spencer.

"Meaning?" He was too busy trouncing her to look up.

"Meaning you're in company *now*."

His expression was unreadable save a warmth in his eyes. "And I've not a complaint about it."

It was an invitation, to what she had no idea, but every inch of her ached to accept.

Alix laid her hand out on the table, palm up without comprehending why; liquor, the moment. Spencer did not hesitate, his warmer, larger one pressing her knuckles into the wood. Like her, he stared at their brushing fingers, joined between the cards. A long moment passed.

Spencer cleared his throat and pulled away. "I've bested you."

"What? Oh." Alix glanced at his discarded hand. "So you have. We didn't lay a wager."

His lips twitched. "I'll name my prize."

Heart pounding clear into her throat, Alix held her breath, both dreading and anticipating his request.

"Come with me into the study."

"And?" There must be more to it.

Firm lips twitched, smile escaping at one corner. "Into the study," he repeated. "I have some letters to attend, and I would appreciate the company."

"Yes." The word drifted from her lips with the resistance of smoke. Under his spell, she rose from her chair and followed him out, not pausing to question the wisdom or the danger of it.

*   *   *

No other woman of his acquaintance, not even Laurel, would take off her slippers and stretch out along the sofa as Alix was now. On her back, she held a book above her face, reading and blocking the afternoon sun from her eyes. Spencer offered a moment of thanks for the sofa's placement under a small bank of high windows across the study. There was a sturdy burgundy arm chair against the wall to his left, by a book case, and another planted before his desk. He'd hoped she would choose that one, sitting close enough to make conversation. Now, reclining against the sofa's red velvet, her blue train sweeping the floor and one arm behind her head, he was glad she hadn't. He stole a glance in between sentences, indulging himself the soft planes of her face and the long lines and curves of her body.

Quill forgotten in-hand, he puzzled over her. Without more than rough exploration, he admitted she had snared him that first night, disarmed him with the same unnamable quality which had first caught his eye. He dared hope, as her soft lines draped with ease along his sofa, that she felt it too.

Her nose wrinkled up and dashed his sentimental moment.

"What are you puzzling at over there?" he demanded, eager for any opportunity to talk with her.

Alix sighed and rested the book across her belly. "I want to like this book. I *do* like it, but I cannot grasp the moral. Is sense superior to sensibility, or is she saying both are necessary?"

He was out of his depth. "Does it matter either way?"

"I feel it does. Redemption and growth of the characters are both affected."

55

Wanting to prolong their conversation, Spencer waved his quill at her thick, leather-bound book. "Perhaps she has purposely concealed her motives, leaving it to you, the reader, to conclude her lesson. Shall we ask her?"

"You know her?" Alix half sat up, propped on one elbow in a pose agreeable to her neckline.

"That edition was a gift of her brother."

"How exciting." She fell back and folded both arms behind her head, unkindly making him more aware of her figure. "You know a great many interesting people. Laurel says that you've been to dinner with the Prince Regent."

They were a step into territory he preferred to avoid, but with Alix it felt different. She didn't pry for details with a look of empty adoration. "Four times, in fact. Any occasion when the Duke of Wellington is made to go, I am mandated to sit between them."

She draped an arm across her eyes against the sunlight. "They don't get along?"

Spencer dipped his quill, at last scrawling a name across his forgotten letter. "A little too well, on the prince's side. Hero worship in the extreme."

Alexandra's body vibrated with laughter. "You have some keen ability to mitigate it?"

"Diplomacy. An ability to tactfully remind one that he is not a king, and the other that he's not a general."

"Perilous," she murmured.

Spencer sat back, resting palms on his desktop. Ordinarily this was where he'd get up, happy to be done with business, off for a ride or more diverting activities. Today there was no hurry leave. The usual tension between his shoulders conspicuously absent, he was relaxed head to toe. Alexandra should have had the opposite effect. She was practically a stranger, after all, and what they had shared in the garden might have made things awkward. Her easiness in his company kindled a feeling inside which he'd struggled to name.

He spared a glimpse at his watch, crushed by how little time they had left. "I could do with something to eat. Care to join me?"

Silence.

"Mrs. Rowan?"

Gentle breathing reached his ears, and nothing else.

Spencer got up, creeping around the desk as though she were a wild animal waiting to pounce. He pressed her wrist and raised her arm, heat radiating through the silk of her sleeve. "Alexandra?"

Fast asleep.

Laying her hand over her chest, he watched her a moment. Lust should come easily; how close had they been that night? It was there, deep in his gut, second to a confused pressure in his chest. He could stroke her cheek, chase stray wisps from her brow. *Lean in*, a voice whispered. *Brush a kiss to her temple.* It sounded reasonable. Spencer braced his hand against the sofa, bending to her mouth.

"Reed!" Heavy boots out in the hall snapped him up.

Bennet.

Limbs shaking with guilty nerves, he rushed the study door, determined to intercept his brother. The door flew open between them and Spencer braced arms against the frame to block Bennet's view.

Bennet stepped back and furrowed his brow. "What are you doing?"

"Finishing up. Something to eat?" He tried for and failed at nonchalance.

"Why so hasty?" Bennet raised up on tiptoes and ducked his head left to right, angling for a glimpse into the study. "Who is that?"

"Nothing." Spencer shook his head while the hole swallowed him deeper.

Bennet raked him with a narrowed gaze. "*Nothing* looks suspiciously like Mrs. Rowan."

He bumped Bennet out of the way with his chest, shutting the door in his wake. "So it is. And it isn't like that."

Bennet's grin held a trace of irreverence, his hand coming up to grasp Spencer's shoulder. "I wouldn't have thought otherwise."

"Hm." Spencer swept a hand down the hall, eager for a change of topic, and they started for the dining room. "Where have you been, today?"

57

"Serving Isabel her walking papers," Bennet grumbled, boots striking harder at the marble.

"That didn't last long."

"Approximately the amount of time it took Ponsonby to come up from London. How many nights have I been turned away for him?" His jaw stiffened. "Like buying a horse for another man to ride."

"Bennet."

Hands flew up. "Poor choice of metaphor, but you take my meaning. Isabel and I have a business arrangement. I've kept up my end."

They settled at the table, already set with cold meats, thick brown bread and village cheese. Spencer had underestimated how hungry he was until presented with the meal. Matching wits with Alexandra was hard work. He snatched an apple, wagging a finger at his brother. "She was never going to please you."

"Why the hell not?" Bennet managed through a mouthful of chicken.

"You've had a taste of that wild lady-captain. The first woman in your life who hasn't fallen at your feet. No hothouse flower is going to satisfy your appetite now."

"Ridiculous." Bennet shoved a handful of meat and cheese onto his bread with enough force to do it harm. "Miranda. I can't be trusted on the subject. I'd wring her neck just as she tried to wring mine, were I not relieved at never having to speak to her again."

Spencer tried to mute his chuckle by stuffing his mouth. Not that Bennet would think, even for a moment, that he believed a single word of the protest.

"Oh!" Bennet's hand smacked the cloth, signaling a change of tune. "I saw old Tremont keeping Mrs. Siddons company. We changed horses at the same stop."

"Oh?"

"Oh. And she was pleased to see me."

He looked Bennet over, artfully tousled hair and smart blue coat, and admitted a jealousy accrued over the last two decades. "I'll wager she was."

"Hush." Bennet paused and stuffed in more food, manners abandoned. "I know you'd rather gut yourself than take her invitation, but if Paton's aim is scaling the social ladder, she'd do him some good."

Bennet was correct. Mrs. Siddons was kind enough and theatrical, naturally, as an actress. But her salon had a queue to the street, packed with the sort of prattling dilettantes he was set on avoiding. Exactly the sort Chas Paton *needed*. "Not certain she'll do him good when she meets *Mrs.* Paton. Sarah has no patience for that woman's brand of snobbery."

"And she'll say as much, if it comes to it. Bring Mrs. Paton down a stair and give her husband a kick in the arse." Bennet rubbed his hands together. "I hope to witness it."

"That sounds appealing," Spencer admitted. "It also sounds exhausting."

Bennet pushed away his plate and slouched into the chair at a limp angle. "No one says *you* have to be there to see it, old man."

He aimed a retort, then shut his mouth. An idea had struck like lightning; a devious, tactical idea. Bennet was correct; he did not *have* to go.

And if Alexandra were sick enough, she would not have to either.

CHAPTER NINE

Alix clutched her straw bonnet tighter as the horses picked up speed on the hill, a warm breeze fanning her cheeks. Spencer's yellow curricle bounced over the road, its two wheels lending it a racy impropriety that couldn't have pleased her more. He was handy with the reins, steering his matched pair of grays around the low spots faster than he probably should, giving the sense he was showing off to impress her.

It was working.

The hills above Oakvale were blanketed by broad green oaks, making the rises appear deceptively low until Spencer wheeled the little chaise to give them a view of the estate's panorama. The thin gray line of his house below said plainly just how far they had climbed. Hopping down, he stopped first with the horses and then made his way around to help her down.

She accepted his hand, studying him all the while. Men at home didn't dress like him; she wasn't certain men at home were even *made* like him. American clothing was practical, dependable; so much brown wool and off-white homespun, with coat tails too long and footwear too short.

Knee high boots with enough polish to look new made Spencer appear taller, if that was possible. The tails of his smart navy-blue coat concealed the more scandalous lines of his tan buckskins, much to her disappointment. Plenty of ladies, including Laurel, referred to the pants as 'inexpressibles'. She had immediately grasped the allusion and was eager for a glimpse of their sinful tailoring.

"Out then." Spencer tugged at her hand, heat pressing between their gloves while he lowered her. Until he'd confessed and returned her glove, she'd dedicated him only a reasonable amount of thought. That had changed since their day together in the study. A brush of his arm, the pressure of his fingers; anticipation strung constant between them. Discovering that Spencer Reed and her stranger were one and the same had magnified the best qualities of both.

He tucked her hand into the warm crook of his arm and led her further up the hill, past where the road faded into high grass. "I'm sorry if my interference deprived you of company or amusement. I could have asked your leave before implying to the others that you were too sick to join them."

She jostled him with an elbow. "You could have, but you didn't."

Spencer ducked his head, lifting his hat to her in salute. "No," he admitted, something kindling in his hazel eyes, something which was not genuine apology.

He settled on the chipped remains of a felled tree trunk, patting the wood beside him.

She studied him in profile, heart pounding faster with each feature she traced. He caught her gaze with a half-smile.

"Lord Reed."

"Spencer, if you would."

Alix sat and shook her head, not certain that she *would* just yet.

He took off his hat and rested it on the log, raking fingers through silky chestnut hair. "May I ask you something?"

Her breath hitched. "Anything you like."

"Why did you go with me?"

Alix pressed a hand to her lips, fighting a smile, struggling to conceal burning cheeks. "The way you touched me. Like I was beautiful, desirable."

"So you were. Though you had plenty of admirers, as I recall."

"Admirers who assumed their titles would impress me into lifting my skirts. That I would be flattered or desperate. There was more warmth in your single touch than in all of their empty platitudes."

"Green," he chided, clucking his tongue. "Heavy handed. That's no way to seduce a lady."

He would know; he'd done a skilled job of it.

61

Leaning in she bumped him with a shoulder. "Such a strange way to begin a friendship."

A bump in return. "Is that what we are?"

"You've spared me from Paulina two days in a row, so yes." She grimaced, imagining her day without Spencer's interference.

He laughed. "She's not stupid, by my estimation. Mrs. Paton is bound to figure out we're dodging her eventually."

He had named her anxiety, a worry that had sat on the edge of her consciousness since yesterday. Paulina wasn't smart, but she was clever. Alix hated the idea of losing what they'd shared the last two days. She'd forgotten what it was like to be free, unburdened. "I have no idea what can be done about it."

Resting elbows on his knees, Spencer tossed her a boyish smile off his shoulder. "We're going to have to like other people, Mrs. Rowan. Or at least pretend to, if we wish to be in each other's company."

"You're asking a great deal," she grumbled, slipping from the tree to the ground. Leaning her head back against the spongy wood, she followed wisps of cloud brushing the sky. Spencer thudded beside her a moment later, sitting close enough that she felt the heat of his body without touching. She wished he would touch her, even the smallest brush to help make sense of a jumble inside.

A rustle of summer leaves passed the time for them, the breeze fanning her cheeks under an afternoon sun. Her attention fixed on Spencer, as it had so many times over the previous days. He became the point at which she started, spreading from him to their surroundings like ripples in water.

"Alexandra." Her name murmured on his lips gave Alix a small thrill. "I didn't single you out in the ballroom because you appeared desperate. Just the opposite, in fact."

"Tell me."

"Impossible. I don't possess the eloquence."

Eyes closed, she exhaled slowly, steadying herself and trying to form feelings into words. To explain a warmth she felt deep inside.

Spencer cleared his throat and got up. She expected him to say it was time to go. Footsteps moved off, crunching into the brush.

Something struck her, a sharp impact above her left breast. "Ow!" She snapped up.

"Oh, dammit all." He raised his hands. "I hadn't considered its staining your coat."

She glanced from a purple blotch on her lapel to the blackberry in her lap, then to Spencer frozen at the edge of the clearing. She stood without a word, stamping first toward the curricle to mislead him and veering into the bushes at the last second. Pinching off two fat blackberries, she wheeled and slung, lodging one in the folds of his cravat. Hers left its own mark, stain bold against the fine white linen.

Spencer raised a brow. "My aim is *accurate*, Mrs. Rowan."

"I've been warned." She snapped more berries as she spoke. One pegged his cheek, and one missed entirely. Winding up for a third shot, she realized she'd discounted his mobility.

First he matched her, a stride forward for each one she took back. Then he was running. She waited for his lunge and turned to flee. His boots were thunder hammering the ground at her back as she circled the horses.

His finger snatched the skirt of her coat. Alix threw herself forward into a long stride, certain she'd lost him rounding the back of the carriage. An arm hooked her waist and tipped her back. "No, no!" She gasped, wriggling against his grip and certain that whatever came next, it would not be pleasant.

His next move proved her right. One broad palm scrubbed wet pulp and coarse seeds across her cheeks and chin, somehow missing her mouth even as she panted and shrieked.

Flailing out an arm, she returned the favor, catching Spencer's jaw and earning shouts of her own.

In the struggle, she managed a foot between his legs. Instead of offering leverage, her effort to get free tumbled him. The ground came up, smarting her backside. Spencer came down, and only her quick dodge avoided a blow from his elbow.

They lay tangled in a heap, gasping, until Spencer groaned and rolled away. She looked him over, reaching above

63

her head with one arm for a missing bonnet, laughing. The same daring energy which had drawn her to him at the ball coursed her veins now, and it was wonderful. Grass stuck in his crisp hair and clung here and there to his berry covered face, and she grinned and admired her handiwork. "You look awful!"

"Do I?" he murmured, rolling onto an elbow and eating up space between their bodies. His question was smoky and filled with challenge. Her heart clenched and throbbed in her chest. "That is unfortunate," he leaned over her, "because you can hardly be tempted to let me do *this*."

It was just a brush, so brief and insubstantial that she might have mistaken the whisper of his lips for his breath. The barest increase in pressure blazed a memory of warm hands, a firm mouth and a cold stone wall. She closed her eyes and cherished those sensations, coupled with his hip pressing hers and his breath fanning her cheek. After a long moment, when he didn't try again, she dared to peek up at him.

He narrowed an eye, grinned and shook his head. "I look awful. You look *worse*."

"We can't go back like this," she breathed, still studying his lips.

Fishing inside his grass- and berry-stained coat, he produced a handkerchief and waved it just out of reach. "This is all we have." He snatched it from her grasping fingers. "And *I* get to use it first."

CHAPTER TEN

Spencer leaned over the table, resting an elbow above the pocket and took his shot. Balls rolled, clicking together, but he was in no better position when Bennet's turn came around. Most nights they were an equal match at billiards, but this evening he was agitated with far too much on his mind.

He'd devoted a lot of time to his dilemma with Alexandra and still managed only a basic solution. If their current group of acquaintances were a problem, then he would construct a party for Alexandra to put her more at ease. Women Paulina could hardly object to, ladies with whom he was familiar enough to be in company without raising eyebrows. Then he would wait, allow a few days to pass and take advantage of their newly formed mutual acquaintances.

Paulina was already more of a sentinel than usual, and he'd allowed five days for Laurel to introduce Alexandra and for Paulina to lower her guard. Ladies Conyngham, Ralls, Villiers, and Cowper formed a center to Alexandra's web. From there he hoped she would make friends of her own and put distance between herself and Paulina.

Bennet leaned in, screwing up his face and sticking out his tongue. Spencer would have laughed at his brother's efforts except that his shot sank with ease.

"You're practically handing it to me, Reed. A little sport for my trouble would be appreciated."

Bennet's 'trouble' was not making the trip to London as he'd originally intended, instead staying in to ease a cloud of boredom that had settled over Spencer. He gave his brother a withering glare, unmoved by Bennet's plight. He'd done enough nose wiping and wound cleaning over the years to feel entitled to some company.

Ignoring the black look, Bennet bent back to the table. "I should thank Mrs. Rowan for all the coin she's winning me this evening."

"How do you estimate Mrs. Rowan has anything to do with it?"

Stopping mid-draw, cocking his head, Bennet rolled his eyes.

A fair response. Bennet was not a child, and Spencer appreciated that he was not as circumspect as he pretended sometimes.

"She fascinates me," he admitted. "Though I haven't decided if it's a thrill of the chase or something more."

Bennet took his shot, propped his cue and leaned against the table to draw on his port, conspicuous by a lack of ribald quips.

"What?"

"What?" Bennet shrugged.

Spencer massaged his forehead. "Out with it."

Laughing, Bennet drained his glass. "We have crossed far beyond my territory."

"Having opinions, welcomed or otherwise? That is well within your territory." Since childhood, in fact.

Abandoning their game, Bennet pulled a chair from the card table, stretched out his legs and entrenched. "Does she know?"

"She does now."

"Did you tell her, or did she figure it out on her own?"

Tossing his stick onto the green felt, Spencer snatched his glass, resigned to joining Bennet at the table. "She's clever enough to have put it together eventually."

A finger rapped the table. "That's not what I asked."

"I confessed to her." It felt as though Bennet had dragged the admission from him, leaving behind a raw spot.

Toying with the edge of his glass, Bennet was thoughtful a moment. "That is the first detail which you should mull over."

He stared back, confused.

"You didn't *have* to say a word."

"I concede your point." He hadn't been caught, not even suspected.

"Hm. So what was her reaction when you did?"

Swallowing, he studied the table, sliding his glass in an aimless pattern. "I'm not certain."

Sitting up, leaning in, Bennet cocked an ear as though he'd misheard. "You're not certain? Did she, bawl? Take a swipe at your trousers?"

Spencer leaned his head back, exhaling some of the thrumming tension straining his ribs. "She's made no secret that she enjoyed it. And has made no move to repeat it. I'm not certain where we stand, precisely."

Bennet's wide eyes were incredulous. "Even a woman as notorious as Lady Frances would put you at arm's length for such stone. But here are you and Mrs. Rowan, whiling away your days together. That counts for something."

Spencer pressed lips tighter, wondering if he was being bluffed. He doubted Bennet was around enough to know for certain how much Alexandra figured into his day.

Laughing, Bennet relaxed in his chair. "I come and go two, three times in an afternoon. Lord Reed nowhere to be found, Mrs. Rowan allegedly ill in her room. No one takes anything up to her, no one comes down. Either you have a poor staff, or Mrs. Rowan is not in her room at all."

He made a furious study of the tabletop. "I fail to take your meaning."

Unfolding, Bennet palmed both their glasses and set off on a course for the sideboard. "Perhaps I don't have one. Just consider your answers this evening, more than my questions."

For all his cryptic, Sphinx-like prattling, Bennet was the only person who'd ever been able to accomplish what had just transpired, and it had been that way since he was young. Spencer found his thoughts organized by his brother's prodding, his provoking. He was old, set in his ways. Now and then, a fresh set of eyes was needed.

Bennet reappeared with full glasses and a chessboard balanced on an arm, planting everything between them on the table. "So, what do you do, then?"

"Hmm?" Still lost in thought, he'd missed the question.

Bennet rolled his eyes. "You and Mrs. Rowan. If it's not a liaison, then what do you do?"

"Oh." Spencer moved their pieces from a small cloth bag. "Nothing particular." The words felt wrong. It didn't feel like nothing when they were together.

"Sit staring until the clock chimes?"

Spencer sighed, arranging pieces. "No. In fact, we do most of the same things you and I do, and with notably less irritation."

"Oh, I am never irritated." Grinning, Bennet tipped his glass and claimed his pieces. "So you drink, play cards, and ponder the curious advent of ladies' drawers."

"Essentially, yes." He allowed himself a smile at Bennet's laugh. "I'm serious. Sometimes we just occupy the room for one another."

Bennet's face contorted while he looked over the board. "What does that mean?" Out marched a pawn.

"I enjoy her presence, and she enjoys mine." Spencer moved, claiming Bennet's piece.

"Ahh, yes, the elderly equivalent of lovemaking." Bennet dodged a cuff to the ear with deftness Spencer hadn't expected of a man so deep in his cups.

"Teasing! I'm only teasing," Bennet protested. Another pawn moved up. "Hours in a woman's company without the promise of so much as a bare ankle. There's something very heartening about it."

Despite the teasing, Spencer considered his brother's words. There had been a time in his life when the idea of an illicit touch was consuming; a hint of flesh, a stolen kiss, maneuvering the whole day for minutes alone in a darkened hall. A younger, brasher time. What had changed?

He came to the same answer as always: He'd grown old.

Things were different with her. It wasn't as if his every thought were noble where Alexandra was concerned; that was impossible now. Despite that, his primary sensation when she came to mind was an encompassing calm.

He'd yet to determine where such a new and foreign experience fit in his existence. It was struggle enough, accepting that somehow it *did* fit.

68

CHAPTER ELEVEN

She had fought tears all Monday morning, wedged as a corner of Chas and Paulina's frigid triangle and suffocated by their silence as Oakvale grew smaller at their backs.

The better part of two weeks passing since their visit to Spencer's home had tempered her feelings just enough that Alix had gathered her joy and passion and tamped them down inside. A firm rein on her emotions had made Paulina's scrutiny less dangerous but hadn't touched a dull ache over her heart. Spencer fed a hunger she had denied, ignored long enough to forget its existence. He fed more than one, if she were completely honest. Quiet comfort, childlike mischievousness, and a woman's passion; he stoked and kindled each in turn. A fortnight of his absence, rather than diminishing her need for Spencer, allowed a dangerous space for yearning.

Disappointment at leaving Spencer and Oakvale was lightened a shade by the distraction of her new friends. Their warmth and conversation soothed her longing when she recalled that it was Spencer who'd sent them to her. The women were hardly a substitute, but she lost herself in their company now and then.

The same held for Paulina. She and Lady Caroline Ralls were a matched set of harpies, so eager to be alone and gossip about the others that they spared the group their haughty looks and raised chins. Alix found Caroline slightly more palatable than arsenic, but had to admit gratitude to anyone who kept Paulina away.

Caroline had done well today, towing Paulina out early so the other ladies were permitted unfettered enjoyment of each other's company. Lady Emily Cowper was an easy charmer. Wild, tawny waves of hair, bright eyes and a naturally alluring smile warned of a free spirit that Alix found was paired equally with kindness. Laurel had shared, on their way home to Broadmoore, that Emily was mid-amour with a Corsican diplomat, to the seeming relief of her own dull, frail husband. The gossip might have been titillating if Emily were a vulgar woman; Alexandra thought her nothing but joyful and refined.

She was still a paler shade than the notorious Sarah Villiers, Lady Jersey, closest to her in age of all the women. When she had whispered to Laurel how beautiful Sarah was, the hushed answer was *'She's a Villiers.'* It was a name apparently synonymous with beauty, whether by birth or marriage. At first, with her sleek black curls and winged black brows, Lady Jersey seemed mysterious, observant, and as aloof as a raven. That was, until she spoke; Emily called her the magpie, a kind dig at Sarah's inability to stop talking. Alix didn't mind. Everything Lady Jersey had to say was interesting, her words soft and rounded by a seductive note. She was allure without effort, and it wasn't difficult to puzzle out the discarded trail of men in her wake.

Alix's favorite of her new friends, by far, was pretty little Lady Amelia Grey. Barely eighteen, she had enough girlhood in her newly mature features to remind Alix of a living doll. A cherubic oval face and brown satin curls exactly matched her doe eyes. She was forever clad in pastels, ruffles, and enough ribbon to keep a milliner employed for a lifetime. Alix struggled to grasp that Amelia had been married a year already, and to a man twice her age, at that.

It was a match anyone would have to shake their head at, insisted Laurel. Lord Grey was a glib, persuasive politician, and Amelia, the shy baby of ten children, was apolitical and a little deaf. Alix had the sense Amelia was used to being ignored, a fact made sadder by the girl's obvious eagerness to please. Amelia was joy and innocence, unabashed enthusiasm. It was real effort at times, not to pet or hug her delicate frame.

Alix watched for Amelia, seated with the others in Broadmoore's fine parlor. Laurel had arranged all the best furniture from two drawing rooms, among them a yellow silk sofa and some curvy-legged oak chairs cushioned in dusty pink damask. Heavy green drapes had been traded for ivory satin from the dining room. Poor Laurel had been so busy that she looked almost too fatigued to enjoy her company.

Paulina, insisting that too much tea was upsetting her stomach, had gone out early with Lady Ralls and Lady Elizabeth Conyngham. No doubt she was eager to show off her riding as much as her snobbishness. Alix was glad to be rid of her, of all three.

Laurel dropped into a chair perched at Alix's end of the sofa. She looked composed, though Alix knew better. Her eyes weighed everything, lending as much weight to the room's arrangement as she did a speck of dust floating through the shafts of sunlight. Reaching out, Alix rested a hand on her shoulder and gave a comforting squeeze. Laurel answered her with a wan smile.

Alix groaned at a familiar voice out in the hall and exchanged a crushed glance with Laurel. Paulina had returned with her coven in tow. Laurel was already nervous to make a good impression, and every woman in attendance boasted volumes more social status; the ladies' good opinion would do as much for the Hastings as it would for her own family. Unless, of course, Paulina behaved in her usual fashion.

They came in like a small army with Paulina as their commander, all clad in ridiculously similar riding habits; scarlet wool fastened by a yard of silk-twine frogs, like a British uniform stretched into an ugly dress. Lady Elizabeth Conyngham's was trimmed in gold, and Caroline and Paulina were hilarious twins with collar and cuffs of dark green velvet. They swept in with all the bearing of the mistresses of the house; it would have been amusing except for haughty glances thrown Laurel's way.

Caroline Ralls at least managed herself in conversation. With no greater claim to fame than a banking fortune left behind by her father and a minor title left behind by a destitute husband, Alix had observed a glimmer of self-consciousness in Caroline

71

now and then. She was determined to prove she belonged in the upper echelon.

Elizabeth Conyngham was cut from the same cloth, a common background and poor connections overlooked thanks to a pile of sterling. Unlike Caroline, Elizabeth had no doubts that she belonged at the top, having announced frankly over tea one afternoon that the Marchioness of Hertford was occupying her bed and she intended to turn the woman out. Confused, Alix had cocked an ear to Laurel, who bit her lip and whispered that Lady Hertford was the prince's mistress. The ambition had shocked her more than the sentiment; until that moment Alix hadn't believed Elizabeth possessed a single idea in her head. She seemed little more than wrists and a neck, a collection of limbs for displaying jewels.

Elizabeth perched beside her on the sofa as though it were dirty, but it was not to be for long, to their mutual relief.

"Elizabeth!" snapped Caroline, pointing to an empty chair Paulina was dragging from beside Laurel to her own spot across the room. "Come and sit! Emily doesn't mind trading places with you."

A sour look said Emily minded very much, but she bit her tongue and moved opposite Alix on the sofa's far end. "My word, look at the three of you. What a sight!"

Alix saw the compliment for what it was, a dig, but the three newcomers were too busy fussing over arranging their chairs and each other's trains to comprehend.

Caroline swept a hand over their ridiculous preening. "Mrs. Paton has borrowed my original so that we would look smart on our ride, without a sore thumb in our bunch."

Anyone else would know enough to be insulted. Paulina beamed, lapping up Caroline's backhanded praise.

Sarah, arching her sharp brow, looked them over. "Wool in June, Elizabeth? It's sweltering already. Really," she clucked, "How ridiculous."

Elizabeth screwed up her chipmunk face, glancing over her riding habit. "Sheep wear wool in June, Lady Sarah."

One was stupid, one vapid, and they had found Paulina to be the malicious glue in between. Alix shook a throbbing head. Three minutes among them and she was already exhausted.

72

Caroline, suddenly aware of more than just herself, skimmed the gathering and patted at her mound of carrot-colored curls. "Where is Lady Amelia? Is she not joining us this afternoon?"

Elizabeth clutched her chest at the mention of Amelia. "Is she shut up now that word about Grey has broken?"

Word? Alix held her breath, afraid to hear more and equally fearful that the women would go on in vague ciphers.

Sarah came half out of her chair, spearing the hateful trio with her rubied finger. "Amelia does not know a thing about it, nor does she need to be acquainted with it just now. London will do its worst soon enough."

Pressing a fist to her heart, Emily blinked at her lap. "How can she not know? It's everywhere, poor thing. Can you imagine?"

Alix worked a hand beneath her hip, grasping a pinch of the silk sofa and holding fast against an impending blow.

"She left London just before the letters were published," Sarah ground out. "I have to wonder if her father had caught wind of the scandal, or her aunts. Sent her north ahead of it." She flicked an imaginary crumb from her skirt with a snap. "I cannot imagine Grey himself had the forethought to spare her."

Caroline sniffed. "How humiliating. And such low class, Miss Fields sending their letters to the papers."

"Julia Fields is a whore, Caroline," retorted Sarah. "Class is not her primary concern."

Letters. Miss Fields. Alix's stomach churned, a squeezing in her chest and throat wringing tears up into her eyes. She had never considered it possible for infidelity to be worsened, that there could be layers to unfaithfulness. Lord Grey had managed to add a bold red footnote of shame to his indiscretion.

Caroline sniffed, trading knowing sympathy with Paulina. "Sad, all the same. Who could have expected Amelia to keep her husband's affections, even at the beginning?"

"Swallow your tongue, you sour old goat!" Sarah's narrow eyes pierced Caroline, who flailed as though physically struck by the curse.

Braided stiff with nerves, Alix leaned in to get Laurel's attention while sharp conversation ricocheted past. "What in heavens are they clucking about?"

"Grey has dallied with Miss Fields for almost the whole of his marriage to Amelia, can you believe it?" Laurel squeezed her eyes shut, shaking her head at the idea. "When he refused Julia's demands for a greater allowance and tried to break things off, she sent their letters to the papers. My mother's note yesterday said nearly *two hundred* billets, full of the most ardent, shocking lines."

"Oh God." Her stomach churned harder, a sour hint of bile nearly preventing her question. "But Amelia has no idea?"

Laurel nodded slowly. "It will be waiting for her, when she returns to London," she spared a glance for the Stygian witches opposite them, "If it doesn't spread north like wildfire or boil over here first."

Wheels clattering up the drive sliced through all conversation and set a sad, strange play into action. Emily adjusted herself at different attitudes, trying to appear relaxed. Elizabeth and Caroline picked at one another's' clothes, fussing in a dull murmur. Sarah, silent for a change, was still and regal, bold features set in grim determination.

A sick feeling buzzed between her heart and her head, and Alix almost wished Amelia would never appear while wondering if their gossip had summoned her. She listened to a bustle out in the hall, indistinct voices followed by the butler's footsteps, her heart pounding at each one.

Elizabeth jumped at the door's opening as though it hadn't been a source of crushing anticipation for five minutes.

Amelia stood in the entrance and they all held their seats. She smiled, and Alix swore she heard dust gathering in the silence.

Finally, she looked to Laurel. Alix nudged her with an elbow and reanimated their hostess to her feet. "Lady Amelia. Come in. Sit down. Make yourself at ease." Laurel's instructions were measured, small safe turns meant to navigate the perilous cliff on which they all stood.

Everyone else felt the awkwardness, but between Amelia's poor hearing and her temperament, she only caught the invitation and her smile brightened. She settled between Alix and Sarah on the sofa, looking pleased just to be seen.

74

Alix looked her over, not able to resist patting one willowy arm despite a grim pall in the air. "Look at you! A very picture of the season." Amelia wore green velvet and green satin from her slippers to the brim of a petite bonnet which was crowned with a little garden of red and pink roses. Amelia colored, staring at hands laid just so in her lap. "That's very kind of you to say, Mrs. Rowan. Mama never approved of so much frivolous color, but I long for it," she admitted.

"You are a *married* woman," Caroline threw out, smirking. "You may do as you please."

Alix narrowed her eyes in a glare that couldn't be undone even by Paulina's quelling gaze.

Amelia pressed on, oblivious. "I'm ashamed at being tardy. You all look so lovely and set for an afternoon. I'm sorry to have kept you waiting."

"No time was fixed for our gathering," reassured Laurel, "Not enough to cause anyone inconvenience."

"We did nothing until you arrived but make idle conversation," Emily offered smoothly. "No one was the least put out."

Alix reached out and claimed Amelia's bonnet, passing it down to rest on a table between her and Laurel. "We're glad for your company. You have made our little party complete."

"Any news from town?" Elizabeth snickered, swatting at Caroline's prodding finger. Paulina pressed a laugh with her hand.

Alix could only stare, frightened by their callous enjoyment of Amelia's predicament. They would stop their baiting any moment, wouldn't they? Then her eyes fell to Paulina, and Alix knew there was no limit to what the trio might say or do, not if her sister-in-law had any say.

"Refrain from gossip in Lady Hastings's parlor, dear." Sarah's smile was brilliant but her words were acid.

Caroline opened her mouth then snapped it again, eyes fixed at a point over Lady Sarah's shoulder. Alix felt the newcomers before she heard them, sensing eyes on her back. She had been too absorbed in the Greek tragedy playing out in the drawing room to catch the sounds of an approach.

75

John, Spencer, and Lord Jersey hovered on the threshold, presumably waiting to be invited in, but Alix saw something in the furrow of Spencer's brow, the way Lord Jersey glanced between his wife and Caroline which hinted at more to their arrival than a social call.

"Villiers, come in here and let me look at you," Sarah drawled, tossing her husband a heavy-lidded glance.

"Not exhausted from looking at every other man in the county?" he quipped.

Theirs was a strange pairing, from what Alix gathered. Lady Jersey had affairs of her own, and Alix presumed her husband did too. But when the two were in proximity she would swear that *they* were lovers. George strode in, presenting himself for his wife's inspection and she began to understand Laurel's comment about being a Villiers. Lord and Lady Jersey were attractive book ends, his features equally striking. Broad forehead, hooked, regal nose and lips perpetually on the edge of a wry smile did him credit against a stoic persona. Jersey was undeniably handsome, a gentleman turned from the same mold as his friend Lord Reed. The comparison drew her eye to Spencer, who arched a brow at her unbroken stare.

"You look positively wild. Sit down." Sarah snapped the command, breaking Alix's study of Spencer. The words were sharp but Alix caught a spark in George's eyes hinting that if he was being horsewhipped, he enjoyed it.

Out of seats and not being invited to do likewise, John and Spencer stationed themselves beside Laurel, who cleared her throat delicately at a protracted silence. "Did you enjoy your sport?" she asked John finally, breaking the quiet stalemate and giving obvious relief to several of her guests.

He tried and failed at a frown. "Jersey and his supernatural horse. Put me and Reed in the dust."

Spencer nodded his agreement, holding her eyes all the while. "Put up a racehorse, Jersey, and you'll have my wager every time."

"I'm after it. Be patient. A few more seasons and I'll have a champion." Jersey's words were rough stones of thought, curt replies while his brain turned over something more consuming.

By his slitted eyes fixed on Caroline, Alix guessed that *something* was not his thoroughbred at the moment.

More silence chased Jersey's bravado. John shifted foot to foot, and Spencer in his charming fashion took stock of the gathering. "Ladies, you look each of you lovely. How are you?" Nods and murmurs. He met her eyes again. "Mrs. Rowan. You look well this afternoon. How is your cough?"

She bit her cheek to pin down a smile. "Much improved." *Cad.*

Silence descended once again and unease stretched taut across the small room.

Tea being brought in relieved Laurel to the point of near collapse. It kept everyone busy and on topic, initiating a round of *pleases* and *thank yous* and *'mind, the cup is hot'*. It occupied exactly five minutes of the next quarter hour. Alix wished she could convey to Spencer with a look the silent agony hanging over the room.

As if reading her mind, he turned to Amelia and raised his voice. "Lady Amelia. How are you enjoying your time in the country?"

Amelia smiled and nodded. Grasping by her look that she hadn't quite heard him, Alix leaned in and repeated the question.

She beamed up at Spencer. "Oh, it's breathtaking. I haven't come up with Grey before, to Rosemont. The house is perfect and we're both enjoying it. Grey has been a little ill, but I'm certain that the fine weather will mend him." Her smile broadened, showing a dimple. "We are enjoying it," she repeated.

"More than town?" Paulina clawed at Amelia, showing off for her tittering companions.

Poison, strangling. No punishment was fast enough or fitting enough in Alix's opinion.

Amelia beamed. "Oh, I doubt there's much Grey loves more than town."

"I can imagine *one* thing," Elizabeth muttered, giggling with her companions, hissed down by Sarah's shushing.

Alix felt decorum crumbling into a landslide. Laurel, not permitted by the vice of good manners to stand up and order everyone out, was casting increasingly desperate glances at John.

Sarah balanced a high wire between imposing decency and revealing too much in Amelia's presence. Caroline, Elizabeth and Paulina grew bolder, too in love with their own hateful cleverness to give Amelia's feelings any quarter. All the while the poor girl smiled and nodded, confident of being among friends. Alix could only sit, an unwilling spectator while the final, terrible act unfolded.

Emily scooted forward on her cushion, interjecting herself and aiming for a distraction. "I hope you'll claim your vouchers for Almack's first thing this season. Our soirees at the assembly rooms would hardly be complete without you in attendance."

Amelia gasped and grabbed Emily's hand. "How wonderful. I will be so delighted!"

Elizabeth, half listening and half paying attention to Caroline's poisoned whispers, shoved a shortbread between thick lips. "You won't be able to show your face there, Amelia! Not with all the scandal!"

Alix heard air being sucked from the room, a collective inward gasp of every person present except Amelia, whose face clouded at Elizabeth's braying. Of all the times for her hearing to work perfectly, Alix thought, it had to be now.

"What scandal? What do you mean?" Wide brown eyes searched their faces, leaving Alix the sick feeling of tormenting some baby animal.

Elizabeth, at least, had the good sense to look shamed and a bit green at her horrible breach. Paulina and Caroline, flanking her, sat stone faced and obstinate. Cowards, forcing someone else to deliver the deathblow while they feasted on Amelia's misery. Alix refused to play along.

"What scandal?" Amelia repeated, voice trembling as she pleaded with Emily, who swallowed and looked to her lap.

"Amelia," Alix said firmly, snapping the girl's attention to her. "You look tired. I'm going to see you home." She stood and held out a hand which Amelia clasped with her smaller one. Towing her limp little frame to the door, Alix pushed her out into the hall. "Go and fetch your gloves. I'll be along directly."

Amelia nodded, moving on stiff legs down the hall.

78

She crossed the room when Amelia was out of sight, seeing red by the time she reached the others. "Every one of you," she hissed, jabbing at even Paulina's tight-lipped expression, "owns some blame for what just transpired here, by your words or by your silence, but *you*," she sliced a finger across Caroline, Paulina and Elizabeth, "ought to *burn* from the inside with shame that only the hand of God himself can extinguish." She bit off the words, choking down more, and turned on her heel toward the door. Paulina, Silas, and their punishments be damned. She'd take her lumps with pleasure.

A word was spoken behind her, a desperate command, but her feet pounded in her ears as much as her thundering heart and Alix couldn't make it out. Amelia was her sole focus now, hunched in the hall, dwarfed by its high columns like an imprisoned miniature, eyes wide and red rimmed. "Mrs. Rowan," she whispered, "please tell me what is happening."

Alix's heart clenched, choking off her words until she could gather herself. Then she wrapped an arm around Amelia's narrow shoulders, sweeping her toward the door. "On the way home, when we can speak more freely." They shuffled out together under a sun that was hateful in its brilliance, callous to poor Lady Grey's impending heartbreak.

"Settle in. I'll get my hat." She passed Amelia off to a footman, who handed her up into the carriage.

Only when she turned back to find Spencer waiting on the top step did it register that what she'd heard in the hallway was her name on his lips. He grabbed her wrist with long fingers as she passed by, forcing her to turn around. She wasn't angry with *him*, just angry, and she didn't want to talk. "I'm getting my hat," she repeated.

Nodding, Spencer brought an arm from behind his back and held out her bonnet.

*   *   *

Spencer settled the hat on Alexandra's head, certain she would pull away before he could find his voice. He swallowed twice before managing out the words. "What you said inside was brave, Alexandra."

79

She raised her chin a fraction. "And could have, *should* have been said by any one of the others. Someone less apt to face Paulina's wrath."

"But it was you." The words tumbled out unchecked. "You have my thanks, my admiration. And someday, when Amelia is able to look back on these days, I expect it will be you she thinks of with gratitude. Her father is a friend to me; he'll appreciate what you've done."

Softening, Alix pressed his fingers with her other hand, glancing back at Amelia's gaunt face peering through the carriage window. "Those days are very, very far away."

Gripping her wrist tighter, he tugged her down one step at a time. "Come."

"Come where? What are you doing?"

"Going with you. Now stop dragging feet and come along."

Full lips pursed, leaving no question of her disapproval, but Alix followed along. He wasn't eager to join her, but suspected she might need him more than she was letting on. He certainly wouldn't allow her to face this task alone.

Lord Jersey had broken the news to them that morning, just as they passed the first clearing out of Broadmoore's view. No one believed Grey's dalliance with Julia Fields had ended with his marriage to Amelia. He behaved more as a parent to her than as a husband. As John had pointed out on their ride, it was assumed that Grey might seek out his mistress from time to time, while remaining discreet.

Jersey's quick synopsis of the daily papers proved Grey had been anything but, and the printing had not spared his words to Julia. That he had groaned over her, passed days in agitation at the thought of her, taken her in his carriage, the very one they were alighting now, one afternoon when parliament had let out early. Julia had shared every red-tinted detail, recalled in her lover's hand.

They hadn't comprehended the real danger in an immediate sense until Jersey spotted three ladies coming down a far hill and John identified the dangerous mix of Ralls, Conyngham and Mrs. Paton. Their horses couldn't draw up or wheel about fast enough. Jersey had made it readily apparent that racing was indeed in his thoroughbred's future, but not at the promise of any coin. Still they were too late; they'd arrived at the house to find a fuse already lit among the women. Alexandra's face had dashed the last of his hopes, saying as plain as any words that Amelia's fate had been decided.

He took the carriage's empty seat. Alix settled opposite, beside Amelia, who burrowed into the crook of her arm without invitation.

The carriage lurched forward, more jarring than it should have been, and Spencer realized he was stiff with nerves head to toe.

Alexandra held his gaze in silence until they had passed under the front gate turning out onto the main road. He was out of his depth, never the unfaithful one and never jilted, and by Alexandra's expression, her frame of reference was not any broader.

In the end, Amelia took the matter out of their hands. "Is it Grey?" she whispered.

"What makes you think so?" Alexandra's voice brimmed with compassion, so much that he also felt comforted by her words.

"I didn't until this moment. A letter came last week. I went to his desk to borrow a nib for my quill. Flowers, roses I think. An envelope was perfumed with them. I wondered but I didn't...I would never think so of him."

No doubt the envelope had been Julia's plea for more money, her demand for his unflagging attentions. He wondered if Grey now regretted his moment of conscience.

Alix squeezed Amelia tighter; Spencer recognized it as a warning to brace for what came next. "Amelia, did you know that your husband has a mistress in town?"

A piercing animal wail magnified by their close quarters said plainly that she did not know. Amelia's shoulders heaved, but no more sound came out, not even breath, and he feared she was having some sort of fit. Then one ragged sob opened a gate for others; face buried in Alexandra's shoulder, Amelia muffled the sounds of her innocence dying. Alix closed her eyes and bounced Amelia out of time with the carriage's haphazard rattling, shushing softly against the girl's ear.

She was stronger than he; Spencer appreciated it in that moment. He could hold an infantryman's guts in both hands, pull shrapnel from an eye, or bayonet his enemy with countless blows until he fell and didn't get up. He could never do what Alix was doing now, holding together pieces of Amelia's heart. That was true bravery.

Lost in the thought, it took several moments before he comprehended Alix's fingers raking at him, beckoning for something. He glanced from his hand to his watch fob, finally grasping what she was asking of him. Feeling like a slow-witted idiot, he tore his handkerchief free, shoving it into her waiting palm.

One hand cradling Amelia's head, Alix unfolded his cloth with the other, frowning at how tiny and inadequate it must seem compared with a growing dark spot on her brown silk bodice. "Amelia," she instructed, "We're nearly home. Sit up and get hold of yourself a moment."

Her words met with only partial success. Amelia pulled herself away, still hunched and face to the foot well no matter Alexandra's efforts to raise her chin. A few passes of his handkerchief got a top layer of tears and snot cleaned before Amelia fell apart again.

"I want..." she gasped between sobs, "I want to go to my father in London."

"Your father is coming here," he offered, glad to be of use and thankful he had gleaned something of value from Jersey's recounting of the London scandalbroth surrounding Grey.

"I don't understand! I don't understand." Amelia gasped the phrase between sobs, head shaking and her eyes pressed closed.

Another person might have drawn things out, tried to soften the blow. Alexandra by some intuition seemed to appreciate that it was kindest to get things over with. "This woman has printed your husband's letters, Amelia. In the papers. So, your father will come here, and you will stay in the country and spare yourself from idle tongues."

"What do I do?" Tears stretched into panic, Amelia comprehending that her husband had not only shamed himself, but her as well. Spencer tucked a hand beneath his thigh to keep from making a fist. "What shall I do?" she cried again, sitting up, eyes darting from Alix to him and back.

"You're going to go home, go inside, and that is all you're going to worry about just now," instructed Alix.

Amelia clawed at Alix's sleeve. "He's there! He's going to be there when we arrive. I can't look at him; what will I say?"

Alix's eyes went to his, an unspoken question in them. He nodded. "Leave Grey to Reed. The men can sort that out; you and I will start by going in."

"I can't see him; I can't! I don't want him to touch –" Hysterics erupted in earnest, Amelia tottering wildly between crying, shrieking, and choking out unintelligible parts of words. Alix looked stricken, and he felt useless. He'd once knocked a hysterical corporal out cold mid-battle, but the application of such a tactic now was useless, and that was the extent of his knowledge.

It took Alexandra and two of Amelia's aunts, summoned by her father he guessed, to drag her limp-legged and wailing from the carriage and into the house. A sound over his shoulder as Spencer followed them in revealed a dust plume far down the lane, a tiny black carriage growing larger at break-neck speed. Lord Darby, he'd put money on it. Spencer picked up his pace; Amelia's father was not a man regarded for moderate temper.

The sobbing drifted farther away upstairs, and Spencer put more distance between himself and the gut-wrenching sound. Staring at the floor as he stalked toward the study, he counted black and white marble tiles; ten of each to the study door. Somehow it helped cage his anger.

George started at his intrusion, arms and legs spread akimbo as though pinning his red leather arm chair to the floor. Green drapes pulled tight cast a sickly light between the room's shadows and over George's blandly handsome face. It didn't help that he was already haggard by a night of hard drinking, guessing by a stale, rummy odor hanging on the air. Creases in George's coat, from knee to thigh on his trousers, announced that he still wore yesterday's clothes.

Identifying his intruder, George raked fingers through wild blond hair and slumped back in his seat. "Reed. I'm in no mood for company."

"I couldn't give a damn, Grey." He paced a few steps in. "And you're bloody well about to have it in spades, so prepare yourself."

The news brought George up in his chair. "What the hell does that mean?"

"That if I don't wring your sodding yellow neck, Darby behind me will."

"Oh God." Burying his face, George scrubbed at swollen eyes. "He knows." Spencer was pinned by an accusing glare. "How do *you* know?"

"Everyone has seen your bare arse, clear to the border. *Everyone* knows."

"Oh God, Amelia!"

Spencer miscalculated how quickly he could cover the room and how forcefully George had bounded from his seat, his arm driving the man back down and cracking something in the chair's frame before nearly toppling it backwards. "You either have excuses or apologies, and Lady Amelia wants neither one. Save them for her father."

His words summoned Darby, bellowing down the hall under a cloud of Scottish vulgarity. "...do not require an introduction! He will damn well ken who I am with my boot in his arsehole!"

A face as cragged as the hills of his homeland coupled with a silver sheen to his once fiery sweep of hair was camouflage; Spencer knew better than to believe Darby was decrepit or tame. Anxiously plucked sideburns stood from his weathered face like gills, mute testimony to his anger and worry. Darby's glacier blue eyes pinned Grey as he stormed in, set to freeze the man where he sat. He was absent his hat but not, Spencer noted, his thick oak walking stick.

"Grey, you unaccountable whoreson." It rolled from Darby's tongue with the same factual monotone as a comment on the weather. "Where is my daughter?"

Spencer pointed. "She's been taken upstairs by Mrs. Rowan and her aunts."

"Mrs. what!"

"A friend," Spencer placated.

"It sickens me," he ground out, gathering a few menacing steps towards Grey, "to think of her breathing the same air as what flows from your pox ridden mouth!" The walking stick slammed to the desk for emphasis, and Grey did not help his cause by flinching. Any sign of weakness was blood in the water for Darby. "Unthinkable, that she should be shamed by a muslin-lifter such as you."

Grey found his feet now, pinning them both with a trembling finger. "No whores for you, I presume! Pure white robes of a saint. And you, Reed? Not a dalliance once in your past?"

Spencer straightened and rolled a shoulder. "Plenty of them Grey, but I never took a wife to bed with my mistress."

"Hypocrisy abounds!"

"Doesn't it?" Spencer stepped ahead of Darby. "Plenty of gentlemen keep comfort on the side with their lady's knowledge." Jersey came immediately to mind. "Why didn't you tell Amelia?"

"Are you daft? Because it would gut her!"

"And now she is gutted. Lo, the irony." Crossing his arms, Spencer kept quiet and let his point stand between them.

Darby was less content. "I'm calling you out, Grey! Battersea fields, day after tomorrow. Be sure to bring a second so I can shoot him too, for his poor judgment in calling you friend."

"You cannot." Spencer raised a hand. "I've already demanded satisfaction from Lord Grey."

Grey crossed his arms. "You've done no such thing!"

"It was my purpose in coming here; my claim takes precedence." Grey was probably not clear which end of a pistol lobbed a bullet, but Darby had the aim of a blind man. Spencer was nearly certain the wrong person would be struck, to say nothing of substantial danger to anyone within fifty yards.

Grey swallowed and his ruddy cheeks blanched. "You're accounted as a dead shot, Reed."

"I fail to see how that is a problem."

Silence stretched between them, tight enough to fray, and Spencer wondered by George's renewed airs if he thought the challenge a bluff. He determined to set the matter straight. "Darby stands as my second. Battersea fields, dawn after next. Or I shred what remains of your manhood."

"Reed." Alexandra's voice was a cool breeze, slaking some of his rage. He realized, turning to find her wide-eyed and hovering in the doorway, that she must have heard his ultimatum to Grey. "It's time we were on our way."

He caught a weight to her words and nodded.

Grey stepped in, red-faced and humiliated. "Is half of London in my house! Get out! I would speak with my wife."

"Don't force yourself on her, Lord Grey. Preserve what's left of your dignity. And hers." Alexandra's sigh was tired and thin. "Learn to practice some unselfishness. *Sir*."

George lunged at her insult, and Darby grabbed a fistful of his shirt, hauling for the door on stout legs. "At present, this is Amelia's home. You'll bunk elsewhere."

Grey kicked against Darby's efforts. "You wanted this! I have never been good enough!"

"Well, you've proved that point, lad!"

Grey went on twisting and flailing against Darby's iron grip. "You're high on your oats, driving a wedge into my marriage at last. You bastard!"

Their exchange escalated quickly to a rough embrace, Darby's arm a vice around his son-in-law's neck while they grunted and strained down the hall.

Each time Spencer believed shame and humiliation had reached their peak today, he'd been proved wrong.

He pressed a hand to Alexandra's shoulder, telling her to stay put, and followed Darby's commotion to the door. A meaty arm tossed Grey outside, and skidding gravel and a mouthful of swears echoed back. He came up behind Darby just in time to see Grey dusting off, drawing back for a charge. Spencer snatched the walking stick and positioned himself on the steps between the men. "Try it, Grey, and I'll break your goddamn ankles. And I'll still put a ball in you and not lose sleep."

George backed away, arms wide. His lips parted in a sneer and then he froze, eyes fixed to windows high up on the house. His hand shot up, grasping. "Amelia, wait! Wait..."

He couldn't see Amelia in the window, couldn't hear the curtain fall, but Spencer knew the moment both had happened.

Head hanging, Grey's arm fell limp, and for the first time there was something like contrition on his face. He turned and crossed the yard toward the stables without another word.

"I'll be here tonight, if he shows his face again," barked Darby, loud enough for his son-in-law's ears.

Spencer took in the slump of Grey's shoulders, the shuffling gait of his retreat. "He won't."

Slender fingers pressed at his back. He closed his eyes and let Alexandra's nearness sooth him.

"Mrs. Rowan, I take it?" growled Darby, shifting his not inconsiderable attentions to her.

To her credit, Alexandra stood tall at his scrutiny. "Lordship."

"A Yank lass. Hmph. Reed says you did Amelia a kindness."

"I imagine she feels otherwise."

"You have my thanks, just the same," Darby muttered, high praise from a proud man.

Alix stepped between them and laid her hand on Darby's arm. "Lord Darby, plenty of people will call to offer Amelia sympathy. There isn't much you can do to ease her suffering, but turning away Ladies Ralls and Conyngham might prevent more."

Caterpillar brows twitched at the information, weighing it, and Darby's broad shoulders slouched. He gestured upstairs. "Into the trenches, then. Reed, if you change your tune about the Fields, no one will think the lesser of you. You can act as my second just as well."

"I won't, but thank you." He took Darby's hand and shook it, waiting until the door had closed in the man's wake to claim Alexandra's trembling arm. "How are you?"

"Don't ask me now." She tried sweeping loose strands back into her disheveled bun. "I'm biased and outraged beyond rational conversation. Disagreeable at being hungry." She scrubbed a sleeve over her eyes. "Don't ask me now," she pleaded again.

He led her across the dooryard in silence, wondering at how she was now a fixture in his days, as though she had always existed. Alexandra's warm evenness created a sort of amnesia, so that he nearly forgot what life had been like before. Friends, she had said, but they had tangled somehow into confidantes, into more.

Her fingers pressed reassuring warmth into his when he handed her up, and Spencer held on longer than he needed to. Alexandra's gaze was questioning, and then she patted the seat beside her. He understood.

He couldn't explain it in words, but he understood.

*　　*　　*

Spencer pressed beside her in the carriage, silent and patient. She held some distance between them, despite their proximity and the carriage's bounce conspiring to make them touch. Alix wasn't certain her heart, red and raw from the afternoon's misery, was in proper shape to handle more complex emotions.

And there was a line between them, for days now, that she was hesitant to cross. Not her scheme, not even Paulina; it was something more profound and filled with risk that gave her pause. Despite that, she appreciated the comfort of just being in Spencer's presence. Deciding she was overthinking the whole thing, she turned to him. "I wish you could spend the evening at Broadmoore."

He jerked beside her. "Why?"

It was not the response she'd hoped for. Alix swallowed, finding her nerve. "I need your company." She met his eyes.

"I confess, I dared not hope that was your reason." His gaze was steady, measured, and it stole any reply. Spencer cleared his throat. "I'll speak to John when we arrive."

"You will?" It was her turn to admit a fear of hope.

He inched closer along the seat. "You will have whatever you wish, anything you need."

She breathed deeply and turned away from him, and tried to sort her roiling emotions. She watched the scenery pass outside without blinking, afraid to invite tears that had threatened all afternoon. "Where is the line?"

"Hmm?"

88

"Fornication is condemned, adultery. Yet plenty of people do so, even those who claim to revile it."

"They damn it in one breath and indulge it with the next," he agreed.

"What are the differences between the Greys, George's lies and Amelia's humiliation, and the Jerseys, who don't trouble themselves about infidelity? Is there a possibility in every union, no matter how joyful, for one to stray?" She sighed and pressed her eyes, wishing she could press the flood of thoughts back into her mind. "Where's the boundary line for hurt and derision?"

"I keep thoughts to myself on Jersey's peculiar arrangement. For my part, the line looks distinctly like a wedding band. But you're a woman of business, Mrs. Rowan." His acknowledgment cheered her. "Marriage at its most base is a contract. No party wishes to sign their name only to discover they've been swindled." He was quiet, but she felt a weight to the silence. "And no, I do not believe broken-heartedness is a foregone conclusion. Some men's character is molded from sturdier stuff."

His character. She thrilled at his sentiment, and Spencer's words put her at ease.

She dared to rest her hand atop his on the seat, studying her pale fingers against his darker ones. Something in the way he made her feel recalled the woman she had been once, vibrant colors instead of muted grays. Alix rested her hand completely against his and looked up to find his eyes on her. The rise of his chest quickened, timed with her own, and a spark in his hazel eyes made her believe he could read her thoughts just then. She tried and failed avoiding a glance at his lips.

"Paulina is going to be furious." Furious at what she had said, what she had done in the drawing room. At what she was doing now, wherever it led.

His jaw twitched, and he shifted eagerly against the squabs. "Leave Paulina to me."

CHAPTER TWELVE

A pink cast from the sun, now well below the hills, danced above copses beyond Broadmoore's garden wall, fading to orange and up into a spectrum of blue where the first evening stars winked down. Alexandra had gone to her room, as much to rest as to avoid Paulina's wrath, but she needn't have. Spencer had enjoyed dinner with John and Laurel, Paulina choosing to stay in her room and Chas, he guessed, mandated to join her.

"One hell of day," muttered John, putting the whiskey between them atop the garden wall. It was hard for Spencer to listen or to feel much empathy at John's words. He had fond memories of the wall, and despite his best efforts, they occupied a good measure of his attention just now. He shouldn't have kissed her at Oakvale. He ran a hand along the wall's crumbling stone. Or he perhaps he shouldn't have stopped.

"Grey," began John. "You really mean to call him out, Reed?"

He nodded, downing his second glass.

"Make a widow out of Lady Amelia?"

"No." Spencer grimaced at the burn and spilled more whiskey into his tumbler. "Make a *point*."

John shook his head, then raised his glass. "If I treated Laurel thus, you'd rip my bollocks off."

Now he turned to face John. "You wouldn't treat her thus, so it's a moot point." He leaned back and stretched tight muscles in his neck. "Besides, unlike Grey, I'm reasonably certain of *your* having some bollocks, given Laurel's present condition."

90

"God," groaned John, chuckling. "Broadmoore, a baby. Can I tell you how bleeding ready I am for the Patons to be gone? They've been nothing but a rash on my arse for weeks."

Spencer opened his mouth to argue, but John's flailing hand cut him off. "Mrs. Rowan, I except from that. She and Laurel are fast friends now. And the stones on that woman! Tell me that even you, Reed, didn't applaud her tirade in the drawing room."

He would *not* tell John that, no matter how true it was. It was hard enough admitting to *himself* the heat that had raced through his veins at her shredding of the other ladies. Her confidence mixed with a dose of righteous anger was more arousing than he might have guessed. She was a formidable woman. A beautiful, tempting, haunting, formidable woman.

Spencer cleared his throat. "On that subject, I have a favor to ask."

"About Mrs. Rowan?"

"Ah..." It was the closest he ever came to stammering. "Indirectly."

"Oh. Of course."

"I had originally intended to be in London this week on business, and gave Bennet leave of the house. Oakvale now resembles the temple of Bacchus and shows no signs of improving. For my sanity, I hoped to impose on you and stay the week at Broadmoore." He clanked his glass to John's. "I know your rooms are crowded as it is." Spencer held his breath.

John tapped back. "It's not imposing when it's company you can tolerate."

"You tolerate me? Hastings, that is the most endearing thing you've ever said."

"Don't let it go to your head, Reed," John slurred. "You're not pretty enough for my taste."

*　　*　　*

A rapping at the door brought Spencer from his book, surprising him because he'd been certain almost everyone had long gone to bed. He was more surprised to find Mrs. Paton hovering in the library doorway.

91

Sliding up in his seat, he gestured to an arm chair across the desk.

Paulina, on the rare occasion she wasn't sniffing or scowling, was an attractive woman, thoroughly Dutch. She had a broad mouth with a long nose and almond eyes, features that were enhanced by a smile more than her usual perpetual glare. He noticed it now, catching her face at rest for the first time.

She perched her long frame on the edge of her chair, hands folded primly. Spencer wondered if she ever did anything that was not tailored for appearance or for an audience.

"How may I be of service, Mrs. Paton?"

"I'm concerned." She pressed a hand over her heart, "Deeply concerned about my sister-in-law. And you as well, Lord Reed, if there is cause."

Bristling, he straightened in his chair. "I'm not certain I comprehend."

She reached for him, then drew back her hand. "Alexandra is not a well person. I know that you have observed what must appear to be my heavy-handedness with her during our time here. It is regretfully necessary where she is concerned."

Crossing his arms, he studied her and kept silent. Whatever she was peddling, he was not buying.

Paulina shifted in her seat, meeting his eyes again. "She has likely told you a story about being manipulated. How she has been ill used by us." She buried her face in her hands. "If I could express to you the humiliation we suffer. Her loose talk, her impulsiveness. She claims to care about family, our business, but..." Her hands raised, pleading. "We tread lightly with her. How many stories have we been forced to tell our neighbors? There are times she is so irrational, so unaware of how dangerous her choices. You witnessed her outburst in the drawing room; so forceful and edged with violence over the affairs of a stranger. I fear she will be a candidate for the asylum one day."

Spencer thought he had already found the most likely asylum candidate. "Why share all of this with me, Mrs. Paton? I too am practically a stranger and this can only add to your humiliation."

Paulina's spine snapped straight. "Let me be frank. She has attached herself to men before, and money is always her

92

primary object. I would be on guard against her advances, Lord Reed."

She had been watching, hawkishly observing, he realized now. Their attempts to dodge Paulina, even his excuse for staying the week at Broadmoore had not escaped her notice. "Allow me to put your mind at ease, Mrs. Paton. Mrs. Rowan has not approached me in an untoward way. And even if she had, marriage is so far beyond my horizon that her efforts would be fruitless anyhow. Bachelorhood has suited me for four decades."

Paulina deflated, pressing cool fingertips to his hand. "That relieves me sir, more than I can say. Please do not judge us, for Alexandra's behavior, or our own in protecting against it."

Scooting away from her touch and eager for her departure, he offered a nod. "I bid you goodnight, Mrs. Paton."

"Lord Reed."

To her credit, Paulina got up with composure. His silence hadn't unsettled her, and he grasped how her story must have easily influenced others. Even he had tested, fit the pieces together as she wove her story, curious for any grain of truth. Alexandra's relief any time Paulina left the house might have been an eagerness to run wild, except she never had. Her rebellion had manifested in the form of perusing a near empty library. His attention in the garden might have been an unimaginable boon to the sort of woman Paulina had described, but Alexandra had never capitalized on it.

He had underestimated Paulina's level of calculation, underestimated the woman in general. He would fare better from here on out, applying every caution Paulina had offered, but to her rather than to Alexandra.

*   *   *

Alexandra waited, making certain that Paulina had gone to her room and was in for the night before slipping downstairs. By the silence blanketing the house, she feared that Spencer had also turned in. She rounded a corner and her worry receded at the lamplight spilling from beneath the library door. Holding her breath, she turned the handle and stepped in.

93

Poor Spencer had clearly not expected any more intrusions after Paulina's departure, probably assuming she too was asleep. Deep in his chair, boots up on a little wooden stool, he startled at her late appearance. "Mrs. Rowan."

She rested a finger to her lips, seating the door in its frame without a sound and twisting the lock. Pressing her back to the door, she looked him over. "Are you ready?"

The speed with which he sat up, nodding, was her answer.

"Me too." She indulged a smile, welcome after a long day of misery, and her breath gained a pace. "Where should we…?" She raised her hands.

"Here," said Spencer. "Here will be fine." He patted his coat. "I have the cards."

"Perfect. I'll get the brandy and you deal."

While he moved a side table from under the window and repositioned their chairs, Alix fished along a bottom shelf for the liquor which Laurel had admitted John kept tucked away, handy for when he was avoiding Chas and Paulina. The drawing room boasted a little sideboard and cabinet with other delicious temptations, but it was too close to the foot of the stairs. They risked being heard anywhere beyond the library, and she wasn't willing to give up the next unhindered hour with Spencer for a few treats. Smooth glass met her fingertips; she gripped the bottle, palming two thimble glasses beside.

"Have you found it or not?" he demanded, failing to sound the least put out.

"Hush." Laughing, she settled at their makeshift spot and drew the cork with a satisfying pop.

"Look at that." He leaned down, peering at both their glasses as she poured, then tapped his own. "That is the most imaginary quantity of spirits I've ever beheld."

Snatching her own from his reach, she shook her head. "Drink from the bottle then."

"Tempting invitation." He held her eyes until she looked away and then fished a slender silver case from his coat. He flipped it open with deft fingers and produced an expertly rolled cheroot, and raised a brow.

"No," she replied to his silent question, feeling tempted by Lucifer himself. "Never once."

"Hm." Next came a thin red wooden box, easily lost in his palm.

No idea what to do, she stalled. "I had no notion you took tobacco."

"Only with brandy," he clarified, nodding to the bottle, "and only occasionally."

Spencer struck the match. It sputtered, then blazed, its light catching in the gray-green depths of his eyes and hypnotizing her a moment. The rolling paper glowed and then smoked, and he held out the cheroot. Alix claimed it, feeling young and wonderfully nervous.

"Slow," he cautioned, grinning. "On account of your delicate lungs."

"Hmph." She pulled warm smoke first into her mouth, letting it billow to the back of her throat and burn her nose. Then she dared a hint into her chest on a slow breath. She felt a fullness and a sensation between her temples, and that was all. It was nothing more illicit than standing too close to a campfire. She shrugged, blew out a breath and handed it back with a smile. "Safe from yet another of your temptations."

He winked. "Trial by fire."

Made bold by the moment, Alix studied him in the dim amber light. "How long is your brother in London?"

He snuffed the cheroot, cutting a hand through its smoky protest. "Three days. Army business."

"Three days." She slid her glass in a circle for distraction. "Must be hard for Bennet to entertain his houseful of guests from so far away." Alix lifted her gaze.

He shrugged, caught, and relaxed in his seat with a hint of a smile in his eyes. "Perhaps I fibbed in order to make a little time with you."

She fought to keep her expression placid against a thundering in her chest. "How long?"

"A week at least, save my trip to London tomorrow."

The duel had occupied her mind all evening and somehow, she'd still managed to forget. Now it erased her joy at Spencer's stay. "You're truly going?"

"I am. I must."

Her heart lodged in her throat, and she could barely speak. "Can we play cards some other night?" she managed.

His hand was abandoned on the table, and he leaned forward. "Of course. What would you rather we do instead?"

"What we're doing now." *In case you don't come back.*

"Always agreeable." Spencer scooted his chair around the side of their table, his long legs nearly brushing her skirts.

Now that she had her opportunity, Alix had no idea where to begin. She fumbled for something neutral to get them started. "How long has Bennet lived with you?"

"Nearly his whole life. My father died suddenly when Bennet was three. It was January, damp and frigid. Bennet's mother hadn't been well. A chill became pneumonia and she never recovered. I was..." He looked to the ceiling, "Twenty? Returned home from the army to a strange, sad, irrational little creature. No memory of our father and too much want of his mother to be consoled. He pleaded for warm milk. 'You won't drink it', I'd say. Then he'd cry and I'd warm the milk and he would fall to the floor wailing that he didn't *want* milk." Spencer rubbed his head, chuckling. "And so, he didn't; he simply wanted my attention. Hasn't changed a bit in two decades. Anyhow," he slouched, lacing fingers over his chest, "We get on all right."

Her heart ached at his story. "Better than all right, in my estimation."

Spencer nodded. "Very perceptive. Bennet is my brother and my child, in a sense. A strong reminder of our father. I love him fiercely for all those reasons and more."

The picture was endearing, and Alix couldn't help the pang of jealousy at their bond. "I've never been close with Chas," she offered. "We had entirely opposite temperaments as children, and after our mother and sisters died, he fell into a melancholy which he took out on the rest of us. When my father fell ill, he truly began to struggle..." She closed her eyes, trying to think back that far. "I have no idea where he was for those years. I can't recall his ever being there. I took care of father round the clock at the end. After father passed, Chas devoted himself to Paulina, and you see how that's fared for us." Alix sighed, resting an elbow on the table and cradling her chin. "Chas can go days on end with the tedious work, but the truly difficult tasks?" She shook her head. "He vanishes."

"You must have missed out on a great deal, with your father's illness and your brother's absence."

She hated admitting to anyone, especially Spencer, how sad and humbled she'd become during those days, how she had made it near effortless for Paulina to sweep in and take over. "I did miss out. My courtship ended. I couldn't bear to leave my father and Edward tired of waiting. I suspect he also tired of Chas, who nattered Edward to death every visit. I stopped taking much of a hand in our company. The world passed by outside and suddenly I was twenty-six. Weddings, babies, funerals; they all kept time and I had missed out." She answered Spencer's frown with a smile. "I set out to do plenty of other things. And I did, until Paulina truly dug her claws in."

He frowned. "A common theme where she's concerned."

"I know that she came to speak to you. I don't want to know what she said; I can probably imagine. Just," she exhaled slowly, "weigh everything she tells you."

Spencer sat up, leaning in close enough that heat from his thigh transferred through her petticoats. He slid a hand over hers and fit their fingers together. "I've formed my own opinions."

She stared at the point where they were joined, wanting to remember the garden and to push it away. "Lord Reed –"

"Spencer," he corrected.

"Spencer." Alix tried it out, whispering his name and thrilling at how easily it slid from her lips, protest forgotten.

"Alexandra –" His thumb stroked the back of her hand, idle at first and then suggestive in its rhythm. Then his face changed, and Spencer pulled back whatever he'd been about to say and separated their hands. Without warning, he stood up. "I'll bid you goodnight, for now."

She cast away her disappointment at the abrupt shift, searching his face and feeling reassured by what she found there. He was likely as wearied by the day as her. She couldn't fault his being too tired for serious conversation. She stood up, taking delight in his formal bow.

"Goodnight, Spencer."

97

"Alexandra?" Her hand was on the knob as she glanced over her shoulder.

"I'll be waiting here tomorrow night, too."

*   *   *

Spencer pulled the bottle close and began to deal for solitaire. He certainly wasn't getting sleep anytime soon. There were moments with Alexandra when he felt they were crossing a line. Not kissing or touching, exactly. He knew what it wasn't, but he couldn't name what it *was*.

Turning over another card, Spencer studied his move. A mantle clock kept patient time, ticking over the house's silence as he tried and failed to sort out their short but convoluted history. They'd gone from a layer of fabric away from lovemaking to an easy, almost necessary camaraderie. The events seemed out of order, but somehow, they made sense. It didn't help when he reached an impasse, as he had tonight, not wanting her to leave but having no idea how to take a step forward. He sighed and laid down the last ace.

What was Paulina's motivation? He could understand her father's detached treatment of Paton Shipping; business was not an arena for emotional decisions. Her tight-fisted grip on Alexandra though... He sensed more at work than loyalty to the family. They had built enough intimacy that he felt comfortable prying Alexandra for details, and resolved to do just that at the next opportunity.

Spencer abandoned his cards at a rumble of hooves thundering up the drive. It was a sound he had expected, though not until later in the morning. He slipped out into the hall and waved off the Hastings's shuffling, gritty-eyed butler.

He caught the front door just ahead of a dusty, panting courier. The man raised a battered felt top hat under the hall lamp. "Lord Reed, urgently." Spencer nodded and traded his coin for an envelope, the courier loping back to an anxious mount before the door had closed.

Darby's wide slanting signature marked the first of two thick sheets of paper. His note read only 'For publication in this morning's papers'. Thin, nervous letters lined the second page, handwriting he recognized by content rather than form.

Lord Spencer Reed has called upon me to give, for my conduct, that satisfaction which a gentleman has a right to require, and which a gentleman never refuses to pay. Admitting offence given to his lordship and a concerned lady, Lord Grey accedes to disgraceful and insulting conduct against both parties. A public apology is merited, and offered to prevent a more hostile transaction.

Ld. G. Grey

"Coward." He crumpled both sheets. Not that he wasn't relieved at avoiding dawn at ten paces; if anything, he was grateful sparing fifty miles to London and rising at an obscene hour. He felt no joy at the prospect of injuring the man, but something about George's casual disregard for Amelia had stoked a fury in Spencer which he hadn't known was there. There was not an ounce of contrition to Grey's apology, just disgraceful self-preservation. In the army, men like him weren't given the gentleman's way out. He missed that simple justice now.

Whatever his feelings, the matter was settled. He relaxed and, relieved at having pried at least one weight from his mind, Spencer stuffed the letter into his coat and headed upstairs to bed.

*   *   *

Alix dressed for breakfast at an unprecedented speed. Usually coming down to face her brother and Paulina first thing in the day merited a lot of stretching and rolling over, several wardrobe changes, and enough attention to her hair that she could be presented at court.

This morning she had tripped on her petticoats and torn a shoulder seam in her gown, all in her eagerness to see Spencer. He would leave for London in the afternoon and she dreaded his journey as much as the outcome.

She could hear Paulina's yammering as she reached the foot of the stairs, which was strange on two counts; Paulina made an art of frosty silence, and she sounded a shade less miserable than usual. The one-sided conversation ground to a halt, however, the moment Alix set foot in the dining room. She found seven pairs of eyes trained on her, Elizabeth Conyngham's only marginally more hostile than Paulina's. John and Laurel stared blandly, Chas sat resigned, and Spencer unreadable as he looked her over head to toe. Despite the attention of so many, it was his study which quickened her pulse.

A man seated beside the pink satin abomination of Elizabeth, her unfortunate husband, were Alix to hazard a guess, toyed with a hank of dark hair in open boredom.

Alix met each pair of eyes in turn, waiting in silence until more than one chair creaked under discomfort. Then she curtsied. "Lady Conyngham."

More silence. Lord Conyngham jabbed his wife with a broad elbow. Elizabeth's full lips tightened into a squished heart, eyes staring at a point beyond Alix. "Mrs. Rowan."
Wearied by the pregnant silence, Alix moved to the buffet and put her back to the group.

"Lord and Lady Conyngham have come with an invitation." Paulina dropped the information in the center of the room, hanging it by a taunting thread.

Again, silence while she managed an egg onto her plate. They were waiting for an *'Oh?'*, or an *'Is that so!'*. She wouldn't give them the satisfaction.

A feminine throat cleared behind her several times, Elizabeth requiring full attention and frustrated that Alix refused to turn and face her. Appreciating that she had all the ears possible and that Alix could go on forever choosing a pastry, Elizabeth finally spoke. "We have come to invite Mr. and Mrs. Paton to Hamilton Place."

Damn the woman if she was going to make anyone feel cut out. Seizing the opportunity, Alix buried her face in the crook of her arm, producing a wracking bout of exaggerated, unladylike coughing and stumbled to her seat. "I'm sorry I'm not well enough to join you all." Thudding into her chair, she grimaced and hung her head to one side.

Elizabeth pursed her lips and her cheeks flushed, but good manners and witnesses kept her from saying that Mrs. Rowan had *never* been on the guest list. Paulina was less circumspect, eager to build her up before tearing her down. "You can suffer a carriage ride, Alexandra."

Spencer, rendered headless behind the papers' crease, cut in. "I have business in London tomorrow, Conyngham; perhaps we can arrange an evening."

His duel. Alix swatted away the idea, sick over it no matter if he was accounted a 'dead shot.'

"Capital," drawled Conyngham, staring at the far wall and twisting away on his hair.

"I did not know that *you* would be in London, sir." Paulina's motives were so tactless that Alix nearly laughed out a mouthful of toast. The moment she believed Spencer would be fifty miles from Broadmoore, Paulina's relief was palpable. "Alexandra, you will stay behind, for your health."

Transparent hardly did the moment justice.

Laurel, bless her, brought everyone back to the beginning. "Hastings and I are too committed with improvements here to join Reed. Alexandra will convalesce with us, and the rest of you will be free to enjoy London."

"There," resolved Chas with an unprecedented measure of backbone. "Everyone is settled. Reed, will you travel down with us?"

"No. I have some marching orders for Bennet to carry out in my absence. I'll leave late this afternoon, before supper."

"This breakfast is too heavy for my nerves!" declared Paulina, shooting up. "Arranging and packing; it won't sit. I must begin directly." When no one made a move to acknowledge her outburst, she snapped bony fingers at Chas's ear. "Charles." Mid bite, Chas set down his fork and groaned from his chair, any trace of spine now absent. Alix was never certain who merited more disgust.

Elizabeth rose next. "Lady Hastings, you may show us to the parlor."

Alix didn't miss the sideways glance, Elizabeth's haughty unease at their being in close company. Though her condescension stung, Alix took pleasure that Lady Conyngham felt a need to escape her.

Laurel didn't bother concealing a frown at the imposition, at having no choice but to entertain the woman. "Of course, Lady

Conyngham. Hastings, come. You can share your plans for the north wing with his lordship."

John, midway through breakfast judging by his plate, looked to her and then Spencer, then finally to his wife, eager for a sympathetic pair of eyes. Finding none, he wiped his mouth with violence and followed Laurel out.

Spencer met her eyes and pulled a serious face. "And then... there were two."

She smiled without reservation now that they were alone. "I take a little pride in my victory, facing more opposition from the room than anyone else."

He clutched his napkin to his chest. "You mean you aren't heartbroken, being cut so fully by the charming countess?"

"Hah!" Alix poured coffee into her cup, punishing it with a frown intended for Spencer. "Her going to London is eclipsed by my anxiety at *your* going to London."

No answer. She finished pouring and glanced up to find dancing hazel eyes watching her. Spencer produced a creased envelope from his coat, laid it on the table and pushed it across to her with a finger to his lips.

She unfolded it close to her chest and skimmed its few lines. "An apology?" she whispered. She glanced up again, hope blooming in her chest. "This means you don't have to go?"

"I could still call him out," Spencer whispered back. "Few would cry foul, though it would be rather ungentlemanly to press things now. Grey is humiliated, humbled. And his troubles are far from over." He smiled and claimed the note. "I won't inconvenience myself to do what London can accomplish more artfully."

She frowned. "But you told Paulina that you have business in London."

He sat back, looking triumphant. "So I did, and I also said that I have business at Oakvale. Which I do *not*."

Alix gasped, heart pounding harder by the moment. "That means!"

He nodded. "Five days at least."

Five days in Spencer's company with no one more obtrusive than John and Laurel to take a bit of notice. Equal

102

measures of relief and anticipation dashed her composure, and she pressed a hand to her chest and fell back in her chair.

Spencer nodded again. "Precisely."

CHAPTER THIRTEEN

He had found her at last, his woman from the masquerade. Perhaps even more than that, Spencer thought, watching her tease John and then duck her head at his colorful retort. However alluring, his garden lady had been one color where the woman before him now was a whole spectrum.

Alexandra was the sun after a cloudy day, and it was impressed on him what a powerful affect her brother and sister-in-law had. Even her way of dressing had changed since their departure. Smooth bare arms and a neckline somewhere lower than her chin revealed creamy skin in frustrating quantity. She wore crisp ivory satin which set off a mountain of black waves swept up to reveal a slender neck his fingers remembered well. There was a renewed light to her beautiful face, and Spencer thought her a match for London's most celebrated belles.

Laurel stood, stifling a yawn against one hand and massaging the green muslin that shrouded her growing belly with the other. "Walk me up, John, or you'll be carrying me."

"Hmph. In that case at your current size, you'll stay where you are."

A whack from Laurel earned Spencer a helpless look from John. Spencer raised his arms in reply. "If you fear her size, I wouldn't provoke her, Hastings."

Laurel grabbed a fistful of John's coat, heaving with all her willowy might. "Your friend is wise. You should heed his advice."

That put an end to it. John caught her around the waist, swept her legs and gathered her to his chest, Laurel giggling and shrieking all the while. Alexandra doubled over with laughter, meeting his eyes and shaking her head.

104

"Spoils of war, Reed!" John called back over his shoulder. "You're my witness. Won fair and square." Laurel's giggling could be heard all the way down the hall, punctuating John's indistinct murmurs.

Still laughing, Alix raked their cards together. "I suspect neither of them is as put out as they let on."

He tapped her slipper under the table. "Whatever gives you that impression?"

"Hm." She finished stacking up the deck and glanced around. "I thought we were old, but here we are, the last ones up at an embarrassingly early hour."

Pulling out his watch, Spencer saw she was correct; just past ten.

She reclined into a languid stretch, painting him with a lazy smile. He wondered if she grasped the effect her pose was having, until her foot brushed his calf beneath the table. "What should we do with ourselves?"

Anything. Everything. Spencer had no idea how to answer. The only thing he was sure of was that he didn't want to leave her yet, that he wanted every possible moment in her company before the Patons returned. "Get your coat," he instructed, not certain what he intended. "I'll meet you in the hall." Like everything where Alexandra was concerned, the moment was impulse and he was happy to make it up as they went.

Looking as perplexed as he felt, she cocked her head and smiled, skipping his heart. "Are we running away?"

Swallowing twice, he still couldn't find a reply, and shrugged.

He felt like an idiot, but she nodded and spared him. "Playing coy. Very well. Though, I warn you, I'm prepared."

He watched her go, the graceful sway of her skirts holding him captive until she was out of sight. Taking her outside had seemed like a clever idea until this moment; now he had the distinct sense of saddling himself with biblical temptation. There was no telling yet if that were terrible, or wonderful.

When he met Alix in the hall minutes later, she was covered from neck to ankles in a sensible brown velveteen coat, and Spencer exhaled. Made safe by the garment, mostly from himself, he offered her an arm.

They went left around the staircase where he opened the ballroom's wide double doors and led her through the dark, their footsteps tapping at marble until they reached the terrace's high doors. A few lamps blazed along the wall and Spencer took advantage of their light, as they moved down the stairs, to steal glances at Alix. They retraced steps they'd taken into the garden on that first night, and he studied her as they went for any hint of recognition. She looked more concerned with navigating deepening shadows, no acknowledgement for their surroundings.

"It's just up here," he whispered when they had passed the orangerie and his beloved wall, and moved into the garden proper.

"Why are we whispering?"

Spencer chuckled at himself and shrugged even if she couldn't see him. "Because it's dark?"

"Oh." A soft laugh. "Of course."

"Here." He stopped them atop a low rise beyond the garden's hedges where Broadmoore's lawn rolled away toward wilder country. Lights from the house caught the edge of a small pond, painting it in amber ribbons, offering a hint of illumination until the moon rose. Sitting, Spencer braced back on his arms, stretched his legs out along the small hill, and patted the grass. Alix fell beside him without warning, hip to hip, one arm inside his own so that their fingers just touched. She was close enough for him to catch the warm, sweet perfume from her hair, to hear her slow, even breathing. The magical ward of her modest coat began to dissolve.

Spencer fixed his eyes overhead, studying the night sky and clearing his throat. "Do you know your constellations, Mrs. Rowan?"

"In fact, I do." He caught a delighted bent to her words. "I think anyone who has a love of sailing must. My father taught me each and every one." Her laugh was girlish. "Sometimes we made up our own. It became a contest."

"Is that so?"

"A toad. A fountain. Snake; my father always tried snake, which of course you can make out of exactly any four stars." She snorted and pressed their shoulders together.

He inhaled, exhaling her name slowly. "Alexandra."

"Mmm?"

It was more a sensation than a word. He had meant it as a preamble, an introduction to a speech he had practiced countless times over the last week. It was a concise and finely worded explanation of his attraction and confusion, her beauty and quiet strength, and how he feared her as much as he chafed in her absence. He had even written it out on a scrap of paper and whispered it to himself before the glass while dressing, two mornings in a row. Face to face with her now, he could hardly recall it and the parts he did remember sounded rote. *Wrong.* Finally, he settled on: "I'm glad we have this time together." He caressed her cheek with his thumb and hoped that she could hear his sentiment behind the words.

"I am glad you found it for us." Her head fell against his arm in reply, putting their faces in dangerous proximity. "A month," she murmured.

It barely pierced his awareness, distracted by her heat through his clothes. "What's that?"

She didn't speak for awhile, long enough that he wondered if she had heard him. "Chas means for us to return home. Settle the accounts he's started here, and then we'll be on our way." Her words were hollow, toneless.

"You could stay on," he argued. "The Hastings enjoy your company. Stay as their guest." While he spoke, he grasped for more answers, more solutions, arranging arguments in advance against any protest she might raise.

Her head was already shaking against him. "Chas and Paulina would never have it. It isn't so simple."

"Tell me how it is, then," he growled, frustrated. "You're a woman of a certain age. Your brother cannot still have so much hold over you."

"My brother? No." Anger burned in her words. "Not my brother." He sensed there was more, that she was about to continue, but then she deflated. "Things *will* change, soon. For

107

now, let's enjoy the time we have. I certainly am, at the moment."

He wasn't done fighting her departure, but a husky note to her last words mollified him. Letting his palms slip over the grass, Spencer fell onto his back. Alix joined him, twining their fingers in the space between their bodies. Her smaller hand fit inside his, palm smooth against his calloused one.

"Funny how you can come to depend so much on something you've otherwise managed to live without. Something you never knew existed."

He knew exactly what she meant, had felt it for days. What Alix had called friendship, except it ran into gray areas along its borders. He turned his face to her and cradled her cheek. He hadn't intended more, but Alix closed the space between them with a kiss, her lips warm and soft against crisp night air.

He held her there, still cupping her face and not daring more or retreating.

She was the first to pull away and, sighing, nestled against him. She shivered and pressed closer, igniting a slow burn.

"Cold? Would you like to go in?"

"No," she murmured to his relief, raising their joined hands and resting them on her belly, "not just yet."

CHAPTER FOURTEEN

Rap-rap rap!

She'd heard him the *first* time, but had rolled over and covered her head with the quilt and ignored him. His knock was heavier, more insistent this time, and Alix wriggled from her bed, stomping through a smaller front room and throwing back her door.

Spencer grinned and looked her over. "Were you awake?"

She raked fingers through tumbled hair, staring back and letting her appearance answer his question.

His grin spread, and he was undeterred. "Well, when are you getting up?"

Alix narrowed her eyes. "Now, it seems." Her frown couldn't hold and she broke into a smile. "I'll be down shortly. Give me a few minutes."

"Perfect!" His smile was serene, and he turned and leaned against the wall. "I'll wait here."

Of course he would.

"We're going out!" he called through the door as she shut it.

"I haven't eaten yet!" She protested.

"You'll manage."

Alix rifled through her trunk for something she hadn't risked wearing with Paulina about. Tossing through her wardrobe, she came upon a crisp white muslin gown with deep flounces to the knees, more extravagant than she was usually permitted. Next, she claimed a raspberry velvet pelisse trimmed in white satin braid, a coat Paulina insisted was gaudy but had asked to borrow twice. Last came a straw bonnet with a matching pink ribbon. She looked herself over in the glass, losing and finding her nerve twice at the combination. Then she turned away and grabbed her reticule, deciding not to overthink a matter just this once.

Coming out the door she nearly plowed Spencer over. He held out a white linen napkin in one hand and a blue porcelain cup in the other. Toast, and judging by the aroma, coffee.

He studied her with a slow nod which gained momentum, and Alix's hesitation at her choice of clothing faded away.

"Butter," he announced, holding out the napkin, "and cream." He raised the cup. "You can eat them on the way downstairs."

"Ugh." She sighed, claiming the toast now hovering in her face, not quite awake enough for his enthusiasm.

Spencer didn't seem to notice. He took the steps two at a time ahead of her, pacing the hall while she managed to drink without spilling. He claimed her cup and empty napkin as she reached the bottom and set them atop a narrow table, the only convenient surface at hand.

"What?" he questioned at her disapproval. "Someone will get it." He grabbed her sleeve, moving off again, bounding for the door like an enthusiastic puppy.

The morning was clear and blue, sunlight spilling golden over green treetops. A summer breeze whispered away its heat and fanned them with a sweet perfume of honeysuckle bordering the drive. It was absolute fantasy but, for just a breath, Alix dared to imagine it as reality, her future a delicious string of similar days, all at Spencer's side.

A groom fussed over Spencer's yellow curricle, checking its hitches and patting down both horses. With a little bow, he opened the door for Spencer, who helped her up and climbed in behind.

Her curiosity was piqued, realizing that they were riding out together. "What are we about this morning?"

Spencer snapped the reins, leading them around the yard and down the drive. "Are you acquainted with our annual Lady Day?"

"No, but it sounds as though gloves are involved."

Spencer chuckled, pulling his hat lower over his eyes. "As in our lady, the Virgin Mary."

"We're moving further and further outside my purview."

"Mid-March," he explained, "leaseholds are renewed and rents are paid. Normally, I settle business in the village with my steward Mister Sheldon. Only, this year I was busy conquering France."

Alix clucked her tongue. "Inconsiderate of you on several counts."

"The French army agrees with you." He wheeled them left, away from the main road toward a series of low slopes. "Now that we're approaching midsummer, the village will hold fairs. Men come for work, cotters trade, and so on. Today is the first of such gatherings, and an opportunity for me to meet with my tenants."

She had teased him thus far, but Spencer's explanation impressed on her his importance, and the importance of his villagers. Still, she refused to be deferential. "Goodness. You're like a king!"

He shook a fist. "And a ruthless king at that. You'll have the best view of the beheadings."

"I can hardly wait." Alix closed her eyes, breeze whipping over her face and enjoying Spencer's nearness.

"No sleeping," he ordered and nudged her with an elbow.

She nudged back. "Shh! Don't ruin the moment by speaking."

He made a wounded sound, then laughed.

The horses slowing their pace brought her eyes open again. The road's brown ribbon dropped, curved, and spilled between neatly arranged rows of stone cottages and shops. Golden thatch roofs glistened in the sunlight with colorful specks of people passing up and down the main street. The thoroughfare ended at an old stone church, its wide wooden doors thrown open for the crowds. Fields of striped green, bronze, and black earth formed a patchwork border outside the village. Roly-poly sheep, white again after spring shearing, meandered between low stone walls.

111

Their surroundings were easy, natural, and peaceful in a way that spoke to her soul. Alix allowed it in and dared a step away from her old self.

Spencer drew them to a stop alongside one of the walls, raising his hand at the approach of a white-haired man. He stood slightly stooped, his frame thinned by the passage of at least sixty years, by her guess.

Spencer rose a hand in greeting. "Tom Thornton."

"Lordship." Tom bowed, taking Spencer's hand, stealing glances at her all the while through creased blue eyes.

Spencer nodded, acknowledging her. "Lord Hastings's cousins have come to Broadmoore. Mrs. Rowan was good enough to join me today, offering us a chance to show off our talents."

Tom nodded to her and to Spencer, head going like an old rocking chair at the pleasing information. "Me and the elders are glad for it." He patted the chest of his brown homespun coat with gnarled fingers. "I've a short list of folks who've asked to speak with you, when it's quite convenient." There was a pride in Tom's voice hinting that the list making had fallen to his lot, as one of the few literate elders.

"Mrs. Rowan and I will have a walk of the village. I'll find you when we're done."

Tom lunged off, carried by long strides, swatting a hand and grumbling instructions to the crowd ahead of his master. Men and women stopped their labors, and even a group of giggling children ground to a dusty halt. Everyone lined the street in front of well-tended buildings, bowing and curtsying at Spencer's passing.

The scrutiny of so many pairs of eyes felt like a punishment to Alix rather than respect. She settled her gaze somewhere near their waists, wishing their processions over as quickly as possible. When they reached a little side lane heading off towards the fields, Spencer muttered something to Tom, who then turned and made a gesture she didn't catch. Everyone reanimated behind them and tension unknit from her shoulders.

Under the noise of the crowd she dared a whisper. "How do you tolerate that?"

112

He shrugged. "They are my band of civilian soldiers; I would hardly say I tolerate them. They show gratitude for work and dwellings, and I tip my hat in thanks for all their hard labor and loyalty."

"They are beholden to you," she argued, not certain if she was asking or telling.

"I am their lord, true enough. But I cannot plow the fields or tend the sheep, harvest crops or mend thatch all on my own. Armies have generals, towns have mayors, and vassals have lords. Any man who believes such a post grants him leave to be haughty or cruel…" He shrugged, turning them back onto the village street. "Ships have mutinies and armies, rebellions. He should expect a stern reminder that no man rules by his own will."

Satisfied, she tugged on his arm. "Well, I'm not curtsying to you, even if you did bring me coffee."

"It's tea that causes all the trouble with you people," he quipped, glancing round. Then he tugged her arm in return, pulling her with purpose through the crowd.

"There are so many people," Alix marveled, wondering at a steady stream of pedestrians which flowed up and down the main street.

"Visitors," he tossed back over his shoulder. "Neighboring villages come 'round to trade or find work. They'll return again in the fall, when crops are in."

They stopped first at a narrow wooden stall tended by an old woman with a face like a potato, her rough brown skin contrasting a wealth of snowy hair tugged up into a knot. She fixed Spencer's appearance with a gap-toothed grin. "Lordship. We're all more than pleased to see you home, fit and in one piece."

"And I am pleased at being seen so." Spencer bowed his head with respect. "Mrs. Collum."

Two girls flanking her ducked their heads. Sisters, Alix guessed by their faces, with oceans of blonde ringlets, twin pert noses and large blue eyes. One was no more than seven or eight while her older sibling was well on the path to womanhood. It was she who dared glances at Spencer while he studied chunks of honeycomb and jars of golden amber. "The honey is very fine,

113

Mrs. Collum," he complimented. "Particularly so early in the year."

Mrs. Collum drew up proudly, smoothing her coarse linen apron with a broad hand. "Patrick's done right with the hives since my son's been away. Not like as Mister Collum used to, but he'll progress." She rested fingers on the older girl's shoulders. "All my grandbabies is growin'," she offered. "Sarah's sixteen now, lordship."

Spencer raised his hat, oblivious, and smiled. "Then happy birthday, Miss Collum."

"Thank you," was muttered from smiling lips between scarlet cheeks. Alix bit her lip and fought a smile.

Mrs. Collum looked her boldly over, head to toe. "Mrs. Rowan. Tom Thornton says you're Lord Hastings's kin."

She paused, surprised to learn that she'd been the subject of gossip to people she hadn't known existed an hour before. "He's told you right, Mrs. Collum."

"And a Yank!" She clapped surprised hands as though swatting away a shock almost too much to bear. "You've intentions to stay here then?" Alix didn't miss the pointed glance between herself and Spencer, nor the pursing of elder Miss Collum lips. "No, not much longer. My brother's business is nearly concluded."

"Shame," muttered Mrs. Collum, without a hint of disappointment.

This time Alexandra didn't bother covering her amusement. "Here," she counted out her shillings into Mrs. Collum's leathery palm. "I'd be delighted to take a jar home."

Their transaction concluded with a dismissive *hmm*, and Spencer tipped his hat to the ladies.

"Lord Reed," she chided when they were beyond hearing, "You'll have Mrs. Collum out shopping for wedding dresses."

One brow raised. "Meaning what?"

"Truly, Spencer?" She shook her head, ignoring his confusion. Frightening that a man his age could be in such a fog.

She drifted next to him, letting her mind wander along with the crowd. There was so much to take in, seemingly endless tenants and craftsmen calling for his attention over the din, pressing him with their wares; a good winter ale that had just come ready, or a pie of last fall's apple preserves; straw baskets, butter and candles. Pots steamed above rock-ringed fires, savory odors hinting at sausages and rich stew. Everyone was eager to impress their landlord with produce and appearance. A thick rope stretched between the posts outside of one house, hung with three wedding-band quilts in pink, yellow, and blue calico prints. Alix marveled at the skill and patience it must have taken to sew them, brushing soft cotton with her fingertips.

"Do you like it?" he asked.

"I'm not partial to yellow, but this is really lovely."

A brown-haired woman in the doorway smiled, nodding appreciation and patting at her cap and apron. Spencer took down the quilt and folded it over his arm. "The lady will have this one," he said, digging inside his coat.

"No." Alix pressed his shoulder. "I can't let you..." No man had bought her a gift since her courtship with Edward years before. Coupled with being beholden to Chas and Paulina, Alix felt uncomfortable. "No," she repeated, "I can manage."

"I did not say otherwise." At first, he was aloof, exchanging coin and gathering the quilt tighter. He claimed her fingers, pressing the heat of his hand between their gloves. "Your stubbornness is endearing any other time, Alexandra. Just allow me this one thing."

Flustered, Alix held her tongue, nodding and staring at the ground. Her stomach betrayed her with a protesting rumble, and she laughed.

"I see," grumbled Spencer. "No gratitude for my toast." His chuckle warmed her, and he tugged her arm. "Come on then. Let's have something to eat."

There was plenty to choose from: boiled fresh eggs, ham and sausages, boiled potatoes and leeks. A meaty, spicy odor of mince pies nearly concealed the scent of her absolute weakness, strawberry tarts. Nearly, but not entirely; she'd claimed two in-hand by the time Spencer had gathered the rest of their meal.

Spencer led them to a wide field just beyond his horses and spread her quilt on the grass. He worked on uncorking some ale he'd purchased while she undid the twine binding their brown wax-paper parcels. Alix bit the crispy, salty rind from a slice of ham, chewing thoughtfully and sighing. "This has been the most wonderful day."

"Has it?" He downed a mouthful of ale and passed her the bottle. "I was afraid you'd be bored to tears."

"With you? Impossible."

Spencer ducked his head, looking for all the world a little shy. It was an appealing contrast after an hour of the entire town doting on him.

After a second sweet, yeasty mouthful of ale, Alix found her nerve. "I want to ask you something."

Leaning back on one arm and claiming an egg with the other, he nodded.

"What made you notice me that night?"

He chewed thoughtfully, squinting against noonday sun. "I had determined to enjoy myself with a lady. When I found the most beautiful one, I advanced."

She snorted and shook her head.

"You may well dismiss it, but it's true." Spencer drew knees to his chest, sitting forward and bringing them closer. His eyes closed. "True, but not the entire truth. If I dare complete honesty, I'm not certain what caught my attention." Spencer met her eyes. "But I recall the moment it happened. There was a gentleman standing behind you. He remarked upon something and you laughed, threw him a look over your shoulder. I swear, you stopped my heart for a moment."

She didn't remember the gentleman, or the moment to which Spencer was referring. Not that either one mattered against his words. Alix ducked her face to hide a blush.

Spencer claimed the ale from her. "Curse John Hastings and his good manners."

Before Alix could offer her agreement, something slammed her from behind, snuffling hot breath into her neck.

"Sampson!" cried a tiny voice. "Sampson, no!"

Sampson, she discovered, was a dog, and not just any dog. He was a Dane, and the biggest animal she'd ever seen not pulling a carriage. He nuzzled her harder, licked her cheek, and began snorting along a scent trail to their food while Spencer waved his hat at the giant beast.

Huffing and panting combined with tiny footfalls drew her attention away from the behemoth, and she turned to find a petite little thing of six or seven, brown braids flapping, chasing after the dog. Waving a chunk of sausage, Alix did her best to distract him from the rest of their fare.

"Bad Sampson!" the girl scolded, making a half-hearted dip for Spencer's benefit. "No running away." Alexandra was chastised by a pouty frown. "You can't feed him sausages; they make him sick."

"Oh!" She pulled a grave face. "I am very sorry."

Sampson, for his part, wagged eagerly, a happy gesture in opposition to his morose, drooping black and white face. The girl stretched up on tiptoes, wrapping slender arms around her dog's neck. "It's all right. You can have just this one, even if it is naughty."

"Why not two?" offered Spencer with a wink, already feeding the beast.

Looking pleased with so much attention, Sampson finally gave into his tiny master's grunting and chiding and loped off, dragging her behind.

Laughing, she glanced to Spencer and found his eyes already on her. She smiled and raised an eyebrow, inviting the question she read on his face.

"Do you have children?" he asked.

"No! Of course not. You?"

His mouth quirked. "Bennet is my perpetual child."

"For all your digs, I like your brother," she protested.

Spencer's brows wiggled. "And he likes you."

"He does?" She sat forward, excited that a member of Spencer's family approved of her. "What did he say?"

"Nothing I'd repeat in a lady's company. They weren't platonic declarations, I assure you."

Flattered, she laughed through a mouthful of strawberry tart. "Be certain to send him my *regards*."

"Don't toy with the lad. You'll crush him."

Alix cocked her head and drank him in. "And what about you?"

"What about me?" he challenged.

"Will my toying crush you?"

His smile was slow and wolfish. "Where I am concerned, madam, you had better be prepared to make good on your threats."

"Oh," she breathed, and leaned back on her arms, "I believe we've established that I am."

CHAPTER FIFTEEN

They had been sitting together silently in the parlor for more than an hour, judging by the clock's chiming out in the hall. It was a perfect, contented silence, without anxious remarks or outside intrusion. It was Spencer's favorite brand of silence.

It had become a quick tradition, tonight marking their fourth evening together in the sitting room after John and Laurel had retired for the night. The first few nights they had played cards, conversed; he'd drawn a battle map for Alexandra while telling a story, and she had added artist's details to his poor sketch. He had traced her fingers while she drew; fingers led to knuckles and then a wrist and then he was brushing her throat. Lips a breath apart, they had resolved to keep a safer distance the following evening.

Spencer had no idea what made him look up from his letter at Alexandra, curled onto a small blue sofa directly across from him. Whatever it was, he found her watching him. Spencer took a long draw of his scotch and raised his brows.

She closed her book and tossed it onto her lap. "I want us to have an affair."

He sputtered, smoky liquor burning his throat. "What!" he wheezed, coughing to expel liquor from his lungs. He couldn't have heard her properly.

She spoke slowly, words husky and annunciated here and there by a teasing pause. "I *want* to have an *affair* with you." Her gaze was frank, honest.

His chest spasmed. He coughed again and rubbed a fist over his heart. "I think you did me an injury," he croaked.

Alexandra rolled her eyes. "I'm serious."

"So am I," he panted, wincing. "I think I'm having an attack."

"Well?" She looked unconcerned by the prospect of his impending death.

Yes; a hundred, a thousand times yes. Spencer cleared his throat and sat back, slapping his ribs and still dodging her. "You cannot just *ask* to have an affair."

Hands went up. "Why not?"

"Alexandra, have you ever *had* an affair?"

"No." The information surprised him, and he thrilled at her eagerness in the garden.

He nodded. "That explains your asking to have one."

"Well," she started, crossing her arms, "Were *you* going to ask me?"

"No." Because one person couldn't simply ask another. It was a dance, a choreographed string of encounters which he hadn't managed to arrange with her, at least not yet.

Her frown stretched into silence, and he raised his palms. "Because I hadn't thought of it," he amended. "Not because I am not interested."

"You've proved my point! If I had not asked you, and you were not going to ask me, how were we going to have one?"

Not much to argue with in her logic. Still, there was an art to the whole thing which she seemed to be missing, something he struggled to quantify. "You can't ask," he repeated. "That's not how it's done." As quickly as the words were out, Spencer wondered why it mattered. Why did people go to such lengths, do such a ridiculous dance? Was there any harm in the sweet, earnest way she risked herself now?

"Well," she fired back, "have *you* had affairs?"

"Yes," he mumbled into his knuckles. "Oh, yes."

"Well then, *you* tell me. When would you call on me? How would we go on? Tell me how it's done by other people."

Tediously, he admitted, running through the sequence. "They meet. Share a few dances. Are sat together at dinner. They find one another attractive, and hopefully enjoy some conversation. Then some innuendo, a flirtation, and each returns the other's banter. The lady offers her card and invites the gentleman to call at an opportune hour. Perhaps he even asks for her key."

"Oh," breathed Alix. "I thought we were already doing most of that."

He opened his mouth, then closed it into a frown, dumbfounded. He really had been buried in the wool. "So we have."

"But you never thought of me...?" She shrugged.

"As I said Alexandra, not because I don't think of you in that way. I don't believe I appreciated how much territory we've covered." He wondered that it had felt painless, natural, and not a bit like the effort he'd described.

She perked up, a smile dimpling her cheek. "Then we should. Why wouldn't we?"

Spencer raked fingers through his hair, refusing to believe that Alexandra grasped what she was asking. "It's not a ham or a birthday party. You don't simply *have* it." *And you certainly couldn't take it back.*

Her sigh bubbled with frustration. "Well, explain it again, then."

"It's not an open sort of thing. Meeting after dark, sneaking away before dawn." Affairs involved a great deal of contortion and cloaking about, things which tried his patience. Then again, watching her bite her lip as she considered his words, he had difficulty remembering why he objected so much.

She frowned. "But we already have an 'open sort of thing'. John and Laurel invite us everywhere. We can still sit together, dine together, dance together. Ride out together. Plenty of young men take ladies to the park and no one seems to raise a brow. If we were younger, or married, someone might fuss." She winked. "But we're just old Lord Reed and dusty Mrs. Rowan. Even Paulina will be hard pressed to object, if we keep company with other people."

It was nearly frightening, how much sense she was making. And how anxious his body was over it. Spencer sat up, pressed his fist to his lips again and looked her over. "I have an idea, but you're not going to like it."

She sat up, too. "What is it?"

121

"You're not going to like it," he warned again. It was dangerous, built on impropriety and fraught with risk, where Paulina was concerned.

Her arms flailed. "Just tell me!"

"My family has a small parcel near the Scottish coast. It's tiny, and I think my father only stubbornly hung onto it because it was contested for centuries. There's nothing there but an old chapel, some wild horses and a stone cottage." He leaned forward and rested elbows on his knees. "I had planned to go for perhaps a fortnight, next week. Some quiet for both inside and outside my mind."

Alix was leaning forward, beautiful face lit by a grin. "And when you return, we could commence?"

"We could commence while *we* are there." He reached for her hand. "Come with me, Alexandra."

She exhaled sharply, sat back and then fell completely into the sofa, eyeing him. "It's risky."

"Aye. But we would have time. Time to sort this out, and make a start out from under prying eyes." Days and nights alone with not a soul around.

"I like it."

He didn't trust his ears. "You do?"

"I do." She nodded slowly. "Can you wait that long?"

In that particular moment, the truthful answer was 'no'. "I don't know."

Her half-lidded smile hammered his resolve, and she shrugged. "Neither do I."

*　　　*　　　*

Spencer lay in bed long after the house was silent, well past the final creaks of servants drifting specter-like through Broadmoore at their final night time tasks. He had wrung every moment of Alexandra's time from the day, before retreating to relative safety inside the shadows of his bed. With the velvet curtain drawn tight, he'd hoped for nerve to examine his feelings about her. Instead, he had shifted restlessly beneath the quilt, afraid of daring into such unfamiliar territory.

122

Afraid to venture *alone*, he amended. For all her teasing and flirtation, Alix had made few overtures before tonight, no meeting him halfway as she had in the garden. He needed to hear that he consumed her thoughts, her body and her mind, as much as she did his.

Slapping his way out of the bed, Spencer claimed his breeches from a chair beside the door and wriggled into them. Determination carried him down one staircase and through darkened halls, promptly fizzling when he came to a stop in front of Alexandra's door. Minutes passed, ticked out by a clock somewhere far off in the house, and Spencer began to pace. His thoughts were sorted and composed in increments of five steps down and five back. He lost count of passes, muttering scraps of feeling he couldn't piece together.

Her door flying open startled him and stopped his progress.

He took her in, head to toe, receiving the same treatment in return though he hardly noticed. More than once he had indulged a fantasy with images of Alexandra as his harlequin from the masquerade. Her appearance now eclipsed those, a delicious new imagining for his private moments.

Dark waves tumbled over her shoulders, their length drawing his eye to the swell of breasts beneath her white muslin shift. A half-moon spilled through windows inside her room, bathing her in ethereal light which caught the depth of her blue eyes. His heart ached at her loveliness, body following suit.

Alix swallowed and broke their silence first. "Have you any notion how much noise you're making out here?" She had meant to tease, he guessed, but a tremble pulling at each word stole her mirth and hinted that she felt at least a fraction of what he had, pacing alone in the hall.

"Alexandra..." He'd meant to say more, to explain his reasons for coming and plead his case like a rational man. Reason burned to ash as his fingers twisted between silken strands of hair, and he drew her in, their bodies meeting with more force than he had intended when she didn't resist. His shirt and her shift; two layers of fabric were a poor substitute for willpower when her breasts pressed his chest.

123

Her slender fingers gripped his neck and finished the distance between their lips. Full and sweet, her mouth was every bit the pleasure he remembered. She matched his every slant and press, catching his lower lip between her teeth when he mustered the strength to pull away.

She pressed the back of one hand to her mouth, panting. "Oh, my goodness." Her cheeks flushed and he caught a smile in her eyes. "I've told myself a thousand times that it would never be as good as I remembered."

He grinned broadly enough that his jaw ached. "It is."

"It is," she agreed, her words little more than a whisper of breath, hot against his throat.

He darted from her shoulder to her waist, her hip and then her cheek, trembling fingers reacquainting him with her shape, and then he stepped back. "Good night, Alexandra."

"What? ... No." Her head shook, brows drawn into a puzzled vee. "What do you mean, *good night?*"

He moved back a few more steps and bowed low. Her unspoken invitation nearly did him in when he met her eyes.

"Where are you going?" she demanded in a husky whisper.

He stopped backing away. "To sleep." Now that he could sleep, certain that her feelings mirrored his own.

"You...what? *Sleep?*"

"There are times," he murmured, closing the distance again a pace at a time, "when a man has need of an answer." At arm's length now, he stopped and ran fingers over her throat and cradled her neck, thumb brushing her hair. "And he can rest once he has it."

Her eyes closed, and there was no missing a hitch to the rise and fall of her breasts. "What was the question?"

"You were," he admitted, tracing the curve of her cheek.

She swallowed, fingers perching on his wrist without enough pressure to encourage or deny him. "What was your answer?"

He put space between them, palms tracing her shape one last time. "You were."

"Can we wait?" she asked again.

124

He drank her in, soft and flushed and well within reach, and swallowed some doubt. "Can we?"

CHAPTER SIXTEEN

Haywood Village, English Coast – July 12th, 1814

As it turned out, they *could* wait. Alexandra wanted to be impressed by their willpower, but truthfully, they had seen almost nothing of each other in the two days before Spencer headed north.

A convenient invitation from Lord Darby, inviting her to Scotland to visit Amelia, could not have come at a more opportune time. Alix took silent enjoyment in Paulina's struggle, not wanting Alix in company with her new, more fashionable set of friends and not wanting to relinquish her grip.

The agony was waiting two more aching, chest-thumping days to follow behind Spencer while shaking Chas and Paulina off of her skirt hem, insisting that she wished to visit Stirling for her cough. Laurel, her unwitting ally, had insisted it was for the best and hinted that she and John could chaperone.

Lady Conyngham's invitation to Bath had put an end to the matter; Paulina, seeing her chance to be a big fish in a small pond, settled the matter at once. She agreed to Stirling, openly pleased at going to Bath for a fortnight in Alix's absence.

Alexandra was left in peace, Paulina too absorbed with preparations to harass her. Thankfully, not one of them had been up at seven this morning to see her off; likely because she had told them all she was going at noon in order to slip away unharried. She had bounced up into the coach secure in the knowledge that Paulina was too terrified of Lord Darby to try and spy on her.

Little sleep the night before, or for days now, turned out to be a blessing. She managed to last until the first time they stopped to change horses. Fresh air and milk, coupled with the carriage's renewed swaying, put her entirely out, and what she'd imagined being a long and lonely trip passed by in oblivion.

They arrived at the salty, sand-blown little village of Haywood just before three in the afternoon. Alix repinned her hair, wiped her face with a damp handkerchief, and did her best not to look like she'd slept for four hours in a torturous u-shape between narrow seats. The carriage lurched to a stop before a two-story shop, its walls constructed entirely of silvery driftwood. Judging by the contents in the front window, it was a general store. It was also a boardinghouse and ferry, based on an ominous sign impaled beside the door which read: 'No tarts or drunks, in beds or in boats'.

"A respectable establishment," she quipped, gathering her valise. The door popped open, bathing her in a gust a sharp sea air, its cool breath welcome after miles in a stuffy cab. She thought nothing of it, and opened her mouth to thank the coachman when a voice a froze her in place.

"Mrs. Rowan."

Alix sighed, her back to the door, and inhaled her name on his lips. "Lord Reed." She turned to hand Spencer her bag, and stared. Barely shaven, bronzed by the sun, he grinned up at her like a perfect rogue. A shirt open at the throat was cinched into buckskins which left nothing to the imagination. Her heart thundered, recalling why she was here, and Alix pressed a palm to her chest to mute its rhythm. "Did you wait long?" she managed, letting him take her hand and guide her out into the blazing afternoon.

"Half an hour," he murmured, brushing the corner of her mouth, "That's when you were expected. I stayed here in the village last night, so it was nothing really." Spiced rum caught in her nose, hinting that perhaps he'd been as nervous as she was now. Alix ducked her head and was silent.

Spencer led her to a pair of horses, a stout chestnut and a delicate dapple mare, that were hitched and shuffling beside the shop. He lashed her valise with deft fingers, then rifled through his saddle bag and produced a bundle of off-white cloth and a pair of battered leather boots. "My room is paid up. Go inside and put these on." He grinned. "We have some ways to go."

She claimed the bundle with trembling hands, moving in a daze toward the mercantile. She was here; she was truly here. And the reason...biting a smile, she shook her head. Coming to Haywood felt as natural as following Spencer into the garden. How far was the cottage? What would they discuss along the way? She wondered how they could talk about anything with the reason for her visit standing boldly between them.

Her eyes took a moment to adjust inside the dim shop. Tobacco and dark sugar filled her nose, wafting from a wall of barrels and cartons. The main shop was clean but crowded by more esoteric goods, liver salts and lead ball molds hinting that it must serve villages for a long way in every direction.

A crag faced old woman looked up from a counter at the back, her wild bun as coarse and silver as the shop's wood. Alix anticipated a scowl, but instead received a kind, thin-lipped smile and a nod toward the staircase. She had been expected.

There were only two doors at the top of a creaking staircase. One stood ajar, the corner of a neatly made bed just visible. The other rough door was shut and was hung with a loop of weathered rope to indicate that it was occupied, she guessed. Alix stepped into the first room and shut the door, not bothering to lock it.

Spencer had obviously done some tidying. The blankets had been stripped back to bare a mattress' blue and white ticking, which was surprisingly clean. They were bundled in a neat stack beside a wash stand. Beyond simple furnishings, the room was plain. She might have overlooked a sturdy table in the back corner, except a scrap of paper fluttering on top caught her eye.

Long hooked letters joined by lines and curls formed her name across its face. Breath catching, Alexandra claimed it with a finger, pulling it to her and unfolding the crease. Inside, the words were written smaller, but with no less artistry:

I accept.

-S

Two words filled with so much intent. Asking Spencer for an affair was an offer of her body, and so much more. She had told herself while still at Broadmoore that she could change

128

her mind at any time before taking the first step. She could see plainly now, miles away, that getting into the coach was hardly the first step, no more than Spencer's midnight visit to her room. They had made the first overtures months before. Whatever she had risked by coming here, Spencer had risked it too.

Her cheeks ached with a smile, and she rested his note in plain sight atop the mattress while she changed. Sliding into ivory duck breeches and working at the buttons with trembling fingers, Alix wondered where he had come by clothes that were obviously not his. Struggling a shirt over stays and a chemise she realized too late couldn't be removed alone, she shrugged and decided to let it be. Last came the boots. They were on the large side, like everything else, but she had no intention of riding side saddle. They would do just fine.

Grabbing her clothes and shoes in a wad and gently claiming the note, she headed back downstairs with a thank-you to the landlady and stepped outside.

Spencer was leaned against the wall, arms crossed, an absolute picture of repose. She watched him a moment, enjoying the sight of him so relaxed. That, along with the wonderful anticipation in her belly, reminded her of the first rushing breeze before a storm. Heart in her throat, she walked to him.

He straightened and greeted her with a lazy smile.

"So," she began, self-conscious, "here I am."

"Here you are," he repeated, nodding and looking her over. "Now I see why women are proscribed from wearing men's clothes. It would be bedlam within the first hour."

Her cheeks, already hot from the sun, burned. Alix held out her old clothes, ignoring his blatant compliment. When Spencer had stowed them away, he helped her up onto the dapple and claimed his own mount. They spurred along the building, past a few ramshackle houses, then veered left off the road and onto a sandy, scrubby trail winding out to the horizon.

There were no half-measures to the land around them. Swirling water was not simply blue but vibrant cerulean; dancing grass glowed a verdant green in defiance of slate cliffs. Stark white clouds billowed across the horizon making her believe that their small bit of the world went on forever.

"I've traveled," she murmured, looking left and right at the beauty around them, "but I have never seen a place so striking."

"No one would ever point me out as a romantic," he said. "In fact, Bennet will assure you that I am a statue." He paused a breath for her laughter. "We've agreed to something which carries a responsibility. No fumbling in a musty bedchamber." Her face burned under the heat of his gaze. "I want to make this good for you, Alexandra."

Waves hushed against the rocks below their path while overhead gulls made lazy arcs, crying to one another. Her head spun, both at Spencer's words and a struggle to believe that this was real.

They had reached the hill's base and could more easily ride side-by-side. "I found your note," she volunteered when she could manage to speak.

Squinting out ahead, Spencer flashed a smiled. "Did you? I thought you would appreciate it."

"I do, very much. Think if I'd come seven hours only to find *'Lord Reed regrets to inform you...'*"

His laugh was deep, sonorous, different than when they had been on the estate or in company. "In that case, I would be a fool, and sending you away would be a kindness."

Flustered again, Alix kept quiet as they fell into companionable silence. A sharp wind kissed her cheeks. Waves crested white and spilled onto the rocks again and again while they trotted along the path. At some point the wide lane had become intermittent patches of sand, and then wiry dune grass with no discernible trail at all. Spencer steered his horse without the slightest hesitation, obviously familiar with the wild terrain.

"How much farther?" she asked, glancing back and finding that the village and its hilltop had almost passed from sight.

Spencer nodded ahead with his chin. "That craggy cliff is Darrow Point. Just around the end and we'll be nearly there."

On a fair day like today, the narrow skirt of sand they now trod allowed for travel around the point. In foul weather, a storm, it would be impassable. "What do you do in winter, or when the winds come up?"

130

"Already plotting your escape?" His boot tapped hers. "There's a road, south from the cottage and then inland for a ways. Eventually it rambles through the forest and back to Haywood."

"A bit in the wild," she mused aloud, taking in the geography.

"It is," he agreed, then looked her over with a meaning she could never mistake, "but it has its charm."

Alix studied her reins and bit her lip under his continued gaze.

"Do you regret coming?" he murmured, voice nearly swallowed by the sea.

She snapped to meet his eyes. "No! No. Why would you say that?"

Uncharacteristic worry painted his face, and his shoulders held a tension she hadn't seen all day. "It's not like you to be so quiet. And I admit I cannot read you at all today."

Emotions battled against her thoughts, not one pairing into anything reassuring. At a loss, Alix brought her horse in closer and nudged his thigh with an elbow. "I'm here, Spencer. You can read that well enough."

He reached out and thumbed her chin. "So I can."

They rounded Darrow Point at last, and Alexandra saw that he had not been jesting. The stone cottage stood on a hill which was set back from a low, sandy embankment being slowly reclaimed by the waves. Its high, narrow face looked out over the sea with a row of wide windows, like gentle eyes softening an otherwise austere facade. Two thick chimneys staked it to the ground and dared the fiercest ocean gales to do their worst. Lush emerald grass waved in fans on hillsides all around, offsetting dusty pink heather that clung tenaciously to the house's foundation and spun out on both sides of the door.

And that was all. As Spencer had promised, not another man or building was in sight. A gentle thrill tremored through her at the privacy, and she bit her lip, looking to Spencer, who nodded. He led her around a slope, skirting a loose embankment and circling the cottage.

As it happened, there was another building hidden behind the house. It was a small stable, its planks weathered by sun and tide. Spencer dismounted at its low stone fence and helped her down, then gathered her bag.

"We can leave them for now," he explained, nodding to the horses and gathering the valise. "They know the land, and they'll stay close."

He took her hand and twined their fingers. Alix gave a squeeze, and Spencer responded with equal pressure. Her heart slammed, thrumming in its cage as they reached the door.

The front room doubled as a parlor, the wide, rough oak planks of its floor softened by a thick blue wool rug.

At the far wall, a spindle-backed rocking chair held court before a smooth river-stone fire box. Split wood half-filled a high alcove made for the purpose. Its mantle sailed a hand-carved ship, its proud lines painted white and dusty blue. That was the extent of the room's decoration. Its tables and chairs were sturdy and natural, polished by time rather than fussy craftsmen. The room was clean and cozy, with not a speck of dirt to be found.

Spencer rubbed his hands together, watching her carefully. "What do you think?"

Alix turned slowly, taking it in, catching swelling waves through a window beside the door. "It's perfect. Beautiful."

His shoulders relaxed, and Alix sensed her words had lifted some weight. "See your way around. Go up and change if you'd like. I'll bring in more wood and tend the horses."

She stared at him filling the room from floor to ceiling, not entirely recognizing him. He was easy and unbuttoned with an absence of frustrated lines, making him look young.

He stared back, and for a moment Alix felt a palpable cord of tension drawing their bodies together. Then he swallowed hard, nodded at something only he understood, and went out.

She exhaled in time with the door's closing, a breath she hadn't realized she'd been holding. Everything felt awkward, her nerves throwing her off, and she hated it. When he came back in, she vowed it would be different.

First things first, she would learn the house, get comfortable in it. Resolute, she moved from the front room into a narrow hall. A doorway on her left revealed a kitchen which was nearly medieval in construction. A cavernous fireplace dominating one wall was hung with an iron kettle, small embers already winking from the grate below. It also boasted barrels and tubs, a high nicked-up counter for cutting and bread making, and another smaller one beside it, stone-topped for butchering. A pantry and larder filled a wall opposite the fireplace.

To her right off the hall was a small dining room. A comfortable looking gray, wing-back chair sat beside the fire, a small plank table and two chairs not far away. A pale oak sideboard and cupboard hugged either side of the wide window, offering up sturdy white crockery for inspection.

A narrow door led from the end of the hall outside, facing kitty-corner from the stables. Peeking out, she spied a knee-high stone wall which enclosed a surprisingly well-tended kitchen garden. Alix immediately recognized spikes of chive and velvety sage. Mint had claimed an entire corner for itself.

Satisfied with the lay of the land, Alix returned to the great room, gathered her valise and went upstairs. First, she came upon a study of sorts. Front and center was a finely made, cherrywood desk, easily the most expensive bit of furniture in the whole house. Another book shelf sat along one wall, twin to one at the foot of the stairs. A telescope stood sentry at the window, ready for a night sky. A few things littered the desk: a medal, coins certainly not British in origin, a small medallion enclosing a lock of dark hair, a pen knife, and wood shavings. Alix guessed that Spencer spent a lot of his time here.

The next room, the bedroom, was her favorite the moment she stepped inside. Larger than the study by half, two of its walls held little more than windows. They would be impractical in winter, but a rough stone fireplace nearly as big as the kitchen's occupied a third wall, ready to chase away the deepest chill. Beside it stood a square, dependable looking wardrobe.

The bed was a sort of sleigh shape, with a tall, cherry headboard and no canopy. Wide and high, it was stacked with plush quilts beneath a blue and crimson block coverlet. Alix ran her hand over its soft, well-worn fabric, then slipped a hand under the blankets into the cool space beneath and traced a silky cotton sheet. Moving upward, she pressed into a plush down pillow and imagined it below her head, warmed by Spencer's body. It took two steadying breaths to pull away, to put the bed and Spencer from her mind. Hefting her valise, she managed it onto the bed and began to undress, finding it impossible not to imagine it was Spencer doing the work.

*   *   *

Spencer planted his axe blade-first into the stump and claimed his shirt from the grass. He paused and panted, the sweat beading in his hairline a reminder of just how long he'd been without drill and the army's exertion. Riding and shooting on the rare occasion Bennet nagged him into it was not getting the job done, physically.

He moved his freshly split pile an armload at a time to the front door, peering in the front windows on each pass for a glimpse of Alexandra. Bryn and Rory stood in the hillside's deep grass, heads hung beneath their blowing manes. The pair shuffled and snorted at his approach, hinting at displeasure that he'd left them waiting to be put away. "I'm here now, you cantankerous nags. Come on, then." He cooed and snapped their reins, cajoling both animals up to the barn.

Finished with horses and firewood, he turned attention to his final chore. He worked the creaking iron pump handle, splashing frigid water into a wooden pail at his feet while he considered her. Why had it been so much easier in town? Conversation had flowed. Quips and glib remarks were handy, and they had been easy in each other's company. It had all felt so natural.

He shook his head and tried to clear it. He was over-thinking matters, suffering from the nerves of a man two decades younger and a military need to run every damned thing. Spencer grinned at himself and snatched the bucket's fraying rope bail.

It had been simpler with other women. They had followed the steps, minded the rules. Encounters were comfortable, but lacking passion.

He didn't want to follow those steps with Alexandra, and she certainly could give a damn for rules. That put him in unfamiliar territory, but that didn't mean he couldn't enjoy himself. Exhaling, relaxing, Spencer grabbed the door handle and went in.

The great room was empty, and there were no creaking floorboards overhead. It wasn't until he reached the hall that sounds caught his ears from the kitchen. Staying silent, he passed into the kitchen.

When his eyes found her, he had set down the bucket to take her in. Her dress was a few layers of white lawn and little more than a heavy chemise swirling at her ankles. Sleeves just reached her elbows with no trim or lace to obscure creamy skin. A wide sash caught her waist, drifting behind her as she moved. The gown had a soft effect on her, showing no fuss or formality. Its gauzy white fabric lit Alix's face, making her look much younger. Then she smiled, and his breath caught.

"I don't know about you, but I would like to eat at some point." She scooped a handful of potatoes and threw them into a kettle he didn't recall owning. "Soon," she added, tossing in an onion and some oats. "And I hope nothing in here is off limits, because it's all been touched."

Not sure what to say, Spencer moved behind her, close enough to catch the heat of her body without touching it. Alix reached a hand behind her back and slipped her fingers inside his.

She stopped cutting and relaxed, laying her head back against his shoulder. Smooth skin along her neck teased him and her hand pressed his hip for balance. His body's response was total and immediate.

Not now, not yet. He pecked her temple and tore himself away. "There's ham in the burrow and some aged beef."

"Ham," she answered, watching him now over her shoulder with a stormy gaze that made it hard to look away.

Shaking himself loose, he bent to raise the small stone door. He took the ham from its cool earthen cave and rested it on the block. "Shall I?"

Alix shook her head, her back to him and bent fetchingly over the fire. "No, I can manage."

"How long will you be?"

She glanced back. "Just the ham and then I'm done. Why?"

135

"Come outside when you've finished."

Her smile was wary and sly. "What for?"

"Come outside," he whispered again, backing away one step at a time, returning her smile, not willing to turn away until she disappeared.

*   *   *

She missed him at first, seated in high grass beside the house. His hand waved, giving her a hint, and Alix made her way down from the porch with eager curiosity.

Spencer was wrapped in a quilt, and he held it open at her approach. "This is my favorite spot," he said, snuggling her into the warm crook of his arm. He pointed out over the water. "On a crisp day you can just spy the headlands over there, usually only in fall, but today the view has been obliging. Any other time, it's just the tide, cresting and swelling."

She squinted, barely spying the proud slopes of land through an ocean haze but grasping why he loved the spot. If they had settled more to the right, a near cliff would steal their view; more to their left would subtract part of the panorama.

The sun was dropping to the horizon on their left, spilling in at a warm golden angle that obliged her to shade her eyes. Spencer turned his body, pressing her and moving their backs into its heat without diminishing the view. Alix inhaled his scent drifting up from beneath the blanket. It was salty and citrus, crisp like lemons and something oily, bergamot and a hint of wood smoke. She laid her head against his chest and inhaled, dizzied. "I have missed you."

"Aye." His shoulders rocked with a nod. "It was hard, coming up alone. Harder to spend the days waiting."

Exactly the way she had felt. Inside the blanket, she found his hand and wrapped their fingers together.

Spencer leaned away, fiddling with something beside her and then held out a little glass in front of her face. She took it in her free hand and smelled it. "Woo! Scotch." She raised an eyebrow at him. "Traditionally a spot of trouble for me. I can't take much. Well," she brought it close to her lips, then away, "I *shouldn't* take much."

"Good," Spencer chuckled, holding up his own dram. "I won't have to spend all my best malt on you, then."

She snorted, pulling out from underneath his arm to better manage her drink. "That sounds like a challenge."

Spencer gave her a once over, warming her head to toe. "Perhaps it is."

Alix groaned, bringing her thimble-glass close again. "This cannot end well." She tipped it back with a flick of her wrist. Smoke filled her nose; it burned her throat and warmed her chest. Exhaling, she shook her head and glanced to Spencer, staring back wide-eyed beside her. "What?"

"God, woman. I meant for you to sip it! We're not at Barnaby's tavern," he cried, pinching her hip under the quilt.

Rather than admit her embarrassment, she held out her glass and smiled. "Stop crowing at being unmanned and fill me up."

"Lord and saints, Alexandra. Pace yourself." His chastising fell flat; he was smiling and already refilling her glass.

She was giddy, and the scotch made quick work of an empty stomach. She raised a mock toast. "Pace your *self*, sir."

Spencer made a big show of seating the cork back into the green glass bottle. "That is quite enough for you, Mrs. Rowan. Nurse what you have or do without."

She took a small mouthful of her second round, suddenly confessional. "It isn't Rowan."

"What?" She might as well have slapped him, by the look on his face.

"It isn't Rowan. Just Paton. Rowan's just a name I adopted after my behavior humiliated Paulina with some imagined scandal. A name I was *forced* to adopt," she corrected.

He scooted further back, and leaned in to study her face. "I don't understand."

"Silas had got control of our business, thanks to Chas. He had control of us, too. He wouldn't brook my *nonsense* and neither would she. Of course, Chas had no choice. So I was marched home from Carolina to discover that I had been 'gone on my honeymoon with Mister Rowan, who had tragically fallen overboard and drowned'." She raised her voice theatrically, throwing arms wide from under the quilt.

137

"Carolina. Where had you truly gone?"

"To Carolina," she asserted, a surprisingly raw ache in her heart. "Tempted by a man I was madly in love with."

Spencer's gaze cooled. "And now?"

"And now he's a memory. I have no idea what became of Edward. If he wrote afterward, I never saw the letters."

"He never came for you?" demanded Spencer.

"Silas was waiting when we put into port." She swallowed and closed her eyes, wishing the images didn't hang behind her lids. "I saw him on the docks, brutish and glaring, with Chas beside him. He dragged me ashore."

"And no one stopped him, no one interfered?" he demanded.

"Not with his hands," she clarified. "With a leash of fear and a heavy palm on my brother's shoulder." She breathed deep and let a swell of nerves subside. "I felt he would be at every port, waiting any time we came ashore and using Chas as leverage. Edward had been so patient through my father's decline, tolerating Chas's abuse. He grabbed my arm at the gangplank and said that if I left him now, it was for the last time." She dabbed her eyes with a sleeve. "I didn't even offer an excuse, just walked past."

Spencer was up on his knees, raking fingers through his hair. "Well, did he come after you at all? Try to stop you? What did Silas want with it all?"

"What he has always wanted: my shares." She shrugged. "To own Paton Shipping, and the obedience of everyone around him."

"Why didn't you run? Flee where he couldn't find you?"

Her laugh rattled hollow in her chest. "I thought I had, with Edward. I'd been so careful, and still, there was Silas." She pressed her eyes with trembling fingers. "If he had beaten me any less I might have found the strength to escape. He drove home his point with every blow of his walking stick. Silas truly beat the rebellion out of me."

"That's madness," Spencer rasped, mouth agape.

"It was. And I had to play along. He holds a majority of our company. Convinced the investors to make him trustee of my shares, in my absence. Just as a precaution, he assured them, in case something should happen to me." She spat the words and swallowed down bile at their memory. "We do whatever he wants, because we've *no* idea what he will do if we disobey."

"Alexandra, he's holding you hostage. It cannot stand."

"It won't," she promised. "Not much longer. I've bought back nearly enough shares to have a real stake. Chas can take over, and I can cash out. I'll finally be free."

"What a wonder you are," praised Spencer, kissing the top of her head and warming her with a note of pride in his words. "Not that you need me, but I am here. We will sort this out together at every turn."

She leaned into him again, terrible memories calmed by his nearness and the rest of her scotch. They watched the waves come on relentlessly. Spencer's fingers played idly with tendrils of hair at her nape while she worried at a seam of his shirt. His other hand brushed her forehead, cradled her cheek and he turned her to face him.

Alix knew what came next. She closed her eyes and tipped her head back into his palm. His lips only played at first, brushing, pressing gently before they finally slid firmly against her own. He leaned into her, urging her back until she fell into the rough grass. Spencer fell beside her without breaking their kiss. His hand traced her waist and toyed with her sash. She braced his jaw with a palm, scraping over the barest hint of a beard. She drew him in close, tasting peat and smoke on his tongue. Driving fingers into his hair, she caught a line of sweat beading at his collar, trailed it into his shirt and raked nails over his taut shoulders.

Spencer sucked a breath against her lips, twitched and then pulled away. He sat up, knees to chest and stared across the water until she heard his breathing slow. He was fighting for control; she wished he wouldn't.

Lying in the grass, Alix watched him, running a finger up his back and trying to read the set of his shoulders. She wanted him to come back, to lie over her and kiss her again. Instead, he stood up, eyes moving over her, head to toe. He stretched out a hand. "Let's go in. We should eat."

A serious note to the words made her frown as he pulled her up. "Why?"

"Because we both need our strength," he teased. His lips buried in her throat without warning.

Alix didn't recognize the moan as hers, not even when her knees buckled and Spencer dragged her close. He held her that way a moment, then reached down for the quilt and gave her arm a tug. "Come," he pulled again. "It's time we went in."

*　　*　　*

He was too hungry for continued seduction, and apparently so was Alix. Their dinner conversation devolved into teasing and good-natured arguing, all of it punctuated by concern over why they hadn't made more to eat. Smoked ham and earthy white potatoes, sweet onions and rich broth conspired to make him lazy. A pint of golden ale hadn't helped matters.

"Hmm." Alix pressed a hand to her chest and leaned back in her chair. "Good food. Good drink," Her foot kicked his beneath the table and her eyes were warm and content, "Good company. I couldn't name a better day if you asked me."

The compliment flustered him. Spencer drained the last mouthful of ale from his glass, sat back, and looked her over. "Alexandra."

Her brows raised, and she cast him a sideways look. "Yes."

"Why did you ask me to have an affair?"

Her head shook and she sputtered. Lips worked but nothing intelligible came out. "I thought we already sorted this out."

"Obviously not." He couldn't fight laughter straining his ribs. Taking up the bottle, he leaned and filled both their glasses one last time. "Or perhaps I want to hear it again. I'll give you a moment to answer."

She shrugged, laughing now, too. "I like you." Alix claimed her glass and drew an unladylike mouthful. Setting it just so beside her plate, she fiddled with the rim a moment and then met his eyes. "Why *not* you?"

He shrugged, not under any pretenses. "I'm old."

"Old?" She laughed and scrubbed hands over her face. "Forty is not old." Blue eyes studied him a moment. "You're tall.

Fit. You've long fingers and lips to tempt a saint. No one would call you *old*."

Her praise started a slow burn. "Some do," he argued, watching her.

"To hell with them, then." She polished off her ale in one swallow. "Old," she scoffed. "*Experienced*."

His pulse doubled at her implication. "You *like* me; is that all?" he prodded.

She leaned across their narrow table, in his face and looking fully aware that she was being baited. "No. You're handsome as Lucifer. I love the way you smell. You kiss like a libertine, and sometimes your gaze makes me feel naked." Her finger was pinning his chest now, and if her rant hadn't been so arousing he would have laughed. "I enjoy your conversation nearly as much as I enjoy you in a pair of buckskins. The books you read are educated. Judging by John's account of you in the ring, you could put a man's face through his head, and I have no idea why but I find that *very* appealing."

"You damn me with faint praise madam," he teased softly, brushing the tip of his nose to hers. Spencer tipped his head, set to kiss her and aching to stop dancing around why they were here.

"Now you," she panted against his mouth, still worked up by her tirade.

He snapped back, putting space between them. "Me what?"

"You." She waved a finger over him. "You tell me why you accepted."

He hadn't imbibed enough to share her level of confidence; the question unbalanced him.

Looking impatient with his silence, Alix crossed her arms. "*I* am *old*."

"No," he breathed, taking in her flushed cheeks and sea-blue eyes, an errant black curl or two caressing her cheek in defiance of her bun. "No, you are not old."

He reached across the table, unknit her arms and took her hands. "I think that is a word that is only applied by the very young. When I was twenty, forty was decrepit," he admitted, recalling what a brash ass he had been. "The finest points of my military career came in my thirties. I am the most content I have ever been. And I have no patience for the uninformed mind and idle chatter of a girl half my age."

He pressed her fingers harder. "I wish to sit at my table and do as we are doing now. To be entertained, satisfied. Not wrung for compliments and otherwise ignored. I want to take a *woman* to my bed and want to be made to feel like a man." Spencer smiled at wide eyes, brushed her cheek. "I enjoy all of that with you. Or, I *will*."

"Spencer."

He ached at the way Alexandra breathed his name and his heart hummed at her soft invitation. He got up, still holding her hand, and drew her towards the stairs.

*   *   *

Spencer had already made up the fire; before dinner she guessed, by a deep gray char to the logs. Small tongues of flame cast an amber glow over an otherwise dark room. Alix stood at a window, squinting out into the night, but there was no telling sea from land with the sun fully set.
Only Spencer's reflection filled the panes; her heart skipped and she turned around.

He shut the door with meaning, slouched against it and pressed it with both palms. Head leaned back, he watched her from across the room. "Here we are."

She caught his smile and nodded. "Here were are."

He straightened and beckoned her with a finger. Hesitant, she took him in a breath longer, knowing that the moment she moved, things would be in motion neither of them could stop.

"Alexandra," he commanded, his voice gentle authority, "come here."

She did. Her *body* did, delighted to obey whether her mind agreed or no. A thrill shivered through her.

They met at the fireplace. Spencer rested an elbow against the mantle, taking her in. She twitched at fingers raking her arm. "I want to have an affair with you," he teased.

She stared at the hollow of his throat, following the open vee of his shirt. "I do. More than anything."

Hands cupped her shoulders and Spencer turned her away. His fingers tugged the knot in her sash and his nose followed the curve of her neck. Alix gasped, tensed, then fell against his chest while her sash whispered to the floor. A stout hand worked between them; he popped each button with deft fingers. Cool air swept her bare shoulders.

Spencer drew lips over her nape, stubble rasping her flesh.

She began to unravel.

Palms curved down over her arms. With little encouragement her dress gave up, pooling with the sash at her feet.

Four sharp tugs got her stays loose. Spencer worked them over her head, taking quick liberty as he went, catching her breast through a thin chemise. And just like that, it and her stockings were all that remained. A hand at her waist turned her back to face him. Arms hung at his side, and, after a moment, Alix realized Spencer was waiting for something.

Settling at the mattress' edge, she leaned back onto her palms and looked him over. "Come here."

He stepped between her knees and forced her shift up higher.

"Take off your shirt."

She had expected him to take his time, make a show of it. Instead, Spencer grabbed the tail and untucked it, and pulled it free in a single fluid motion. It fell discarded with her own clothes. Reaching up, she raked fingernails at his throat and brushed from his chest to the flat plane of his stomach, and stopped just shy of his breeches.

"What," she breathed, sitting up, "is that?" Angry and red, the scar banded beneath his ribs, a gash with thick skin healed over it. Alix ran a finger over the recent wound. Spencer's flesh twitched beneath her thumb.

"Musket ball," he panted. "Not the first or the last."

He was being truthful. Running her hands over him in dim fire light, her fingertips caught three more ragged scars and a dozen smoother ones, carved by blades or bayonets. Each was a brush with fate, a near miss which might have cost her Spencer before she had known to miss him, and robbed her of their

143

future. The patchwork of his flesh was sobering, and she caressed each mark with reverence.

She pressed a hand to the small of his back and leaned in to brush kisses up from his hip. Sweat and sea salt stung her lips. Spencer's fingers crushed her hair a moment, muscles taut under her tongue, and then he drew back. A straining in his breeches was unmistakable. Alix ducked her eyes, stealing glimpses while Spencer bent to pry off his boots.

Tucking her legs, she crawled up the bed and wriggled beneath the quilts.

Spencer stood up and froze. Grinning, he shook his head. "Absolutely not. What do you think you are doing?"

She glanced over the bed, confused. "I thought … If we're going to," she cleared her throat, "then we should be in bed." Her experience might be limited but that part seemed fairly obvious.

Spencer was already shaking his head again. He pinned the mattress beside her with a knee, and grabbed the quilts and dragged them all the way to the foot of the bed. "I'm not making love to you like a dowdy, under the sheet in my night cap and dressing gown."

She bit back a smile at the image, heart racing at how easily he took charge.

His rough palm bridged bare flesh between the top of her stocking and the hem of her shift. Fabric bunched helplessly in his path to her hip, and his fingers brushed over her ribs. The chemise gathered around her face, and then it was gone, tossed from view.

She didn't meet his eyes, instead staring at shadows of flame dancing on the wall. Alix had never really thought of herself as self-conscious, but then, no man had ever seen her nude. It was a foreign, wondrous feeling.

"Alexandra," Spencer beckoned, obliging her to look up, "take down your hair."

She obliged him, under a spell. Eight pins; she drew them slowly, reveling in the way he watched her, caressing her with his eyes while she worked. Bold, she held both arms higher as she went, aware of the effect it was having by the slant of his gaze. A moment later her teasing was rewarded by a low groan.

Finished and triumphant, she tossed her pins to the floor and pinged them off of the wood without caring. Hair brushed her back and shoulders, a sensation she had experienced a hundred times before. Tonight, though, it was different.

Spencer pressed her back against the bed and raked fingers through her waves to fan them over the pillows. When he sat back to survey his handiwork, Alix turned her face away from the scrutiny. Fingers circled one wrist, then the other; he raised her arms and rested them above her head and hummed his approval.

When he stood up the mattress shifted, giving her the courage to look at him again. His eyes didn't leave her body while he worked his breeches open with the same deftness as he had her gown. Long planes and sharp angles were silhouetted by the firelight and she watched unabashed as he stripped the pants away. He came back to her, sat, and then stretched out beside her along the bed. His hard frame crushed her softer one, and she sighed.

Spencer wrapped her with an arm, tucking a hand into the small of her back. Then he stopped, head bent halfway to her mouth. "Do you feel that?" he whispered.

She felt a lot of things. Uncertain, Alix shook her head and he smiled.

"I can just feel your heart against mine."

Exhaling, she closed her eyes and smiled. She did feel it, and contentment washed over her. She breathed his name, exhaling the last syllable against his lips.

There was no preamble to his mouth's force. He crushed lips against her teeth until she winced, but she had no desire to pull away. Something about a little pain made her heart thump harder, and she gripped his shoulder and pulled, silently begging Spencer to cover her body with his. He obliged with one easy shift, settling between her knees.

He assaulted her neck and shoulders, the tops of her breasts. Teeth nipped, his tongue soothed, and Alix struggled to catch a breath.

She traced the corded lines of his back, his buttocks, memorizing the shape of his body. She'd never seen, let alone touched, an entirely unclothed man. Something primitive

145

whispered for her to scrape, to knead, to learn. She wanted to learn him with fingers and legs and tongue, to touch every inch.

Spencer stiffened between her legs, groaned into her breasts, and pulled away. He stared down at her, chest heaving. He was asking; she understood by a hungry look he fixed on her. Alix closed her eyes, raised arms above her head in surrender, and arched against him.

Spencer's weight shifted on her, transferring onto one arm, crushing her while lips painted her shoulder with hot gasps. Knuckles brushed the inside of her thigh. He drew back, and then pressed her with infinite gentleness.

"Mmph!" She arched further, winced, and sucked in a breath. It hurt, and then it passed, washed away on a surge of need.

Spencer stiffened. She didn't hear him so much as breathe, and then he pulled back.

"No! No, no!" Alix grabbed at his shoulders, his hip, holding him.

"Alexandra," he panted, pulling harder.

"No." She locked a leg over his back, and when that didn't work, raised her hips to sink him fully inside. "No," she gasped again, knowing she'd won when Spencer weighted her back against the mattress. He came into her again, pushed up the length of her body with a pressure near to pushing through her. He tore a cry from her chest, coming on again at the same delicious pace.

Sweat beaded between their bodies. A knot in her belly moved lower, heat spreading to her thighs and coupled with a tender throbbing already lingering there. "Please," she whispered against his damp temple. "Spencer, please..." She ran a toe up the back of his calf, twined their legs together.

He grunted, bucked against her, chuckling into her throat. Slow and relentless, he ignored her plea.

Now she begged in earnest. Thought fell away under sensation. She *needed*. Alix had no doubt Spencer was doing it right. He just wasn't doing enough; he was withholding on purpose. Lungs burning, she panted and raised harder against him. She writhed, arched. Fistfuls of his hair twined between her fingers, thick and silken. She clenched them, tugging him into a kiss. His lip was too fetching a target, and Alix caught it between her teeth and pinched.

His groan filled her mouth, vibrating in her throat; she had won. Spencer gripped her thigh, raised her knee and pierced her with a force which punished even as it fulfilled.

This. This was what she wanted. Small 'ahh's' of frustration were shredded into cries of pure, mindless satisfaction. She clutched at Spencer with trembling limbs, bracing herself.

His hips jarred hers, groans caught against her nipple. "Alexandra. Oh God, Alexandra..." Her name was sweet and urgent on his lips. Spencer went rigid between her thighs, hands cradled her back, and he raised her until her flesh stung. His body trembled ahead of hers, a warning she had only a breath to heed, and then she snapped. Spencer's movements ripped something from her, and spasms wracked her head to toe as the world melted away. His name on her lips was a wild sound, a sound she felt in her throat more than a fully formed word.

He shuddered out a cry of his own against her breast. Heat spilled over her thighs and he fell against her, trembling out of time with her own weak limbs. Air couldn't come fast enough, but she was in no hurry for anything else.

The crackling fire reached her ears as their breath slowed, reality setting in once more. Sweat cooled on her skin and Alix tensed, anxious about the moment that Spencer withdrew and left her empty.

She had no idea how much time passed. Her eyes closed and she drifted, content just at the edge of sleep under his warmth. At some point, a sound drew her back. She realized it was her name when he spoke again.

"Alexandra." Spencer raised up on his elbows, staring down at her from a heavy-lidded frown.

"Mm."

"Why didn't you tell me?"

"Tell you ... oh." Her first impulse was to say she thought she had, but then Alix realized she hadn't said anything one way or another. "I told you I had never been married. Never had an affair. I thought it seemed obvious." She swallowed. "Though, in hindsight it's clearly not."

"Clearly," he sighed, then brushed her cheek with his lips.

"You don't owe me anything," she protested as he pulled back.

"No, perhaps I don't. I'm not exactly dashing out to fetch the parson, but this is serious, Alexandra."

Not to her. It had just been something she'd lived with, like the color of her hair. Or perhaps it was, and giving herself to Spencer was so right that it had felt more natural than momentous. She was in no condition for rational thought.

Spencer shifted, his eyes on hers. "London teems with men who find virginity a prize. They take *bets* on it, Alexandra; I have seen the wagers. Once they've taken it from her, they wouldn't tip the girl a nod when crossing the street. And still others avoid it like a pox, thinking it a synonym for prudishness. I am neither sort." He slipped a hand up beneath her shoulder, raising her to him in a slow kiss. "It can only be given between a man and woman once, and I think that carries some weight."

"It does," she breathed against his chest. "But I wanted you, wanted to make love, and carry on as we have."

"It wouldn't have stopped me," he grinned, "but it would have spared me a nearly fatal moment of surprise."

"I'm not a nun," she muttered. "It's not as though I've lived three decades as a hermit."

"No," Spencer brushed kisses over her cheek, her bottom lip, "that much has been apparent for some time. But the act itself..." His grin was cheeky now, skipping her heart. "It's in a gentleman's best interest to take a little care, to make sure the lady enjoys herself. Ideally she should want to do it again."

"Oh," she twined her arms around his neck, kissed him and bit knees into his sides, "She does."

*   *   *

They lay twined together nearly in the center of the bed, having finished at the foot and not quite making it back to the top. He was sixteen and in the hayloft again, and nothing about Alexandra was slowing the charge. She was all curves and softness, firm thighs and womanly hips. Her sweet perfume

148

clung to him and the husky way she'd begged at the end made him want to start all over again. And they had, until the fire burned out and he lost count, until his parts ached and then passed beyond aching, forgotten in the frenzy of arousal.

Alexandra had been quiet, her cheek pressed to his chest. Now she stirred, slipped onto her back and caressed his thigh. The touch garnered an impressive response, by his estimation, given the near pulped sensation he felt from the navel down.

"What pleases you?" she murmured against his ribs.

"What?" He wondered at this point if her question could be serious after the last few hours.

"I read a smuggled copy of 'A Gentleman's Diary', years ago. Have you read it?"

"No. Why, am I in it?"

She snorted, poking him. "He indulged in all manner of activities, but one or two things in particular gave him the greatest pleasure."

He blinked slowly, taking her in. "I want *you*, Alexandra. To make love to you, to press you and debauch you in every way. Wear you to exhaustion until you tremble, and then sleep against me." He drew a thumb over her nipple and relished her gasp. "Whatever wins me that, pleases me."

A slender arm draped his chest. Her fingernail traced his lower lip, raked his jaw. "Knowing what pleases you, wins you that."

"Very well." He couldn't deny an inherent appeal to instructing her. Spencer settled against the mattress until he was entirely comfortable and folded one arm beneath his head. He beckoned Alexandra with a finger. "Up."

She knelt beside him, her smile an invitation to sin.

"Over," he ordered, raking a hand at her.

"Hmm." She straddled him. The perfect weight of her thighs was torture. "This?"

"Mmhmm. The man who thought of this was a genius," he murmured, looking her over. "I can touch every inch of you." Cupping her shoulder, he traced her curves; the weight of her breast, flare of her hip. He pressed a thumb to the crisp black hair between her thighs and hardened at her ragged gasp.

"Every inch." Gripping her hips, he raised her up slowly and denied himself the pleasure of her for an achingly long moment. Sheathing slowly, rational thought melted away at the point where their bodies joined. Alexandra's moan vibrated through him. He pressed her backside, moving her until she caught his rhythm.

"Like this?" she murmured, hands splayed over his chest.

He nodded, taking advantage of their position to explore her. Wild black waves covered her face, teasing his chest when she leaned into his touch. His words felt ragged and out of breath. "If it feels good to you, I promise it's the same for me."

Groaning, he admitted the information might have been a mistake. She shifted, a wicked smile on her face, and for a moment he thought he might lose control.

Alix arched and her fingers gripped his thigh. She was relentless, pressing him to the point of mindlessness. There was something sweet and heedless about her deliberate pace, an innocent disregard for how quickly she was pushing him to the edge.

"This?" she whispered again, palms brushing his chest.

Spencer laced fingers behind his head, arched into her and let himself be thoroughly used. "This."

*   *   *

Two days passed divided in equal fashions: utter domestic failure and exhausting romantic success.

Spencer estimated that no part of the shy little house had been spared. They had burned a loaf of bread while taking advantage of the kneading board's convenient height. His treasured, and until now, pristine cherry wood desk boasted a few well-earned scratches in its surface. A trip and fall on the staircase while chasing Alexandra to the bedroom had presented an entirely new opportunity for both of them. Food was reheated two and three times, and sometimes finally abandoned out of exhaustion. Window ledges, table tops, the rug; nothing was safe.

They were only being driven out of doors today by a heat which not even a stout ocean breeze could chase from the cottage.

"I need a bath," Alexandra murmured into her pillow, sprawled over the mattress. Spencer sat next to her and traced the nude the lines of her body with his eyes. She looked no more eager to move than he was for her to do so. But it was sweltering, and Spencer admitted that after two days of near crippling exertion some sort of ablution was in order. That realization had planted an idea. "Bring your shift," he instructed. "And a wrapper if you have it."

"I do," she smiled, brow arched in a question.

"Then get them," he said, lacing his fingers through a handful of wild black locks, forcing her lips apart with his tongue. She matched him blow for blow until it took real effort to sit up. "And be hasty about it."

A swat to her backside earned a half-hearted glare. He dodged her blow just in time, blocking it with a clean shirt.

"Do I have to wear them, or get them?" Alexandra tossed over her shoulder.

"We're entirely alone, so I'll leave that to you, madam. If you're asking for my preference..."

She turned and faced him, pressing a rumpled shift ineffectually over her nakedness. "In fact, I am." She began to lower her cover.

"No." He backed away, a whole step outside the bedroom door. "At ease, Alexandra. A quarter of an hour. Just … Bite your tongue that long. Keep hands to yourself."

One step, then another, she closed the distance relentlessly. "What's a quarter of an hour now, or later?"

"No, Alexandra." *Yes*, his body insisted.

"Spencer..." She lowered the shift, dropped it on the bed.

He swallowed, restraint slipping like sand through his fingers. "I'll be downstairs."

He took the steps two at a time, considering whether he'd made a mistake. Alexandra was a monster of his own making, and he wondered if he'd survive her.

When she joined him outside, he was disappointed to see that she hadn't made good on her threat. She was close, however.

151

She carried a chemise in-hand and was swallowed by a white muslin wrapper stitched with tiny lavender sprigs. Sunlight caught its loose folds and silhouetted curves beneath.

He coughed and kept his gaze to her face. "A rather short walk just grew a bit farther."

Staring at the ground, she smiled and didn't meet his eyes. "Where to?"

A breeze tousled her hair, sweeping it across flushed cheeks. She was so beautiful; he couldn't take enough of her in, touch her enough, breathe her enough. Spencer reached to brush strands from her face, burning at the barest contact.

He took her hand, walking side-by-side with Alexandra in silence until they reached the barn. Bryn pranced, eager beneath his canvas duffle, and Alix ran a hand over the horse's dappled coat. "Sending me home already?" she teased.

"It had crossed my mind." He tried to hide a flat tone at her mention of home. How could they go back? Seeing one another two or three times over a week – they could never dare more. Minding their looks, their conversation, hiding their feelings. Spencer felt the first pangs of frustration strain his ribs.

Not now. He wouldn't let that spoil their day. Taking Bryn's reins in one hand and Alexandra's fingers in the other, he started them off inland.

*   *   *

The walk took longer than a quarter hour, but Alix didn't mind. Aching hips and tender thighs slowed her pace. Heat burning down from above made her lazy. A languid slackness in her muscles battled the grip of high grass, and she was in no hurry to be anywhere except with Spencer.

They gained the top of a third and final slope that stretched past the house, coming even with the world above. Green in lush shades rolled out as far as the eye could see, interrupted only now and then by sharp gray cliffs cutting the landscape like stone blades. It was less arid here, tangled and wild. Hesitant trees formed arching copses, out of reach from all but the worst ocean gales. Roses of a variety she had never seen sweetened a light breeze that swept over them, and their thick fuchsia blossoms formed hardy clusters of velvet that carpeted the grove.

Spencer led them between the proud arms of two wide oaks and down a low hill into a flat meadow. A mirror pond kissed its stony edge and caught the reflection of ruined stone arches on the opposite bank. Just when she thought she had seen all the land had to offer, Alix was astounded once more.

Spencer stopped, dropped Bryn's reins, and hauled a pack down from her saddle. "Ready?" he asked, grinning.

"For?" For him to lay her under the trees, kiss her?

He jerked his head at the water. "Let's go in."

"Oh. *Oh*." The idea of cool water on her skin sounded heavenly. She unfolded her shift.

Spencer's fingers on her wrist halted the process. "What are you about?"

She grasped a fistful of muslin. "Putting it on. Going in?"

"*That* is for after." He pulled the shift away and tossed it on top of his bag. A finger hooked her belt, snapped free its loop. Hands slid inside her wrapper, cupping her shoulders and gathering it down her back. "And so is this."

What was she doing? She'd traveled to the borderlands alone; that was scandal enough. Then alone with a man she adored for the express purpose of making love. Naked in the heath for anyone to see. What was next? She'd suffered moral erosion in a matter of days. Alix dropped her clothes, satisfied with where impropriety had led her thus far.

She turned to find his eyes on her, and a warm flush ran through her body. She lived for the way Spencer was looking at her now, his silent regard more flattering than any compliment.

"Go in," he rasped, swallowing hard. "It's shallow, just there by the stones. I'll join you soon enough."

It took effort, not wrapping arms over her body as she crossed to the pond under his gaze.

At first the water was comfortable where she dipped her toe at the edge. Not very deep and undisturbed all day, it had been warmed by the sun. Two steps in, a brisk current bit at her knees. Goose flesh prickled her limbs, and she welcomed it. Wading in up to her hips, she shivered.

"Frozen yet?" Stripped down to only his breeches, Spencer watched her from the bank. His scars stood out in the daylight, a patchwork map drawn over taut muscles. Alix wondered at the story of each and how he would take her asking. She met his eyes again. "Come in and find out."

He set to work removing his pants. She didn't look away this time. Two days had taught her the shape of him, head to toe. Shyness washed away on a tide of anticipation, and she studied him until he was bare.

When he reached her, Spencer trailed damp fingers over her breast, gripped her backside and pulled her close. "Better than being shut inside now, isn't it?"

She slid a hand beneath the water and along his thigh, pressing just so at crisp hair in a way she'd discovered always made him gasp. "Mm. I'm still undecided."

"I can make up your mind." He waded past, raised his arms and dove, gliding through deeper water to the pond's center. Long, confident strokes pushed him out beyond the middle of the pond, and Alix realized she had better get started if she were going to keep up.

Spencer was already out of the water when she reached the far shore, knees to chest, skin glinting like wet bronze in the light. She stopped short in the deeper water, flipping onto her back and floating out of his reach. "I would wager you've done this before."

"Swimming?"

"No." She fanned fingers through the green water, drifting closer. "Wandering about like it's the garden of Eden."

She caught his laughter over her gentle splashing. "Never once, if you can believe it. Not out of doors, anyhow. Runs contrary to a soldier's every instinct."

It was just for her. The information shivered through her, concluding as a sweet ache low in her belly. She pulled herself from the water and Spencer stood up. He ducked beneath a medieval arch and she followed, smooth bits of marble digging at her heels as the warm sun dried her skin.

Spencer stopped, and his broad hands circled her waist. He lifted, laying her back on an old stone pediment. Hot stone seared her back, wicking the dampness from her skin. The backs of her knees burned where they hung against the block's side.

"Here? I don't think we –"

Spencer's palms smacked the stone above her shoulders, saying plainly that he didn't care if they should or not. Alix wriggled under his weight, lost to the pleasure of the moment.

He fanned her wet hair, chin scrubbing at her neck while his lips went to work beneath her ear. It was a dirty tactic, something he had used against her countless times since he'd discovered its effectiveness. And it worked. She gave him credit for being a good soldier, employing tried and true methods to win her.

"I have to wonder," he breathed against her throat.

"Mmm."

"How no man has ever caught your eye."

She thought back for a moment. "There have been one or two." Edward. Chas's friend David, a dashing lieutenant. "A French captain," she murmured out loud, Spencer's tongue muddying her thoughts.

Palms raked over her ribs, and he drew her arms over her head and onto the smooth slab. "A sailor." She felt his grin against her breast. "And yet you guarded your virtue."

"Not easily," she admitted. "He was very good with his hands."

"Of course he was. Tugging on his rope all day."

His fingers on her thigh cut her laugh and replaced it with a gasp. His knee worked between her legs, followed by a hand. Alix knew his cues by now, what would follow. Stretching farther underneath him, she closed her eyes and fought an impulse to rush. He came into her slowly, pressing until it reached a sharp pain deep in her belly.

Alix rose up, welcoming it, lost to sensation.

Trees rustled, intruding on her reverie, and for a moment she worried at being discovered. Then Spencer pressed again, found her mouth, and worry melted away.

*   *   *

Stretched out along the blanket, Spencer cradled Alexandra on his shoulder, watching ripples in the lake and fumbling his breeches closed one button at a time.

Slender fingers swatted his hand. "Let's not be so hasty," she murmured into his chest, words bent by a smile he couldn't see.

"For your own good," he mumbled, "and for *my* own good, we must. For now."

She rolled away, onto her back beside him, an arm under her head. Spencer ran a hand from her throat over her breasts and wondered again how they'd found themselves together, how fate had thrown them in each other's way.

"I've been thinking." Alexandra yawned, stretching up into his palm. "Now that I *can* think."

"Sounds ominous."

That earned a black look.

"You aren't married." Her voice was rich and sleepy, making his heart race.

"No, I am not." He wondered if she caught the relief in his voice.

"Never?"

"I was in danger of it, twice. But no, never."

"Why haven't you?" she asked.

Content, exhausted, he wasn't keen on deconstructing the choices that now found him alone. "Why haven't *you*?"

"I believe I've explained why." A chill flattened her words.

"Before Paulina and Silas. Why didn't you marry then?"

"I'd rather rely on myself."

Not the answer he had expected. "Meaning what?"

She wriggled impatiently beside him. "We're not speaking of me. We're speaking of *you*."

"Not anymore," he dodged. "Explain what you mean."

Alix sighed and rolled closer, bringing her body into dangerous proximity. "Until Van der Verre, I don't think any man had ever told me what to do. Not even my father. He *asked*, but he knew better than to make a fight for himself."

He smiled, imagining the strong-willed young woman she must have been back then. "Wise man."

"Mm. It was an attractive quality to more than one suitor. It was fine that I went about unescorted. Desirable that I could work a trap line or had visited the native villages. Adorable really, unconventional even!" There was a bitter edge to her words. "But, of course, *all* that foolishness would come to a stop when we were married."

"Suffocating," he added, grasping the depth of her apprehension.

"An embarrassment," she countered, then lay quiet a moment. "I enjoy having company to dinner. I can mind my manners and keep still at the theater. But I won't be ordered about, and I'm too set in my ways now to change. There's a whole world outside of mother's parlor."

Spencer folded his arms beneath his head, not a word to say, lost in thought. He couldn't say that he'd never met a woman quite like her. There may have been one or two in all his travels, but no one who'd knocked the wind from him in quite the same way.

She sat up and pulled her shift over tousled locks. "Now, answer my question."

"About marriage? Oh." Spencer shrugged, more to himself than to Alix. "I don't know what circumstances conspired for my bachelorhood." He turned the idea over in his mind, considering all the things which had set him against marriage. A vague impression formed. "No," he corrected. "That's not completely true."

"What, then?" Alix had leaned herself against the rough trunk of an oak, legs drawn up, watching him intently from her little post.

"I was fifteen, perhaps sixteen, when my father married Bennet's mother. She was three years my senior. A long story to how it all came about, but it was really more of a business arrangement. They got on well enough, but father was twice her age, almost more of a parent than a husband. Sarah was sweet, ignorant, and a little dull. Luckily, they were eager enough for each other in the beginning; otherwise, Bennet would be a nonsum. Unrest in France, and then revolution, took up more and more of my father's time. He traveled almost constantly, and when he was home, there was no one for him to talk to. Sarah

157

resented his being away but hardly made him feel welcome when he was there. It might have been different, if she'd understood his work. But she never did. I'm not sure she could."

"So choose better for yourself. It isn't like that for everyone," said Alix.

"No, but you could distill my views on the married state from all of that. I didn't know any better. Sarah prattling on about Lady Jersey's ball. My father nodding and hmming, trying to compose a letter. Cold silence in between bites at supper." He sat up and rested an arm atop his knees and poked at their small fire, renewing its thin wisps of smoke. "The army was my first love. What I chose anytime there was a choice to be made. Then I discovered enjoyment of a woman, and without the crushing vice of contempt for one another. Lust and some affection with an end in sight. I could have the army, a relationship, and my peace in between."

"How practical of you."

"It was," he retorted, not grasping her jest until her face fell. Spencer realized he was agitated and shrugged. He couldn't form the words to tell her that practical was all it had been.

Alix nestled deeper into the soft gathers of her shift and leaned her head back so that he couldn't see her eyes. "I'm grateful for it. Is that unkind?"

"Why?"

"If you had married, or I had, we wouldn't be here together."

The words gave him pause, and Spencer recalled with a pang how little time they had left. "Come here."

Alix crossed the quilt and knelt beside him. Spencer skimmed his hand over her curves through the soft chemise, then tugged her into the crook of his arm. A faint smell clung to her garments, her familiar blend of amber and musk. Thick strands of black hair kissed his bare shoulder. He rested a hand to the small of her back and pulled her fully against him. She nestled into the embrace, sighed, and then they were quiet. He turned the problem of her leaving over in his mind, and tried to wrap his head around the time they'd spent together. Five days had sounded like an eternity, before she'd arrived. Now it was nothing, a drop in an ocean. He struggled to understand why.

158

Sun filtered in through the trees, low on the horizon, finally lending the air a comfortable warmth. Wind rushing through leaves in sharp gusts pricked his instincts, warning of a storm. He brushed kisses over her forehead, pressed one to her temple and sat up. "We should start back."

She didn't answer, or move. Spencer rested two fingers on her cheek and turned her face toward him. "What's the matter?"

Alix inhaled slowly, exhaled almost as slowly, and shook herself. "Nothing."

Something had been the matter, he was certain. But she smiled, sat up and leaned her head on his arm. The moment passed, and Spencer let it go.

*   *   *

They hunched over the narrow dining room table, and Alix wondered by their proximity and distraction, why they made any pretense of hiding their cards. She had seen Spencer's hand no less than four times, and he had seen hers.

Wind rattled the panes beside them, hinting at a storm she couldn't have predicted earlier at the pond. "I think we'll be confined indoors tomorrow," she offered, drawing a card without being certain it was her turn.

His fingers pressed the bend of her arm and traced a rough path to her wrist. He claimed her cards and set them on the table. "We'll muddle through."

"We have cards," she chuckled, pointedly ignoring the meaning in his words.

"I enjoy cards, a great deal in fact," he swept their abandoned hands into the discard pile. "But I believe that is true of many men. I would play them with you every day, but for fear you'd grow bored."

"There's such a variety of games!" she protested. "You cannot bore me with cards. Father and I played them every night until he was too ill; I never tired of them."

"No cards with your brother and Mrs. Paton?" he quipped.

159

"Chas and Paulina have as little to do with each other as possible. When they do interact, I am not often included."

"How do you fill the hours? Books, I recall. And what else?"

Alix held her breath and weighed the danger of what she was about to confess. "I read every bit of business correspondence in the house, any ledgers Paulina keeps about, anything she brings in regarding the company."

"Sounds dry," he teased.

"At first it was just for my benefit, to see if my shares were being managed and where the money had been put. One night, I found a letter from a shareholder tucked into the ledger; he was deep in the pockets and begging Silas to buy him out."

Spencer shook his head slowly, brow furrowed.

"The amount he was asking was a pittance, and I have no doubt Silas wanted those shares back. But he never does a favor for anyone, wouldn't help someone unless he was helping himself. So he hadn't answered, probably biding his time to get the shares for even less."

A small smile played at his lips. "I perceive this wait was a boon to you?"

"What I did was dangerous, but I was desperate. I pawned my mother's ruby ring and got twice what the shareholder was asking. Not without a great deal of bickering," she grumbled, "and not nearly what it was worth. But I sent the money to my father's solicitor with instructions." She swallowed at the memory. "I hadn't spoken to him in years, not since my father died. I had no guarantee he wouldn't tell Silas, or give me away by accident."

"My God, Alexandra," breathed Spencer, claiming her hand.

Awe in his voice thrilled her head to toe, and a pang in her chest stung at how brave she'd been, once. "I engineered my coughing powder, to be assured of time alone and then, I wrote. Even while we've been in England," she dared, "I've penned all the offers I'm able."

Spencer leaned back in his chair, idly shuffling the deck and grinning. "I admit I'm terrified of you at the moment. Perhaps we will not play cards anymore."

"I've been letting you win," she said.

He set aside the deck and leaned in, taking both her hands. "And I've no complaints about it, so long as I have your company in exchange."

"You know I wouldn't arrange it otherwise," she muttered to the table top, too shy to meet his eyes. "That's why I am here."

"I want this with you, Alexandra; every day, more than anything. This moment could comprise the remainder of my life and I would die content."

She wished he hadn't said it, hadn't planted the hope in her heart. "I don't –" she stopped and blinked back tears. "I've learned not to think about tomorrow or next year, but we have each other *now*. This moment *is* my life."

He was staring at her with a look that filled her heart to bursting. "How can I give you back, when it's over?"

"I don't have an answer, not for you or for myself. I have an affair with you," Spencer ducked his head at the word and made her smile, "and that is the point at which my life begins and ends."

"You cannot *ask* to have an affair, Alexandra," he chided, mimicking his words at Broadmoore.

"Why not?" she demanded and squeezed his hands.

"Because by the time you had asked me, I think we were already having it."

*   *   *

Alix raised her fists higher. "Just a swing. One." Spencer was accounted a masterful boxer, at least according to John, and she was eager to see how it was done. She was also bored with her book and ready for Spencer to be done with business for the day.

Spencer, for his part, was less interested.

"No!" he barked, focused on scribbling out a letter.

"I won't hit back."

He smirked, still not looking up. "That does not concern me."

It was clear he didn't appreciate just how determined she was. She reached out and pulled his second piece of paper away and tossed it to the floor.

"Alexandra." More scribbling.

She pressed a finger to the brown glass inkwell, raised it by the rim, and threatened to tip it.

"Miss Paton!" Spencer's chair scraped the floorboards. He shot to his feet, grabbed a discarded handkerchief, and held it at the ready.

Seizing her chance, she leaned across the desk and jabbed him in the ribs.

"Stop."

Another jab, this time in the midsection. She ground teeth into her cheek to quell the laughter straining her chest.

He grabbed her wrist, brows set into a frown, and stalked her around the desk. "I won't strike you, but I *will* make you regret your provocation."

Laughter tore free, at the absurdity of his words and a suspicious twitch at the corners of his mouth. "I would absolutely love to see you try."

Spencer swung with his free hand, loose knuckles biting her ribs through the fabric of her dress.

"Ow!"

He grinned and raised his eyebrows.

Alix steeled her courage, smiled sweetly, and sunk her teeth into the meaty webbing between Spencer's thumb and forefinger.

"Goddamit!" He shook his hand and she darted away, raising her arms in triumph. "I think I'm bleeding!" he cried, not looking half as distressed as he sounded. "You fight dirty."

There was an ominous drop in the way he pronounced 'dirty', as though he really had no problem with it at all. As if, she shivered, he had no qualms *following suit.*

"You," he wagged a finger, circling the desk, "are in very dangerous territory, Miss Paton."

Days together along with a little wine this afternoon had made her bold. Alexandra spread her arms wide. "Do your worst."

Spencer lunged.

162

She only dodged him thanks to a tell she'd learned over their days together, a twitch of his jaw indicating that he was about to spring. He got the back of her dress and she squealed, a fit of giggles stealing her breath. Jumping three steps was all that freed her, snapping the fabric from his grip.

She nearly ate floorboards when she reached the hall, taking the turn too quickly so her stockings lost traction. Running into the pitch-black dining room, she pressed herself beside the cupboard and willed her breath to come slowly.

She listened intently, but there was only silence. Not so much as a footstep echoed through the house. Her ears strained until they filled with the sound of her own blood pounding through her heart.

Then there was a cough, followed by a long groan. Boots scraped against the floor. "Oh God, Alexandra! My ribs." Another cry. "I've broken my ribs."

She snorted. What a load of hog swallow. Still, she could use his position to her advantage. She would risk a quick glance into the hall to see what could be seen. Creeping to the doorway, she braced.

Fingers twisted the fabric of her bodice and dragged her through the doorway with a force that snapped her from the room.

She drew back a fist, prepared to jab again, and Spencer held up his hand, grinning. "I wouldn't." He grasped harder at her neckline; a button popped from the back of her dress. "*You* are in enough trouble already."

She shivered at his threat, then followed through anyhow and swung. He seized her wrist, stopping the blow and plowing into her with unstoppable force. It drove her into the shadowed dining room and tumbled her against the table.

Spencer rucked up her skirts. Cold air kissed her legs, and the rough tabletop bit the backs of her knees. He brought his lips to hers with violence, pinching the flesh of her bottom lip between their teeth.

Alix held her breath, anticipated the hard pressure against her leg. Instead he dropped low, and moments later his lips brushed her knee. He bit the inside of her thigh, digging until she cried out and clutched his hair. It was a feeling more than pain,

163

beyond pleasure; it was pure sensation. He traced the band of her stocking with his nose, panting hot against her skin.

His hand pressed into her belly and urged her back. Alexandra fell against the table and dug nails into its underside. "Please," she whispered, prompted by a throbbing between her legs. "Spencer, please."

His laugh was the deep sound of pure male satisfaction. It vibrated through her thigh, redoubling the ache above. "Beg, Alexandra. Plead with me." Hands ran under her skirts, gripping her backside and forcing her knees apart.

"No." She pressed harder against the table, sucking breath after breath through her nose. "I won't beg."

Spencer's tongue dragged a wet trail from her hip along the crease of her thigh. His shoulders opened her further. Alix realized what he was about, began to protest, then bit her tongue. The idea was illicit, and wonderful; why should she stop him? Pressure from his mouth between her legs tore a moan from her chest, raised her back from the tabletop. "I won't beg," she rasped again, feeling the hollowness in her own words.

He made another slow pass and pressed until she squirmed to get away, all the while digging her heels into his back to keep him close.

Then he laughed. "You will."

*   *   *

Spencer had no notion of time when the sound woke him. It was dark, and no fire burned in the grate. A rumble separated itself from the thunder that had bellowed off shore all night, something more immediate, more dangerous than the weather. Muscles taut and heart pumping, he sat up, Alexandra following suit.

"Someone is in the house," she whispered.

He nodded, not certain she could see him in the dark. "Can you manage a pistol?"

"Give it to me."

He had never stayed at the cottage unarmed. Leaning down beneath the bed, he claimed a brace of pistols from its underside. They were not in London, or even inside the relatively

164

safe borders of Haywood. A lone house, one or two occupants: the equation equaled ripe pickings for a thief or highwayman. He passed one pistol to Alexandra. "In the wardrobe."

"What!" she yelled in a whisper.

"Inside. And stay there until I come for you."

"I am not hiding in a cabinet."

"Until I come for you. Not for any other reason." He sat up and fastened his breeches, planting feet on the cold wood floor. He eased forward a bit at a time, transferring his weight from the bed to keep the boards from creaking. His ears strained all the while.

Whoever it was, they were downstairs. In the front room, by his guess. He listened carefully, catching the familiar off-balance creak of the rocker's treads. Someone bumped a chair, scooting it into the wall. Judging by the sounds he was hearing, there were at least two of them below. He swung the door just far enough to pass through and heard Alix slide from the bed behind him. A candle blazed to life somewhere near the fireplace; he caught its flicker and glow up the stairway. He made out whispers, but not words.

He crept down a tread at a time until he could peer into the front room through the banister. Empty. Whoever was there, they had moved deeper into the house. Spencer drew a breath, then another, forcing his chest to take them in and let them out slowly and quietly.

Two steps from the hall, back to the door, he heard it: the click-click of a pistol lock behind his head. "Stay right there and go no further."

Spencer lowered his arm and turned slowly.

London, he thought, by the way the soldier dropped his r's, an educated polish to his words erasing a Cockney heritage. These were not local men.

"In here, captain!" Ruddiness in his cheeks spread farther over a bony face, making the private's already red-tipped nose glow cherry in the candle light.

At least three pairs of boots rushed the hall, and Spencer dared to turn and face their approach.

"Captain Dudley," he drawled, recognizing wild gray sideburns before he could clearly see the man's face.

Dudley stopped ahead of his men, crossing his arms. "And just who the devil are …" He squinted in the dim light, taking in Spencer's features. His eyes widened. "Oh! Oh, my apologies, Major-General!" he said, beckoning for the soldier with the gun to aim it somewhere other than at Spencer's head.

"Accepted. Now explain what you are doing in my house."

Dudley's beady raccoon eyes widened. "We didn't know it was your house, as such. Come to fetch a lady. Family's put in a report she's missing. Abducted, in fact. Hackney driver claims the scoundrel brought her 'ere."

Spencer planted hands on his hips, looking to each soldier in turn. "Horse shite."

"All the same, lordship, witnesses' statements are in agreement. We're to have a look about." Dudley's low voice was apologetic, trembling with a thread of fear, dreading his superior's answer.

Alexandra saved him the trouble. "You've had your look, Captain Dudley. Here I am, and of my own free will."

She presided over them from the top of the stairs, clutching a sheet closed at her breasts with one hand, pistol still grasped in the other. Rebellious waves tumbled to her shoulders, sweeping her brow. For a moment, he forgot that they were not alone and stared.

Dudley's staccato throat clearing snapped Spencer back to the here and now. What was she thinking, standing in front of six bawdy, loose-lipped soldiers? Had he been anything but clear in his instructions for her to stay hidden? The soldier behind him pushed eagerly, pressing him out of the way to get further inside the front room. A sick knot weighted in Spencer's gut.

Captain Dudley shuffled a few paces closer, leaning in to be heard and staring at Alix all the while. "Brother's wife says she ain't well, sir. Tells stories about bein' married or not. I can't follow it."

Spencer's lanky captor had shuffled a half-step at a time, nonchalant, while his officer had been talking. Rolling stiff shoulders, Spencer put himself deliberately between the man and the staircase, and drew back on his pistol's hammer for emphasis. Movement stopped, but the private continued stealing hungry

166

looks at Alexandra. There was no one around for miles; if Dudley's men chose to turn on them, it would go poorly.

"A bit touched, accordin' to Mister Paton's wife," finished Dudley.

Spencer tensed, not at the accusations, but at Paulina's having calculated them so well. "Some bad blood," he offered to Dudley. "Fluff. Don't trouble yourself over it."

Dudley nodded, looking lost now that his purpose had been dashed.
"My steward will be here any time now, if you'd like to question him as well. He was expected in the evening; I imagine the storm has slowed his progress from Haywood." He spoke loudly, for the benefit of Dudley's men. Information that a visitor was expected, could arrive at any moment had the desired effect. Two soldiers drew back; shoulders and muskets alike drooped in resignation.

Relief bowed his knees and then something occurred to Spencer, who turned his full attention back to Dudley. "What set you looking for the lady in the first place?"

Eyes drooping, Dudley pressed his cap to his chest. "There's been a mishap."

"What mishap?" Alexandra's voice was raw, small beneath a wind howling outside.

"Mister Paton. Suffered an injury touring Bath. Head wound."

Alix stared, lips working, but no words came out. Spencer asked the question for her.

"Does he live?" he prodded. "What is his condition?"

"They thought he was dead at first. Looked as though he'd fallen into the water. But a ledge caught him, spared him goin' in the drink. Nasty gash, but Lord Hastings' physician thinks he'll fare all right. Lady Hastings thought Mrs. Rowan'd like to be with her brother."

"Did Lady Hastings raise the fuss that sent you here?" Kidnapping, hysteria. None of that sounded like Laurel.

"Mrs. Paton was the first to mention it, by the constable's account of things."

Without another word, Spencer took down a wooden box from the bookshelf, a case meant to hold letters. He scooped a handful of coins from the bottom and pressed them into Dudley's palm. "You all have come a long way, expended a great deal of effort under –" He hesitated to say *false*, not wanting any confrontation between the soldiers and Paulina until he was back in London. "– *mistaken* information. You've been put to no small inconvenience. See to your men's comfort on the way home. Your own as well, captain."

Dudley took the coins, cradling them and staring at his hands. A struggle played out on the man's face as he tried to make the money anything but a bribe. "And what is my report, upon my return?"

"The truth, of course. That you found Mrs. Rowan hale and whole, and very much *not* abducted. That you saw her with your own eyes, and delivered your grave news. That is *sufficient*."

Dudley's frame slackened, and he nodded slowly and saluted. "Sorry to have caused a commotion for you both." He turned his body but not his eyes toward Alexandra. "Mrs. Rowan."

"Captain," she murmured, eyes far away as the company filed out.

He moved to bar the door behind them, watching to be certain that all six men were leaving, then heaved the door with his shoulder against a screaming gale.

When he turned back to the stairs, Alix was gone, but their business was entirely unfinished.

*   *   *

Alexandra must have brought the candle from his study. She was placing it atop a trestle-legged night stand and just shaking out a match when he entered.

He stood a moment watching her and trying to master his anger. "What are you doing?"

"Gathering my things, packing. Going to London."

Spencer put himself between her and the wardrobe. "You're doing no such thing. Not until we've spoken. Running out in the middle of the night isn't going to help matters, anyhow."

168

She bent down, claimed a few stray hairpins from the floor, and snatched a lost stocking from beneath the bed.

"Alexandra, please help me grasp what in bloody hell you were thinking tonight."

She didn't look up. "About what!"

"Coming out there in front of those men, like *this*," he growled, waving a hand at the paper-thin sheet eaten through by candlelight, "when I fully, expressly told you to stay put."

"I seem to recall my interference helping you. Bailing you out of that 'abducted lady' mess."

"I did not ask for, nor require your help. You might have been hurt, savaged."

She snorted. "They were soldiers."

The last red strand of his temper snapped. "Raped, Alexandra!"

She raised fists. "They were *soldiers*, Spencer!"

"Because they are soldiers doesn't mean they meant well. Not every man came back from the Continent a bloody hero!" He raked fingers through his hair, desperate to make her understand.

"Officers in wilder parts pay their men *protection money*. Bribes to keep their obedience. In Newcastle, or Trenton there is mob rule among the detachments. The men do as they please, asking a great many *favors* of the citizens. And they are not always polite about being denied something."

Alexandra's chin raised a fraction. "We could have stood against them."

"No, we could not! Six men with pistols, muskets, knives. I'm not even flattered that you think so. It's foolishness."

"Foolishness?" She came away from the table, still claiming the sheet with white knuckles.

"One instruction, Alexandra: to stay where you were told!"

Her voice was hot, angry, and her eyes blazed like he'd never seen them before. "I don't take orders from anyone, *general*!"

"That is apparent!" he bellowed back. "But you do not seem to grasp how it would *ruin* me to watch them hurt you!" He threw the pistol down onto a ladder-back chair beside the door, panting for breath to cool his temper. "You might not take orders at home," he turned back slowly, grinding his words between clenched teeth, "but out *here*, in these moments, you will damned well take them from me."

Alexandra's eyes clouded, her shoulders slumped. For a moment, she wouldn't meet his eyes. He hoped she finally understood. Then she shook her head.

She might understand, but she was too damned proud and too beaten down by Paulina to admit it, and admission was what he needed to hear. He took a step toward her.

"No. I am going back to London." She backed away, tripped up by the sheet.

Spencer took a strange pleasure in her widening eyes. *Fear.* And if she was feeling even a fraction of what he had with the soldier watching her, *stalking* her, that put them even already. "You are not going anywhere." He let her swallow hard at an imaginary threat, not bothering to point out that she *couldn't;* the night was pitch black and pouring rain.

"I'm sorry," she whispered. She was, he had no doubt, but it wasn't enough. He took another step.

"I'm going," she murmured, glancing behind with open surprise as her back came up against a window. Her jaw set, and Alix squared her shoulders, not an ounce of intimidation on her face. She was fiercely beautiful.

Spencer admitted that maybe he *shouldn't* touch her, right then. He wasn't feeling rational, and she wasn't helping.

He had struggled to confess his fear. Alexandra hadn't seemed to grasp what the soldiers could do to her, and what he would suffer if she'd been brutalized and violated while he stood helpless. More than anything, he needed to hear that she would never put him in that position again. She was contrite; it showed in a tender frown creasing her face, but no words were offered to match it.

He snapped out a hand, taking her wrist, willing his own fear into her with fierce pressure.

"Don't ..." she protested, but she didn't pull away. A hot blush burned her cheeks, and her full lower lip rolled out in a near pout. Her scent perfumed his every breath. It didn't quell his

170

anger; instead it pulled at his insides. Stoked his lust and fanned something else he'd felt, but for days had been unable to name.

She tried pulling her arm away. He snatched it back, pinned it to his chest and held her fingers to his heart, holding her eyes. Clutching the sheet beneath her fist, he drew down with even, uninterrupted tension. Her fingers relaxed their grip in surrender.

"Spencer, I'm sorry," she breathed, relaxing and leaning into him.

Tension drained away at her words.

"I live to touch you," he whispered back, watching the slow reveal of breasts and hips, swallowing hard. The torrent of the last hour threatened to undo him, and the storm outside was nothing compared to what he felt looking at her now. "I'll put my hands on you, take you here on this bed." Thunder rattled the windows, punctuating his promise. The sheet pooled over his bare feet in a whisper.

Slender fingers circled his wrist in response, tighter until her nails dug half-moons into his skin. Her eyes narrowed to slits, raking him. She stepped in and ate up the space between their bodies. "You will take what *I* offer you." Her arm bent, a vice around his neck, and forced his lips to hers while the soft mounds of her breasts pressed him away.

Grasping Alexandra by both arms he turned her, drove her steadily down onto the mattress. "I'll take you now, or you me." He had no patience for buttons and tore at his breeches until their flap fell away in surrender. He worked a knee between hers. "And again after. Either way, say you'll have me." He murmured his plea into the silken curve of her shoulder. "Please Alexandra, say it." *Was it for her benefit, or his own?*

She raised both arms to him in silent invitation, stealing victory for herself. He drove into her, forgetting the question.

In a flash, there was only the searing heat of her body gripping him. When he'd got himself inside of her all he thought possible, he pressed harder still. He would possess her, even her deepest parts. Spencer pounded at her, short and sharp, as though he could drive a claim onto her very soul.

Alexandra lay still beneath him, not touching any more than their joined bodies required. Eyes pressed closed, her lips barely parted as though she were napping. *Retribution.*

No woman had ever equaled her for exasperating him, or quenching something inside. He was desperate to be touched, to please her, catch his name on her lips. Her refusal spurred him on.

He traced her belly, the curve of her hip, gripped her thigh and raised her leg to his waist. He murmured against the warm ridges of her ear, the skin of her neck; mindless, illicit confessions punctuated by urgent groans.

She gripped him deep inside and cried out at last. A trembling started in her limbs, and Spencer felt her transformation beneath him, taut and ready. Her body communicated to his that she had shown him his place, forgiven him. She arched and raised to meet his hips.

His heart hammered against his ribs, trapped in a too-small cage. Sweat plastered their thighs and peeled at her belly each time he drew away. He sucked a breath at her finger tracing a damp path along his spine, and anticipated her brutality. Nails bit deep into his buttocks and scraped up his back in a path stung by cool air. Tension in his gut pulled, frayed, and unraveled.

His effort shifted the mattress, scraping the bed frame over floor timbers and into the wall. He couldn't get enough of her, be enough inside her. "Look at me, Alexandra," he managed, panting.

Alexandra turned her face away, pressed the back of one hand to her mouth, drawing desperate breaths through her nose.

He jerked the hand from her lips and raised her leg higher onto his hip. "There's no one to hear. Only me, love."

At his words her head turned, and she cried out in earnest then, sobbing, igniting his determination. She clutched fistfuls of the sheet beneath them. "Spencer, *Spencer...*"

His name on her lips picked the thread of his will and undid the last of his control. He ducked his head, took a nipple in the vice of his teeth and tasted salt, coaxing out a sharp cry.

Breath from Alexandra's soft animal groans fanned his chest. She raised fully now, as if too proud to allow him down onto her. He had no say; she took him as deep as she pleased.

She pleaded, chastised. He felt but didn't hear the words. Alexandra quivered, her body clutching at his, wringing him ruthlessly for the cries he spilled into her mouth as he spilled himself inside her.

Alexandra took something from him in those final moments. He felt it in the silence after, listening to raindrops spatter against the panes ahead of each gust. His heart beat slowly in his chest, too slowly for what they had just shared, as though she'd made him content by force. Her own heart beat back, steady against him, reassuring.

What had changed?

Attrition. They'd beaten at each other's will until they had both won. Or lost. Spencer wasn't certain which had occurred, and which was welcomed. He only knew that it was *right*. He fell to the mattress, gathering Alexandra's limp frame to his. She nestled against him and he caught her yawn. Then worry drifted away, and he slept.

*   *   *

As quickly as the storm had come it passed, both inside and out. They'd fought out the night's animosity, inflicting punishment on one another until exhausted and resigned to sweet surrender. Tension had drained away like raindrops along the gutter.

Alexandra lay on her back in the crook of Spencer's arm, cradled by the mattress and warmed by quilts, watching cotton wool clouds billow over the ocean's wide blue line. Sun glinted off wave crests and lighted the clouds silver at their edges.

He was awake beside her; slow, even breaths gave him away. She reached up and cradled his face in her palm.

"Alexandra."

"Mm?"

"No. Alexandra, look at me." His rich voice trembled over an urgent bent to the words.

She sat up, rolled onto him, and brushed the hair from his forehead.

Spencer returned the favor, raking strands from her face, tracing her back from shoulder to hip, holding her eyes all the while. "I do not believe that we are having an affair anymore."

"No?" Alix thought she understood, by his expression and by the tense thread that had drawn between them for days, a thread which forced them to cling together or snap apart.

"I'm angry," he said in response to an unspoken question, "but not with you."

"Then what?"

"London." He sighed and scrubbed a palm over his face. "Crowded, noisy, clinging with all its busyness. Not a moment's peace to be had. A hundred pairs of eyes watching. You and I in the middle of it, shaving our words, hiding our glances. I think of being forced to spend days apart and ..." He raised hands into trembling fists, eyes pressed shut a moment. "I could strike something."

Alix leaned onto one elbow, clasped his fist and smiled. "Spencer?"

His eyes snapped open, wide and questioning in time with his hand, and he twined their fingers.

"Are you saying ...?"

Nodding, he raised his head from the pillow and caught her lips. She barely registered the sensation, heart pounding until her head swam. *He loved her.*

"Madly, Alexandra."

"Then what should I do? Chas, Paulina ...I have to go back, for him."

"Would Chas do the same for you?" he demanded.

"No," she admitted. "No, I don't think so, but he is still my brother. I can't postpone going back forever." She sighed at an ache in her chest when she thought of her brother alone with Paulina. "It's all so tangled."

"I would never ask you to turn your back on your brother, but I also don't believe that flying to London is necessary. Or wise, considering Paulina's hand in last night's visit."

"What do I do?" She repeated, desperate.

"What do *we* do."

Alix shook her head, not understanding.

174

"I want to be married," he blurted, looking as surprised as she felt.

Alix held her breath, waiting for the spell to break, to wake up. One moment continued into the next unbroken, and she stretched further along Spencer's frame. "Are you certain?"

"Yes." He nodded with a grave slowness. There was a desperation on his face, to his words which Alix felt mirrored in her heart. "Will you have me or no?"

It was a dangerous question, treasonous and defiant, tempting her to do the very thing she had feared for years. Only now, Silas seemed much smaller in her recollection, his reach shorter and Paulina's thumb not as heavy as it had been just a week earlier. Spencer could protect her, would fight for her. Love her.

"You ask as though I have a choice." She pulled their hands apart and laced her arms behind his neck, trailing kisses across his mouth until he growled and fit their lips together for a long moment. "I will," she breathed. "Of course I will."

"I'm sorry for last night. It wasn't gentlemanly behavior."

Spencer had every right to be less than a gentleman. She had caused him real fear, and worse, her pride had gotten between them. Her heart ached at the idea even now. Still, they'd met in mutual combat, both making amends, of a sort. Chuckling, she tucked her toes behind his ankle, drew them up his calf, enjoying the rapid rise and fall of his chest. "If I didn't want you, you would not have taken me." She dragged lips over his cheek and nuzzled his ear. "Certainly not more than once."

"Bollocks, Alexandra. How will I keep my hands from you until we're wed?"

"Don't."

"We've agreed to marry. I'd like to make an effort to honor that, hypocrite that I am."

He had apologized, but she intended to make him pay at least a little for last night. Alix ran a hand under the quilt, traced a rigid thigh and pressing until Spencer jerked beneath her. "That, *my lord*, is entirely your problem."

*   *   *

175

Morning sunlight after the rain was always warmer, more golden in his estimation. It poured in through the dining room's narrow windows and bathed the room in a soothing glow which perfectly suited his mood.

Alix banged and clattered in the kitchen while aromas teased his nose and grumbling stomach. For just a breath he slipped into a fantasy; Alix preparing their meal while he saw to chores outside, both unhurried, confident of their days and nights belonging only to each other.

Her cheerful call pulled him up from the day dream, and, despite an ache in his chest, he managed a smile.

"What a domestic marvel you are," he said, rubbing his hands together at her appearance and a bowl of steaming golden-brown biscuits. "All this time I may have been overlooking your greatest talent."

Grinning, Alexandra dropped into the chair across from him and snatched the cracked stone lid from a butter crock. "A surprising revelation, considering what you whispered to me upstairs."

He poked her with a toe beneath the table. "A lass to warm the sheets is well and good, but a man can find *that* sort of comfort on campaign. Good food," he proclaimed, snatching a biscuit and shaking burning fingers, "is what a soldier misses most."

She slid the crock over and passed him the knife. "When my parents married, my father was still a struggling captain trying to convince anyone to let him haul cargo. My mother had never had to do anything domestic. By both their accounts, the first few months were …" She shook her head and frowned. "Anyhow, she made us all learn to cook. Sew a button. Kindle a fire."

"*All?*"

"My sisters, Nan and Sarah, too. They died young." She offered the information frankly, between bites of ham.

Still, it tugged at his heart. "She did well."

"Thank you." Her cheeks colored, and she poked at her food.

"Alexandra, I love you." The words were out before he comprehended that they had entered his thoughts. Relief was followed by contented joy at finally having spoken them.

Her face snapped up and she nodded. "I know."

"I didn't say it earlier, and I wish to now." He'd wanted to feel the words on his lips, try them on. They felt right.

"I love you, too." She took his hand, fingers cool against the heat of his palm. "I thought it would be more difficult to say," she mused.

"Maybe it is, when one is young and proud and fearful." He answered her smile with one of his own.

"We're both too sensible for all that." She broke their gaze and sat quiet, staring at the table and pressing a pattern with her fork into the soft top of her scone. "You're set on being married, when we return?"

Her words were drawn with hesitation and gave him pause. "I bloody well am. Why?"

"You're Oakvale's heir."

"It's a profitable estate," he offered. If income or comfort were giving her worry, he could put those fears to rest in a single breath. Forty thousand a year would buy her anything she desired.

Her hands waved, cutting the air between them. "I don't care about money, Spencer."

He caught her hand, took away her fork and squeezed her fingers. "What then?"

She swallowed. "I'm older, obviously. My mother struggled for *two* children well before my age. Don't you think that perhaps you should find someone younger and –"

"No, I do not," he stopped her and squeezed harder. "Bennet will have children. Bennet probably *already* has children, England and abroad. I'm not marrying you for practical reasons, Alexandra."

In fact, his reasons were entirely selfish. He wanted her close at every moment. He loved the way she made him feel, and that she may be saving him from an empty, solitary existence. But there was no translating the wild joy in his heart to words. "Besides," he waited until she met his eyes again, "I'd say we've hard tested your ability to get with child."

"Oh my God," she whispered, pressing a hand to her mouth.

"Had that not occurred to you?"

"No!" Then softer, "No. To be frank, not much of anything occurs to me when you're near."

It had occurred to *him*. First, when he realized he'd forgotten his little wooden case of sheep gut condoms. Not that they would have been a sufficient amount. They were well and good for a night here or there, but Alexandra's effect on him would have exhausted his supply before their second sunrise. And then, it occurred again, the first time he spent himself inside her. Just once, he'd reasoned, raw and unadulterated, passion over reason. But they had come to it a second time so quickly. Then his heart began to ache for her in earnest and he'd stopped caring. If Alexandra gave him babies so much the better, though the idea of fatherhood at forty pulsed in his temples. And if no children were forthcoming … He studied her face, brushed knuckles from her chin to the soft curve of her cheek. Then, nothing changed. They stayed perfectly as they were now.

Alix chewed her lip, still considering his words.

He refused to let her fret over matters beyond their control, and according to Captain Dudley they had more immediate concerns. "I have a worry, about your brother."

"That makes both of us," she muttered, crossing her arms.

"You know your brother's wife far better than I, but I'll be blunt, Alexandra: I think she's up to no good. Something outright sinister."

"I don't believe his injury in Bath was an accident," she whispered, ducking her head as if they might be overheard. "Silas has made some coupe, or something has made him believe that my brother is expendable. In the past he needed Chas as the face of Paton; it was reassurance to my father's accounts, to the investors. But if Silas were to lay the right groundwork, Van der Verre Freightage could practically own Paton & Son outright."

He gnawed his lip, head aching at the depths of so much scheming. "I wonder how Paulina trailed you here."

"I don't." She shook her head. "Well, I do wonder at the specifics. Just not at her ability. I thought Edward and I were so careful, so circumspect. Silas found us anyhow, and Paulina has been his eager pupil all her life."

He had sworn, on their first day at Haywood, to help Alexandra break Silas's grip. He'd meant it, but appreciated now that their efforts would be necessary sooner rather than later. "We have to sort this out. If we return prepared, you and I can strike more quickly, rob them of a chance to do more harm."

"Chas," she offered flatly. "His marriage contract with Paulina has harsh conditions if they divorce. The excuse for it was to clearly set terms for his estate, since they have no children."

He was beginning to understand. "But really it keeps him hostage."

She nodded. "Both of us."

There was still something that didn't make sense to him. "Why is Van der Verre so desperate for Paton Shipping? His business seems solvent enough; why go through all the trouble?"

"Silas takes a great deal of pleasure in that trouble." A shadow crossed her features. "And he doesn't want to own Paton. He wants to *dismantle* it."

"You cannot be serious." He didn't question her business acumen or her grasp of the situation; if anything, her information underscored Silas's madness.

"Entirely serious. Silas was my father's partner, years before I was born. My mother's encouragement separated them, once she convinced my father that he could succeed on his own and remain… *ethical* in his business practices."

He raised a brow. "Ethical?"

"Slaves," she whispered back, eyes downcast. "Van der Verre made their fortune in the Dutch slave trade. When my father left, gained success, *and* exposed Silas's main source of income, it put a bitter taste in Van der Verre's mouth."

Scheming and machinations enough to write a novel. He took it all in. "So how, by God's bollocks, did your brother find himself wed to the man's daughter?"

Alexandra's sour expression turned outright hostile "Chas always had a weakness for her, ever since childhood. She would hold court in the yard demanding he fetch her hoop, get her lemonade." She shivered. "And he did, for any scrap of approval. Even then she knew how to manipulate him."

"And Van der Verre was not specter enough to put him off?"

"Just the opposite, at first. When my father died, Silas was contrite. He swore a desire for our families to reconcile. That was about all the encouragement Chas needed to ask for Paulina's hand."

He admitted grudging admiration for Silas's commitment. A decade or more of laying the groundwork, biding his time, playing a calculated long game to his greatest advantage. It was a level of cunning few men could boast. "So, what has changed?" he puzzled aloud. "Why is Paulina so intent *now* on doing your brother harm?" Spencer pressed fingers to his eyes, trying to see the problem in the same way he viewed the battlefield, arranging lines in his head.

"Go to the source. Chas may be her husband, but Paulina takes her orders from her father, make no mistake." She popped a last dainty bite of scone into her mouth, dusting away crumbs with her napkin. "I don't think John has provided Chas the lucrative contacts Silas demanded of him. Van der Verre wants more Prince Regents and fewer Old Baron Crowleys."

Spencer thought he finally grasped Silas's aim. "Clients for Paton & Son, those will ultimately be clients for Van der Verre, when Silas disassembles the former."

She nodded. "It's brilliant, really. Use the more successful company's reputation. Attract all you can and then claim it for yourself. Faster ships, hearty crews. Our load masters calculate ballast-to-cargo down to fractions. Silas deserves credit for recognizing our advantage. Even if he loses ten percent over brand loyalty, twenty percent, he'll have made out like a king."

He was impressed by her grasp of the business. *Very* impressed, but not surprised. "You know a great deal about your father's company."

"I do. I had hoped he would split it equally between us. He did see that I was taken care of, the house and some shares, but not as I'd have liked." Bitterness colored her words.

"I wager you deserve more than half. Your brother's hand doesn't belong in any of this." He wondered if his opinion would offend her.

Alix nodded, chewing her last bite slowly. "Chas is handsome, polished, and clients take him seriously. But he's too weak to manage by himself. Paulina is the gears in that machine." She tossed the napkin onto her plate as if throwing away Paulina herself.

Her eyes were far away now, staring out the window. "Chas never applied himself at school, never paid attention to father's lectures. He is the master of all sport, all things outdoors, but his pursuits are *clean*. We only ride in the park, and we only play Bocci on the lawn, wearing our gloves and minding our hem. In that respect, he and Paulina are equal snobs. He never even once traveled west with me and father."

Alix shook her head and held up a finger. "No, that isn't right. One time. Sometimes father imported goods and then took extra coin to transport them. Forts, trading posts, that sort of thing. He oversaw those himself. We stopped in the native villages along the way, bartering here and there."

He was jealous, Spencer realized. Men who had served in America during 1812 had come home with all sorts fantastic, unfathomable tales about the wildness and beauty of the land and its people.

"We came to a camp of Delaware near Ohio," she continued, "And they were punishing a woman outside the chief's lodge. For adultery, we came to learn. The elder women held her down and an old man, a shaman or some official, slit the tip of her nose with a bone-handled knife. When my father asked, one of the braves said the wound was meant to resemble the part of her body by which she'd committed her offense."

So at least some of the stories had been true. "Brutal," he acknowledged.

Alix shrugged. "Perhaps, but that is their law. I never felt it was my place to judge, but Chas was horrified. He didn't speak to anyone the rest of the night, and he never traveled out with father again."

"So, he wasn't much of an obstacle to Van der Verre."

181

"Useful," she agreed. "To this day I have no idea why father thought Paton should belong to Chas. Wishful thinking, I suppose."

"I have no sons of my own," he raised his hands at Alix's look, "but being the older of two boys sired by a demanding sort of man, I think that in some men, there's a hope that his son will rise to the occasion."

"Not always," she muttered.

"Not always." It was time to broach the topic neither of them wanted to consider. "Which brings us to your brother *now*, and what the hell to do about our returning to London."

"Our returning to London," she repeated, staring past him with eyes narrowed. "That is why Paulina is looking for me. Or you."

"I don't follow."

"Paulina hasn't survived so long or pushed Chas so far by being stupid. She's perceptive enough, and she's obviously caught our attraction."

A blind man could have. Spencer held his tongue.

"If we courted, if we *married*," she added meaningfully, "it would be a threat to Van der Verre. You would make a formidable enemy."

An unfamiliar feeling gripped his gut. It took Spencer a moment to identify it as protectiveness.

He strangled his knife handle, knuckles aching. "We'll face him together, Alexandra. This ends *now*."

CHAPTER SEVENTEEN

London – July 20th, 1814

Alix sat in the carriage, staring up at the number '24' on the townhouse's whitewashed face. She had been there at least ten minutes, putting off going inside. She felt different, so changed after her week with Spencer, and was certain that everyone would be able to tell.

Her dread wasn't helped by Paulina knowing the truth, or knowing at least that she had not gone to Stirling. She'd put off their encounter for part of the afternoon, collecting business papers Spencer had asked to have sent to his townhouse. She wished for all the world that the stage had not been full at Longbridge, that bad weather and worse roads had not conspired to trap other travelers and fill the seats so that she and Spencer were separated. If only they had traveled back together, to face Chas and Paulina now as one. One more day, one more night apart, and they would never be separated again. Drawing a last steadying breath, she opened the door and climbed down.

Stepping inside, she was nearly barreled back out into the street by a stout, silver-haired butler with slits for eyes. "You will knock and present a card," he growled.

"Mrs. Rowan!" she shouted in reply to his snatching fingers as he tried prodding her outside. Her name halted his assault, but that was all it gained her. He stood, silent, staring at her no doubt in accordance with Paulina's instructions.

"Where is my brother?" she demanded finally.

"Upstairs." His tone was curt, and final. He turned and strode off through a shadowed doorway. *The usual treatment*, she sighed; relegated to below-stairs.

Several doors off the landing were closed, and only one showed a strip of light along the crack. Knocking but not waiting for a response, she went in.

Small but extravagant, the room was taken up mostly by a bed, its elaborate red velvet drapes concluding in a canopy held aloft by gold-gilt plumes. Everything was in the French style, from the pot-bellied cabinet inlaid with exotic wood to round-cushioned chairs perched beneath the window, set like miniature thrones.

"Chas?" she hazarded quietly, unable to brush off a hunted feeling.

"Mm." His grunt came from inside the cavernous bed.

She peered in, settled on the mattress, and looked him over. Blue bruises ringed both eyes, brown- crusted scrapes painting one side of his firm jaw. Thick linen bandages wrapped his head in two directions. "What happened." She didn't bother asking; it wasn't a question.

"Where have you been?" he accused, not meeting her eyes.

"Ah ... away? I left before you went to Bath."

If that wasn't what he meant, Chas didn't correct her. He lay still, eyes half-closed, reeking of stale gin.

"Where's Paulina?" she pressed, far less inclined to tolerate him since her time with Spencer.

Silence.

"What happened in Bath, Chas?"

He sighed as though it were the most tedious thing in the world, talking with her. "Paulina and I had breakfast. We went out to the ruins ahead of the Conynghams. I was taken by a spell. Dizziness. Lost my footing."

"Or poisoned scones."

Chas snapped up and winced. "You can be hateful, Alix. Paulina was nothing but attentive to me the whole of our time in Bath."

She got up. "Her attentiveness should be warning enough."

His glare was bleary, not quite finding her eyes. "Meaning *what*?"

184

"Meaning I'm through suffering both of you. And Van der Verre. I'm not going back to New York with you." Her ribs strained, chest full to bursting with the pleasure of telling Chas off and joy at what lay ahead.

He sat up further, pawing his temple. "We have discussed this, Alexandra," he ground out, wild- eyed. "Don't make trouble. It won't go well. For either of us."

How many times had she heard those same words repeated, the same threat prodding her back into her cage? She backed away a step at a time, disgust filling the distance. "I'm not going back," she repeated. "Paulina, Silas. They should never have been my problem. That is being rectified now."

He writhed up onto his knees. "Goddamit, Alexandra –"

She slammed the door on his abuse and swept the staircase with no direction in mind save away from the house and away from Chas.

She rounded the foot of the steps, gained the hall and skidded to a stop just short of barreling into Paulina, who pressed herself to the door, smile thin and eyes hot. "Alexandra."

"Get out of my way."

"Come now. Before you go, we should speak."

Her courage nearly faltered, molded by years of brutal conditioning. She swallowed down a lump and raised her chin. "I have nothing to say. Move."

"But I have something to say that you'll wish to hear." Paulina tugged a crumpled letter from inside her reticule and waved it like a threat. "Come into the parlor," Paulina hissed, the stone-faced butler appearing beside her. "We should speak."

CHAPTER EIGHTEEN

London – July 27th, 1814

Spencer paced his study's length, arms and legs trembling with unspent frustration.

First, there had been no answer to his letters. Then, they had been returned, unopened. Next, he'd visited five times in two days, and conveniently, the Patons were never at home. There had been not a sign of Alexandra since they parted a week earlier, and his temper and patience were frayed through, fear gnawing at his heart.

Tonight, he would not be so patient. Either he would force his way in and find her at home, or he would wait until she returned.

Convinced at last that plowing a fist into something was a useless solution, he forced himself to sit behind the desk and take out a sheet of paper. Rank and celebrity might limit how much of a scene he could make and how many doors he could put a boot through; his friend Ethan Grayfield's shadowy brand of influence put more clandestine means at the man's disposal. He scrawled out a note, doing what he should have days earlier.

One way or another, he would gain entry to her house and discover what the hell was going on.

He threw down his quill, interrupted by the clatter of hooves out front. It was her, it had to be. Alexandra would come at any hour of the day. It took effort not to dash for the stairs, his heart demanding he run while his mind reasoned that the butler was already showing her upstairs. He paced again instead, wearing down the rug's thick pile.

When the study door opened, however, it was Paulina who hovered at its threshold.

For a moment, his chest squeezed with a pressure which made breathing impossible. "Mrs. Paton." Not bothering to conceal his crushing disappointment, Spencer took up his armchair in the corner.

"I hope you'll forgive the hour," she offered nervously, perching in a chair near his desk and looking ready to flee at any moment.

"And that you've come unescorted," he added, knowing she hated to be on the outside of etiquette.

"My husband is injured." She smoothed her skirts, not meeting his eyes. "Urgency is my excuse."

"And your sister-in-law?" Paulina's eyes snapped to his, and he had the distinct sense of being plumbed, shook out for information. "How is *her* health, in comparison?" He slouched deeper in his chair, waiting for whatever fantastic story she had concocted.

She drew a long breath, eyes turned down. "We have spoken before about Alexandra's illness. Her instability."

"Mm."

"She is worse, Lord Reed. So much worse." Paulina buried her face in her hands a moment. "I worried at allowing her out into the world alone. I told my husband as much! And now, here we are."

"*Where*, precisely, is that?" he hissed.

Rather than answer, Paulina shook her head and wrung her hands. Ever the consummate actress.

If she was willing to entrench, then so was he. "You do not feel that you and Mister Paton have a responsibility in all of this? Or should I say, culpability?"

Paulina huffed a bitter laugh. "She spins a fine yarn about how we have robbed her, imprisoned her, forced her to live in reduced circumstances. Yet, I have never interfered in Alexandra's affairs. None of us have. She makes a mess of them all by herself. There were times when we tried to *help*, to spare her and spare ourselves from her outrageous behavior." She wrung her hands together, pleading. "My father's generosity is the only reason she has anything left of her family's legacy. She

187

is not well, sir. Her mother, too, suffered bouts of madness near the end."

He wondered if the madness were hereditary or catching. Paulina must have it in spades to imagine he would believe her tale. "Your account is exceedingly different from the Mrs. Rowan I have encountered. Alexandra is hardly cold. In fact, she claims to love me."

"You aren't the first." Paulina assured him, reaching out a hand. "She plays demure very well, all smiles and doting looks. She's seduced many men in that fashion." Her face flushed. "We had to bring her to England, where no one knows of her scandal." Her expression softened. "It is her delusions which are to blame. I must remind myself often that she does not act with malice."

He stifled a yawn. Her words were a fabrication and not a particularly interesting one. Told with a lot of feeling, he admitted, but little plot and hardly a crescendo. "Mrs. Paton, I fail to see what Alexandra thought to gain from me, besides a battered reputation."

"Wheedling her poor brother has not worked, though she has even tried taking his business by force. So she comes 'round to many others with her hand out." She waved, gesturing to his study. "She wants your fortune, simply put. That much of her, at least, is calculating."

Alexandra was laughter and passion, love and anger and spontaneity. She was many things, none of them calculating. He smirked and leaned farther into his chair. "The only way for her to secure my wealth would be through marriage."

"Yes," agreed Paulina, eyes wide in confusion.

"I have no intention of marrying." He gauged her reaction. "Mrs. Rowan or anyone else."

"Sir!" Paulina clasped a hand to her heart and slumped. "Oh, sir. That is a relief, and I am glad to hear it. She would not do you credit as a wife."

"Not as you do your husband," he offered. "So concerned and… industrious."

"My husband!" She crossed her arms and slouched, rolling a pouting lower lip. "He would never pay me such a compliment."

188

"No?" He toyed with her now, amused and decently frightened by how quickly she had turned the conversation to her own suffering.

She stared at the ground, shoulders slumped, her voice small. "First, he must remember that I exist. He must care."

"No attention from Mister Paton?" He swallowed a chuckle; Chas's every waking moment must revolve around her.

"He does, but only when he is cross." She ducked her face. "The blows are not so severe. He and my father … Some days I cannot comprehend why I am necessary to either one."

"I am sorry to hear it," he lied, passing bored. "Let me walk you out."

When they reached the hall, he paused with a hand on the knob. "I will pay a call on Alexandra tomorrow, to see this for myself. And I *will* be admitted."

"Tomorrow," agreed Paulina, nodding and dabbing at her eyes. "Of course."

He watched her alight her carriage and clatter off down the street followed by her lies, and questioned the wisdom of letting her go. The wisdom of not following.

*　　　*　　　*

The morning dawned gray, dreary, and raining, a perfect fit for Spencer's mood. He'd spent a sleepless night worrying about Alexandra, and turning Paulina's words over in his head, looking for hidden meaning. He'd finally given up before sunrise, and six hours of nothing but coffee, whiskey, and pacing had done little to improve his mood. When an acceptable hour to pay call on Alix had finally come, he was already in the hall with hat in hand, and dashed from his home, almost commandeering his carriage when his driver was slow to clamber aboard.

Arriving at the Paton's house, he'd paused for the first time that day, dread twisting his insides. He knew that Paulina's words were little more than lies, but something was clearly wrong. He couldn't imagine a situation that would have kept Alix from writing him, even if she couldn't pay call.

189

Mustering his courage more than he remembered doing on a battlefield, he climbed out of the carriage, marched to the door, and knocked.

She was waiting in the parlor when the butler showed him in. Spencer had expected Paulina to be present as a chaperone, but Alexandra was alone. She paced the dim room, her movements agitated but slow. She didn't look up when he stepped in. Clad in a shabby brown calico dress that looked like it had come from a cast-off box, she pulled at a loose strand of hair hanging behind her ear from a haphazard bun. She was thinner than he remembered, dark half-moons beneath her eyes. Swallowing growing fear that wormed its way up from his gut, he took a steadying breath. How could she have deteriorated so much in only a week?

"Alexandra," he probed, watching her as he took a seat.

"Why are you here?" She still didn't meet his eyes, didn't use his name.

"To visit with you."

"No visitors. Not today." Her words were clipped and impersonal.

"Alix, I'm …" he pressed a fist to his chest, "Please, just a few moments to put my mind at ease."

She laughed and hung her head, eyes half open. "I'm perfectly well. I don't need your thumb over me."

"My thumb?" He braced, tried not to be wounded, and failed. "I'm not here to frustrate you."

"Then go!" She threw her arms out wide. "Respect my wishes, and leave me alone!"

"You don't mean that."

More pacing, but her eyes met his for the first time. What he saw there frightened him more than any words Paulina could concoct: she recognized him, but nothing more. He might have been a face she'd seen before in a crowd. There was no emotion, no warmth in dim blue eyes. "Try leaving and see if I stop you."

He'd come determined to prove Paulina a liar. To find an Alexandra intimidated by her sister-in-law and held prisoner, or something close. It galled him beyond reason to take any of Paulina's words seriously, but it was clear that something was very wrong with Alix.

190

They could spend the last few minutes of his visit in tense animosity, but Spencer was certain the friction between them wouldn't be improved by forcing Alix to endure more of something she'd already rejected. Sighing, he rubbed his eyes and stood up. "Get some rest, Alexandra. You'll feel better tomorrow."

CHAPTER NINETEEN

She did not feel better, not the next day or a week later when he stopped by on his way to the Exchange. Today she didn't leave her chair, casting him wild and nervous glances, whispering unintelligible strings of conversation under her breath. He had tried to settle near her only to have her bounce and slam her chair across the rug away from him. Moments later, her mood shifted yet again, and she hung her head and fell asleep.

Paulina insisted that Alexandra's haring off and her brother's brush with death had been the final straws piled atop an already fragile psyche. It was a lie, one he refused to accept whole or in part, but he had yet to find evidence disproving Paulina's theory. While they battled with frosty silence, Alexandra wasted away inside the prison of her mind.

Despite the Paton's assurances of physician visits and proper care, Alexandra was getting worse. With each passing day she recognized him less, made less sense. He lost patience with the Patons' methods, and with them. Storming out almost as soon as he'd come in, he shoved past a surprised Paulina just coming off of the stairs. "Lord Reed, leaving so soon?" Her voice was carefully neutral.

"I'll be back," he promised, snatching his hat from their hovering butler. "With a constable, if I must. Alexandra is coming with me."

She stepped in, throwing her long arms wide. "How dare you! Alexandra is our family. We care for her night and day and you have the gall to treat us thus!" Paulina's eyes flashed pure hate. "As though your suffering is greater." She backed away from him up the stairs. "Bring your constable. Mister Paton and I will fight you every step."

Spencer tipped his hat, teeth clenched. "I look forward to it."

*   *   *

A constable had been called, but it hadn't produced the result he'd wanted. Forced to listen to the uninterested drone on about how Alix was obviously sick, and therefore should stay with her family, he'd ground his teeth silently, trying not to glance up at Paulina's smug expression. Finally, he'd stormed out.

If they thought that was the end of things, they were very wrong.

The next step had been to elevate matters to the courts. Chas had arrived, as Alexandra's brother, but Paulina was close behind, and she'd immediately taken command of their side of the proceedings.

For three days, they had all gone round and round until civil conversation had passed into spiteful bickering, and then it had escalated to shouting that obliged Magistrate Adams to drive his gavel until it produced inflamed silence. He peered at them now with beady bird-eyes, almost a silhouette against the chamber's only window, his thin lips pursed and a hand hovering over his desk, waiting to strike again if necessary.

"Lord Reed," said Adams when he could finally silence Paulina, "your reputation carries a great deal of influence with the Courts. While we are convinced you've approached this matter with the noblest of intentions, we must agree with the Patons. Mrs. Rowan is not fit to make her own decisions, certainly not regarding marriage."

"Forget marriage, then," he argued, growing desperate. "Guardianship. Let me see to her physicians, her day-to-day care."

Adams massaged a temple beneath the edge of his powdered wig. "There is nothing, in our estimation, that you can do for Mrs. Rowan that her family cannot. And domestic upheaval seems ill advised, given her state of mind."

193

He was losing. As impossible as he'd believed it, as much as he'd thought Paulina would make his case for him, Alexandra was slipping away, beyond his grasp.

Spencer drove his walking stick into the marble and jammed a finger in Chas's face. "We are not finished!" He made a cursory bow to the magistrate. "This is far from over."

"Lord Reed." Adams' warning grabbed him at the door. "The matter is very much over. I have issued my decision. From this point on, Mr. and Mrs. Paton have legal recourse against your interference."

"Your ruling is not the last one in England." He jerked open the door, but Paulina, of all people, stopped him with a hand on his shoulder.

"Visits!" she shouted at his back. "If you will stop all of this, I will allow visits with Alexandra. Every day, provided you arrange a time."

He noticed that Chas was not included in the offer. "I will have visits." He refused to give any hint that she had done him a favor. Visits with Alexandra would have to do, for now, and he would not stop fighting to get her back.

Without another word, he left.

CHAPTER TWENTY

London – September 16th, 1814

He had visited every day except Sundays, for two months. Outside, the seasons had changed from pale green buds to lush leaves, to bare branches. Rose and lilac had blossomed, scattered their blooms across the walk, and been blown away on a fall gust. Spencer had made the walk in baking summer sun, and under the drenching, frigid downpour of August. It all passed him by unnoticed, muted by the ache of a broken heart. Bennet had been his only rock, binding his crumbling sanity with a word or a steady shoulder.

Today three steps to the door felt like a whole flight, and a walk from the hall up to Alexandra's room, miles. They had stopped allowing her to sit in the parlor after a tirade which reduced a small table and half a bookcase to scrap.

Alix hunched, left side drawn up, bouncing arrhythmically in her high-backed chair. Her blinking was repetitive, deliberate, out of time with a lock of hair she'd twisted near to breaking.

"Alexandra." Spencer pulled his chair across from her, reached out and grasped her free hand. It hung limp and clammy inside his grip, but the moment they touched she grew still. She went on staring out the window, motionless, but he wanted to believe that she knew that he was there.

Each time, he prayed that the Patons would hand him a victory, that she would be dirty or bruised, in soiled clothes. He prayed for something that would tip the scales, but today, as on all the other days, there was nothing more sinister than Alexandra's usual state.

195

For a while, he stared with her. A gust shook the trees now and then, caught curling golden leaves a handful at a time and drifted them to earth. Their color lent a glow to the sun, low on the horizon despite being just past midday. It shone through with a pale white light of autumn, illuminating the landscape while leaving it cold.

"I went to the Exchange today, early. Got business out of the way. I saw the Duke out on Copenhagen; that animal is meant to be a famous warhorse. You can tell he takes such pleasure in being ridden." Spencer laughed and shook his head. "His ears perk up and he makes such high steps when anybody takes notice of him."

Alix's eyes went on blinking. Her breathing didn't change.

"Laurel is shut up at home, now. I think she would be glad for your company. The physician says the baby will come in early January, but she's eager for it to come the last night of the year."

Spencer heard his voice fraying. He took the hand from her hair and held both of hers. "Please say something, Alexandra. Today is no different than all the others, but …" He studied her face for a sign. Nothing. He looked down at their hands, twined loosely together. Her fingernails were torn, red with unhealed rips along her fingertips. Skin across her knuckles was dry and chalky.

He choked down a sob and wiped his eyes. "I'll come tomorrow. We can sit longer. Bennet's due home tonight, and …" He stood, jaw clenching down on more words. He claimed his hat, and brushed her hair one last time, then stood in the hallway a moment, closing the door slowly for every last glimpse of her.

Paulina was waiting when he turned around. "Lord Reed."

"Mrs. Paton," he managed.

"Doctor MacPhearson was by today."

There was weight to the sentence. He shivered inside his wool coat. "Is that so."

"Your visits … I'm sorry, Lord Reed. You will have to stop calling."

"The hell I will!"

She rested a hand on his sleeve, for all the world looking sympathetic. "I am sorry, more than you know. When you leave she is an animal. Screaming, dashing off of the walls, agitated for hours. It drives Mr. Paton from the house in anguish." She fished a cloth from her sleeve and pressed it to her eyes. "I'm so sorry," she whispered.

He didn't want to believe her, but he'd seen Alexandra's fingertips, her tirade in the study weeks earlier.

"Let me take her!" he begged, grabbing Paulina's sleeve, cool blue silk escaping his fingers when he grasped harder.

"No! Charles has already told you as much. The magistrate will again, too. Alexandra is all my husband has, besides me. He will not abandon her, not even now." She took a deeper fold of his coat. "Not one person in this house bears you ill will, lordship. You love Alexandra, as we all do. But she cannot be even as a child to you. She must stay with her family."

And just so, it was over. At least, for now. His jaw twitched; he didn't bother struggling for a reply or even a 'good day'. Planting his hat hard atop his head, he pushed past Mrs. Paton and left the house for the last time.

*   *   *

"Absolute pig shite," Bennet spit his disgust. He leaned forward in his chair and rested elbows on his knees with enough force to slosh his brandy. "You're not going to listen to her..."

He wanted to agree, wanted to march up to the house right now, but he couldn't. He had no choice but to listen to Paulina. Until he convinced Magistrate Trumble to attend with more sense than Adams, he risked a stay behind bars at Newgate. A fortnight locked in the gaol wouldn't do Alexandra any good, or make him look more fit to care for her.

"You have to do something," demanded Bennet.

"My hands are tied, Bennet! I live by their leave, at least until I find some leverage. Waiting is all I can do."

Bennet slammed his glass to the table top and leaned in. "And what happens when Paulina decides that the best thing for Alexandra is taking her back to New York?"

He stared at his brother, agape. She was so sick, so frail that it hadn't occurred they might try to move her, but it should have.

"They won't be obligated to grant you piss back in America, and the courts there will laugh you back out to sea. I know of what I speak. What then, Spencer? What will waiting have gotten you then?" Bennet demanded, pacing.

He didn't answer, instead throwing back his tumbler and swigging deep, sad to see its bottom. As he lowered the glass, something caught his eye: a sticky plum colored spot on the webbing between his thumb and forefinger. "What in the hell ..." he sniffed at it, "is that?" It had a sweet smell with a boozy finish, but not from the brandy.

Bennet snatched his hand and examined it. Then without warning, he pressed his tongue to the spot.

"What in bloody hell, Bennet!"

Bennet spit into his empty glass, jabbed a finger at the substance, and fell back into his chair. "Laudanum." Bennet stabbed with his finger again. "*That* is laudanum."

He didn't take the medicine, didn't even keep it in the house. "And how would you damn well know that?"

Bennet shook his head, exasperated. "Because Captain Riley is an addict and he sodding spills it on every goddamn thing in his quarters. You can't open the tent flap without finding your fingers glued together. Ugh!" He scrubbed his tongue with a sleeve. "Something else mixed in it, though. I've a numb spot on my tongue."

Spencer sighed, too drunk and far too depressed to care much for this particular mystery. "Well, I've no sodding idea where it came from."

"Was the Paton's house the last place you visited? Did you touch anything on your visit today?"

He raised both hands, weary and certain that Bennet wouldn't give up. "Plenty of things."

"Without your gloves on, you great ass."

"No. Yes. Just Alexandra's hair, her hands."

"So it could have come from her ..." Bennet widened his eyes to near owl proportions.

"It could. Perhaps they give it to her to make her comfortable." He recalled her torn nails and wild antics in the parlor.

Bennet's head was already shaking. "Just the opposite. Laudanum is only soothing in short. She might float a cloud for a few hours, but later she'd be an absolute hellion. *If* all they'd given her was the poppy."

"How do you know any of this?"

"Miss Foster. She was the one to uncover Riley's habit."

"The woman doctor?"

"Aye. She's a damn sight sharper than the pair of withered hands prodding Alix."

"What's your point?" They had reached one of those moments when he desperately hoped Bennet would be the voice of reason.

"My point, brother, is that, if I didn't know better, I would say that someone is trying to harm her."

A wild hope had sprung up in him, but weeks of being stymied left him cautious. Spencer resisted latching on to Bennet's theory, precisely because he wanted so badly to believe it. "For months? They could have done the job long ago, so why didn't they? Why wait?"

Bennet shrugged. "I'm no scholar. *You* will have to answer that."

"If I had answers, I would have given them to the Court weeks ago."

"And you can't possibly go looking for them now?" Bennet scoffed. "Holding back was a benefit when they allowed you visits. Now that they've cut you off, really what is there to lose?"

"Ah, go to hell with it." He wouldn't be tempted by Bennet's conspiracy, wouldn't raise his expectations only to have them dashed for the hundredth time. Spencer spit and scrubbed the spot from his hand.

"Out, out damn spot," muttered Bennet.

He raised from his seat. "What did you say?"

Bennet matched him. "I said you are a *coward*."

199

He hadn't drunk enough to keep his knuckles from outright searing. The blow jarred his arm, clanked his teeth. Spencer shook his hand, to mitigate the throbbing.

Bennet's brow hadn't fared any better, red and angry, split and trickling a crimson line down his cheek. Spencer reached out his other hand and hoisted his brother up. "Say it again and I'll strike you twice as hard. It's what you deserve."

Bennet shook his head, one hand on a chair for support. "I *will* say it again. Paulina Paton is a scheming bitch, rotten to her core. You're a fool to trust her a moment longer with even a shred of evidence that she's harming Alix. If you would truly go to any lengths for your woman, Spencer, you should damn well sort this out."

"What do I do, barge into the house and start bellowing accusations? That met with spectacular success the last time."

"Truly, Spencer? You can defend your men against a gun battery with two sticks and a sail cloth but you cannot reckon this out?" Bennet raked his fingers for a handkerchief, then pressed it sound against his temple and winced. "You really sodding hit me. Did it have to be so hard?"

Spencer took up his chair. "Line it out for my simple mind, then."

"You've already given yourself the answer: motive. What would be the reason for keeping Alexandra alive, but her mind crippled? And who gains from it? That part should be the easiest."

Bennet cocked himself at an unnatural angle to hold his head, and righted the leather armchair. "I'm foxed. My head's split and I'm going to bed. But I am just up the staircase if you need me."

He did, more than anything. Spencer reached out and shook his brother's hand. "Thank you."

"I forgive you for canning me."

"I wasn't apologizing."

"Not aloud, but you meant to."

"No. No I did not."

"It's no matter," Bennet called back through the open door. "I know you meant to."

"Brat." He shook his still aching hand and pressed a torn knuckle. He was furious, and he really had hit Bennet hard.

Coward. He was furious, and now, motivated.

Bennet, you clever sod.

Spencer shook his head, taking stock of the room and where to begin. *His desk.* He settled against his chair's plush burgundy upholstery, scooted in, and laid his hands palm down atop the dark polished wood. He always thought better at his desk; his mind coached that it was a place for serious consideration.

He took the complicated web of Alexandra's family and began to pick strands away. The shipping company, Silas Van der Verre, the hidden shares. Alix had said her father took care of her in his will but not as she'd have liked. So, what was her stake in Paton & Son?

He opened his desk drawer and pulled out a brown leather folder which housed her copy of the business papers, documents she'd had sent to him after their week in Haywood. Thumbing through pages of minutiae, he stopped when her name caught his eye.

'Alexandra Rose Paton, being of the age of majority at this signing ...'

He skimmed the lines, once and then again to be certain. Alix retained her shares unless wed, in which case they became property of her husband. At her death, without any children, they devolved to a Mister Thomas Meacham, 'able solicitor,' her father's attorney.

In two sentences Bennet's mad theory had grown far more plausible. For months, Silas and likely Paulina, and perhaps even Chas, had no doubt been digging into Alexandra's affairs. They had probably learned of the hidden shares, though he doubted they had quite put the pieces together to discover where and what name they were owned under. When they did, they would still need Alexandra; at least until Paton & Son belonged fully to Van der Verre. Then she would be nothing more than an inconvenience.

Bennet had been right; the time for waiting was over.

CHAPTER TWENTY-ONE

London – September 22nd, 1814

Spencer stepped back to allow Constable Bowen more room for another assault on the Paton's door. The delay was frustrating but not surprising. It was just past four in the morning; most of the household staff would sleep for another hour or two.

"Open up! Crown business," Bowen shouted again, bending his ham of an arm and jarring the door until flecks of blue paint chipped away. Spencer mused idly that the man resembled a bear wrestler he had once seen in a Russian circus; tall as he was broad, bald as a stone, and with a thick brow ridge bent to a perpetual angry line over slit eyes. Not a man any sleep-addled butler wished to find at his door before sunrise. "Last warnin'," Bowen barked, "or me and the lads'll step in uninvited!"

On cue, the lock grated in its tumbler and the door inched open. A bed cap and one weathered, suspicious eye was all the space revealed. "What business?" croaked a leathery voice.

Bowen hooked a sausage thumb in the band of his mile-long blue wool trousers, presenting his crisp, neatly-creased prize. "A warrant, served on Mr. Charles Paton and his lawful wife Paulina, and any domiciled within." Bowen's wide chest puffed at 'domiciled', and Spencer got the sense the man had been practicing for just this moment.

He exchanged a knowing glance with his friend Ethan Grayfield, who had helped secure their legal papers on short notice. He'd sent a note to Ethan that first week, when his letters and visits had gone unheeded, and though he'd received no reply, there wasn't a doubt in Spencer's mind that Ethan had been digging. The man was an unmatched spy master, had himself dabbled in espionage for a time. Ethan could do little to sway the Courts or change a law, but when Spencer needed information, Ethan could procure it in spades.

"Wait here." The sharp instruction was followed by the butler attempting to close the door. Bowen checked it with an elbow, throwing it wide and tumbling the butler onto his backside.

Once through the door, Bowen stepped aside and Spencer followed behind. He raised his hat to a host of owlish eyes, ending with Chas Paton on the third stair, bracing Paulina behind him.

"Reed. How did I know you were the cause of this?"

"Mister Paton, we are of course acquainted. And this is Magistrate Arindale, Constable Bowen, and his trusty leftenant, Noble. And my friend Lord Ethan Grayfield, as witness."

Ethan crossed his arms and did not remove his hat.

"Witness to what?" ground out Paulina.

Bowen raised his prize again. "To escort you and your husband to Bow Street, unmolested, and to take custody of a Mrs. Rowan, sister of Mister Paton."

Paulina scoffed. "There is no one here by the name of 'Rowan'.

Spencer leaned forward, raising in his boots to see the warrant over Bowen's shoulder. "Paton. It also says Alexandra *Paton.*"

Chas's jaw clenched, blanching his pale cheek. "You are an unfathomable ass. You have been denied at every turn. We have tolerated you, your boorishness, your effect on my sister –" His voice hitched and he swallowed. "And still you force your will on us."

Spencer almost applauded. That speech must have taken more courage than anything he'd said all year.

Arindale broke in. "I understand your concerns, Mister Paton, given the court's earlier findings. However, Lord Reed brought forward new evidence late last evening. We have reasonable suspicion that your sister is being held against her will."

Chas lunged. "My sister!"

Bowen menaced forward at a sign of unrest and Chas lowered his voice. "My sister cannot dress herself. We keep a nurse to feed her."

"Do you administer laudanum to your sister, Mister Paton?" This from Ethan, still lurking just inside the door.

"What? No!" Chas shook pleading hands at them. "She wouldn't tolerate its effects. She is barely lucid as it is."

"Interesting." Spencer leveled his gaze on Paulina, who glared back. "Herbs and potions, Mrs. Paton? I believe that is how Alexandra described it."

Silence stretched awkward through the room, and finally she dropped her eyes.

Arindale waved a hand as though shooing stray dogs. "Constable, take them in," he mumbled through his silver brush mustache, "and we'll go up and fetch Miss … Mrs… whatever her name is." He turned back to Chas. "My men will take you up to dress. Be hasty about it."

"Dress!" Chas's voice rose an octave, settling just below hysterical. "Why in the hell must we go anywhere! Taking Alix is insult enough. Where are we to go?"

Spencer wondered who Chas was more worried about: Alexandra or Silas. He'd had enough of the attacks on his character and of Chas's anguish, genuine or manufactured. "Mister Paton, what happens to Alexandra's shares while she is incapacitated?"

"What!" Hands flailed. "Why …?" Chas scrubbed his wild blond hair. "My father-in-law manages them."

"And if, say, Alexandra were to have more shares somewhere, those would also fall to his care, would they not?"

A nod.

"But if she dies, unmarried," Spencer stared at Paulina now, who looked a bit ill, "do you know what happens then?"

Chas tried to speak, cleared his throat. "No. The legalities do not, um, fall within my purview."

"Mrs. Paton! You know, perhaps?"

A murmur.

He cocked an ear. "I cannot quite make you out. Mister Paton, turn and ask your wife if she has an answer."

Chas's jaw twitched. His pale face flushed from neck to hairline, and he turned on the ball of one foot. He didn't look up to meet her eyes. "Paulina. What happens to the shares?"

"How would I know?" Her trembling mouth formed words too weak to pass her lips.

"You manage more of Paton's documents than anyone else." Chas's arm snaked out. He grabbed her wrist and jerked her down two stairs to stand below him, clutching the banister to keep from tumbling behind. "You manage it," he added deadly soft, limbs shaking inside his night shirt, "so do not say you *don't know!*" He screamed the last into her face, spittle flying with each word.

Bowen lunged forward and got hold of Paulina, and Spencer followed behind, hooking Chas's arm, driving him back until they were nearly lying on the staircase.

"What happens, Paulina! You damn well answer me."

"Don't make trouble, Charles!" she pleaded, "Don't make trouble!" The last word cut through the room's commotion as a shriek.

"Paton!" Spencer shook a sinewy arm to keep Chas from trying to strangle his wife.

"Tell me, Reed," Chas panted. "I know you already know."

"Van der Verre loses the stocks. They go to Mister Meacham, unless Alix is kept alive."

Chas pressed his free hand to his eyes and began to sob. "You bitch!" he cried. "You horrid, incestuous bitch."

"Charles!" Paulina's eyes flew to every man in turn, an actress gaining the attention of her audience. "As if you didn't have a hand in it all!"

Spencer shot a glance over his shoulder and nearly at Paulina flapping in Bowen's grip as though she had any hope of getting away.

"How can you lay blame against me, Charles?" she demanded. "This man has destroyed our peace, abused our family! And suddenly you take his word over that of your own wife?"

Chas sat up mechanically, not meeting anyone's eyes. "They'll hang you," he murmured, sounding dead himself. "We're in England, Paulina. They're going to goddamn hang you."

Paulina flailed in earnest, feral noises tearing from her throat.

Arindale snapped his fingers. "Take her out, Bowen. Noble, hitch her in the wagon."

"I am not decent, you great ass!"

"Your maid will bring you clothes." Arindale swirled a thick finger. "Out."

Paulina raised her chin, shrugging in Bowen's grip, pinning them each with haughtiness as she passed.

Spencer watched the spectacle, cold inside.

As Bowen dragged her out the door, Ethan raised his hat for the first time. "Madam."

Chas slumped back into the treads and hung an arm across his eyes. "Am I to be taken with her?"

Spencer turned to Arindale, who only raised his brows. With a last glance to Chas, Spencer nodded, no idea the extent of Chas's complicity. "I think you should go with these men now, and you should answer their questions as truthfully as you can. If your wife has done something criminal here, now is the time to set it right." Spencer lowered his voice, "And to distance yourself from it."

"Yes." Chas's nod was slow, in a trance. "Yes. All right. What will happen to Alix?"

"I will take her." Spencer was unequivocal, brooking no argument. "She'll stay with John and Laurel. A physician has been summoned."

He wasn't convinced Chas understood what was being said. "Go with Lieutenant Noble," he said finally. Hooking Chas beneath the arm, Spencer hauled the man to his feet.

"Reed? Oh, Mister Paton!" Laurel appeared in the doorway, spinning in a circle as Chas passed out and Bowen came back in, obliged to shuffle sideways past her growing belly.

Spencer stepped forward and put a hand to her shoulder. "Laurel, what the devil are you doing? John will geld me if he finds you've come here."

She yanked her bonnet ties with deft fingers. "I'm here for Alexandra. You cannot allow a strange man to come in and prod her without a soul she knows at hand."

"She knows me," he muttered, stung by her words.

She set her hat on a narrow table inside the door, and rested a tiny hand on his lapel. "No, Spencer. If she has been abused as you say, she will need you after. But this," she put a hand to his face, and her eyes glanced upstairs. "You will need comforting as much as she does."

He took Laurel's hand, relieved by its warm pressure. She rubbed her back and sighed, mouth set in a grim line. "Well, let's go up."

CHAPTER TWENTY-TWO

There was no doubt that Paulina had been sedating Alexandra, perhaps even poisoning her. The only question more pressing than what she had used, was where she had *not* hidden her weapons.

Behind a crock of salt in the kitchen; inside a hatbox in her wardrobe; occupying the place of an ink bottle in her writing case; all eight bottles recovered thus far had been found scattered throughout the house, a bottle of death standing shoulder-to-shoulder with a bottle of wine, innocuous.

Doctor Ashby swept a hand over the last tuft of white hair atop his egg head, squinted through his spectacles at a final brown glass bottle, and set it on the window ledge with the others. Then he turned kind, sad eyes to Alexandra, heaped on her bed, sleeping or too sedated to be aware of what was happening around her.

"In their defense, Lordship, it is understandable how several of my peers could have missed such a poisoning." He waved a hand at the small pharmacy gathered up during Bowen's search of the house. "As you can see there are a *number* of tinctures and elixirs here." He knocked a few bottles with a fingertip. "Dogbane. Laudanum. Bits of what appear to be mushrooms. Given in combination, slowly and over time, it would be hard to pinpoint any one of them as the culprit." He tapped at a scrap of vellum that had neat lines written in pencil down its face. It had been discovered in Paulina's dressing room inside, of all things, a bible. "Mrs. Paton was very skilled in her dosing and administration. Hidden from the staff; even her husband, if he's to be believed. With a family history of madness..." He shrugged. "The missus fooled us all rather well."

Spencer didn't care. None of that mattered now. He pointed to Alexandra. "What do we do for her?"

"I'll examine her. She ought to be given tea and broth only." Those instructions he directed at Laurel. "Stop the laudanum at once. That alone will be a hard path; God knows what these other concoctions might do to her now they've been terminated."

Spencer shuddered. Laudanum hunger was not foreign to him. Plenty of wounded relied on it long after they'd fully healed. They became addicted as they convalesced and later found themselves drummed out and shunned by their families.

Laurel's hand pressed his back. "What should we watch for?"

"Agitation, paranoia. She cannot be accounted for what she says and does. There will be severe body pains, probably vomiting. You must not give anything until this has passed."

Spencer swallowed, watching the slow rise and fall of Alexandra's chest. "Will she..."

"No," Ashby reassured. "I cannot speak to anything else, but flushing the laudanum from her cannot cause death. And for that reason, you must not comply with anything she asks. She will beg, plead. She may try to escape the house." His sad expression deepened. "It will not be easy to watch."

Inhaling, he looked to Laurel and steeled himself. "When?"

"As far as I can tell, her last dose was between one and two o'clock this morning. I expect her symptoms would begin after noon."

"We have to move her quickly. She cannot remain in this house." Alexandra might not recall what she had suffered here, but Spencer couldn't bear to think of her staying a moment longer than necessary.

"I would advise against it, but I know better than to run contrary to your lordship." Ashby smoothed his ample waistcoat. "Let's look her over, and you can be on your way. Though I'd advise you to bring along one of those stout lads I passed on my way in. If she wakes en route, you may well regret being in such close quarters. And Lady Hastings should not be alone with her at any point for the next day, at least."

209

Spencer nodded and was silent. Ashby stared, and Laurel stared, seeming to expect something from him. Finally, Laurel cleared her throat. "Spencer."

He stared back, waiting.

Laurel cocked her head toward the door.

Crossing to the far wall, he took the little ribbon-back chair where Alexandra usually sat, brought it up close to the bed, and planted himself in it, ignoring a silent exchange between Laurel and Ashby. They might fetch Bowen to drag him away, but short of that, he was not leaving.

Ashby sat his patient up, and Laurel went to work on Alexandra's buttons. The wrinkled calico was filthy; it hung on her torso, mute testament to weeks spent without proper food.

At the first glimpse of a shoulder that looked far thinner than when he's last seen it, Spencer lost some of his nerve and turned his eyes away.

When she'd been stripped, they laid her down and Laurel drew a quilt up over Alexandra. Ashby raised her arms in turn, studied her nails and hmm'd, stopping now and then to scribble on a page in his little brown leather journal.

He flipped back one side of the quilt, down to her hip. "Mmph."

Spencer sat up at Ashby's sound of disgust, craning to see around the doctor's arm. He pushed Laurel's hand from his shoulder and rose half out of his chair.

Sores. Some were old and red, white flakes of sloughed skin. Others, newer ones, were scabbed by a yellow crust. He clenched his fists, willing slow breaths in and out through his nose. Paulina was fortunate that Arindale had taken her away before Doctor Ashby's arrival.

"Lift her up. Let's get a look posterior."

Outpacing Laurel, Spencer slid his hands under Alix's hip and tried to ignore her flesh against his hand. He pushed her backside while Ashby raised a shoulder, and they turned her half onto her belly.

Laurel had been right; he should have listened, kept his eyes away. Angrier blisters covered Alix from shoulders to the small of her back. Cuts, small nicks carved by knife or razor, underscored some of them.

"*What* are those?" Laurel breathed, while he ran a finger around an oval pattern.

"Oh!" Laurel buried her face in her hands, turning half away from the bed.

"What, what is it?"

"A candle," she groaned. "A candle would..."

Spencer hid his own face and fought to keep the image from his mind. He had wondered at times if he were capable of killing a man, off the battlefield. The answer weighed on his heart now.

Ashby went on scribbling, punctuating each entry with thoughtful noises, then closed his book. "I've seen all that I require. I'll go prepare my report and deliver it to the magistrate this afternoon. Lady Hastings should have some help dressing Miss Paton, and then you may take her off."

Spencer stood, more than eager to be away.

Laurel raised an arm. "Out! You've interfered enough. See Dr. Ashby to the door; one of these skittish servants can help me get her ready." She planted herself between him and the bed, shooing him out with sweeping hands. Nearly wide as she was tall, Spencer realized he couldn't have circumvented her had he wished to.

He followed Ashby out into the hall and closed the door. "Your report?"

Ashby looked wary, and then his shoulders relaxed. "Whether Miss Paton suffers some mental disturbance remains to be seen. Clearly, I cannot assess that now. That she was given substances to keep her compliant? Undoubtedly. Those suffering mental disturbances do themselves harm, but Miss Paton is hardly able to inflict the injuries I observed. And one wonders," Ashby's voice lowered to a somber rumble, "that there are no injuries to the *observable* areas, such as the face and limbs." Ashby sighed and smoothed his thin tuft of hair. "Whatever Miss Paton's condition, I have no doubt that something sinister transpired in this house."

Spencer followed Ashby downstairs, shaking his hand and closing the door at his exit. He pressed his back to the cool plaster, closed his eyes, and tried to gather himself. Tried not to see Alexandra's wounds again and again in his mind.

211

Chas had warned Paulina that she would be hanged. Spencer clenched a fist, stretched out his fingers. Lucky for her, just now, that was probably true.

CHAPTER TWENTY-THREE

Broadmoore – September 23rd, 1814

The screaming came again, ripping like a gale through doors and hallways.

Laurel raised from her seat; John's palm atop her shoulder pressed her back gently. Spencer took another long draw on his whiskey and fought the urge to be sick. None of them spoke; keeping vigil in the parlor, the noises coming upstairs pressed them into silence.

Fists hammered against the door out of time with one another. At first Alexandra had screamed incoherent things, and occasionally he'd caught Chas and Paulina's names in the garbled string. Now she was begging again and again for Laurel to ease her suffering, seeming to know who and where she was. Spencer wasn't certain if he should feel relief at her increased awareness, or fear that she was delirious despite it.

Many of her pleas and cries were muffled, but those that weren't took many forms; she was dying, they all wanted her gone, they were killing her. She had even screamed about 'all the blood', though he had no telling if it was a hallucination or a plea for sympathy.

"Please, please!" she moaned. And then a long bout of sobbing echoed from the floorboards.

It wore at Spencer's sanity; he had to do something, had to try.

"Go out," he ordered finally. "Grayfield has made his house open to one or all of us."

"She's our family," Laurel protested, but he caught her anxious glance at John.

He put his hand on her arm and squeezed. "So she is, and you've done a great deal already. But there's nothing you can do now."

John hesitated, still staring at Laurel; Spencer watched the conflict tearing at him.

"Hastings, your wife is in a delicate state. The servants have all gone out; there's no one to wait on you," he reasoned. "This cannot be good for her. Go to Grayfield's. Rest. You can relieve my watch come morning."

He locked gazes with John, who nodded. "Thank you, Reed."

Laurel took his hand and kissed it, resting her cool forehead against his knuckles. "You are a good man, Spencer. Thank you."

"Spencer!" Alexandra's banshee shriek snapped Laurel up, rocking her chair. "Spencer," she moaned again, hammering the door one solid blow at a time.

She went on that way for half an hour while John and Laurel gathered themselves to leave the house, agitated by their commotion.

Spencer held himself in check until the rumble of their carriage faded down the drive. Then he mustered his courage, planted one boot after another on the staircase, and went up.

For a few minutes, he stood in the hall and listened. Alexandra whispered furiously to herself, and something rustled like clothes brushing the floor. He turned and sat down, leaning his back against the door. All sound stopped and the house was silent a few breaths.

Spencer realized after the kick that he should have thought better about resting his head on the door. The wood jarred ahead of her foot, rattling his teeth.

"I know you're out there, you son of a bitch! Open this door!" Another kick. "You cannot keep me here." He heard her suck in a breath, braced for a scream. "*I hate you!*" She ejected the words with a force that vibrated against his back.

Spencer drew knees up to his chest, clasped his hands and bit his tongue. Keeping silent tore at his chest and wracked him with guilt, no matter how necessary.

Screeching and swearing, Alix pounded through the room. Something crashed to the floor and rolled. That was intriguing, since they'd removed every possible object from reach. She went on hitting walls and pounding the door, calling him every sort of a devil for long minutes. The meaty thud of a body falling to the floor reached his ears, and then panting.

"Please," she gasped. "Please, Spencer. If you won't let me out, just come in. Please, I'm so frightened."

He struggled with the entreaty, remembering Doctor Ashby's caution. He knew she was still heavily under the influence of the drugs. In the end, he could handle himself. He was not letting her out, and he was damned well not giving her more laudanum.

Spencer stood up, took the key from his pocket and turned it in the lock. He snapped the door open just an inch, jerked it back and then swung with the full strength of his arm. It caught Alexandra's charge long enough for him to hook her with an arm. His grip knocked her from her feet and sent her sliding on her backside almost to the window.

"You bastard! You are the son of a whore!" She struggled onto her elbows, spitting in his direction.

He closed the door, locked it again, and sat against it once more. "You can paint me black with your tongue all night, but if you take to spitting and biting, I'll muzzle you." He trusted the threat to be enough, not trusting himself to follow through.

"Of course you will!" Her laugh bubbled with hysteria. "You're just like them! I hate you." Alix struggled to her feet and climbed up onto her bed. She turned her back, sitting cross legged, and faced the wall.

Spencer guessed they passed nearly an hour that way, unnerving silence in comparison to her earlier raging. Now and then her breath rasped, and after awhile her shoulders slumped and he wondered if she slept. Then: "Spencer."

His name sounded sad and desperate on her lips. "Yes, Alexandra?"

"I love you."

He closed his eyes and exhaled, hoping that the worst had finally passed. "I love you too."

215

She wriggled down from the bed, crawling on hands and knees to where he sat. His hope deflated; she was still not in her right mind.

Alix stopped just at his knee, raking fingers through her wild mane. He swallowed. She was so pale, made worse in the moonlight. Thin. Hollows around her eyes were deepened by scant light, and in silhouette she resembled a scarecrow. He rubbed a fist over his aching chest.

She reached out slowly, fingers plucking at his cravat. "I'm sick, Spencer. I'm dying." A hand pressed over her eyes and she sobbed. "I'll die without my medicine."

"I've sent John into the village to get more. He'll be back directly."

A cocky smile curved up one side of her mouth, her whole frame relaxing. "That is very kind of you." She inched closer, until his leg was wedged between her knees. "*Very* kind."

"Mmm."

She pulled his cravat again, ran a finger down the front of his shirt. "You are a very handsome man." Her eyes were vacant in the dark, holding nothing but her hunger. When she looked at him, she might have been looking *through* him.

"Am I? What is my name?"

A shrug. Up on her knees now, she reached again for his throat.

Spencer snatched her arm, pushing so that she fell onto her backside.

"I need my medicine," she demanded, and her lip rolled out in a pout.

"Soon enough. I'll have it brought up the moment it arrives."

Alix fingered a button along the side of her bodice. "We're alone in here."

"So we are." Spencer fixed his eyes to the window, tracing a half of the moon not hidden from sight by the casement.

Fumbling her way along, Alix freed each button in turn. He could feel her eyes on him and refused to acknowledge it. "We could do a great many things, all alone."

"No, we mustn't," he cautioned, "The servants will hear us."

She giggled, undeterred from opening her bodice.

Servants. It was all he could think to say. Despite days of anguish, Alexandra's state of mind, his rage at Paulina, when Alix whispered his name and began to remove her dress …

He sucked in a breath, trying to keep one eye on her without truly looking. The dress was all she wore. No stays, for her own safety, and no chemise.

She grasped the hem, started to wriggle it over her head.

"John could return any moment," he warned. "You would not want to be in such a state."

No reply. Her dress smacked the wall beside him, landing in a heap. She inched closer again.

Spencer stretched out his legs, holding his breath while Alix fumbled her way into his lap. He rested a hand on each of her hips. It was instinct; he hadn't meant to do it. Her skin was clammy and stuck to his palms.

Heart thundering, he struggled to listen, to keep his guard. He swallowed down a lump in his throat and regretted ever opening the door. Alix fumbled his hair in a disjointed caress. "You're killing me," she whispered. "I need my medicine."

"Nearly here," he murmured, turning away from breasts almost pressing his face. Alexandra's familiar shape, even thin as it was, weighed his thighs. When she turned his face back and leaned in, Spencer let her kiss him.

It was a mistake; he knew before it happened. Her teeth seized his lip, digging harder and harder until he snatched a fistful of hair and snapped her head back. Blood trickled over his chin.

Alix tensed, threw back her head and cackled. Then she slumped against his chest, buried her face in his shoulder and wept like a child.

He ran a hand up her back, calming her as hot tears soaked his shirt. With his other hand, he brushed away his own. As time passed, her body calmed and he dared to hope that she'd fallen asleep at last.

He waited, Alix cradled in his arms until the moon had passed beyond the window's narrow opening. Tense, he was ready for the next assault, for her to hit or scream, for her rest to be another ruse. She lay slack against him, breathing slowly and evenly. Finally, Spencer worked up his courage and tipped her back a little. Her eyes were closed, chest rising and falling no matter how much he shook her.

Letting out a breath he hadn't realized he'd been holding, he scooped her up, abandoned the idea of putting her dress back on, and settled her on the bed. Tugging a quilt over her, he watched her for a long time, gaining control of the tumult inside.

He went out and locked the door again. Stretching out across the hall rug, he braced his head atop an arm and slept.

CHAPTER TWENTY-FOUR

Broadmoore – September 27th, 1814

Spencer. He had been telling her something, reassuring her. He wasn't a face or even words, just sound in the darkness. She hadn't heard him anymore after that, sad that she couldn't remember the last thing he'd said. She hadn't been able to listen to him, too thirsty, and no one brought her water. Sometimes she heard Laurel, or other hushed voices, but they never brought her a drink. Hungry too, but not for food; for something that would feed the crazed cyclone between her temples, an ache between each joint which made her want to run and kept her from rolling over.

She had been awake for days, but not truly aware. Foggy scraps of conversation, of people coming and going swirled in her mind, but today was the first day Alix felt that any of it truly made sense.

She remembered Laurel's smooth hand rubbing her arm, bringing her awake. Someone she didn't know had come in and out, first with a tub and then buckets. Laurel had tried to get her excited about a bath, but the tub seemed so far away. Alix wasn't certain she could sit herself up.

The maid left the room with her empty pail, and Laurel came in. "Ready?"

Alix nodded, feeling that she was supposed to. "If you wouldn't mind closing the door on your way out."

Laurel scrunched her face. "I was going to stay. I thought you would need –"

"No." She hadn't meant to snap. Her head throbbed almost too much to keep her eyes open, but she didn't trust

219

anyone to touch her yet. She might need someone's help, but she certainly didn't want it after months of forced dependence, not even from Laurel.

She managed a smile for Laurel's benefit. "Thank you, but I'd feel better doing it alone. Can I call for you, if I need help?"

The compromise pleased Laurel, who nodded. "Just call out. I'll be in the next room."

Alone again, Alix scrunched her belly and tested her ability to sit. Finally, she rolled onto an arm and pushed herself up. Sparks erupted at the edge of her vision; she was going to be sick. Panting, she closed her eyes and after a moment it passed.

Getting her feet onto the rug was easy enough. Putting weight on them was an entirely different matter. It took the help of a nightstand, a curtain, and the mantle to get herself to the tub. Trembling arms braced her against its wooden edge, requiring an exhausting amount of maneuvering to step in, sit down and not dump the whole thing. The process left her gasping and sobbing quietly, but she would not give up.

Steaming water seared her skin, biting her wounds and turning her red from her toes to the tops of her breasts. She welcomed the sensation. Any feeling other than numbness was a blessing, made her feel awake and aware. Taking a towel from the hearth, she rolled it up, stuffed it beneath her head and leaned back as much as the tub would allow.

A bath would make her feel better, she'd told herself, but despite the hot water on her skin, it didn't really help. She gave herself a cursory scrub with the soap from head to toe, and then she lay in the water until it was cold, waiting for something to happen. Mind unoccupied, her attention settled on her wounds.

She tensed, pulse hammering in her throat. Panic beaded into sweat along her forehead. It was the second time in as many days, when thoughts of Paulina tried to slither inside her mind. She couldn't summon up one single recollection of the torture, but a churning in her gut and the urge to run screaming in any direction told Alix that some part of her had been aware as it happened.

It was over now, done. Thanks to Spencer, Paulina was imprisoned and Chas was finally being made to face his part in things, however passive.

Spencer. He felt so far away; had he forgotten her? She couldn't really conceive of how much time had passed. It felt like years. Her memory wasn't just a flash of blank space. She almost wished it were; that might have been easier. Instead, she had just enough spots of lucidity, enough memory to light the darkness, to feel how much had been stolen from her.

She took the towel from behind her head, rested it atop her knees, and buried her face in it to hide the sobs. Terror lashed at her from the shadows. A part of her could sense heat burning her skin, or stabbing pain piercing her flesh. Fingernails tearing at her neck, or forcing her head back to drink. They were just sensations, vague hints of memory. Somehow, they felt worse than clearly recalling every moment.

When she'd got hold of herself, Alix wiped her face and dared standing up. It was a little easier this time, though her stomach clenched and her limbs trembled. Toweling off, it occurred that she was hungry. She could call for Laurel, ask for something to eat. She opened her mouth to call out, but couldn't make the words come. An emptiness welled up inside her, drowning her courage.

Instead, she ignored clean clothes and fell onto the bed. Rolling onto her side, she drew the blankets up almost over her head, and lay there. She stared at the wall, blinking, willing sleep to come.

*   *   *

Two mornings later she woke ravenous, less delicate and more determined to put space between now and her awful memories. Laurel consulted Doctor Ashby, who agreed that she could be allowed downstairs for breakfast which sated her desire for company, the first she'd felt since waking.

No one avoided her eyes or made a fuss, and Alix was grateful. John and Laurel picked things up as though she had just seen them the day before, including her without singling her out.

221

She had held her breath down the stairs, hoping that Spencer would be there, afraid to ask and be disappointed. He was not at the table, only John and Laurel. For a moment, she thought tears would come, and disappointment strangled her words. Swallowing an ache in her throat, she nodded to John, who was just getting up. "Leaving already?"

"Business in the village. Someone has to pick up all of Reed's slack," he teased.

Laurel swatted as he passed, shaking her head and casting Alix a look. "Secretly John enjoys it."

Alix kept silent until he'd gone, overly focused on slicing a boiled egg. She worked up her courage, exchanging a few glances with Laurel. "Where … Where is Lord Reed?" she asked, hating how weak and yet formal the words sounded.

Laurel blinked, surprised. "You mean *Spencer*? He's in London testifying against –" Laurel glanced away, "Testifying in the inquest."

"Oh." Crushed, Alix stiffened her face and went on scraping at her egg. She couldn't name her gratitude, her love for him and what he must be suffering now. Fear at his absence melted away.

"John had a letter from him early this morning." Laurel sounded surprised. "Third this week, and he is not much of a writer. He starts each one by asking after you."

The news warmed her, and something like peace settled in.

Laurel leaned over, laying a hand on hers. "If you'd like to write, John can send it with his answer tomorrow."

Alix stared at her plate, thinking of how she would begin, of what she should say to him. Wondering what she *had* said to him when she wasn't herself. The simple human contact of Laurel's hand was a welcome comfort, and she pressed back.

"He would not stay away for anything less, Alix. He visited you every day when … He never abandoned you. But his bloodlust is up, as John puts it." Laurel's green eyes narrowed to slits. "He'll see Paulina gets what she deserves." A squeeze, and Laurel took her hand away. "It's hard on him, but he would do anything for you."

Alix groaned, burying her face in her hands. "God, I don't remember it. It's as though we've been apart forever. Sometimes I hear things in my mind, inconsequential things. Who bought a new horse, the price of corn." She laughed. "I hear them in Spencer's voice. From his visits? They don't feel real."

Laurel shook her head, eyes wide. "Such a nightmare. What *is* the last thing you recall?"

Alix pressed her eyes shut, struggling for anything. There were fragments of London, of an argument with Chas, Paulina and a letter, but nothing fused together. "My last easy memories are of my week at Haywood."

"Stirling, you mean," corrected Laurel, pouring more tea.

"No, I mean Hay –" Her eyes snapped open, meeting Laurel's, "Wood."

Laurel's eyes narrowed, and she leaned close as though trying to read Alexandra's mind. "*Lord Reed* was at Haywood."

A smile spread against her will, and Alix looked away. "You are correct. He was."

"Hmph." Laurel pursed her lips, folding in a grin.

"What?"

"Nothing. It's no great matter."

"What?" Alix demanded again, hating that she had been baited.

Laurel shrugged, studying her nails. "It's just that Spencer never invites anyone there. Not even John."

"Oh."

"How did you pass the time during your week at Haywood?"

Laurel was her only close friend; if she could confess herself to anyone, now was the time. "How would you and John pass a week at Haywood?"

"Little clothing and plenty of wine."

Alexandra nodded, not fighting a grin. "Precisely."

Laurel's smile was triumphant. "Mm. You should write him this afternoon."

CHAPTER TWENTY-FIVE

The Old Bailey, London – September 29th, 1814

Spencer squinted at Paulina from the gallery's second row, grinding his back teeth as another frustrating bit of testimony concluded. A gavel rapped against the judge's high bench and a bailiff called in his long monotone for the gallery to empty. Feet pounded the scaffolding overhead, both the idle and the curious public shuffling out.

The longest trial he could recall had lasted just shy of forty-five minutes. Proceedings today had become so convoluted that the judge had been obliged to retire everyone for lunch, reconvening at four thirty that afternoon. He stared at blotches of sun on the room's white plaster walls, the stars of dust drifting from the ceiling's high peak, and took some comfort in the silence. London had never been the great love of his life, as it was for so many of his peers. The trial's noise, agitation, the sickening bites of testimony he was forced to swallow had made him resentful toward the city.

"You should go home for a bit." Ethan folded himself onto the bench, setting his hat between them.

"Not a chance." Spencer damned himself with a yawn, then shook his head. "The streets are beyond congested this time of day. I'd only have to turn around and come right back."

He glanced at Ethan, polished from his short black hair to his smart blue wool coat and high boots. The man could easily have just woken, but Spencer knew better. "Where have you been today?"

Ethan grimaced. "Seeing to Chas Paton. Utterly foxed and taken in for being disorderly at the coach station."

Spencer groaned. "Going where?"

"To see his sister, of course. Despite her pleas in the last letter to be left alone. He was out in the middle of Oxford Street raving that she's mad for saying she doesn't want to see him."

"What did you say to that?"

"I very nearly cocked him in his damned mouth. It's just what we need, when Paulina's lawyer is already doing his best to prove Miss Paton is not of sound mind. He wouldn't shut up, so I dragged him back to the hotel."

"One of the runners alerted you, I take it?"

Ethan nodded. "And he is now posted on Mister Paton's door. Bow Street can be a well-oiled intelligence machine when it chooses."

Spencer nodded, still set on the news that Alix did not want to see her brother, wondering if the same feelings extended to him. "It is bleeding difficult to not feel discouraged. Our evidence seemed perfectly set, irrefutable. That bastard Lawrence has done his job, giving everyone pause."

Paulina's lawyer was naturally the best money could buy, certainly getting every last coin he could from a man like Silas Van der Verre. He was smirking, arrogant, and with enough false bravado to get heads nodding in the dock when he called a witness into question.

"It would help if Alexandra were here to speak on her own behalf." Ethan's words were carefully spoken, the entreaty of a man already sure of an answer but trying anyway.

"Impossible. I'm not dragging her fifty miles over bad roads in her present state. And I'm not making her face that *woman*." Spencer massaged his jaw. "Besides, what would it accomplish? She was heavily drugged the entire time, and Lawrence will just use his forked tongue on her, too."

"It would establish a clear line, if she could describe how she felt while in Stirling, versus the changes here in town. Paulina has claimed her sister-in-law's mental break began during that week."

It would establish *perjury*. "You know as well as I that it didn't start then."

225

Ethan nodded. "But we are neither of us qualified to testify to it."

He held his tongue.

"We cannot *know* Miss Paton's state of mind in Stirling. Precisely what she said and did during that missing week."

He glanced to his friend, but Ethan stared ahead with a bland expression.

Spencer shifted. "Hmm."

Ethan sank deeper in his seat, leaned closer. "It would help if we knew how she behaved during that time..."

Understanding struck with a lightning jolt. "You know where she was," Spencer grumbled.

A smug smile. "I am always digging, Reed. Always digging."

Exasperated, Spencer leaned against the seat-back. "Then why not just say so?"

"Because I was curious to see how doggedly you'd guard her secret."

"To my grave," he ground out. "If Lawrence or the jury discovers the truth, they'll throw the whole case out on principle. Who's going to defend a scandalous American light skirt?"

Ethan patted his shoulder and stood up. "Good man. Be certain you keep that locked in the vault," he said, turning to leave.

"Ethan."

He turned. "Yes, Spencer?"

Ethan's steadfast, sleepless assistance had a been a bulwark against a storm. "Thank you. For everything you've done," he said, looking up at Ethan. "I felt so confident, when I came to testify. Since, matters have been … Your help, your friendship, will not be forgotten."

Ethan smiled. "I have been told that my interference is sometimes a two-edged sword. By the by, your lady has sent a letter. Arrived by courier late this morning."

Spencer stood and grabbed his hat. "How do *you* know that *I* received a letter from Alexandra?"

"I am always digging, Reed." Ethan grinned and swept a hand toward the doors. "Always digging."

*   *   *

Bennet greeted him at the door, Alexandra's letter in hand. "You're earlier than I expected; has something been decided?"

Spencer passed his coat off to the butler and wished again that he had at least brought Huston down from Oakvale. The man had been a keen reader of his moods and wishes for nearly two decades, unlike the stiff help he'd found in town. "No. In fact, things are looking rather grim. Paulina's counsel has pulled such sleight of hand that I'm not certain the judge knows where to look half of the time."

Bennet snorted. "Bunch of powdered prigs."

He claimed the letter and ducked into a room on their right, a study he shared with his brother while they were in London. A fire had been lit, and the card table was made up with scotch and glasses. Bennet claimed the right-hand chair, as usual, and Spencer fell with him in unison to the other, tearing open Alexandra's letter.

My Darling Reed,

I have received encouragement from Laurel to write you regarding your letter of the twenty-sixth, which I did not see, but in which she was good enough to say that you had asked after me.

You alone have brought me through my darkness; let me now bring you through yours. However matters are settled in London (John says the case against P. is not so simple), you have won. By fighting for me, you have already won. Come to me at the first moment you are able; my life cannot begin until you are here.

Yours,
Alexandra

Ps. Give my affection to Bennet, and no teasing. Don't be cruel and tell him I did not think of him.

Spencer skimmed the few beautiful lines and committed every word to memory.

Bennet poured, then craned his neck, first over the top of the page and then left to right while Spencer held the it away.

227

"What does it say?" demanded Bennet, still leaning for a glimpse and managing his drink.

"Nothing for your eyes, whelp. Keep at bay."

"Did she mention me?"

"No." He sighed, and admitted the truth. "*Yes*."

He braced for Bennet's inevitable jest, but received a thoughtful nod instead. "There's nothing I can do for Grayfield, now. Or you. I'm thinking of going up tomorrow, to be with her until you've settled things here."

Spencer was surprised and touched. Not that he would share that information; he'd never hear the end of it. "You? Give up town for the hinterlands?"

Bennet crossed his arms. "For you, for Alexandra, is it even a question?"

Spencer tousled his brother's hair, then pulled him in and pecked his forehead. "You've come out all right, you sodding brat."

That won a smug smile. "So I have, mostly."

Something occurred to Spencer. "What do you mean, nothing you can do for Grayfield?"

Bennet got up, shaking his head. "Can't discuss it."

"What is *it*?"

"Can't discuss it," he repeated, leaning in to fill his glass one last time with a wink. "Grayfield's orders."

CHAPTER TWENTY-SIX

Broadmoore – October 1st, 1814

"I'm all right!" Alix shouted again, kicking the chamber pot farther behind her dressing screen. She threw open the casement as she passed, praying crisp October air would hide the smell.

Laurel's winged brows were pulled into a deep vee when Alix opened the door, fixing herself in the middle of the frame while Laurel raised on tip toes, dodging left and right to see past her.

"What are you doing in here?"

"Resting," she lied. "Just resting."

In an uncharacteristic move for a woman so petite and pregnant, Laurel threw her weight forward, bumped Alix out of her way and strode in. "Ugh!" A handkerchief was scrambled to her face. "Alix, you're ill!"

"Bad food, a fall cold. It's nothing. It will pass," she murmured, humiliated.

Laurel's narrow eyes said she didn't believe a word of it. "You come up to your room countless times a day."

"Because I like to be alone! I live for the moments when boredom and mindlessness overtake me to the point my body will do nothing but sleep." Now that she was started, she couldn't stop, the words pouring out in a torrent of bottled anger and pain. "The moments that let me forget that my brother's wife did *worse* than try to murder me, while *he* stood idly by." She inhaled, opened her mouth again. Before she could continue, her guts lurched out a warning, sending her dashing behind the screen.

When the wave finally passed, Alix fell onto her backside and leaned her head against the wall. With no small amount of effort, Laurel sat next to her and smoothed a cool hand over her forehead. "How many days?"

"Not the first day that I remember coming to, but every day since. My stomach hurts all the time. I tolerate food one meal, and then I don't the next. Tea tastes like poison, bitter metal. Maybe that is how Paulina fed it to me."

Laurel looked stricken, tears glistening in the corners of her eyes. "I think we should send for Doctor Ashby. Perhaps whatever Paulina gave you is still affecting your body. There might be something he can do, recommend."

Alix tried breathing through her panic, refusing to accept that things were so dire, needing to believe that she was getting better. At least, she'd tried to, up to this point. But as the sickness continued, her will had worn down. In the face of everything Paulina had used to drug her, who was to say there weren't poisons in the mix? Not accepting did not make it go away.

Another cramp gripped her belly, and she nodded at Laurel's anxious stare.

CHAPTER TWENTY-SEVEN

Old Bailey, London – October 3rd, 1814

Spencer sat alone among the others in the gallery, Bennet having gone to Broadmoore and Ethan moving from tardy to absent with each passing minute. He jerked out his watch and checked it again, not encouraged by its answer.

His eyes fell again and again in the dim light to Paulina, standing with other prisoners in the dock and conspicuous by her well-kempt hair and clean clothes. Prisoners with money were afforded better accommodations within Newgate's cells than their destitute counterparts. But she had come in by the same door as the toothless pickpocket beside her, and when her trial was over, he hoped to see her leave by the same way.

Now and then one lawyer traded places with another. The jury grumbled and tipped their powdered heads to one another; a clerk flitted from a podium to the bench and back. A gavel banged, a sentence was bellowed out, and without fail the next prisoner along the line buried her face in her hands.

Judge Symonds was not swayed by any of their pleas; false accusations, children, a promise to change. Not even claims of pregnancy spared the women who pleaded the fullness of their bellies; it only delayed the inevitable.

And then there was Paulina. Symonds had been conspicuously hesitant where Mrs. Paton was concerned, which was strange for a man who had sent a twelve-year-old girl to the gallows for thieving. Watching Symonds and Paulina now, Spencer's confidence reached an all-time low. Symonds looked bored, and Paulina unconcerned.

When it was her turn, Lawrence stepped in front of the bench, swishing his black frock and preening, patting his wig and engineering the moment for maximum tension. He hung his narrow head, an already small frame dwarfed by the courtroom's towering architecture. Then he swept an arm at Paulina in a crescendo of silence. "Your honor..." he drawled, words pulled long by a weariness that, his tone asserted, must be felt by His Honor, too. "We have explored the case against Mrs. Paton to an exhausting degree and –"

A bang like a pistol shot echoed through the room, cutting his words off. Spencer ducked, and raised a hand to shield his face in reflex.

Lawrence flinched too, and ducked where he stood. A woman screamed in the gallery above.

A murmur spread through the room like wildfire. Spencer traced its origin, and turned to find that both of the courtroom's high, panel doors stood open, thrown wide with a violence that had crashed them into the wall.

Grayfield's long figure, from polished hat to boots, cut the opening in two. Ethan didn't enjoy orchestration, and as a matter of course he did not enjoy attention, Spencer knew as a fact.

However, he very much enjoyed making a point. Spencer recognized, by a lift of Ethan's chin and an unconcerned set to his shoulders, that he was doing just that.

"Really!" shouted Lawrence, still half-crouched and rightly looking intimidated. "Who allowed this interruption? This affront to justice?"

"Lord Grayfield," boomed Symonds from on high, "I must agree with the honorable Mister Lawrence. Even a man so venerable as yourself cannot be allowed theatrics, not in my courtroom."

Ethan removed his hat, bowed, and took four lazy strides into the courtroom, each movement an obscene reply to Symonds's objection. He took his time, reaching into his coat for papers which might have been in his hand all the while, then dusted his lapel and indulged a few more steps.

The murmuring around Spencer had quieted to whispers which now ignited in every direction. He craned his neck, along

232

with everyone else, to get a good look at what Ethan was about, the clever bastard.

"I come," Ethan paused and raised his papers, "on Crown authority, and under the auspices of the Whitehall Office."

Lawrence held frozen near the dock, and Symonds shifted his corpulent frame against his high-back chair. "To what end?"

Ethan paused just long enough for the tension to build to a palpable level. "Your Honor has been the victim of a scheme."

Excited whispers. A woman behind Spencer gasped with the same thrill she might have felt at Drury Lane.

"And the defendant Mrs. Paton has perpetrated it cleverly," he continued, turning to address all assembled. "So cleverly that I say with absolute confidence that Your Honor has been living in *fear* for some days now."

The look on Symonds face assured that no such thing had been occurring, but his silence told Spencer that Ethan knew as much, and that he was on to something more.

"Mrs. Paton has blackmailed you, and perhaps even Mister Lawrence here, as both of you are shareholders in her father's shipping company. No doubt these are the means by which she has manipulated you."

Understanding formed in Spencer cold and sudden like a douse of water. Symonds and Lawrence owned stock in Van der Verre, but they were not victims. They had made an arrangement with Paulina, and perhaps Silas himself, to pad their pockets and allow Paulina to go free.

Ethan strode toward the bench now with purpose, waving his perfectly creased packet of documents. "What she did not impart to you is the most crucial bit. The shares she's offered in order to buy your silence are not hers to give away. They were purchased months ago by an A. Rowan." He held the papers out for Symonds to inspect, and the man's face blanched with each turn of the page.

Knowing Ethan as he did, and now appreciating Bennet's remark about aiding him, Spencer guessed there was more in the packet than a simple matter of shares.

"No," murmured Paulina, stiff save for a shaking head. "No, no."

Ethan rocked up onto his toes, pointing out one of the pages for Symonds. "Pardons for you both have been secured; you'll see my signature, just there. Your good names will not be tarnished by this unfortunate scheme."

Symonds wrestled his weight up from the chair, hand pressed to his ample chest. He sagged with enough relief that he might have been on stage, and then raised a hand to the heavens.

"I have lived as a prisoner, lo these many days, suffering as much under the machinations of that woman," he wagged a trembling finger at Paulina, whose throat worked like a piston, "as those whose suffering brought her unto Newgate. To be unburdened at last..." He clutched a meaty fist at Ethan, and then dabbed his eyes, "I cannot express to you, Lord Grayfield, my unabating gratitude."

"Oh," drawled Ethan, turning away from the bench, "It was *my* pleasure." Ethan held for maximum effect and made a bow to each juror and counselor in turn. He raised his hat to Paulina in passing and planted it atop his head at a jaunty angle.

Spencer caught a wink thrown his way and then, as Ethan passed beyond the courtroom doors, pandemonium erupted.

CHAPTER TWENTY-EIGHT

Newgate Prison, Old Bailey Street – Evening, October 3rd, 1814

Bit by rain falling outside the protection of the Newgate Prison's high stone arch, Spencer stood shoulder-to-shoulder with Ethan at the crest of a surging crowd. The shouts at their backs were deafening, men and women crying out in condemnation or simply making noises of contempt. Old and new sweat, stale booze, and tobacco wafted up in an invisible haze, adding to the general seediness.

Waving fists behind him toppled his hat to the scaffold's base for a third time, and Spencer ducked to claim it. When he stood, Ethan was blandly sweeping cabbage from the sleeve of his navy greatcoat. "Like Prussian artillery," he muttered beneath the roar, raising a brow meaningfully at Spencer. They had already been pelted countless times by produce and worse under the frenzied aim of a bloodthirsty mob.

"Why?" Spencer jammed an elbow behind him, knocking back a toothless loudmouth he had practically worn for the last quarter hour.

"Why *what*?"

"Why would you wear a Weston to the Newgate gallows?" Spencer narrowed his eyes. "Is this Major Burrell's doing?"

"Major Burrell cuts a smart figure as far as the ladies are concerned. I don't know that I'd mock him so freely. Besides," Ethan patted down his double row of silver buttons, "my wife likes me in this coat. A *great* deal, as it happens."

Spencer opened his mouth for a retort, but stopped as he caught a hush falling over the crowd.

235

The Bailey's iron gate swung open. Two blue-uniformed constables filed out ahead of a gaunt, wild eyed minister who was bald in a patchy way that made Spencer wonder if the man had plucked his hair from nerves just before making his exit.

He was right to look afraid. Spencer estimated a good wind would snap the man in half inside his dumpy black cassock, which was half what the crowd would do if a riot ensued. It was a real possibility tonight, judging by a thrum of hysteria that pulsed from over his shoulder.

Despite a damp sting of a stormy October night, hundreds had turned out for the hanging. Three at once, *that* was something by itself, but a woman, too? No wag-tongue fishwife would miss such a rare spectacle. Yet, despite showing up for the event, a good many *were* missing it. The crowd stretched as far as the eye could see down both sides of Old Bailey, filling a wide cobblestone square at one corner, where it met with Newgate Prison. Wet stone walls boxed them in on every side of the square. Poor rowhouses across from the massive institution were used for coin and entertainment. Families hung from windows and clever landlords had let their roofs for a modest fee, but not every spectator who wanted a closer look was going to get it.

This had traditionally led to arguing, and more than a few colorful insults scented with beer. Onlookers took sides, even when they were strangers to the fighting parties. Someone threw a rock, another a fist, and then a brawl would spread like a barn fire all the way to Ludgate Hill.

Spencer braced at the idea, eyeing a thin number of constables present to address such a riot, and raised his hat to the passing minister who managed a weak nod. Poor bastard.

The two men shuffled out next, arms bound by thick ropes behind their backs. Adams was the tall, greasy-haired one, his horse face as marked by the pox as an 'R' branding his left and right cheeks. Two rapes in Spencer's estimation was two too many, and still there were more he claimed as victims. He had heard the accusations against Adams in the dock, waiting for Paulina to be brought out the first time. Faceless voices in the crowd around him now shouted names of other women. Two men waved kitchen knives calling eagerly for the man's bollocks.

Spencer wished them success; Adams' final victim had been a child.

The second man Spencer knew nothing about, except that he was leering, portly, and in a few minutes he would be half an inch longer than he was now. That was all he cared to know.

Beside him Ethan tensed and braced him with a shoulder. Now it was Paulina's turn. The crowd behind them positively crackled with tension.

In different circumstances, he would have laughed when she stepped out into the street. Her ruff-necked brown satin dress was the height of fashion, and her matching cap pinned to a mound of gold curls that would have done for a ball.

"Long live the queen!" someone shouted. It echoed through the crowd, followed by cheering and guffaws as she was marched along. She stabbed them all with haughty glances, pausing when she passed him. "How does it feel to hang a woman?" she hissed.

"No less satisfying than if you were a man." No pleasure or joy, nothing more than a settling of accounts. Paulina was here to pay as owed, and he would bear witness to see that it occurred. Together with Ethan they tipped their hats in unison. There was more to say on her twisted lips, but before she could open her mouth a guard prodded her, sputtering, on towards the steps.

The gallows were really a coffin without the sides, he thought. Stout wooden beams formed supports and a frame at its top. The structure extended in a long triangle from the wall of Newgate gaol, twelve feet up, and its paneled scaffolding could be brought out or put away at notice. Ropes and mechanisms formed its guts, an empty belly inside waiting to devour convicts above. At its base were six stairs, all that stood between Paulina Paton and a fate better than she deserved.

"Goddammit all," muttered Ethan jamming him with an elbow, pointing to the street at the platform's far end.

Chas Paton, pale and utterly lit, judging by bleary eyes and slack limbs, hung back between two shouting, scrubby-haired women. Spencer was about to tell Ethan that if Chas wanted the satisfaction of seeing Paulina's end, he deserved it. Then he caught what Ethan had been trying to point out: Chas's hand stuffed deep inside his coat front.

237

Ethan rushed out first, being the one with any sort of credentials, as a crown agent. Spencer certainly did not envy him that tonight. Ethan's top hat raised and lowered at the lunge of each constable, obliging him to bark, "Whitehall, Whitehall," over the seething crowd so that the guards let them pass to reach Chas.

Chas spotted them too late. He turned to run, but Ethan's long legs swept his feet from under him and Spencer took a firm grasp on Chas's coat. A few offended spectators shoved Chas as he fell into them, and Spencer used that momentum, hurling him face first into the prison's rough stone wall.

His boots scuffed wet grit atop the pavement. He growled, grunted, and then stilled, panting beneath a point of Spencer's elbow in his back.

"What is in your coat, Paton?" demanded Spencer.

"Go to hell!"

Ethan clucked his tongue, leaning left then right around Chas, shoving an arm between his torso and the wall.

Ethan held hands aloft to display his prizes, and Spencer let Chas go with a whistle. "I can fathom a man carrying one, but what reason could you possibly have for a pair of dogs, Paton?"

Chas snatched at the pistols, but Ethan raised them higher, stepping back and slipping them inside his own coat. From behind them the minister's warbling voice raised above the crowd, reaching the middle of the Lord's Prayer. Chas covered his face and sobbed. "I can make this up to Alix. Paulina is my doing. A man has an obligation to make things right."

"A man does not present himself at the Old Bailey with a brace of pistols as though it's a Newcastle mining camp." This from Ethan, who crossed his arms, bearing all the emotion of marble.

"And the second pistol, Chas. What was the purpose?" asked Spencer, though he already knew.

"I failed!" He leaned in, beating fists against his chest. Spencer winced as Chas's rum and garlic breath fanned his face. "I couldn't protect the business, or my sister," he cried. "Not even myself!"

Now he was crying in earnest, a braying miserable sound waving in and out in time with his drunken swaying. Ethan tipped him a nod, and Spencer hung his arm around Chas's neck. "You will thank me for this, eventually."

He held Chas fast in the vice of his elbow, pressing at two throbbing points on his neck until eyes rolled back and he fell limp to the gutter. Leaning down, he rested fingers at Chas's throat and, feeling the steady beat, nodded. Together they hefted him up against a wall, out of the foot traffic. "There. We've spared him further embarrassment." He leaned back, sizing up Chas's unconscious heap. "Or, at least the awareness of it."

Spencer glanced behind them. "And we've spared him the memory of what's to come."

The hangman had draped all three of his prizes with their ropes. Adams and the other convict were anonymous twins now, heads buried inside fraying and dirty linen hoods. The hangman had stopped before Paulina, the minister taking the same position behind her. There was an exchange between the three, Paulina's lips repeating the same desperate phrase, eyes wide and searching the crowd beyond her executioner. Spencer could not hear her voice over the din, but he could read her lips plainly: *I was obedient.*

And there it was, three words to form the root of all the evil she had committed. There was no penitence or contrition, but blind obedience to her father. It had spurred her on and salved her conscience all at once, until now when it found her abandoned.

Producing a hood for his last victim, the thick fingered executioner struggled with Paulina's hair, trying to pull it down, then reaching for her cap. That unleashed a sharp tirade at the indignity, Paulina bobbing and ducking until Spencer was certain she'd put herself through the floor early.

The minister fished out his own handkerchief, which ignited a new struggle as the two men attempted to cinch it around her head. Paulina's entire face flushed while she hurled profanity at their efforts. Finally, the hangman untied the sweaty, dirt streaked kerchief from around his tree-trunk neck. The bickering began in earnest, Paulina struggling to pull her face away from the hangman in front and the minister's entreaties behind, all at once. The last of her dignity shredded, and Spencer felt some divine retribution in the moment.

Behind them, the crowd rose in pitch and seethed, unhappy with the delay. If they didn't get this settled and proceed, more than the three up on the platform would need to be buried.

Ethan shifted foot to foot, watching Paulina's struggle, grim-faced. "Thank the lord we spared him."

Spencer nodded his silent agreement, feeling more sympathy for Chas than he'd thought possible.

Perhaps faced with inevitability, Paulina stopped struggling so that the stained rag could be tied over her face. The minister stepped back and raised his hands across the three, his small voice reaching just to the crowd's edge. "May God have mercy on thy souls."

Absolute silence fell over all assembled, and it was still enough that Spencer thought he caught a ship's bell out on the Thames.

The hangman grunted out his count: *One, two, three.*

Thump. The trap door slamming open was an offhand remark; a dull, short sound making plain that it had done the same a thousand times without scruple.

Both men's necks snapped, and both went limp. Paulina, being lighter, was not so lucky. Her shoulders rowed and her feet pumped staccato, a drowning woman struggling for air that wouldn't come. Spencer's stomach clenched; after all that Paulina done, he wanted justice but not suffering. He refused to close his eyes; he would see it through. After what felt like an eternity, Paulina spasmed and finally stilled and twisted limp in her noose.

He had watched until it was finished and marked the moment when Paulina had paid her debt. He lowered his head, eyes closed, and exhaled.

A roar swelled over him, the crowd undulating forward as one giant body, pressing them toward the scaffold. Men and women rushed the steps ahead of laggard sentries, and surgeon's assistants eager for their next autopsy, next experiment. They could claim bodies ahead of the family, ahead of the mob, and that caused trouble.

Spencer knew what would happen now; he'd seen plenty of the same violence in France. The crowd expected more than the show they'd received so far. The atrocities that would follow were grotesque: shorn hair and even limbs passed around as amusements, souvenirs. It reduced the living to not much better than the executed, in his opinion.

Spencer drew his pistol, Ethan following suit with Chas's pair. One he aimed overhead, and they each trained a muzzle on the crowd while the constable's men cried for order.

A few daring hands slapped at his barrel, and cries of 'traitor' rose here and there. He was disgusted by the outburst, and his pistol was aimed for self-preservation. He had no interest being crushed by hoodlums in their rush to defile a dead murderess.

With both pistols ahead now, Ethan opened a path through the crowd. Spencer grabbed a fistful of Chas's coat as they passed, dragging him along the scaffold until they reached the Bailey Gate.

Magistrate Arindale, peering between the iron bars, shooed them in quickly. His eyes darted from Ethan to a limp Chas, looking urgent.

A wide hand pressed Spencer's shoulder in the dark passage, Arindale jostling him with a pat. "Well lad, it's done."

Spencer only nodded, no words left for this day.

It was done.

CHAPTER TWENTY-NINE

Broadmoore – October 5th, 1814

Alix gained the yard at the foot of the pond just in time. The sun was brilliant overhead, but fall was fall and a sudden breeze worked itself inside the plush lining of her amber velvet pelisse. She would be just the right amount of frozen by the time she reached the gate.

Broadmoore was a burden on John, but it *was* magnificent, framed by the rust and crimson leaves clinging to its ancient oaks. She had come to appreciate that on her daily walks. Laurel had cautioned her against the exertion, but Doctor Ashby was in Scotland, too far away to agree with her friend, and Alix couldn't bear to sit inside every day. She had been surprised to discover that her time outside was the only time she felt well. Just over a week of long walks, light meals, and Bennet's company had left her renewed.

Turning up the drive, she noticed a sturdy black carriage in front of the house. At first, she mistook it for John's, and felt exhausted on his behalf that he was called away so often. She was nearly at the top of the pond now, and she squinted, realizing her mistake. The embossed arms on its door were all wrong; a rampant argent lion stood silver against a black and white shield. The carriage's wheels were narrower, finely crafted and more expensive than what John and Laurel could afford.

Her heart stopped, skipped, and Alix began to run. Through the gate and across the drive, nearly spilling herself on the steps. She sped into the hall and halfway up the steps before she reined herself in, panting and struggling with where she should look first.

242

"Alexandra."

Alix froze, closed her eyes and enjoyed the small thrill which ran up her back at his voice. She turned slowly and made herself wait until she ached, before laying eyes on.

He stood inside the front door, looking up at her unblinking.

Spencer had changed along with the season. His bronze skin had faded to a bare olive. His chestnut hair, clipped short, barely peeked from beneath his polished beaver hat. A neat cravat, tailored great coat, heavy boots, and thick kid gloves transformed him into a polished London gentleman. Her breath caught just as it had on seeing him at Haywood, and suddenly the empty space between then and now collapsed.

Spencer lifted his hat and bowed. Three gallant strides brought him to the foot of the stairs, and there he stopped. His face said what his words did not; he was waiting for permission, an invitation. She grasped the banister against her swimming head and started down. On the last stair, when they were nearly eye to eye, she held. His body heat drew her in; a wave of cedar and bergamot tipped her over the top, memories flooding back. For a moment Alix forced her breath to come slowly.

Spencer peeled a glove from one stout hand. He ran bare knuckles across hers, achingly slow before fitting their fingers together. His hazel eyes met hers.

Alix appreciated that she should not have thrown herself from the step with such force when his knees buckled. Thank goodness for his athletic grace. His lips pressed to hers with a hesitant pressure, desire held in check. Her arms around his neck elicited a groan which could have been pleasure or pain. Perhaps a bit of both; it certainly was for her.

There was something visceral about the small border of bare neck between his hairline and collar. She pressed it with her fingers and felt a part of herself revive.

Spencer pulled away first, a matter of a few inches which left a physical ache around her heart. Eyes closed, he was still, holding on to her with a stiff grip while the rise and fall of his chest calmed. Then he reached inside his greatcoat and produced two similar-sized letters. They were written on fine paper, she noticed as he held them out, not cheap foolscap. "My second and

243

third most valuable possessions," he whispered. "I put *all* of my time in London to good use."

Alix claimed them with uncertain fingers and studied a bold but illegible signature on the first. "I felt you were there a lifetime," she murmured.

"I hope you'll forgive me, particularly when you've read these."

She pried open the first, crumbling off bits of its already broken red seal. The words were long and slanted, but more legible than the exterior. Alix skimmed its three brief lines:

'In response to your letter of October one, Field Marshal the Duke of Wellington grants leave to wed and habitate. Maj. General Lord Spencer Reed and Miss Paton may choose a day of their own convenience. Felicitations to the pair on this most happy occasion.'

Tears pricked her eyes, and she dared only a quick glance at Spencer's anxious gaze, afraid the dam would break. The second letter was much longer, and more important if one judged it solely on the number of finely scrolled capital letters. But she didn't have to read the entire body; its heading was enough:

'Charles, by Divine Providence the Archbishop of Canterbury...', followed by both their names halfway down the page. A special marriage license.

"Any day we choose," he added, taking the papers back from her trembling fingers. "If you've not changed your mind."

Alix grabbed his face in both hands and brought her mouth to his. It was chaste, as kisses went, between a man and woman with so much ardent history.

That was how Laurel and John found them. Alix wasn't sure how long they'd been like that before a feminine and masculine clearing of throats from near the drawing room door pulled them back into the moment. Alix startled, but Spencer made it clear with a hand at her nape that he would not be rushed.

"Alix, Doctor Erroll has come in Doctor Ashby's stead. He's waiting upstairs to speak with you," said Laurel, a suspicious pull at the corners of her mouth and eyes averted.

Spencer's eyes snapped to hers. "Why, what is the matter?"

Neither the doctor's arrival nor her worry would douse this moment. "It's nothing now." She smiled and brushed his cheek, touching him again just for the pleasure of it. "Absolutely nothing."

*   *   *

It was something.

Despite Alix's assurances, he could not suppress the fear that had held his heart at the mention of the doctor. Spencer gripped his chair's smooth arm, stilling an urge to pace, shout, to shake something or someone.

Instead, he got up, settled beside Alix on the bed, and took her cold fingers. She was still staring, shaking her head with a slow repetition as though she could shake off Doctor Erroll's words. "I still do not understand. It was a matter of weeks."

Erroll's thin lips pursed tighter. "Substance, not duration," he snapped, smacking a white crock labeled 'Leeches' back into his leather valise. Spencer watched them go, convinced the breakdown in the doctor-patient relationship could be traced to Alix's refusing to allow their use. It was common practice, but he wouldn't insist she bow to the whims of a man like Erroll.

"You were administered all manner of substances. They react with food, with drink. Miasmas encourage their potency." He snapped his bag shut, signaling an end to the discussion. "Miss Paton, you are a mature woman. It is likely this malignancy has been increasing for years. This alleged poisoning only helped matters along."

'Alleged' brought Spencer from the bed in one motion. He took Erroll's bony arm in one hand, throwing open the door with his other. Out went the man, out went the bag, and Spencer slammed the door behind him, drowning out his irate sputtering.

Alix had turned on her side and was buried now beneath her quilts. For a moment he watched her, clenching his fists, entirely helpless. Then he lay down and pulled her against him, nuzzling into the sweet smell of her hair. He pressed a hand over her belly. "He doesn't know that it's cancer, Alexandra. He doesn't know his arse from a boot-jack."

245

"What do we do?" she cried softly. "*We* don't know either. That's the hardest part."

"I'll get a second opinion. Ashby or someone else. A third, if it comes to it." He squeezed her tighter. "A doctor who can do his damned job."

*   *   *

A rumble of carriage wheels on the drive brought Spencer to the hall, where he paced until the Hastings' ancient twig of a butler appeared and opened the door.

Bennet's account had influenced him, but Spencer acknowledged it had not been a detailed one. They had mostly barked and stomped over her experience, her skill, her sex. Not how young she was. How dangerously comely for a woman entrenched with eight hundred red-blooded, malefactor, foul-mouthed Englishmen.

The moment that thought had passed, Spencer knew what had saved her.

Everything about Kate Foster's *appearance* was sensible. She wore a plain, blue wool coat over a blue and white calico dress and smart white apron. There were no capelets or embroidery, no bare arms or teasing neckline. Even the brown grosgrain ribbon on her chipped straw bonnet shrugged off any attention, plainly announcing it was only there out of necessity. She was *sensible*, save for rebellious chestnut curls sweeping her cheeks and a perpetual lift to the left side of her mouth hinting at mischief.

Spencer got the impression there was a good deal more than 'sensible' humming beneath the surface when he took her hand and shook it. She didn't curtsy and didn't duck her eyes from his. Skeptical as he was of her abilities, he already admired her frankness.

"Lord Reed." Her voice was rich, American, with a long New York drawl to her words that reminded him of Alix.

"Miss Foster. A pleasure." He was about to offer tea, bring her to Laurel and make the usual trying few minutes of small talk.

Kate swept a hand at the staircase, taking command. "Let's go up."

He gathered her bag and filed up behind her. "You are very prompt, Miss Foster."

"The enemy doesn't break for tea." Hands clapped. "Forward march."

Spencer chuckled in spite of himself and caused Kate to stop before the landing and turn around. One brow formed a cheeky arch above her dancing blue eyes. "Your brother accounts you no sense of humor. I'm delighted that he misled me."

Reserving adjectives on his brother's character, Spencer nodded. "Where the army is concerned, one must learn to laugh."

Kate paused again at the door, and cocked her head. "Reed. You were at Badajoz in 1812."

The information startled him speechless a moment. "I was. Over the 95th Rifles."

She made an *X* with her finger, low on the left side of his coat. "You have a very nasty scar there."

He stared, dumbfounded, unable for even a second to recall a thing about *her*. Though, when he considered it, that was no surprise. The weather that spring was shite, nothing but cold and mud, sometimes sporting torrential rain that lasted for days. A French garrison blasting away. Entering the town itself – Spencer shuddered, willing himself to forget the way his boots had pressed on his fallen brothers, tripping him, a landslide of dead men tumbling out from the walls. He closed his eyes, blotting it out. "You were at Badajoz too, then."

"I was," Kate answered, somber. "That is where *I* learned to laugh."

Laugh, or go mad. He knew the feeling well. "You have an impressive memory, Miss Foster."

The shake of her head was almost imperceptible. "It's not a difficult task, recalling the ones who *live*."

He stared back at her a moment, something in her gaze speaking to him in a way civilians did not understand. Then he nodded, remembering their purpose, and opened the door.

Alix scooted up the bed at their entrance. Her eyes were shadowed by faint bruises under them, and she was dreadfully

247

pale, her color more of a contrast when framed by the little pink roses embroidered on her quilt.

"Miss Foster." Alix was smiling, but Spencer knew her well. Her eyes were measuring, calculating, taking Kate in. The misdiagnosis and ineptitude she'd suffered after Paulina's torment had filled her with a healthy distrust of doctors in general.

"Miss Paton." Kate claimed her bag from him and settled it on the foot of the bed.

"It was very kind of you, coming all the way up to see me."

Kate swatted away the thanks. "The army's in camps, and I detest London. The moment Major Burrell and Major Ford conclude their business there, I will board the first ship bound for Paris. Or swim the channel, if they tarry too long."

"It pains me to hear you speak so of my beloved country," he teased, settling beside Alix on the bed.

Kate laughed while producing a small strip of paper and pencil stub from her bag. "It's not your country that bothers me. I think we're all sorry about the tea by now." She winked here at Alix. "It's just London. The whole city is an invitation to catch the plague. It's nothing but noise, sewage, and soot. Public spitting. Public urination. Rats." She shook, ticking off each one on her fingers. "A sanitation nightmare."

He liked her better by the minute.

A knock at the door interrupted any further denigration of the great city. Laurel's maid Mary poked in her brown head.

Spencer opened his mouth to speak, but Kate beat him to it. "Hot water, just half a kettle please, and a basin." She tossed a smile at Mary's owl eyes. "I've brought soap and towels."

The door snapped shut. He couldn't be certain if it was out of surprise or annoyance.

Beside him, Alix drew a ragged breath. "Miss Foster, I want to know what can be done about this malignancy. If I'll ever get well or go on this way. And if I'm dying then –"

Spencer tried not to hear the words, to keep his mind in perfect stasis and free of thoughts and diagnosis, until Kate's verdict was in. It was the only way he'd discovered to keep his gut from clenching.

248

Kate stopped rifling her bag, reached out, and grasped Alix's wrist with obvious pressure. "The first thing you're going to do is toss from your mind everything that Doctor Erroll told you. His report is not worth the shoddy paper on which it's written."

Curious, Spencer stood up from the bed. He wanted to accept what she was saying, but there was evidence against it. "Doctor Erroll is a well-regarded physician. He tends a great many families in these parts. I believe he went to a very fine school."

Chuckling, Kate set her coarse linen towels and a round cake of soap atop the empty washstand. "Attending a school means you have money, not ability." When she turned back, it was to Alix. "Did he examine you, Miss Paton? Put a hand on you anywhere?"

"He felt my pulses."

"And then he took a history?"

"A short one. He read Doctor Ashby's notes, asked me what I had felt since ..." Alix reached for his hand and he took it, willing her strength.

"Bennet has summarized what you endured." said Kate, earning his esteem by sparing Alix further explanation. "And then I'd imagine Erroll brought out the leeches, to balance your female humors or drain excess blood from the growth or some other nonsense."

If Miss Foster were fortunetelling, she was doing a fine job. She was beginning to sway him.

Mary reappeared with the steaming basin, settling it beside Kate's towels. Spencer caught the woman's furtive glances, craning her neck as she bustled out for a look at the American girl's witchcraft. He, too, was curious to see what she could do that a seasoned physician could not.

When Mary had gone, Kate planted fists on her hips. "The report sent last week to my sponsor, Doctor Addison, says Doctor Erroll believes at worst you've been exposed to bad humors which have manifested in your abdomen. In his opinion, there is nothing truly wrong with you."

"Bastard." He would put the man's nose flat given the first opportunity.

Alix shook her head, fingers trembling against his. "But he said it was a malignancy, a tumor."

"Again, put whatever he said from your mind." What he inferred, and Kate was too diplomatic to say, was that Erroll likely made all sorts of dire and protracted predictions. For money.

Kate turned to the basin and dipped her hands into the cloud of steam. "Down to your chemise," she said to Alix, lathering between her fingers with the soap.

Mystified by the activity, Spencer snapped back to attention. "I am not leaving."

Kate glanced over a shoulder, looking him up and down. "I didn't ask you to. That is Miss Paton's decision."

He was liking her more and more.

Alix squeezed his hand tighter, then sat forward. "Help with my laces?"

He would rather not. Days of behaving like a gentleman, of trying not to look at her body, motivated by a pang at how thin she'd become, had worn on him. Seeing the damage that had been done to her ground at him as nothing in his life had ever done before.

Oblivious, Alix turned her back, raising her curls until her neck was bare. Spencer pinched her ties and pulled, feeling himself unlace along with her dress.

"Spencer, your fingers are trembling." Alix was staring over her shoulder pointedly, and he cleared his throat, glancing from her to Miss Foster's back.

"What is wrong?" she whispered.

"Not now," he ground out. "It is not a complaint for mixed company."

"Oh. *Oh!*" Alix's eyes widened and she smiled, falling back onto the quilt in a smug heap. Let her think it was desire; he wasn't about to tell her that it was heartbreak.

Kate buffed her hands with a towel, rubbed them together and then settled on the edge of the bed. "Arm up." She prodded under each of Alix's arms, pressed both breasts, massaged the right and left sides beneath her ribs. There was a confidence to Kate's touch which put him at ease. Alix too, judging by her closed eyes and even breathing.

250

Kate listed off Alix's symptoms. "Sweats, vomiting, fatigue. What else?" Standing, she folded the quilt down to Alix's hips.

"My heart," said Alix. "Sometimes it cramps and races. I taste copper or metal in my mouth all the time."

Nodding, Kate's three fingers rolled in lines, navel to pubic bone. Spencer couldn't help watching, fascinated by a process infinitely more involved than anything Doctor Erroll had done.

"Monthly courses?" asked Kate.

"I don't know. Not since I've recovered. They've never been timely."

"Mm."

When she reached the bottom of her second pass, Kate paused and frowned. She cupped Alexandra's belly and circled with her palm.

Spencer swallowed a lump and wondered if Doctor Erroll was about to be proved right.

Straightening, Kate held up a hand. "I'm going to press a hand to your backside, the other to your belly. There'll be a great deal of pressure. Speak up if it hurts."

An arm snaked under the blanket, under Alix's legs as though Kate were about to scoop her up. Pointing her middle and index fingers, she pushed in and down, between Alix's hips.

Alix's fingers gripped his and she grimaced. He reached to stop Kate's, but she pushed him away with a tap of her elbow. "Last one." She pressed deep, until Alix winced.

"Doctor Erroll never laid a hand on you?" Kate snorted. "What an ass." Chuckling, she stood up, went back to the basin and splashed off her hands.

He exchanged a glance with Alix, who raised her brows and shrugged.

"I have news," Kate said finally, "though I don't know if it's the news you'd hoped for."

Spencer held his breath until spots exploded at the edge of his vision.

"There's no sign of a malignancy, and nothing I can detect that would make me suspect cancer. But you are pregnant, Miss Paton. Four months, give or take."

251

Closing his eyes, Spencer tried to hear the words again, to absorb their meaning. He tamped a thrill in his heart, too frightened to trust something like good news. When he opened them, Alexandra stared up at him, eyes bright with worry, chewing her lip. He smiled at her, then nodded to Kate. "I think that is precisely the news we had hoped for." Alix exhaled, going limp everywhere but in her hand, which gripped his fiercely.

Kate wrapped the soap in her used towel and stuffed them back into her bag. She cocked an eyebrow at them, a small smile playing across her lips. "By that answer I assume that you, Lord Reed, are the other responsible half in this."

His role was implied but hardly stated. Men and women sired children in all sorts of complicated arrangements. Still, he bristled at the question. "I am."

Kate threw her hands up, placating. "I am certainly not in a position to cast the first stone. But as the father you should be aware of some things." While she talked, she swirled in a kind of dance, putting away her ledger, gathering up her bonnet, and at last coming to rest again, seated on the bed.

First, she addressed Alix. "You are not the oldest mother I have ever attended by far, but this pregnancy is not without risk. You *are* older, and that means taking plenty of care." Her blue eyes fell, full mouth turning down so that Spencer's heart clenched, and she glanced to him. "The real worry is one we can do nothing about. I have no idea what effects the amounts and combinations of things you were forced to take might have on your baby. There may be very little, none at all," Kate shrugged matter-of-factly, "or you may lose the pregnancy."

"Oh God." Alix buried her face in her hands. Her desperate cry shred his heart.

Spencer steeled himself for Alexandra's sake. "When?"

"Well," Kate rubbed hands together eagerly, looking at Alix, "you've been recovered for several weeks. You've had no cramping or spotting, so we're off on the right foot. Now we'll wait for the baby to move. It'll be a lengthy wait; another month perhaps. But I have assignments for you both, and that should help pass the time."

This, he could tolerate. He understood orders, assignments. Anything to keep busy.

"Miss Paton, no London diet for you. Eat only meat taken directly from the animal, fish from the pond, and produce from the winter garden. Eat plenty, but nothing heavy, pickled or preserved. Drink boiled spring water in quantity. Give up the tea." Kate pulled a sad face. "It pains me to even say those words aloud, but I think it's only agitating your belly." Spencer and Alix exchanged relieved glances.

"And you," she stood and pinned him with a delicate finger, "do not keep or allow anyone else to keep her bed-bound. She's pregnant, not paralyzed. A walk, especially in clean air, will help her nausea, her fatigue, and prepare her for labor. Take her out every day, at least until the snow falls."

Some of the pall left Alix's face. "Walks *have* helped me these past few days."

"Good." Kate looked pleased, as much with the patient as with herself. "As a general rule, do what feels best." She stood up, wrestled her bonnet on tighter and took up her case. "If you experience headaches or swelling of the face and feet, someone should be sent for. I have no idea *who*. Ashby, maybe. He seems to have some sense."

Alix had relaxed into the pillow beside him, but now she sat up. "Miss Foster, you won't say anything to my cousins? We aren't …" Alix glanced at him and of all things, blushed. "We would appreciate breaking it in our own way."

Kate snorted, shaking her head as he stood to walk her out. "As I said, my own web is a bit tangled at the moment."

Spencer grinned, relieved and amused that *something* in life discomposed charming Miss Foster. He recalled an aside in Bennet's letter. "British major?"

Kate rolled her eyes. "Portuguese captain."

*　　　*　　　*

She dressed while Spencer saw Miss Foster to the door. Even those few minutes felt like a lifetime in the face of the news they'd been given. Alix paused to cradle her belly, just beginning to trust Miss Foster's diagnosis. A baby; her head swam.

She was finishing with her clothes when Spencer slipped in. Fighting her nerves, Alix avoided the topic of the baby. Instead she glanced over her shoulder and smiled. "I like her. Very much."

"She's American. You all like each other." He seated himself on the bureau and winked.

"We're very likable people."

"Mm."

"I wish she could stay, and we could see her more often."

He frowned. "She's back to trudging with the army. Wouldn't even allow me to pay her."

"What!"

"Gave me a letter and asked that I please pass it along to Lord Bathurst. Apparently, some concerning reports about her regimental commander, Braddock. Anyhow, it's an embarrassingly small amount of effort, considering what she's done for us."

Alix presented him with her back so he could tie her laces, trying to think of something else glib to say, but she couldn't. "I'm frightened," she admitted finally.

Warm hands turned her around, and he pressed her head to his shoulder. "I'm not. We're together, Alexandra. I thought we could be married on Saturday, if you're willing." He cradled her face, and pressed a firm kiss to her forehead. "We'll take care of each other. And the baby. And if it isn't meant to be …" Spencer exhaled, creases deepening around his eyes. "We can try again. We'll keep trying." His lips brushed hers, pounding a heart already aching from today's emotional tidal wave. Then he flattened a hand to her belly. "But I'm not giving up yet, and neither should you."

"Spencer." She cradled his jaw, trailed her fingers over his cheek to his throat.

His eyes fell shut, and he did a very poor job of stopping her hand. "Alexandra, hypocrite that I am, I vowed not to touch you again until we're wed. Which is why I truly, sincerely, am begging you to consider Saturday."

"That's only three days," she grumbled.

"I've a weak constitution. Morally speaking."

"Why rush? You've stolen my virtue, got me with child." Alix stiffened her face against a smile and tried to look sullen. "A ring won't put the yolk back in the egg now."

Spencer sat up a little more at each word, until he slid completely off the bureau with a desperate wideness to his eyes. "You're asking the impossible. Field rations, trench foot, lice. Caroline Lamb. Ask me to endure any of them, but do not ask me to wait." His mouth snapped shut, and he narrowed his eyes. "You're *jesting*."

She laughed.

Spencer took a slow step forward.

Alix squealed at a swiping arm. "You can't chase me! I'm delicate. It's too dangerous," she panted, backing towards the bed.

"I heard Miss Foster say that exertion was desirable." Spencer claimed another step.

Instead of increasing their distance, Alix rushed him and threw her arms around his neck. "Save your strength, Lord Reed. You can exert us both on Saturday."

CHAPTER THIRTY

Oakvale – October 12th, 1814

Bennet strode into the bedchamber like a conquering hero, smoothing the breast of his smart blue frock. "She hasn't fled the house yet, so I'd say your luck is holding." He skidded to a stop at the edge of the rug, and Spencer caught his brother's furrowed brow. "Why are you just sitting there?" Bennet hooked a thumb toward the door. "If you've changed your mind, I'll gladly take your place."

Spencer snorted and rubbed his forehead. "It is a great deal to take in all at once; a wife, a baby. I was sitting here pondering what I've ever done to deserve so much. And wondering if perhaps I'm being punished, too."

"Very philosophical for a man who lives by the musket." Bennet pulled a chair out from the vanity and settled across from him. "I think you think too much. Go downstairs and say your vows. Suffer having a beautiful woman pledge her love to you. Saturate yourself with champagne, dance like a gypsy and then retire upstairs to do … whatever a man of your years can manage."

He pegged Bennet's shin with his boot. "Incorrigible ass."

Bennet bounced to his feet. "Get up, if you can. Let's have this over with so that I can unburden myself. Keeping all your sordid business to myself is moral agony."

"God," Spencer groaned, standing up. "Major Burrell is rubbing off on you." Then he stopped and pressed a hand to Bennet's shoulder, realizing he hadn't thanked him yet, for anything. "Bennet, I'm grateful you did not die in that Spanish brothel."

"There are worse ways to go." Bennet patted his arm and led them out. "Anyhow, I suppose I love you too."

Spencer paused when they reached the top of the stairs and wondered if he could have done more. There had been no time, even after sending word ahead from London, for his steward to do much with the house and grounds. They would hold a ball, eventually, to celebrate the wedding, but for now that was all. Tonight, he had been determined at least to have a lavish dinner. Yeast rolls, boiled potatoes, glazed carrots, baked apples, ham, partridge with marmalade, and if his nose hadn't deceived him earlier, fish were all on the menu.

His stomach protested a lack of breakfast as he mentally ticked off the menu. Cook had chafed at the restrictions he'd had to place on Alexandra's behalf, but judging by the rich peppery smell of roasting meat filling the house, Mrs. Tate was managing just fine.

They went out to the garden by the west hall. Sun glinted off the black and white marble, catching gold gilt on the scroll work iron railing as they passed through high French doors and onto the terrace. Mare's tails streaking a blue fall sky promised more unseasonably warm weather. A handful of crimson maple leaves blew down the stone steps ahead of his boots, welcoming him and Bennet into the garden.

Spencer stopped at the foot of the balustrade. Their little party formed a handsome collection. The newly-minted Lord and Lady Grayfield, a dark-haired and captivating matched pair, stood to one side. John was opposite them, smart in his olive-green frock and hovering attentively at Laurel's elbow, his tall frame dwarfing her rounded body into doll-like proportions. Their minister waited apart from the group, a sore thumb in his black cassock and hat.

He took in those few details, and then nothing more, not when he caught sight of her.

Alexandra had never worn red in his presence, that he could recall. Strange, because it suited her perfectly. His fingers itched to brush the cherry velvet of her pelisse and trace the full skirt falling from her bust, its train sweeping behind her. Wide satin lapels hugged her ivory neck and gathered sleeves draped her willowy arms. A matching silk bonnet framed the beautiful oval of her face, unable to contain dark waves tumbling over her shoulder.

Bennet was crossing to her now, bowing like a prince and holding out his hand for hers. Spencer continued staring, hardly breathing, wondering again how he'd gotten so lucky. She was so beautiful that it ached behind his ribs. Her face, her figure, and that something deep in her eyes when she looked at him.

Alexandra did look at him then, prompted by something Bennet had said. She turned, her movement almost shy. Still and unblinking, she watched him with lips slightly parted. Spencer could only return her gaze, suspended in the amber of a solemn moment. She smiled and ducked her face. Love, anticipation, even lust twined into a reanimating thread and drew him to her across the garden's crisp expanse.

*   *   *

Spencer stopped at arms-length and bowed. Alix looked him over, taking her time. "You wore your uniform." The brilliance of his red coat stamped him onto the landscape. A black velvet collar outreached even his white cravat, stiff with yards of fine gold embroidery. His buff trousers she skipped over, being in the presence of clergy. The omission was brief; Spencer's high black boots raced up to meet the tan fabric. 'Handsome' was too thin a term for the figure he cut, too shallow a sentiment for the warmth in his eyes now. Her husband. Alix smiled and tears pricked her eyes.

He nodded, openly admiring her pelisse and smoothing the scarlet wool of his coat. "I thought we should match. So that everyone will know that we are together."

She grinned. "Like a pair of socks. Very practical of you."

His shoulders relaxed, and he nodded slowly. "Precisely like an old pair of socks."

'Old' was not lost on her. Alix narrowed her eyes.

Reverend Munroe scowled from under the flat brim of his black felt hat, downturned eyes sad and disapproving all at once. "Shall we begin?"

Bennet leaned to her ear. "He's having an apoplectic fit over our locale. Your choice of color, the time of day," he snorted. "Just think if he knew about the *rest* of the commandments you've violated."

"I will throttle you after," Spencer promised in a whisper, and she nudged Bennet with an elbow, giving him a wide smile.

Reverend Munroe raised his chin mightily, looking down on them despite the deficit in his height. His eyes widened and nostrils flared. A grimace spread his plump lips and Alix expected at any moment that he would bellow out actual fire and brimstone. He drew a sharp breath, taut as a bowstring, and then: "Join hands, please," he said, exuding all the fury of a pond on a still day. She exhaled, relaxing.

Alix didn't know that she heard any of the words he spoke next. Her heart brimmed with love, thoughts shot through with nervousness, a hint of fear; only a sonorous mumbling from Munroe's bowed head pierced her fog. She answered when he paused, or after Spencer spoke. Then Munroe's words pricked something.

"Consider the causes for which matrimony was ordained:"

Spencer cleared his throat meaningfully, causing her to focus on his eyes.

"First, it was ordained for the procreation of children..."

Eyes widening a fraction, Spencer wiggled his brows. Heat rose in her cheeks, burning against a crisp breeze. Nothing was sacred.

"Secondly, it was ordained as a remedy against sin, and to avoid fornication ..."

Seizing the opportunity, Alix formed a small "oh," and cocked her head at Spencer's twitching lips.

"Thirdly," Munroe hung dramatically, reaching his crescendo, "It was ordained for the mutual society, help, and comfort that the one ought to have of the other ..."

Spencer clutched her hand, constricting her heart and bringing forth a spring of unexpected tears. She squeezed back and mouthed his name.

"Who gives this woman?" Spencer winced and she almost giggled. 'Woman' was bellowed, as though she were tardy coming to the dinner table.

"I do." Bennet, still beside her, squeezed her arm and let go. It should have been Chas; at least, it was his rightful place. But he had not answered her letters, not for weeks. It hurt, but deeper than that Alix was forced to admit to herself that she was relieved. Instead of dwelling on it, she pecked Bennet on the cheek, and could swear that he colored before turning and joining the others.

They promised to obey and serve, love and honor. Promises made in emptiness for hundreds of years by drunks and adulterers, wife beaters and cheats. Alix had no doubts that her vows with Spencer were sincere, but the words were flat and rote; not what she would have chosen to say in that moment. Nothing about how he had chased and desired her and brought her back to life, how they had willingly risked so much for one another; how they had looked at each other that day in Haywood and *known*, but hadn't realized they had been in love long before that moment.

Spencer held his free hand out to Bennet, who fished in his tail and produced a ring.

"With this ring I wed thee, with my body I worship thee." He fit the band over her third finger without resistance, a tad too large around cold flesh. It was a wide band, hewn from heavy and ancient looking silver. English roses notched its argent metal, set between finely carved scrolling leaves. Alix closed her eyes and judged its weight.

She inventoried head to toe, discovering that despite her doubts she felt different. She didn't belong to someone else, but she was *part* of something else, something lasting.

"I charge you now to go and live together in holy love unto your lives' end. *Amen.*"

Nerves ratcheted a knot in her gut. Oakvale wasn't her home, a voice protested. The small band of people behind them were not her friends, save Laurel. Her body, her interest in Paton & Son, all that she owned or ever would own belonged now to Spencer. For the first time in her life, excluding Silas's

260

manipulation, someone could control her. The old familiar fear, colored by the last week's events, flushed through her.

They had *both* made that bargain, she argued back. *Spencer's* friends were here to celebrate his happiness, and hers. She would *make* Oakvale her home now, out from under Van der Verre's thumb. And, most of all, Spencer loved her.

He claimed her hand more tightly, thumbed her ring and then bowed and kissed her knuckles. She took his other hand, and they were married.

CHAPTER THIRTY-ONE

Once the papers were signed, John took the initiative of opening champagne, half a smuggled crate Spencer had been hoarding since his last campaign in France. In his estimation, there was no better occasion to open the remaining half. He chuckled; it wasn't as though Napoleon could be deposed *twice*.

They had passed their glasses and clinked them, and Spencer estimated he'd blushed as much as Alix at all the cheers and well-wishes. After a deluge of disjointed conversation during which no one person could hear the person speaking to them, they concluded their toast in exchange for his second-most anticipated event of the evening: dinner.

Spencer dropped his napkin beside his plate, wondering if just once, on such a special occasion, he could be forgiven sliding beneath the table and lying on the rug. Canned sardines and stale biscuits, or even the thin but comparatively opulent sauces of the officers' mess, were reduced to a bad memory.

He'd stolen glances at Alix through dinner, pinching himself while Bennet held her captivated by a tale as only Bennet could. When she laughed, she laughed with her whole body; perhaps what had caught his attention that first night. If they were strangers at the table just now, he would do any number of things to win her again.

Now that the meal was nearly finished, Spencer sat quietly and basked in the moment, quietly watching his friends. John teased Sofie about trouble she'd gotten into in Portugal. She looked to her husband for defense, but Ethan only raised his hands, smiling and taking no part. Laurel lifted her voice over the others, interjecting laughing disapproval at parts of Bennet's questionable story.

This was his life now, at home with Alexandra, their friends. Soon, there would be children. A warmth spread through him, contentment, and he reached out and squeezed her hand without thinking.

Even in the midst of Bennet's interrogation about the Carolinas, she squeezed back.

They passed the night hand-in-hand at the table, in the drawing room. Whether they were whispering to one another or lost in conversation with their friends, Spencer refused to let go. He might grow tired of it, or she would, in a decade or two. For now, he intended to hold her every possible moment.

Bennet was the first to make his excuse, engaged to spend the week at Henry Taylor's estate and eager to get started debauching himself. John and Laurel were the last to leave, which suited him just fine. He stood beside Alix on the front step, one hand raised, steady in contrast to her furious waving, until the Hastings were out of sight down the drive. He would have been happy to stand there with her indefinitely, gazing up at the night sky and holding her close, but Alexandra's breath clouding out beneath the lamplight caused him to bundle her against his side and shoo her in.

In the dim foyer, she rubbed her hands together then smoothed the front of his uniform coat. "I really can't express how smart you look," she murmured, wrapping arms around his waist.

He cradled her head against his chest and fought the trembling in his hands. They were well and truly alone for the first time since Haywood. And they were married. Everything felt new, unexplored. He kissed the top of her head. "What would you like to do?"

Alexandra pulled away and slid arms around his neck, playing in his hair. She bit her lip in a fashion he knew well, and his heart raced.

"Laurel told me something about you." Her nose traced his jaw. "Something very shocking."

"Is that so?" The potential for Laurel, married to *John*, to know something shocking about him was rather high.

"Mmm." She took one of his hands and studied it, and traced it a finger at a time with aching slowness. "You're better

263

with your hands than I'd been led to believe." She nipped the end of his index finger. "And I was certain I knew what they were capable of."

He laughed despite the moment, nearly doubling over when he finally caught on. Getting a hold of himself, he twined their fingers. "I think I comprehend." He winked, turning her cheeks a fetching pink. "Would you like me to show you?"

Her smile was brilliant, answer breathless. "Very much."

"It's been a long time," he warned, leading her down the hall. "This may not be as good as you're expecting."

"I'm sure I'll be perfectly satisfied."

"Lady Reed," he chastised, enjoying her new name, bringing a chair from against the wall, "there is a shocking quantity of innuendo in your words."

One slow button at a time, Alexandra unfastened her coat. It whispered over naked arms, pooling into her chair and set his imagination ablaze. She settled in a rustle of crisp ivory satin, sliding down until her breasts pressed her neckline in a demonstration of pure torment. "Shocking," she repeated, biting into a smile.

He settled on the piano bench an arm's length away and flexed his fingers, stealing a few last glances. "Ready?"

"Mmm."

His first key taps were hesitant, but his fingers found their pace soon enough. He was ashamed, upon hearing the pianoforte's rich sound, that he rarely played anymore. Alix clasped her hands, sitting up now and studying him carefully, insuring it would not be his last time.

"My choice of song pleases you?" he asked, still focused on his finger work.

"You could play scales and it would please me." She chuckled, "But yes, it's lovely."

"Hm. When you accosted me in the hall, I did not perceive that 'lovely' was your desire. Shall I play something else, a more seductive piece?" He finished and sat back.

Alexandra applauded, looking more delighted than he could have hoped. "Whatever my desire, that was perfect."

"I'm pleased Beethoven and I could impress you."

"He's no Liszt," she teased.

"Liszt is for the seduction of rich widows only."

She gasped and pressed a hand to her lips. "I had no idea."

"Mmm. Bennet taught me that." He waved a hand over the keys. "So, now you know my secret. What else would please you?"

He anticipated a second cheeky request, but Alix slid from her chair in a whisper of silk and circled him. She rubbed palms up his shoulders, slid hands down into his coat. He held his breath and waited for her next blow. Her palms warmed him through the linen and her lips brushed his cheek, his ear. His heart pounded at his temples. Above his collar, at his throat; she teased everywhere while avoiding his mouth. He groaned when she pulled away.

They were still and he stared at the piano, listening to Alexandra's soft breathing behind him. Her fingers buried in his hair, nails scraping before she claimed a fistful and drew his head back. Her lips slid over his until they fit together.

Spencer fought an instinct to raise up, press her for more, and subjected himself to her seduction.

Her small hand cradled the back of his head while she settled beside him, facing opposite atop the bench without breaking their kiss. She cupped his face and Spencer gripped the bench to keep from touching her, determined not to interfere. He was rewarded when she brushed kisses over his cheek, his chin, and the border of his cravat where it hugged his throat. Then she got up, and stood behind him again.

A slender arm draped him, claimed his hand, and she pulled. "Spencer," she whispered, "How long has it been?"

He swallowed, dry-mouthed, and shook his head. "I don't know. I stopped counting the days without you, for my own sanity."

He got up, wrapping her waist, and swept her feet out from under her. Cradling her against his chest, he laughed down her protests. "Hush, Alexandra. You'll have reason to complain soon enough."

She stopped fighting and frowned, head against his shoulder. "Why?"

He nipped her ear. "For the rest of the night, you have to endure more pedestrian attention from my hands."

*　　*　　*

She wriggled closer to Spencer under the quilt and worked around her belly to get her head onto his chest. "I learned something very terrible from Laurel," she murmured over his heartbeat.

His hand pressed the small of her back. "You learn a great many terrible things from Laurel. Perhaps you two should be separated."

"Did you know," she continued, pointedly ignoring him, "that husbands and wives do not share a bedchamber?" She chuckled. "I suppose my parents' house was too small for me to know better."

"Oh," he started gravely, "Well, it's too late now. Common practice. We'll have to go on sharing."

"Ignorance of sin is no excuse." She fought a laugh, wriggling until she was braced over him. "We should mend our ways."

"I have bad news on that score." Spencer played with the hair at her temple. "The chamber adjoining mine is empty. Entirely cleared out."

She rose up further. "Why?"

He shrugged, still twining her hair and not meeting her eyes. "I thought we could go to London, before the snow falls. Visit the shops," he muttered, shifting uncomfortably.

She swatted him. "You didn't answer my question."

He worried his lip in an uncharacteristic show of nerves. "A nursery has consumed my every thought, waking and sleeping."

Kissing him, Alix slid arms around his neck and squeezed him close, fighting the joy and fear whenever she thought of the child growing inside of her. "What if... should we? If something is wrong..." She couldn't bring herself to finish.

"Whatever happens can't take away from our joy right now, Alexandra."

266

He was right, of course. Worrying now didn't change anything. "What should we look for?"

"Truthfully, I had no idea. I had to ask Hastings."

His confession made her laugh. "And what did you determine?"

"A cradle. One of those rocking horses with a real mane and red painted rockers."

She stared at the ceiling, mentally placing furniture in the empty room. "It will be ages before our baby can use it."

"Doesn't matter. I want it. You can order gowns and swaddling, or fabric if you're inclined to make them."

"I am!" She sat up, sliding to sit against the headboard, excitement bubbling. "That hadn't crossed my mind. Something to do to pass the time."

Spencer worked up beside her, claiming her hand. "Day after tomorrow?"

Alix held up fingers, winking. "Three days." She raked him with a glance. "I can't recover so quickly."

CHAPTER THIRTY-TWO

London – October 19, 1814

Only their second full day in town, and already the gossip mill churned at full speed. If Spencer had dreaded visitors before, Aix decided he would loathe them by week's end.

Today, though, he would be spared the brunt of it. She wanted to make her round to the shops early, avoid busy streets and arrive back home before her back and hips began their protest in earnest. They had risen early, dressed in haste despite Spencer's attempts at derailing their schedule, and breakfasted together as they always did.

It was a fuss in the papers today; Lord R., hero of the Peninsula, marrying an 'American shipping heiress.' Alix chuckled and slid the paper back across the table to Spencer's elbow. "A flattering account. I came with ten dollars and a trunk of smallclothes."

"Perhaps when they talk of wealth they mean it in a biblical sense. Like wheat, or knowledge." He tossed her a look off his own paper, making her laugh. "Anyhow," he shrugged, folding the page, "I'm not concerned with money. You'll earn your keep, in one fashion or another."

Money. Shipping heiress. She nodded, only half hearing Spencer's jest.

"Chas will turn up," he promised, recognizing the worry in her face. "Grayfield has men looking. We'll find him."

"I don't want to see him." She met Spencer's eyes. "Is that horrible? If I could just know that he's well, that would be enough. I would be happy going our separate ways."

"You have every right to feel that way."

Something occurred to her, dark but nagging. "What happened to Paulina's remains?"

Spencer winced and shrugged, then shook his head. "Someone claimed them? Otherwise, they were lymed in the pit with the others."

Bile rose in her throat, both at the thought of Paulina and her fate. "What she deserves." There was no fighting bitterness.

"Her father was influencing the trial, obviously. I'm certain he had someone collect her."

Alix shuddered and pushed the whole idea from her mind. "Laurel has given me the name of a shop with good flannel. I was thinking of going this afternoon. Her directions don't seem complicated."

"I'll take you. Grayfield has papers for Bennet, and I can collect you after."

"Collect me? Like a glove or lost key?" she prodded.

Spencer pushed back, stood up and offered a hand with a grin. "Precisely."

*   *   *

The English method of shopping was still lost on her. First, no merchant seemed to know what to do with a customer set to buy and her mind made up. Salesmanship was put to use despite her protests, their accounting of a fabric's virtues enumerated long after she had agreed to six or seven yards. Then, no goods or money actually changed hands. A merchant agreed to deliver, she agreed to pay, and that was that. It was strange and vaguely unsatisfying. She had to admit there was a convenience to it, though. She wasn't obliged to bundle out ten parcels and wedge herself between them in the carriage. Spencer was forever complaining about foot room, anyhow.

Not that she hadn't enjoyed every minute of the day so far. London was new to her, recollections of her few days in town after Haywood foggy at best. Ladies drifted up and down Bond street in a pastel rainbow, like blossoms on the arms of their men, tall and straight like sticks in brown and olive green. The steady traffic of grand, eight-horse equipages, speeding curricles, and merchant carts rumbled up and down its roads

269

without pause, their drivers shouting to and at one another. She didn't care to make the city her home, but there was a delight in spending a few months each year in London. In London with her husband.

Thrilling at the idea, Alix let herself out into the street, rubbing an aching back and happy to head home. She had browsed longer than intended, and Spencer would be along soon.

"Alexandra!" a voice rasped, nearly drowned by the murmur of afternoon crowds. She glanced left and right, not catching a single set of eyes looking her way. "Alexandra," it barked again. Turning she startled at a figure tucked almost behind the open shop door.

"Chas!" she gasped, hardly recognizing him. "Where have you been? What are you doing?" He looked awful. If she had seen him at a distance mingled with the crowd, she would have dismissed him as a drunken tramp. Stale gin and something more foul assaulted her nose from the folds of his rumpled clothing, and he was unshaven and entirely unkempt. Black crusty scabs punctuated his lip and eyebrow, mute evidence of a wretched beating.

"You have to come with me this very moment," he mumbled, swiping for her hand.

She darted back a step, dodging. "Not the slightest chance."

"Ohh!" he laughed. "You're a fine lady now. I read all about it in the papers. Whore."

It was more than enough. Alix spun on her heel, but this time he caught her. "Wait. Wait! Alix, I'm sorry. I'm sorry, but you have to listen, you have to come back." Chas rambled over himself like a madman, his words and even his tone of voice changed from just a moment before. It was as if more than one person shared his head, and they were all jockeying for position.

"Come back *where*?"

"With me!" He let go of her, grabbed his coat and strangled its lapels. "You have to come with me, back home. Silas is angry, Alix, furious! But we can set it right, we can still make amends if we just go home and do as he says."

"Charles," she snapped, leaning in and ignoring the smell, "you can kiss my arse if you believe I am *ever* going back to that life."

"Stop this rebellion, Alix! Stop it!" He wrestled her sleeve, and a passing gentleman stopped to swing his walking stick, knocking Chas into the shop's wall.

"Can I help you, miss?" The man spoke to her and glared at Chas.

"I was just departing." She muttered thanks and waved the man on his way.

"You are ruining everything," Chas bit out, eyes wet with tears. "We'll lose Paton, the house, our fortune –"

"I don't have any of those things!" she cried, shaking fists at him. Then she gathered herself with a few breaths, and looked over the pathetic heap that was her brother. "Those things are your matters now. They should always have been your matters."

This time when she turned away, she took a wide stride into the passersby, ensuring Chas couldn't pull her back.

"I'm sorry over it, Alexandra!" he screamed through the din. "It had to be done, I'm sorry!"

Sorry over what? Obviously not the same things she was sorry over. She yanked open her carriage door, not waiting for a tardy footman.

"Alexandra."

She was mostly up when a voice inside broke her name into four familiar, terrifying syllables. She turned back, but moist sausage fingers grabbed her arm and hauled her into the foot well with a force that stole her breath.

"Didn't take your brother's advice," Silas bit out in his thick Dutch syllables. "Disappointing, as always." He tsk-tsk'd.

He was bigger than she remembered, larger, maybe because she'd thought herself beyond his reach. He'd grown smaller on the horizon as she and Spencer moved forward. But he hadn't changed, his jowled cheeks red with perpetual ocean wind-burn, muscled arms and legs those of a farmer, though his trunk was a barrel. He glared at her now with Paulina's eyes, hate boiling in their brown, almond depths.

I'm sorry over it, Alexandra.

271

Not as sorry as he would be if she outlasted Silas Van der Verre.

Silas jammed a boot into her hip, shooting lightning up her back.

"Get up, sit." He glared down at her from the high bridge of his nose. "He cannot get your obedience, but I shall."

She wriggled onto the opposite seat, putting as much space as possible between them.

He reached into the dark space beside him, snatched up his walking stick and cut a swath through the air with it. "You're headstrong, like your father." He clucked his tongue at her grimace. "I enjoy your spirit, Alexandra, I always have. One application of punishment was enough for your brother. Three?" He gasped. "Well, that's really something. I haven't broken you yet."

His first blow caught her cheek. A rattle inside her skull was the worst of it. The blow should have hurt more; somehow the memory of his last beating lessened her pain. Maybe it was knowing how quickly the worst of it would fade, how long it would take for bleeding to stop and swelling to subside. She pressed a sleeve to her cheek to stem a hot trickle there, throbbing made worse by the carriage's bounce and sway. Just until Spencer could find her; she had to survive Silas that long. Spencer *would* come.

"Not yet," Silas hissed, drawing back, "but I shall."

*   *   *

Ethan held one side of his desk, while Spencer squared off against Bennet on the other. He had been certain of the meeting going quickly, Ethan giving Bennet his assignment and seeing his brother off in approximately the same amount of time it would take to brew tea. He should have known better; Spencer shook his head. Nothing with Bennet was ever simple.

He noticed that Bennet was unusually intractable for a mission with so much danger attached, usually his first choice. "I received a good many sour looks at the War Office for resigning my commission," Bennet protested

"You're not *actually* resigning it," corrected Spencer.

272

"I know that, and you both know it…" Bennet flexed under scuffed pride.

Spencer had a feeling his brother would take to the prestige of his new role soon enough. "You'll have one of Paton's ships. It's been refitted." Spencer placed his hands on Ethan's desk, rearranging their width and stalling. "Grayfield has arranged some things. Papers; a safe house. You're going to need help from someone there with connections." He spoke the words carefully, preparing himself. His brother wouldn't be sporting about being duped.

Bennet's eyes darted from him, to Ethan, and back. "Why do you say it like that?"

Ethan cleared his throat. "Because there is only one person in Barataria Bay who works with the British army *and* the privateers."

"No." Bennet got up.

"Just use your manners. Say you're sorry, perhaps?"

"Out of the question." Bennet backed away a step. "Not at the fork tines of Satan himself am I apologizing to Miranda Clery." He snatched his hat and his scarf, and stormed from Ethan's office.

"Have you seen her?" drawled Ethan, watching Bennet's retreating back in triumph. "They'll apologize."

"They have history," added Spencer. "She won't have to."

"Mm." Ethan unfolded from his chair. "My stomach believes it's time for supper, even if it is only four-thirty."

"Old habits die hard, Major Grayfield."

Nodding, Ethan gathered his things from the desk, while Spencer checked his watch in disbelief. "I'm tardy. Alexandra will be waiting."

"We'll make good time. Come, I'll walk with you as far as Bond."

When they reached the point of Bond Street and its intersection with a small alley where Ethan would normally part ways with him, they were so engrossed in a discussion of the steam engine that they passed the route entirely. Spencer didn't appreciate it until he realized they were across the street from the dressmaker's, and only then because there was no carriage, and no Alexandra waiting.

Beside him Ethan stopped talking, and frowned, eyes narrowed. "Down the side street?"

He shook his head, searching a bustling crowd passing the shop. Why would she move? If the carriage had moved off the main street and into an alleyway, he reasoned, she was likely still inside the shop. Anxiety twisted his insides as he looked around wildly, hoping for a glimpse of her in the crowd.

"Come," Ethan shouldered him. "You step inside. I'll have a look around the block."

Two old ladies examining ribbon comprised the shop's entire clientele, and the bells in Spencer's head clanged in earnest. A diminutive, beak-nosed clerk fluttering between the printed bolts nodded eagerly at Spencer's description. Yes, he had put some yardage on credit for the lady and had taken down her address for delivery before she left. She hadn't been back since.

A sick knot gripped his gut, and Spencer wondered at the coincidence of their not having seen Chas since the execution. He tore open the door, finding Ethan planted sideways to the entrance.

"She's not inside; any luck?"

"No, but you have a driver with a sore head propped at the rear door." Silent, Ethan squinted into sunlight of a fall afternoon, arms crossed over his chest. After a moment, he tipped his chin and drew Spencer's gaze down the block.

Two men built like bear wrestlers flanked a lamp post at the corner, incapable of being more conspicuous in finely tailored suits that lacked enough fabric to wrap their tree-trunk arms and legs. Thick, jowled faces, slitted eyes, and lips sneering almost to the cusp of spitting made them stand out.

"You have your pistol?" murmured Ethan.

"No."

"Good. They would gut you if you did." He straightened, tossing a surreptitious glance off his shoulder. Then he patted Spencer's shoulder.

A sharp point registered against his arm, the fine tip of a lock pick being driven into his coat lining. "Go with them," instructed Grayfield. "Mister Tilton is just there, by the flower cart. He will be your tail."

Spencer dared a glance without moving his head and noticed a white-pudding sort of man reading a newspaper, the sort no one would notice let alone recall later.

"Burrell and I will work from outside; meet you in the middle."

How was it that they had walked to the shop seemingly without design, and Ethan had already scrounged up an agent?

Spencer swallowed, eyeing his new companions. What if they didn't take him to Alix, if she had already been hurt? He shook off the idea; at the moment he had no information, and no choice. "Be hasty," he muttered, stepping away. "I would hate for either of us to miss supper."

CHAPTER THIRTY-THREE

London Docks – Evening

It was nearly sunset, and despite her coat Alexandra was already freezing. When Silas had her dragged in from the carriage, it had been midday, though fear had chilled her even then. Now a damp breeze from the Thames bit through the warehouse's crumbling brick and rotting timbers, and its earthen floor chilled her legs and backside. Her hips ached at sitting upright for so long, but she didn't dare lean back against the wall and sacrifice more body heat.

Silas waddled across the long room at angles, stopping now and then to check a pair of ropes hung from the ceiling, poking his walking stick into the nooses and tugging for emphasis. She ignored the implication, just glad to see the cane applied to something other than her face for a change.

Throbbing, above her eye and across her mouth, hinted at damage that would be long in healing. Mold and tobacco tickled her nose; Alix prayed more fervently than she had in her entire life that she wouldn't sneeze and split her lip for a second time.

A freight door at the far end of the large room rumbled open, allowing just enough space for a person and spilling thin amber shafts of sunlight into the shadows between stacks of crates. Alexandra wondered absently if it was the last sunset she would ever see. She dared a hand inside her coat to cradle her belly.

One hulking form sidled through, and another behind, goading a silhouette she could recognize immediately. *Spencer.* She would have felt relief, except that his hands were obviously bound like her own. Gratitude filled her at being together, though in the immediate she failed to see how they were much better off.

"Over there," Silas ordered, indicating a stack of discarded pallets across from her. "Don't put them together. I don't want them concocting ideas."

One lumbering goon drove Spencer with a meaty arm, throwing him to the dirt where he produced a terrible, deflating sound. Alix held her breath until he finally groaned and rolled over. When no one made a move to interfere, he worked himself up to sit against the pallets, staring at her across the narrow space.

She answered his eyes with a bare nod, which was all she dared without risking Silas's wrath. Spencer's reply was a slow blink. She sensed more than an acknowledgment; maybe a reassurance, but she dared not hope. Only one thing was certain in that moment: she would put a musket ball in Silas at the first opportunity, if it ever came. Then she would deal with Chas.

"Where are my papers!" Silas shouted at no one in particular, swinging his stick, cutting the air with a quick *zip*. It was a fine line; she sensed things would escalate quickly for her and Spencer when the 'papers' arrived. Too long a delay though, and Silas was bound to grow bored, turning idle attention to his captives. He had dumped Emily in the river, pregnant, bleeding, and broken. Alix shivered at the memories. Emily had been helpless, unaware. She, on the other hand, knew Silas for what he was, what he could do, and would fight him every step of the way.

The issue was quickly rendered moot. Hooves thudded on cobblestones along the wharf and ended with a sharp whinny that echoed through the door. Silas immediately left, leaving his two hulking golems to keep watch.

She strained her ears, trying with every fiber of her being to hear what transpired outside. All she could hear were two voices.

First an unidentified man, then Silas. Alix could hear their tone, but not the words. They climbed one another until it peaked with shouting. There was a horse's anxious shuffling, and then a man-sized thud. Silas went on yelling, the other man escalating to shrill screams. Then it was only Silas and a repetitive, meaty thump that seemed to go on forever. Alix swallowed down a wave of bile, staring at Spencer without blinking.

A moment later Silas appeared in the doorway, blotting out the last burning ripples of sun. Huffing, he dragged something behind him that Alix couldn't bring herself to examine.

"We agreed on a goddamn price!" A meaty blow, boot against flesh, reached her ears. "Don't dare try to cheat me!" Spit flew from Silas's fat lips, caught by the light. "We agreed on a goddamn price," he muttered again, panting. Then he waved over one of his men. "Get rid of it."

The man stared at him blankly. "Where should we take him?"

Silas waved a steady hand out toward the river. "Whatever you do, I don't think he'll complain."

He shook a long envelope in her direction, sweeping dark spots from his waistcoat with a handkerchief. "Abel, bring her here. And Dein, watch *him* with both eyes," he said, vaguely waving as Spencer.

She had no idea which was which. Abel, based on the order Silas had addressed them, came around behind her while Dein grabbed her coat-front and hauled her up. Grunting, he stalked back to Silas while Abel yanked at her manacles. Whispers passed between Dein and his master, Silas staring at her and plucking a wiry straw mutton chop. "With child? We come a little closer to justice, then. One child for another."

She dared a glance at Spencer, but he wasn't looking at her. He studied the ceiling, listening. "Don't compare our children," she dared. "It's hardly the same."

A nod from Silas, and Abel's ham fist jammed her kidney. It drove out her breath, cramping, buckling her right knee. More than feeling pain, however, her mind shrieked with fear; she could only think of her unborn child.

Spencer roared, rising up, but Dein was quick. His fist twisted Spencer's jaw and knocked him back to the floor. She cried out, lunged for him, but Abel smacked her hard enough to make her head ring, and she fell to her knees.

Before she could recover, Abel was dragging her. Silas seemed oblivious to the commotion, smoothing his papers out atop a long wooden box which was set on two crates against a wall near the doorway.

The smell struck her before they'd gone half way across the room, sweet like decaying fruit over rotting meat. It grabbed for the bottom of her stomach, turning it, and obliging her to pull breaths through her mouth. By the time they reached Silas it was near impossible to avoid.

He pushed the papers in front of her and set a quill beside them with a chilling gentleness. "Sign the documents, Alexandra."

Pressing her face into a sleeve, she skimmed writing on the first page. "Sign over my shares to you? I don't have any shares."

"That's not true," he pouted, thick lips pulling into a frown. "You have a great many shares. I've had time to piece together how you stabbed me in the back!" He slammed the box with a fist, each word raising in volume. He sucked in a breath, growing calm again. "Sign the papers."

She pushed the quill away with a finger. "Why should I? You'll kill me either way. Why give them to you?"

Smoothing the wood between them with a fat hand, Silas followed its path with down-turned eyes. "You owe a great deal for what you did to my daughter." He pressed trembling fingers against the box. "I can be merciful, if you sign. We can end things quickly." His eyes fell to Spencer, forgotten behind them. Spencer had risen back to his knees, and a dark bruise was forming under his eye. "If you make this difficult, I will start my revenge with him, and you will watch. How much will you endure, I wonder? It can take a long time."

She heard his words, felt their razor edge, but her eyes fixed on the long crate in awful recognition. The odor, the way he caressed its lid.

Alix swallowed back vomit and glanced over her shoulder at Spencer, face blank save a firm set to his jaw. "Do not sign those papers," he said.

Despair rose up inside. "We're dead anyway. I can't bear to watch him hurt you."

"Alexandra," he barked, widening his eyes, "I do *not* want you to *sign* those papers."

"A pair of idiots," Silas declared.

Abel moved to replace her shackles, but Silas raised a hand. "Hold her. I think she'll change heart quickly enough." He tugged a leather thong which bound a canvas bundled set atop the box. Metal clanked inside.

Swallowing, she glanced behind her. "Spencer…"

He winked, then smiled.

And somehow, impossibly, she felt hope.

Maybe whatever he'd heard was the same thing that had grabbed her attention, while Abel gripped her wrist and Silas went on un-bundling his tools, Dein keeping bored watch over Spencer.

There was a sudden thunder out on the wharf, a rumble that reached her ears from under the ship bells and hushing surf. It grew suddenly, as if hurried by a short distance, and the cargo door slid open with a deafening clatter. Silas shot to his feet as his goons turned, shock on their faces.

Alix knew a privateer when she saw one, and right now there were five. Too rough edged for sailors, they also sported too much of a uniform to be mistaken for pirates. Loose shirts tucked into blue- and white-striped slops, they held pistols at the ready. A smart-suited little man marched in behind them and studied his pocket watch with a frown.

Abel dropped her arm, drawing his own pistol while the newcomers waved arms and shouted in angry French. She had no notion if they were friend or foe, and at the moment she didn't care. They were a distraction, and no one, including Silas, made a move to stop her as she dodged and ran for Spencer.

*   *   *

Spencer narrowed his eyes, taking in the new development and considering how it changed things. Not for the better, so far.

"DuFresne," Silas snapped. "We agreed that I would come to *you*."

DuFresne raked his hand through thin hair over his egg head, then adjusted his spectacles to better peer insultingly at Silas. Unlike his companions, the man wore finely polished boots and a proper wool suit which he smoothed with long, puppet-master fingers. "You *informed* me that you would come to me, Van der Verre. I *agreed* to nothing." The unimposing Frenchman took a few steps into the warehouse, squinting and sniffing with the fussy disapproval of a butler.

It wasn't who he'd expected to see come charging inside, but DuFresne and his men had bought them time. He shrugged a shoulder at Alix as she fell to her knees beside him. He wanted to comfort her, to ask about her injuries, but they might only have seconds with no one looking at them. "Quick, put your arm inside my coat."

She frowned but didn't hesitate.

"Inside the sleeve. You're looking for something like a thick pin, a nail," he said, keeping his attention on the others.

Silas snatched his documents from under DuFresne's probing gaze. "I have matters to resolve before we can conduct our business."

DuFresne's arms went slack, like a disappointed parent. "You assured me those matters were already resolved." His men, still until now, shuffled between agitated murmuring.

"Spencer, who are they?" whispered Alix as she searched through his sleeve.

It had taken him a moment, but he'd finally placed the man's face. "Emil DuFresne is a bureaucrat. I recognize him from my time in Paris."

Her fingers skimmed to his elbow, then started back. "What is he doing here?"

"If I had to guess, a bureaucrat is not *all* he is." DuFresne worked for men with changeable loyalty. He was too incurious to be labeled a spy, but was certainly an agent for *someone*.

"Found it," said Alix. "Now what?"

"Tear it out."

There was pressure against his arm as the lining ripped and her hand flew out. "Good. Get around behind me." He rotated away from the crates, giving her access to his hands. "See a thin spot, nearly in the middle?"

281

"Mm."

"Twist it, just there, until you have two pieces."

"Done."

"The real key is a sort of screw," he explained. "That's what you're trying for. Flat bit goes in until you feel it seat."

Her pin scraped the shaft. Spencer felt when it lodged. "Bend the other one into a U, settle it over the post and press hard as you can, twisting at the same time."

"You're impressively familiar with this process. Something you do often?" she whispered.

"More often than I'd like, thanks to Grayfield," he whispered back, and left it at that.

Alix made small frustrated sounds behind him, until he feared she wouldn't manage the task. He watched the exchange across the room, praying with every fiber of his being that no one turned around.

Fortunately, the conversation between Silas and DuFresne was becoming more heated, and their respective groups of goons were eyeing each other warily. He hoped Alix got him free quickly; he could practically feel the impending violence growing.

Then the bar across his left wrist loosened, and Spencer slipped his hand free.

"Give me the picks," he whispered, never taking his eyes off the drama unfolding across the warehouse while going to work on his right hand. An opportunity would present itself for a weapon; he had to be ready.

"...because *you* wish to make a game out of it!" This from DuFresne, who managed to make his words larger without actually shouting. He grabbed the creased papers from Silas's hand, turned and strode in their direction.

Spencer let the shackles drop between his thighs and tucked hands behind his back.

DuFresne bent his short figure in front of Alexandra, and held out the contract, producing a pen from inside his coat. "Mademoiselle. Sign the papers."

Alexandra met Spencer's eyes, and he nodded. It must be nearly time for Ethan's men.

She claimed the pen, glaring. "If you say 'please'."

Thin lips bent into a predatory smile, and DuFresne nodded. "Please."

Alix laid the papers in her lap, looped her signature on each page and passed them back graciously.

"See, Van der Verre?" DuFresne shook his stack of documents in the air. "Manners, with a lady."

Silas's jowls flushed scarlet. "That murdering, conniving whore is no lady."

"I'll take the woman," DuFresne told his men, ignoring Silas's rage. "Van der Verre can do as he pleases with the vicomte."

He would have to kill at least two men now. Spencer groaned and scouted harder for a weapon.

"No! Absolutely not!" Silas lunged forward, oblivious to the click of four pistols. Spencer narrowed his eyes, counting the people in the room again. The fifth member of DuFresne's retinue was absent. He had a sudden hunch, but wouldn't glance around and risk drawing attention.

Silas drove his fist down onto a crate, eyes still trained on French pistols. "Our deal is the other way 'round, DuFresne! The woman is my matter."

DuFresne stopped mid-stride, raised his chin, and turned a pointed gaze at Silas through his beady spectacles. "Our arrangement is for the *ships*, and the ships only. The emperor has been more than generous on that score. As have I, given how inept you are," he snapped. "And so, if I wish something else for my trouble, I will have it."

"He's taking my ships!" Alexandra's protest was hushed, but she sat up with enough force that Spencer feared she would intervene.

"Leave it. You'll get them back."

"If we live that long," she hissed.

"Have a little faith in me," he teased. "Grayfield is working on it."

She nodded once and looked unconvinced.

"If you wish to be the imbecile," continued DuFresne, "who hangs an English lord and draws the Crown down on his head, I welcome you to it. The lady is my concern."

Silas sputtered, his fists clenching and unclenching. He'd turned an impressive shade of purple, and for a moment Spencer thought one of his problems might be about to resolve itself in a fatal fit of rage. He leaned in to Alix. "See all the trouble you've caused?"

She smiled for the first time since he'd arrived, then winced at a swollen lip. "I'm not done yet."

The barest odor of smoke reached him, wafting lazily on damp air, and he grinned. "You may have a rival."

And then, all hell broke loose.

CHAPTER THIRTY-FOUR

Alix had never believed she would live to see the day when Silas's colossal temper got the best of him. He never went toe-to-toe with anyone his own size and never went into conflict if the odds were against him. It was genuine comedy, then, when he turned his porcine physique on a comparatively small DuFresne and snatched for his beloved walking stick.

DuFresne side-stepped the blow with a dancer's grace. After dodging the stick, one of his men immediately barreled forward, driving into Silas's over-extended paunch. He folded, tumbled back and jarred the stacks of crates and his rough wood box. It slid, slamming end over and splintering, its choking stench wafting over the room. An upended lamp sputtered and bathed DuFresne's men in shadow.

"No! No, no!" Silas screamed, flailing on his back like a stranded tortoise and clawing for his box.

Pistols on both sides rose higher despite uneven numbers, each side bracing for inevitable fallout.

Alix realized, drawing a steadying breath, that the smell she'd earlier mistaken for a far-off chimney had grown stronger, and it was also much closer. Glancing left, she noticed gray smoke billowing from the shadows deeper in the warehouse. She nudged Spencer with an elbow.

"Shh." He gave a half nod, not looking the least bit concerned.

DuFresne snapped up Silas's discarded walking stick. "Take your blood money and your disgusting box of bones and your king-loving bastard over there, and get out of my sight." His swing was sudden and true, catching Silas's jaw without warning.

Silas cried out, lurched, and tore most of the papers from DuFresne's fingers, throwing them high. Silas's men rushed forward, frantic in opposition to a slow drift of pages and DuFresne's men charged ahead in answer. Fists and feet pummeled; it seemed in an unspoken agreement not to use their pistols, neither group looking eager to endure a ball for his master.

Despite the thickening smoke and their current predicament, Alix was stunned. Silas had always had a temper, but he'd also always been a coward.

Grunting and straining, Silas got to his knees. Some measure of sanity must have asserted itself because he began moving between stomping feet, snatching at pages while a shuffling, stooping DuFresne mirrored him from the other side of the fray. Alix could hardly wait to see what happened when each man finished with a handful of papers, neither one with a complete set.

Engrossed in the rapid degeneration, scuffling feet at her back startled her. She turned and swung hard, ready to bite, claw, anything to keep from being dragged away.

A man tumbled behind the crates, groaned, and rolled to his side. "That was a hard sodding blow!"

Whatever she'd expected to hear, that hadn't been it. She turned, taking in the man at her feet. Handsome enough, despite a tight grimace on his face and a red blotch marking his cheek. Tall and fair, and fit enough that she indulged a thrill at having soundly clocked him. "Who...?" she asked Spencer, stealing glances at the mounting chaos behind them.

"Major Burrell is a friend," drawled Spencer, craning his neck to survey the damage to the man's face. "At least, he *was*."

"Why didn't you say anything?" she demanded.

"Ty fancies himself the shadowy sort. Prefers his activities remain clandestine."

Ty sat up, massaging his cheek, a pained look on his face that made her feel just the tiniest bit badly. "I'll bloody well say something next time." He glanced from her to Spencer, then to the fight up front. Several men were down, with Silas and DuFresne raking for pages in the dark. He seemed to measure the progress of the smoke, burning her eyes now, and nodded. "Almost time. Are you ready?"

"The fire?" she asked, wondering at his lack of concern.

"It's small, for now. But that won't last," Ty said, grinning and balancing on the balls of his feet.

Alix rubbed her hands together, wondering if she should trust anyone so casual about a smoldering building. "What are we doing, then?"

That earned frowns from both men.

"I'm not an invalid!"

Spencer opened his mouth for some retort, but the warehouse door thundering open cut their argument short. Bodies rushed in; more of DuFresne's men, by their clothes. Spencer deflated. "Well, shite."

More men pounded in on their heels, bellowing something in Dutch. They flowed into the melee, shouting encouragement to Abel and Dein. Silas raised a fist, sneering and hurling insults at DuFresne through the melee. They were equally matched once more, in the space of a breath. At the current rate Alix estimated the building would be full in minutes.

Ty groaned beside her. "Why is it never *our* men?"

She coughed in answer, pressing a hand to her mouth and eyeing a wall of haze filling the warehouse. Flaming bits of char drifted down before her eyes. Alix looked up, frozen a moment by the tongue of flame licking down the eaves. True to Ty's word, it had spread quickly despite a slow start. Grabbing a fistful of Spencer's coat, she shook him. "We have to go."

Spencer, in turn, took a handful of Ty's coat. "Goddamit. Burrell, what was the rest of the plan after you lit the place on fire?"

Ty clasped a hand to his chest. "Don't complain to me about how long it takes the army to turn out! I am well aware."

"We have to scatter them now; we cannot wait for aid," said Spencer.

Sighing, Ty scrubbed a hand through his blond hair. "Hold here a moment. I'll see what I can do about a distraction."

She reached for Spencer's hand, watching Ty's retreating back. His fingers squeezed in answer.

"En fue! En fue!" Ty called out in French, jostling and pointing through the fracas of at least twenty men. Their blood was up, and they went right on slugging; it was the masterminds who were the first to take notice.

DuFresne caught on first, his neck craning, the dancing flames reflected in the discs of his spectacles. Alix expected him to run, but he backed into the fighting, unperturbed. When he was nothing more than a hand and papers above the swearing, straining men, DuFresne waved his prize at Silas, who swore furiously. In a final coup, DuFresne disappeared out into the night. She was torn between relief and anger that he'd got away.

Something stung her cheek, and she looked up once more. Smoke filled space between the timbers overhead, fire roiling back on itself in a hungry inferno, then fanning lower in a spray of hot ash.

"We can't wait any longer!" Spencer sprang to a crouch, casting about wildly for something. "Alexandra, get behind these crates and stay put. Those bastards are both going to get away, and we *still* can't get out past this mob."

Nodding, Alix pressed behind the boxes and peered out just enough to follow Spencer's path.

He ran for Ty, who was ducking and weaving the blows of a man twice his size with impressive dexterity. Watching their exchange, she grasped Spencer's caution: if Ty tried running now, the man fighting him would give halfhearted chase, and then turn his efforts to a target closer at hand. If she ran through the fighting, men on both sides would make a grab for her, pursue her.

A groan started somewhere farther back in the warehouse, a single deep report which peaked as several shrill protests. Ships and wharves made a similar sound; it was the cry of creaking wood. The first timber crashed into shadow, a deafening noise and spray of hellish sparks flying up into the dark. She bent one leg to plant a foot on the floor, braced hands against the dirt and prepared to run. She would take her chances with the crowd, if it came to it.

The men went on fighting, ignoring the peril around them.

Silas had a head start on Spencer, thanks to the fire. She lost sight of him well before Ty had extricated from the mob's center, before Spencer's long strides had put him at its edge. He lumbered between the crates, behind the fighting, and through their fingers.

Heat cracked the glazing of a narrow window above where she'd earlier been kept. The explosion of glass penetrated the hoodlum's awareness as nothing else had. Shouts went up between the men. A few hung stubbornly from each other's necks, striking or choking, but in short order they flooded outside.

She stood, catching Spencer's gaze and he nodded: *Time to go.* Pausing just long enough to snatch up a discarded pistol, Alix grabbed her skirts and ran.

*   *   *

He came outside nearly shoulder to shoulder with Ty. Van der Verre and DuFresne's men were milling about in a confused mass, being herded by the very English sounding shouts of "Halt for his Majesty's army." Privates had scrambled into position and a half-circle of redcoats two men deep were formed up into a choke point, forcing their adversaries to spill against one another, fold on themselves, and, finally, to surrender. Any fight they might have had in them drained at the sight of three dozen cocked muskets. Hands were already up, and iron shackles clanged from soldiers' belts as they detained both sets of men. Spencer searched the crowd as he emerged from the smoky darkness. Of course, Silas and DuFresne were nowhere to be found.

"What did I tell you?" panted Ty, drawing up next to him. "I told you the army would be here."

Only Burrell could reasonably get away with jokes at a time like this. "General Webb was correct," said Spencer. "You *do* have a keen imagination."

Farther down the docks, Spencer could hear a bell's anxious chime and the cries of a fire brigade, too late now to do much more than pour water on a smoking foundation. "Thank God we decided to run when we—" he turned, reaching for Alix

289

to share his relief. There was nothing behind him but empty space, all the way to the warehouse.

He lunged for the freight door, circled now by a hungry wreath of flame. He was an arm's length away when it slammed shut. A rusted latch thudded from the inside while he gripped its iron handle, pulling fruitlessly. Panic gripped him. "Alexandra!" He drove a boot into the stout planks, ignoring chunks of burning wood that seared his hands and face. "Alexandra!"

Why had he run out ahead of her? A distant, rational voice reminded him that they hadn't known that the army was waiting outside, and that sending Alix out into two groups of hostile, armed men would not have improved matters. He'd made a split-second decision, and it had been wrong. If she was hurt, or worse…

Those were thoughts of his *rational* mind. His primal, animal mind, the one in charge now, hungered to maim, squeeze, crush. He fought the door, channeling his anger and fear into every wild kick.

Ty's hand gripped his coat. He expected the major to try and stop him, and started to wrestle away until Ty waved a hand. "Around the side!" Splitting the air with a whistle, Ty swirled his hand at soldiers. "Keep working on this goddamn door!"

CHAPTER THIRTY-FIVE

Alix writhed against the dirt, struggling to pull air into starving lungs.

That damned walking stick. She had recognized its shape hooking her ankle a split second too late. It hadn't occurred to her that Silas would have the cunning, the guts to lie in wait. She'd counted on his sense of self-preservation to take him away from the fray, but obviously his hatred had won out.

Silas had closed and locked the door. Outside, men beat at it violently, making no real headway. It was solid oak, and she didn't believe them capable of budging it. Worse, the efforts of their shoulders brought down more searing ash, leaving her no choice but to get up and move further into the burning building, struggling to conceal her pistol in the folds of her coat.

Silas smirked at her, back to the door, and knocked two sets of crates with his walking stick, crates set at an angle to the exit. "I realized I didn't need his pages." Silas tipped his cane to her chest, menacing her with its silver lion, a pistol dangling from his other hand. "I have the means to craft more."

Spencer was safe; she would sign anything now, anything he wanted. The contract would be a short lived one, when her husband finally caught him. "You can have it, if you let me go. Open the door; I'll sign all the pages you want."

A *whoosh* seared her back, sucking air from the room and leaving her face and hands hot and dry. Timbers popped, and smoke invaded their small pocket.

"And all those soldiers outside will let us go?" He shook his head. "I'm no fool."

"Us?"

"Yes, us! You authorized the sale of Paton's ships to French spies. I have half the evidence and DuFresne has the other." Cold dark eyes caught the flames rising behind her, demonic.

"Tell them whatever you like. You'll still hang, and like Paulina, it's better than you deserve."

His scream was a reeking cloud of hot breath propelling unintelligible words into her face. "She never betrayed me! Never," he panted. "She kept you and your imbecile brother obedient. Managed the books. She did precisely what I told her with the poisons. I forgive her." He slumped, eyes half closed as though he would fall asleep. "For getting herself caught. I forgive her now. Your father, *he* betrayed me." Silas's eyes snapped open, voice rasping at the smoke. "I have never forgiven him. His enterprise, his seed." He leaned into her face again, eyes wild, whispering through trembling lips. "I had to be patient though, so patient. Your sisters were the only ones who ate the cakes, you see. But that was all right. I decided you could wait, could be of use before I took care of you."

Sisters? Despite the inferno, her body and mind went calm, all emotion but one evaporating. His words were a string, a tripwire, closing the world to anything but hatred. They snapped up her arm, drew back her finger. Powder smoke stung her cuts and burned in her nose before Alexandra comprehended that his face was gone, some of it now painting hers. His lifeless body fell to its knees, then the floor. Crimson pooled from shattered bits matted in his wiry hair, soaking the dirt.

Nothing came to her, no emotion touched her as she stood over the man who had terrorized her and ruined so many lives. She worried for her baby, harmed by the poisons they'd forced into her. She thought of Chas, reduced to a shell of a man. Even Paulina, whose only crime, at first, was that she'd been born to the monster lying lifeless now before her. And she thought of herself, and Spencer, and the wonder they'd found in each other, almost snuffed out. At what she'd been forced to do to survive. Grief gripped her heart, at what Silas had done to her family, and what he'd forced her to do.

Grief, and rage.

She jerked the walking stick out from under his bulbous frame, raising it high with every intention of smashing what remained of his skull. She stood there a moment, frozen. First in a trickle, then a flood, Alix recalled where she was. That the tears trickling her cheeks were more from the smoke than anything else now, that the warehouse rocked and caved behind her. A fluttering in her belly, faint and maybe even borne of desperate imagination, reminded her of what was at stake, insisting that it was time to go. She brought the lacquered wood down onto her knee, snapping it in two and throwing them atop Silas's corpse.

Flames raced over the door. Thoughtless and desperate now, she grabbed the iron bale, crying out and pulling her scalded fingers away. Alix wriggled from her coat, wrapping both hands in its plush fabric, and grasped the lock. It scraped, then stuck, refusing to budge in either direction. Heated metal had expanded against itself, and there was no way to open it. Coughing violently as flaming roof fell in against the sidewalls, Alix searched the fire-lit room for another exit and refused to accept a growing truth: she was trapped.

*   *   *

He raced ahead of Ty, along the warehouse's north side. They tugged coats up over their heads against a rain of ash and hot soot. The roar of flames was deafening, and something exploded inside the warehouse, cargo or a crumbling section of its roof. Ty propped a ladder they'd scrounged beneath a lone section of wall nearly halfway down, where flames licking through the eaves had yet to spread lower.

Toes braced for all he was worth on the ladder's top rung, Spencer leaned into the window. Sucking in a breath, he pulled back, hacking at smoke and seared lungs, face burning from the inferno inside. "Alexandra!" he cried, forcing himself to lean further.

"Spencer! I'm here!"

His heart stopped at the sound of her voice, relief a torrent in his mind. "Alix, get up on these crates! Hurry!" Planks against his chest creaked and began to buckle. Ty, steadying the

293

base of the ladder, called out a warning. "Make time, Reed! We have flames at the ground."

"I can't see you!" called Alix, voice sounding farther away than before.

"This way! Keep coming! Feel for the draft!" He kept calling out instructions, encouragement; anything to lead her through the smoke. At last, there was a stomping sound below, punctuated by worryingly harsh coughing. "Climb as high as you can," he ordered, peering through the haze.

"The crates are on fire!" her words were desperate.

He leaned further through the window, risking buckling wood. "Climb as fast as you can!"

The top of her head appeared, and she looked up at him. Time froze for a second as he took her in, her beautiful face spattered with blood from her from neck to hairline. Black bits clung to her cheek and temple. She was alive, and she was *here*. Still, his relief was tempered by fear. "Are you hurt?"

"No," she panted, wiping a path through blood and soot with her sleeve. "No, just pull me up."

"Both hands." He leaned in as far as he dared, already precarious on the rickety ladder. He grasped her wrists, praying his dry hands would compensate for her wet ones. "Push off as hard as you can on three." The warehouse shook. "Never mind, go!"

She pushed hard with her legs and inertia got her over the sill to the waist, but at that point her belly halted progress. She turned sideways and he moved down a rung, pulling. He repeated the process over an achingly long expanse of the ladder until Alexandra could finally swing her legs around and follow him down.

The walls heaved. A gust rushed past them and fire belched from the window above. Ty's hand pressed his shoulder and they ran for the wharf, his hand in Alexandra's. He wasn't sure he'd let go for a long, long time.

Out front, the fire brigade ran buckets to and from the river, lobbing pail after pail on a hopelessly blazing warehouse that was imploding faster by the second. Across the way, soldiers were prodding off the last of DuFresne's men.

Ty gripped Alexandra's arm. "Van der Verre?"

Her face hardened in a way Spencer had never seen, not even when discussing Paulina. For a moment it seemed she would remain silent, but then her expression softened, and she simply looked exhausted. "Not enough left to go in for, if that's what you're asking."

Ty's nod was grim, and Spencer caught the pat-pat of Ty's hand on her back. "No DuFresne, either. Though I have a feeling I'll be seeing him again." Then he tipped his chin at shadows past them down the docks. "Here he is."

Ethan materialized from the darkness, a face between black hat and coat, eyes piercing the activity around him.

Spencer brushed knuckles over Alexandra's cheek. "We have words with each other. Wait here." He released her hand, breaking the promise to himself already.

Ty, understanding that 'wait here' meant 'don't follow,' took Alix gently by the arm and led her towards fresh air near the river while she barked out a ragged cough.

Ethan tipped his hat. "Reed. Glad to see all's well."

"I've a mind to cock you here and now, Grayfield."

Ethan removed his hat entirely. "Then do so. I want no hard feelings between us."

Spencer relaxed his fist, swatting the air, mindful of all Ethan had done since the trial. "How long did you know? Tilton waiting on the street, Burrell conveniently at hand when he is never made available by Whitehall. Do me the courtesy of at least telling me how long you were planning this."

Sighing, Ethan moved to a stone ledge bordering a narrow jetty, sat, and placed his hat just so atop the wall. "When you came to me with accusations against Mrs. Paton, naturally I began to dig. *Always digging.*" He shrugged at the phrase, tacit acknowledgment that it had stuck of late. "I kept that up until I found what you'd asked for. And then, as is my wont, I continued. It was mentioned to John that Paulina handled many of the documents for both companies, but Charles Paton's name was on the scant few papers they'd produced since they'd arrived in England. They were meaningless papers, too. He has a terrible head for business."

"Hm." Temper simmering, he joined Ethan on the wall, watching men stab down the warehouse with their pikes.

295

"Isn't it odd that such a controlling woman allowed her husband to take the reins, and then for him to do so little?"

He began to comprehend. "Silas had already made arrangements with DuFresne."

Ethan smacked his thigh with a gloved hand. "So he had. A deal with the enemies of a free France. And for an obscene amount of money, too. Silas kept Chas Paton occupied, too busy to note larger dealings, and believing that a sudden increase in revenue was nothing more than the fruits of his labor here in England." Ethan made an airy whistle between pursed lips. "Silas would take on Paton's sleek new ships, and sell Van der Verre's old hulks to the revolutionaries. Dutch merchant ships trolling up and down the European coastline. Who would bat an eye?"

"Trolling doing what, exactly?"

A shrug. "Let's say 'information', and keep it at that."

He gave up prying for anything but bland details from Ethan. "Paton & Son would cease to exist. Chas and Alexandra would lose their shares and their father's company."

"And then he would kill them. The papers were in Paulina's dressing room, along with her poisoning schedule for Alexandra."

"Just laid out like a dinner menu?"

Ethan huffed a laugh. "No. Encrypted, God bless her, and with an old French code. Clearly she had no idea who would be searching her rooms."

Something still dug at him, something he could not let rest. "I'm still not clear on you using my wife as bait for Van der Verre."

"He wrote Paulina during the trial, making it clear he was coming to England. He seemed to think Lawrence would stall and that he could buy Symonds. That she would still be here and he could coach her."

"And?"

"And my men never saw him arrive, or take lodgings. It wasn't even he who claimed Paulina's body. But I knew he was here by the movement of others around him, like ripples in a pond. A female acquaintance of DuFresne's arrived in town, a countess from Germany. Merchant sailors with French accents

296

who didn't seem to belong to any particular vessel milling about in random places. Chas Paton went to ground and he couldn't be flushed out."

He understood now, but his simmering anger hadn't cooled at the realization. "And you knew from the documents I gave you that Silas would need Alexandra to close the deal he'd made. I still don't see why you couldn't at least tell me."

"I think you do, Spencer." Ethan stood and claimed his hat. "You know that is just not how my business is transacted." He placed his hat back atop his head. "God save the king."

Cryptic son of a bitch. He had come to blows with Bennet over less, but Ethan was not the sort of man one crossed so easily.

Spencer stood and offered Ethan his hand. "A decade of friendship can weather a great deal. Even so, don't use my wife again."

"Would it comfort you to know that I had a man on her almost the whole time? His only error was intervening when Chas accosted her outside the drapers. My agent assumed that she was safe once inside the carriage."

"Would it comfort *you*, if I said the same of Sofie?"

"Not a bit," admitted Ethan.

"It does not comfort me, either."

Ethan's nod was slight and grim, promising nothing. Spencer chose to take his silence instead. Glancing at Alix, huddled inside Ty's coat, something came to him. "You said Chas couldn't be flushed out."

Ethan followed his gaze. "Not at first, but with time. Turns out he's susceptible to pretty blondes, and I have such a one in my employ. He was cooperative, played his part in my shadow theater in exchange for a sort of immunity. I felt like an absolute cad, having to break that his wife effectively sold him to the French."

He cocked his head at Alix. "She's going to ask."

"He's shipboard. On his way home to America with fifty-percent stake in Paton shipping. Van der Verre's portion is all forfeit, but I imagine Chas is glad to see it go. What he does now is his affair, not mine."

297

"A man! Sir, we have a man here!" Shouts rose from the fire brigade, a member rushing out through his comrades as they pushed water through the building's front to the embers still cooking inside. In the distance, he saw his wife's face snap up at the words.

"Silas," offered Spencer. "Alix said she left him inside."

Ethan's mouth set in a grim line. "Let's go and see, shall we?"

Spencer moved with Ethan around the building, sparing a glance for Alexandra as he passed. She was still staring into the dark maw of the warehouse's door, her expression unreadable.

A sudden weariness descended over him. His time with Alix at the cottage felt like a lifetime ago. The poisoning, the trial, and now this. If not for their wedding, he would think the last few months were some nightmare from which he could not wake.

He drew on the last of his reserves and turned back the warehouse.

One thing left to do.

He had seen men burned on the battlefield. It wasn't anything new or even particularly disturbing, at this point. This body was the same: no hair, clothing gray and crumbling, charred and dusty where dousing water had failed to wash the ash. Fat oozed, giving Silas's corpse the appearance of a scorched and melting sugar confection.

"Roll it over," instructed Ethan, waving to a man with a pike pole hovering outside the wall.

It took a joint effort between his tool and his boot heel, and a fair amount of grunting, before the blackened remains would turn.

He had been prepared for a lot of things, but not the cavernous hole where Silas's eye and forehead should have been. It was a strange mix of feeling: fierce pride in his wife's courage and sorrow at what she'd had to do.

Ethan took a step in, toeing a trigger guard and lock still clutching smoldering wood. "I would see to your lady, Reed."

He couldn't reply, couldn't even manage a laugh. He could only imagine the desperation which had brought Alexandra to that moment, and what it must be doing to her now. "I'm taking my wife home, Grayfield. If you need me, find me there."

*   *   *

Alix scrubbed away the last traces of tears from her eyes and nestled further back into Spencer beneath the quilt. He had held her, gentled her silently through each storm: her fear, her relief, her remorse. Her anger, that she could never truly unsee what she had done at the warehouse.

Now he pressed a handkerchief into her hand and slipped his arms fully around her. "What do you want, Alexandra?" he whispered, smoothing her hair. "Ask it of me. I will grant you anything within my power."

She didn't have to think about it, not for a moment. "I want to go away."

"To Oakvale?" asked Spencer.

"No."

"Home, to New York?"

"Oakvale is my home now, but no. Not New York. Some place far from here, not tainted by Silas or Paulina. I want to forget before I hate England altogether."

"You shall have it," he promised, just as he had on their carriage ride back from Amelia Grey's.

And so, she believed him.

CHAPTER THIRTY-SIX

Paris – March 4th, 1815

Spencer jerked upright, ripped from sleep, rubbing burning eyes and not immediately certain where he was.

"Did you hear me?" Alexandra grasped his thigh harder. "It's *time*."

"It's *time*, or it's time like the last four 'times'?" he grumbled, adjusting his pillow to settle back down.

"My waters have broken, Spencer. It's time."

"Oh!" He came off the bed tangled in a quilt, nearly falling into the wall. "God, Alexandra, why didn't you say so?"

A small hand whacked his shoulder. "I did! 'Spencer, wake up. It's time'."

He grabbed his watch from the nightstand, squinting. Four minutes past seven. "What's all that commotion outside?"

Alix frowned at noise equal to midday and shrugged. "I have no idea. I've been a bit preoccupied."

"What do I do?" He shouted to her from inside the wardrobe, grabbing garments he had no business taking down from the shelves. He looked to his hands, realizing he was holding two waistcoats and Alexandra's stays. He sighed. *Calm down.* "Should I have Mrs. Devereaux boil water?"

"If she intends to make me tea with it. And send Dorothea, to help me make up the bed. Ooh!"

"What, what?" He darted out, shoving shirt tails into his breeches.

Alix hunched beside the bed, a hand to her belly and a sheet wadded between her knees. "Will you go?" She swatted a

300

hand at him, laughing. "Go fetch Doctor Marceau and leave me some shreds of dignity."

He managed one arm into his coat, pressing a kiss to her temple. "Behave yourself until I get back. It won't be long."

He tore down the staircase and outside, obliged to come back twice in order to get the door fully closed.

Reaching the street, Spencer was forced to swallow his last words to Alix. People churned from the lanes, their faces unreadable. The crowd's noise wasn't joy or displeasure, just random chaos. He stopped a threadbare boy running for the corner with a stack of leaflets tucked beneath a skinny arm. "Is it a holiday? What is all this commotion?"

The boy shook his head, opened and closed his mouth, then smacked a handbill into Spencer's palm, dodging back into a sea of people. Its headline froze him in place:

'Napoleon quits Elba – Marches from Lyons with a force of thousands.'

He read the whole thing twice to be certain, feeling the same expression on his face as that of the people around him: disbelief and a touch of horror mixed with resignation. Like the citizens of Paris, he had faced the emperor countless times before. All they could do was to keep pushing back.

But not today, he resolved, stuffing the bill into his coat. He and the emperor would have an appointment soon enough. Today belonged to him and Alexandra.

He elbowed through the crush of bodies packed between the street's row of limestone houses, convinced that whichever way he was going, they were headed opposite en masse. Flags waved from iron balconies overhead, causing a handful of people to stop in front of him every few feet, to cheer or boo depending on the colors. A glimpse of his watch at each corner confirmed his snail's pace. He prayed for a little more speed coming back with the doctor in tow.

At Rue Vivienne a flower stall had been upended in the chaos, blocking the sidewalk and in turn, the street. Pedestrians teemed around it like a river, blocking wagons and carriages. He missed Doctor Marceau's house numbers three times, pushed along or blocked by the riot.

How many times did he have to knock? Spencer stepped back, watching the house's narrow whitewashed face for any sign of movement in the windows. He'd keep going until paint chipped from its weathered black door, he decided, hammering again.

Finally, a lock scraped and it slowly opened. A woman stabbed him with dark, narrowed eyes, enough haughtiness in her gaze to make it clear *she* did not normally answer the door. A carefully pinned silver bun had been reduced to wild wisps, and her black dress and crisp white apron were at opposing angles, as though she'd been chasing something through the house.

"Doctor Marceau?" At a loss, it was all he could manage.

Anger pulled some of the wrinkles from her face. "He has patients!"

"And I am one of them! Or, rather, my wife. Lady Reed."

"Oh, oh!" The housekeeper slumped, bracing herself against the frame. "It's madness today, monsieur. Half the staff has given notice, run right out! The rest are drunk and –" Her words were prophetic, a crash rattling from a staircase behind her, and she winced. Then she drooped, sympathetic. "Here, I will give you his next three appointments. Perhaps you can catch him somewhere in between."

She disappeared back into bedlam. Down the hall, shrieking began, two women and a man assaulting each other in French. It continued growing louder, to the point where he readied himself to interfere. Finally one, the housekeeper he guessed, shouted the others down under what sounded like an avalanche of books.

Things were falling apart around him. Why couldn't the baby come tomorrow? He could think of nothing more comforting than fleeing the city.

The housekeeper came back with a calling card, fanning it to dry the ink and pulling the door behind her as though afraid a dog would get out. She pressed the card into his hand. "Good day. And good luck." Before he could even thank her, she was already slipping back inside, shutting the door on him. As it closed, she muttered "good day" one more time. It slammed, a lock grated, and Spencer found himself alone outside the impromptu asylum.

Looking over the addresses she'd scribbled on the card, Spencer appreciated why the housekeeper had wished him luck. He'd traveled on foot owing to the crowd, but Doctor Marceau obviously had gone by carriage today. His appointments were some distance apart, and in several different directions from where Spencer now stood.

The second house was the closest. With a last glance to the congested streets, Spencer made up his mind to go and wait. Trying for one of the further houses would take forever, and in the confusion at street level, the doctor might pass within five feet of him and he wouldn't notice.

No one seemed aware of anyone else's existence except in trading shouts of "Vivre Libertie!" and "Vivre Emporeur!" They slapped one another with crudely made flags, pushing and jabbing with elbows. Sometimes one clung to another until they formed a small band within the mob, chanting and shoving, obliging him twice to dash onto a front step to avoid their march. They were as impoverished, as hungry, and as oppressed by the police ministry under the emperor as they had been under the king. Yet, they celebrated his return. Spencer tried to push away thoughts that these rioters were getting what they deserved.

He waited at the foot of wide steps outside a mansion seated at the foot of the Rue des Jardins. It was one of the last grand residences holding on to a time before the revolution. Sculptures sat in the dooryard, and gold gilt shone on its high iron fence. Wide stone balustrades framed balconies that had supported the last public appearances of exiled and beheaded. He wondered who lived there, that they had escaped a fate that others had not.

A lad ran from the house, so absorbed wrestling his hat that if Spencer hadn't seen him they would have collided. Bracing his shoulder to prevent their impact, Spencer realized he was easily twenty. Thin and lanky, he wore a practical blue coat and plain brown nankeen trousers. Spencer spotted a horse hitched near the gate. *A courier.*

Spencer rose his hand and the courier slowed but did not stop. "Doctor Marceau, has he been here this morning?" he asked quickly, before the messenger could pass.

Already pulling away, loping across the yard, the lad clasped his hat atop a shaking head. "Monsieur has died, in the night. Doctor Marceau was told not to come."

Spencer rubbed the bridge of his nose and swallowed a mouthful of profanity. Now there was no telling where to find him. His third patient might have moved up the ranks, or down. Their house was too far across the city, either way, for him to take the risk.

"Wait!" He waved to the courier, just wheeling his horse out onto the street. Running up to him, he rummaged in his trousers for some money. "Name me another doctor who lives close. One near Place de l'Ecole."

"Doctor Baudin, at number twelve," the man called over his shoulder.

Spencer pressed some francs into an eager palm, dodging between pedestrians ahead of the horse.

That was only a few streets over from their house, on the Quai. Doctor Baudin would be close. Spencer chafed at retracing all the distance he'd covered in search of Doctor Marceau, more convinced than ever that the crowd was against him. And always, in the back of his mind, images of Alix, waiting. Pushing between two revelers, he redoubled his pace.

Spying the doctor's door, he loped up the steps and slammed the knocker down two passes, losing a third when the door was wrenched out of reach.

"Monsieur," sighed the butler, white gloves curved halfway into fists. "Doctor Baudin is out. He will *be* out. As you will have observed, there is… *drame*. His many clients are suffering all manner of complaints, owing to the news."

No. No, this was not happening. He had no patience for fluttering and fainting spells. "Where!" demanded Spencer.

"*Out.*"

He smacked a palm into the closing door. "*Where?* I am prepared to pay."

The butler smirked, patting a neat sweep of dark hair. "Monsieur, so is everyone else." A slam cut the rest of their conversation violently off.

Spencer dug the watch from his waistcoat, wondering how long he'd been gone. *Three hours.* He fumbled it back into his pocket, swearing, wiping beaded sweat from his hatband. How had he lost track? He turned and ran for the street, generous with a boot or an elbow for any who chose not to move from his path.

He briefly toyed with the idea of trying to find a third doctor, and just as quickly dismissed it. He had a sinking feeling that no matter how many he sought out, the situation would be the same.

Best to go back to Alexandra; she must be going mad by now and he was bringing only bad news.

CHAPTER THIRTY-SEVEN

They were leaving. Quitting. Her first clue had been the hurried French exchanges she didn't understand which carried through the house. Then, Mathilde had demanded their week's wages in halting English. Lastly, it was the absolute silence in the house after the downstairs door had opened and closed several times.

Alexandra had managed the bedding by herself, following Kate's neatly printed instructions, and risked the three sets of stairs down to the kitchen to set water boiling. As she worked, the first real, breath-stealing contraction had hit her and made her nervous. After negotiating herself back to the bed on trembling legs, Alix didn't dare make the trek again. The baby would just have to come before the pot boiled dry and the house caught on fire.

A first baby would be long in coming, Doctor Marceau had assured her. Perhaps that was why he and Spencer were taking the scenic route back. The joke was on both men; she arched against the headboard breathing through an ache that gripped her back to front. Just a hair over three hours and she was feeling the first faint urge to push.

This time, when the door opened and closed, she knew it was Spencer. It shuddered in its frame and boots pounded in the hall. "Alexandra!"

"I'm here. I'm all right." She held out a hand for him to take, ready when he dashed in. His fingers were cold around her own.

Spencer half turned, glancing around them. "Where is everyone?"

"I'm *alone*. Everyone has gone."

"Bastards." He buried his face in a palm. "This cannot be."

She craned her neck to see out the door. "Where is Doctor Marceau?"

He looked to her, his eyes haggard. "I'm sorry, Alix."

"Is *anyone* coming?"

He stroked her cheek. "It's just you and me."

Doubling up, she writhed under the grip of another contraction, its cramps stealing her breath. They had progressed rapidly from high and dull to sharp waves which had made it impossible to do more than pant out the brief period in between. She dabbed at sweat along her temples, scrubbing damp hair with the sleeve of her shift. When it was done, Spencer sat her up, climbed onto the bed behind her and cradled her against the heartbeat thudding in his chest.

"We're together," he murmured, resting a hand over her belly. "We're not going to worry. We can manage through this, Alexandra."

His words gave her courage, but she had only a moment to appreciate it. She was tightening already beneath his fingers, starting at the navel, a slow, downward pressure that crested in thoughtless sensation. Everything between her legs began to burn. Gasps subsided and she searched for his hand. "We don't have *time* to worry."

He stiffened at her back. "Not yet..."

She didn't want to talk, to explain the urgent pushing which made her hips feel too wide. "Mmhm."

Spencer was on his feet, fussing at her pillows, pacing. "What do we do?"

"Water, in the kitchen. Clean your hands?"

"Right, yes! Water."

She loved him, but Alix was glad to have him gone for the next contraction. She wanted to be alone, to shut the door and close out noise from the street. *"Aaahhhh!"* The cry tore from her gut, borne of sensation too intense to even be pain, just need.

"Oh, God, I'm coming up!" Something clattered and Spencer's voice echoed from far away, deep inside the house and outside her mind. Everything was outside her now. Breaths came faster. Alix twisted fingers into the sheet beneath her backside, bracing. Don't panic, she'd repeated, but she *was* panicking now. Pain, pressure, aching all built to an edge slicing through her resolve. A cry on her lips evolved into Spencer's name.

"I'm here, I'm here. Move down the bed."

His instructions penetrated, but there was no complying. Bearing down, she arched from the pillows and pushed despite her fear, against her will.

"Alix, you have to slide down!"

"Mmmmph!" Glaring at him, she ground teeth into her lip until she registered a salty taste. Stout fingers grabbed her knees, dragged her over the sheet. She hated him for even that slight interference and was grateful he'd taken charge.

It was just in time, she was certain. Flesh between her legs prickled, swollen and numb. He slid her shift to her belly, the room's air cooling sweat that had built beneath the fabric.

Spencer stroked her hip, idle and repetitive until she jerked away. He spoke, shushed her, asked if she was all right again and again.

"Shh! Don't ask me. Don't…" Muscles laced across her back, the tension ratcheting in unison with her belly. She couldn't last through another one. "I can't," she muttered, fullness between her thighs beginning to tear. "Spencer, I can't."

His fingers squeezed hers with a painful pressure. "Yes, you *can*. You can, and you will *right now*."

She dug heels into the bed, shaking her head, strung too taut to answer.

"Do you hear me, Alexandra? Now!"

Pain, frustration; pure annoyance at his goading; she doubled up and pushed.

*   *   *

Watching Alix cry out and strain, Spencer wished he had some definition of normal where childbirth was concerned. He knew that some blood was normal, but a great deal of blood was not. That was the *sum total* of his knowledge, and he had no idea if crimson spotting the sheet now was excessive.

He breathed deep against a pounding heart. Alix would push, and a baby would deliver. That's how it should go, and if it

308

didn't, he had no idea how to go on. Not that he would or could be so rational just now. He couldn't help her, comfort her; could just keep watch until something did, or did not happen.

He was spared worrying about it a moment later when Alix grabbed her knees and gave a low animal groan. Something *was* happening. Her next push came on top of the first, and without warning a head fell into his waiting palms. White and waxy, it was instantly the most beautiful thing he'd ever seen. Alix collapsed against the mattress, but he hardly noticed. Tightening in his throat choked out tears he hadn't sensed coming. "Push," he whispered, then louder when the baby lay still in his hands. "Push Alexandra!"

"I am!"

"Harder!"

"Turn!" she screamed, "Turn!"

It didn't register at first, and then he realized. Gripping a tiny shoulder, he folded and pressed until its mate was unstuck. Blood and fluid rushed out in a pungent, briny flood, and his baby slipped into the world.

He held the baby away, under its head and beneath a tiny buttock, frozen for a moment. "Oh, God. Alexandra." It was fragile and awkward; he didn't dare put it down, or bring it close. He could only hold it in his hands, waiting for some movement. Any movement.

Limp and panting, Alix managed up onto shaking elbows. Her eyes were wide, and he knew her worry matched his. Childbirth was a thing fraught with risk, and hers more than most. They sat that way a moment in awful prayer.

And then, their baby twitched, sputtered out a hacking cough, and wailed.

The rest came naturally, bending his arm and cradling its small unwieldy body. His heart pounded, and he thumbed at a mewling, wrinkled face. He took it all in; a whorl of dark hair, stout little limbs clenching angrily, and a tiny mouth wide in protest. Spencer knew he couldn't have let go for anything less than Alexandra's eager arms. He rested their baby on her belly, already aching at their distance.

She wiped tears with a sleeve, shushing through a smile. With a finger she pried tiny legs apart. "It's a boy, Spencer," she breathed, cradling the baby's head. "It's our boy."

He pressed a hand half over Alexandra, half over their son's narrow back, aching at how beautiful they were together.

"Fingers and toes," she managed in a ragged whisper. "He's all here."

Spencer stared down at his hands, fingers splayed, taking in the blood. Panic of hours before was forgotten, and he gave silent thanks that Doctor Marceau had been nowhere to be found. "What do we do about…" He pointed to the cord, still draping a tiny leg.

"Cut it? Kate said the rest would mostly take care of itself."

"I'll get shears and a cloth and–"

"Come and sit," she whispered, patting the bed, nuzzling their baby. "We'll worry about all that in a moment. Just come and sit."

Heart filled to bursting, he did.

*   *   *

"What was your father's name?"

Alix winced at the hot water, then made a face. "Charles." She loved her father, but had no desire to name their son after him.

"Hm."

"Exactly. Bennet?"

"Don't tempt fate." Spencer had sorted out the bed, and he now sat against the headboard, cradling their sleeping baby to his chest. From time to time, he brushed his lips absently over the tuft of brown hair. Tears threatened every time she paused to take the pair in.

She'd been ready to give up, at the end. She'd been close. And then, like magic, it was over. She was sore, and exhausted, but the trade was worthwhile. More than ready to take her baby, she grasped the washtub to stand.

"No!" Spencer was forceful, startling her, but he settled the baby with a gentle hand. "Don't get up. Wait for me."

310

She opened her mouth to argue, and then stopped. She could get up on her own, of course. Alix smiled; she didn't need to point it out.

Up, dried off and in a clean shift, Spencer settled her with military efficiency. He was a little rough, but very sweet, and he got the job done. When he tried to lift her, though, Alix had to draw the line. "Just walk me to the bed," she negotiated. "I'm too pulped to be carted around."

He got her up onto the mattress where she scooted as far as she could manage, then claimed her little bundle, cradling him close. His sleeping breaths were a tiny purr, heat seeping through his blanket and into the skin of her chest. "He's so…" She didn't have words for the way he filled her heart.

A pounding at the front door interrupted her thoughts, and Spencer started up from the mattress. The door banged open. "Lord Reed?"

She recognized the voice, but could hardly believe it. "Miss Foster! We're upstairs!"

Heavy leather soles raced the steps and Kate appeared a moment later, flushed, all her clothes in disarray. A glance between them, and she grinned. "Major Ford caught me at the coach stop on my way back to the garrison and said he'd seen you running up the avenue like a madman. I assumed it must be time."

Alix bit her lip at that image of Spencer, and patted the bed beside her. Kate settled, peering over her shoulder. "He's beautiful, you two. Well done." She pressed Spencer's arm. "And credit to you for helping him along. I would have been here sooner, but this riot is impossible."

"Riot?" It occurred to Alix that the noise outside had not diminished all day.

There was a look exchanged between Spencer and Kate that stole some of her happiness, and he moved to sit on her other side. "Alexandra, we've had our good news for the day. Now for our bad news…"

CHAPTER THIRTY-EIGHT

Haywood Parish, England – July 26th, 1815

As the cart rumbled away, Alexandra shaded her eyes and squinted at her mountain of provisions against the early afternoon sun. It would occupy a few hours, storing it all away. Caught between the chance for a brief but welcome distraction and the daily agitation which made it nearly impossible to focus on any one thing, she sighed and settled on checking a small bundle of letters that sat atop one of the barrels.

Spencer had been at war for thirteen weeks, and apart from her for four months, two weeks, and three days. Even when the army stopped moving and his letters were something resembling frequent, it wasn't enough. She hoped there would be a note today, even a short one; in her wildest dreams, it would say that he was finally coming home.

The cottage's front room was bathed in cool shade, the sun just low enough to tease through the windows. Slipping into the rocking chair, she was content with the decision to leave the supplies for now. Glancing about, she felt the familiar loneliness that had been her constant companion over the last months.

Miles stirred in his cradle, turning his sable head left and right. Alexandra tipped the rail with one hand, rocking him, drawing coarse brown twine from her letters with the other. By the time she had worked out the knot, he was sound asleep.

First, she checked the casualty lists. Copies sent up from London were at least two weeks out of date, but every page where Spencer's name did not appear was good enough, no matter the currency. There was only so much worry she could manage to worry over. Skipping from 'Redding' to 'Reese', she exhaled and happily tossed the sheet into the fireplace. One more down.

The first two pieces of mail were clearly intended for Spencer; she shuffled them to the back. A third envelope stayed her hand:

'Mister Thomas Meacham, Able Solicitor'

It wasn't the name which gave her pause. Word came now and then from her father's attorney; the confiscation of Van der Vere property and the untangling of Paton shipping had required her attention more than once. It was the thick black border, enclosing the sender's information with an ominous rectangle, which set her heart to thudding like a mourning bell. Its contents would not yield glad tidings.

Trembling fingers pinched, and losing her nerve, Alix moved it behind the other envelopes. But it was there, its paper rough and thickness insistent against her hand.

She struggled to recall the information in Spencer's last letter. It had come late June, weeks after the battle at a small village called Waterloo, and his handwriting on the envelope had collapsed her onto the steps in relief. His message had been less comforting. They would push south to Paris and on towards Spain in pursuit of fleeing French regiments, and try to recover Bennet and his Portuguese guerillas. He feared heavy opposition from soldiers and citizens alike.

Unable to ignore it any longer, she brought the ominous letter back to the front. It was better to know. If Spencer was…
No. She wouldn't think about that, not when the letter could be so many things.

She raised the envelope, which felt heavier now, trying one last time to divine its brand of bad news. Resting both thumbs against the black wax seal, she snapped it with violence and folded back the paper. She skimmed for a name, then skimmed again, eyes finding it at last in Meacham's upright lettering.

At first, nothing came. The world suspended, without the ticking of the clock or even a breeze rushing outside to signal that time continued. Tears pricking her eyes set all things in motion once more.

313

She abandoned Meacham's letter, its pages drifting from her lap to the floorboards in a whisper while she collected Miles from his bed. Draping his warm little body over her shoulder, she patted away his sleepy protests, heart aching harder than she'd thought possible. "For all his faults," she whispered, kissing the downy hair behind his ear, "I think your uncle would have loved you."

She had put away her love for Chas, any feelings she had for him too twined with memories of Silas and Paulina, and his servitude to them, to acknowledge. Now, as her tears wicked hot into Miles' linen gown, Alexandra regretted that there had always been a distance between them, sorrow that it would never be mended descending on her. A guilty shiver up her back whispered that there could have been no other outcome, sending Chas home alone with nothing but his shame.

Cradling Miles' now-sleeping body against her chest, Alexandra realized that it hadn't mattered. Chas could have taken his own life as easily in London, or any other place. If she had failed to reach him during Paulina's reign, there would have been no getting through to him after when he was in an even darker place. Still, she ached for his suffering. The tears would come in earnest, later. She felt them under the constant dull ache which gripped her chest now, trapping them from reaching her eyes as more than a dampness just now.

More grateful than she had been a half hour earlier for some work to distract her, Alexandra abandoned the rest of the mail. Melancholy, she bundled Miles outside to be close while she worked, settling him on the yellow quilt Spencer had bought her in Oakvale. She pressed a hand to her aching forehead and studied the dry goods, a fist on her hips. Sighing, she picked a starting spot.

One crate at a time, Alexandra kept her heart distracted.

*   *   *

Hours later, a cart rumbled up the long, pitted drive while Alexandra wrestled the lid from a barrel of flour. Mrs. MacGreavy at the general store must have realized, at about the same time she had, that the little blue tin of salt was missing from her order. Finally gaining some leverage with a knee and both arms, she went on wrestling, content to let the driver bring it in.

Predictably, Miles began to cry just when she felt certain of success. The cart's lumbering faded off into the distance again, and there was no appearance of a driver or salt. Gripped by curiosity, she admitted defeat and headed out front.

No blue tin awaited her on the step or atop the remaining pile of dry goods. She collected Miles, shushing him to a plaintive hiccup, and shaded her eyes against late day sun to see if the cart had driven away or further up the path to turn around.

The cart was nowhere in sight, but movement caught her eye, and it took her a long moment to make out a silhouette just passing the low stone wall, its shape swallowed by the sea's blue backdrop.

Alexandra chuckled to herself and worked Miles' stout little legs around her hip. The cottage's long drive was hardly more than a trail, having seen more use in her three months' stay than it had in the ten years before. Jagged, weathered stones punctuated its length out to the open dunes, making it treacherous to feet, saying nothing of wagon wheels. She couldn't fault the man not wishing to make the trip up and back a second time in as many days. Sympathetic, she bounced Miles higher on her hip and started out to meet the driver halfway.

It took a handful of paces and an angle which put the sun more at her back to see the man's approach as anything more than shadowed. A red hue ringed his coat now, a glow which she attributed to an aching heart and wishful thinking.

Her suspicions were confirmed a moment later. The cart's battered silvery wood came into sight, having been stopped in a low spot beneath the wall and out of sight from the cottage. *Brown*, she corrected, inspecting the man's coat and dusty walnut trousers. It was Tom; she recognized him now. He'd brought most of her supplies since April. He raised a well-worn gray felt hat when they were within speaking distance.

"Good afternoon, missus!" He stopped and rested hands on his thighs, small pants bobbing his stout frame. Then he hooked a thumb over one meaty shoulder. "Mrs. MacGreavy sent me up to say she's not forgot the salt." Straightening, he panted a moment longer. "She's sending someone 'round with it, this evening." Tom cradled his faithful hat against his chest in apology. "If that's quite convenient to you."

Alexandra laughed, bouncing Miles, who waved a tiny fist at the newcomer. Then she swept a hand around them, at the wild hillside. "I'm at my leisure at all hours, sir. Tonight will do just fine."

Tom was already backing away, nodding and putting space between them with a haste that made her wonder if her jest had offended him. But when he replaced his hat and made a little bow, there was a kind smile finishing the gesture. "Good afternoon to you, then. Good afternoon." Tom turned and lumbered back with the bobbing haste of a man who'd forgotten to put the fire out before leaving.

Shaking her head, Alexandra followed his path back to the wagon, then shrugged and turned back for the house. "Strange, wouldn't you say?" she muttered to Miles, who answered with a coo and an unsteady turn of his head left and right, wrestling to take in everything over her shoulder.

She'd been warned by Spencer, on the docks at Le Havre fleeing France, to be on guard and have a pistol close. A woman and a baby alone, even on the remote shores of Haywood, faced danger. Shivering in a late-afternoon breeze, Alexandra took a last glance behind her, finding the plume of dust from Tom's progress, watching until Miles buried his face in her neck and fussed.

"Hungry?" she asked. "So am I." She patted his back, weaving around the last of the dry goods. "Let's go in and see what can be done about it."

Busy minding her footing over clumps of sandy grass, Alexandra didn't notice the figure looming before her in the shade. She stumbled over him as he threw up an arm and caught her shoulder. She struck out blindly with her free arm, turning Miles away to shield him from the intruder. Panic welled, then dissipated when the man spoke.

"Ow!" *A low groan.* "Not the welcome I expected. But, perhaps the one I deserve."

Her lungs ached with a breath she could neither take in nor release, eyes pressed closed to hold the image of Spencer in her mind, certain he'd be gone if she opened them.

"Alexandra."

She peered slowly, catching first a band of red wool through slitted eyes, a sign which tempted her to open them completely. Her heart thundered against her ribs, pounded at her temples, and Miles protested the stiff grip of her left arm. Finally, she stepped back, and looked up.

Spencer extended an arm and shook a blue tin of salt. "Mrs. MacGreavy sent me to deliver this."

"Oh, God." It came as barely a whisper, words carried on air she released at last from her throbbing chest. She reached out trembling fingers, daring a press at his temple, tracing the familiar line of his jaw. "It's you." Tears blurred her study of him. She pressed them into her sleeve. "It really is."

He looked older, and tired, but it faded under a smile no less handsome than the one in her memories. Scabbed knuckles raked her cheek. Spencer grabbed her sleeve and hauled her to him, crushing her and pressing a confused babble from Miles.

Tears that had refused to come for Chas spilled in earnest now; joy, confusion, sorrow, and relief. "How?" she sobbed, pressing a fist into his back to keep him close.

"With haste," he quipped, a suspicious thickness to his voice, lips dotting kisses at her temple.

He smelled awful. Rotten-egg powder smoke, old blood and sweat, lathered horses practically wafted from him. Still, she wouldn't have let go for less than convincing herself that he really was there.

Alexandra pulled away at last, clutching the gritty lapel of his uniform coat and looking him over head to toe. Spencer was as dirty as he smelled, blotched with stains of every color. A telltale bullseye of dried and fading blood hinted at a wound on his thigh.

It occurred to her how long they'd been standing there, after his arduous journey home. "Inside! Go in. Sit down."

She smacked at a hand when he leaned to claim his bags, earning a chuckle, and then shooed him by a press of his shoulder.

She raked an apron out of the rocking chair, pushing Miles' cradle with her foot and balancing his little body all the while. Spencer's gentle grip on her arm gave her pause. "Here." His broad hands curved around Miles' torso, lifting him. "Go on about your business. We can manage together."

Spencer's words were for her, but his eyes, wide and bright, never left their son. "I thought he would be smaller," Spencer murmured, folding into the rocking chair.

She breathed against a sharp pang, grasping all that had changed in his absence. Claiming one of the dining chairs, she moved it in front of him and settled, taking in her matched set of chestnut-haired boys.

"Look at that," whispered Spencer, sparing her a glance while Miles gripped and pulled his broad index finger.

She went on staring, relearning him, still disbelieving and certain she'd never tire of looking at him. A hundred things came to mind, questions and stories, worries. "I've missed you," she managed at last.

"Do you know," he whispered, studying Miles, "that I am always acutely aware of your watching me?"

Her heart drummed a rapid tattoo at his words, recalled from so long ago.

A telltale bob to his adam's apple filled the silence, and then he met her eyes. "I'm not certain all the days between now and the end of time can ever mend this ache." He pressed a fist to his chest.

Leaning forward, she slipped fingers into his collar and pressed her lips to his. "I love you."

"I know that you do." He pulled away and smiled. "That is the only motivation you could have for being within arm's length just now."

Hiding a laugh behind her hand, she shook her head. "I wasn't going to say anything." She looked him over for a thousandth time, heart aching. "Are you hungry? Tired? What can I do?"

"Yes," he nodded, smiling and cradling Miles closer and feathering his downy tuft of hair. "But I don't need you to do anything more."

318

Miles writhed, arching and stuffing a tiny fist into his mouth. Spencer's brow dipped into a sweetly worried furrow. "What have I done?"

"Made him wait on supper." She reached out, pulling their baby to her chest. "He shares his father's opinions on food." Thoughtless, she unbuttoned the gusset on her dress and cradled an impatient Miles to her breast.

Spencer was on his feet, clearing his throat almost before she'd settled the baby. Alix pursed her lips to hide a smile at his averted gaze.

"Perhaps now is a good time..." He worked between her knees and his chair, body turned half away, "While you... I should clean up. Sort myself out..." His voice trailed off behind her.

She hated for him to go, and nearly snuffed his protests. Seeing him exhausted and gritty, soot- and blood-caked, she put away her selfishness. "There's a washtub against the garden wall. Fire's ready if you'd like to heat the water."

More muttering, down the hall, was muted by distance and her laughter.

*　　　*　　　*

The front room was empty by the time he'd finished. Not that he'd been hasty. He'd chafed at any separation from Alix right up until the clean, hot water had touched his skin. The unholy pleasure of something better than a frigid, cinched out rag couldn't be forsaken.

The bite of an evening breeze at sunset had finally rushed him into clean breeches, and then into the house. The chill felt bone-deep and lingering after weeks being baked by the Iberian sun. Claiming a few logs from the alcove, he built up a fire, thrilled when the wood flared, and warmed by the simplest of domestic pleasures. Taking a moment longer to toast the front and back of his hands over the crackling timber, he claimed his towel, intending to go in search of Alix. A haphazard pile of papers beside the hearth caught his attention, fluttering when he stood up. He reached down, claiming the stack of letters. Only one lay open; he skimmed its contents and swallowed, reading it

319

again carefully. She hadn't said a word, but there was no question that Alix was hurting. Tossing the letters into the chair, he sought her out.

It wasn't hard to find her; a delicious odor wafting from the kitchen hinted where to look. He stopped short in the doorway, leaned against its frame, and let the moments pass while he took her in. Her back was to him, and she moved from the fire to the butcher's block, adding something to a cast iron pot a handful at a time.

She was thinner. It wasn't the heartbreaking thinness she'd suffered at Paulina's hands, but rather a leanness to her curves earned by splitting wood, hauling water, and hefting their growing baby. If not for that, he wouldn't believe that nearly half a year had passed. Her waves were caught up in a loose knot, silky and soft. How often he'd longed to run his fingers through it while on campaign. How many nights he'd lain awake, imagining the moment he could lay eyes on her again.

Unable to resist any longer, he took a step into the kitchen, soaking up heat from the fire and buffeting the last drops of water from his shoulders.

"Food is nearly done." A smile bent her words. "Took you so long I thought I'd lost you. I half expected to find you laid out cold in the garden." She threw him a glance off her shoulder, revealing a dimple. Then she stopped stirring and turned around in earnest, and he felt a slow burn from the inside out which had nothing to do with proximity to the fire. Alexandra's gaze painted him head to toe and back. She set down her wooden spoon with a deliberateness that quickened his pulse. One dark brow furrowed, and she raked fingers, beckoning him closer. "Come here."

She met his progress at the far side of the kneading board. He braced, waited for the delicious brush of her hands after so long, but for a breath she only stared. When her fingertips did brush his chest, it was a pleasure nearing pain. Spencer sucked in a gasp and closed his eyes. Her touch marked every wound and scar, from a short line of jagged sutures at his throat to spikes of mostly healed slashes at his waistband. There her exploration paused with a questioning pressure.

"Nothing," he answered and flexed his aching thigh. "Hardly more than grazed."

A good bit more than grazed, but he had no intention of adding to her burdens.

"Hmm." He opened his eyes to a narrowed gaze, its suspicion shredding his half-truth.

"I've come through it well enough," he placated.

Her chin raised a fraction, a challenge. "*How* well?"

An ache from gut to knees nearly doubled him over. His mouth parched and he struggled to swallow. "Well enough," he repeated, taking her in and pausing over-long on full lips.

A fingernail pricked the flesh at his hip and dragged a searing line to the hollow of his throat. Warm fingers rested atop the ridge of his shoulder. Then her stomach grumbled.

Alix doubled over, half giggling, half sighing.

Catching her laughter, he pushed her away. "Curse these mortal forms. You'd best go finish before we die of starvation. I'll finish dressing."

She raised up, brushing his lips with a pressure that started the troubles all over again. "Sounds like a lot of unnecessary effort." Her teasing concluded with a sharp swat at his hip that would have settled matters then and there, had his own belly not felt inside out.

Groaning, he retreated out into the hallway under her appraisal. "I'll be back," he threatened with a grin.

Alix turned and claimed her spoon, rewarding him with a wink. "I'm depending upon it."

*   *   *

Alexandra turned onto her side, wriggling deeper into the mattress' plush down. Spencer rested against the headboard, knees drawn up to bounce Miles in his lap.

"They really aren't so difficult," he observed, clapping Miles' tiny hands together.

"Not particularly. Give them plenty of rocking and cuddling. And feeding. Beyond that, he's pleased if I narrate the wash for him."

321

"Like his father." Spencer jabbed her with an elbow, then gathered the fussing bundle of eye-rubbing to his chest and jostled.

"Precisely like his father." She rubbed his arm, then Miles' tiny foot, curling his toes.

"I remember holding him so, that first morning."

A wonderful, terrible morning, like so many days to follow.

Working herself against him, Alix buried her head in the warm crook of Spencer's arm, inhaling him. "You're home now."

There was a long pause. She could tell he was chewing over something and was content to wait until he was ready to discuss it. Finally, he cleared his throat. "Alexandra, I saw the letter. I'm sorry about Chas."

"I'm not certain how I feel," she admitted. "Sorry that he suffered so, just when he had a clear slate. But..." She swallowed, dredging up the courage to confess herself. "Is it horrible, thinking the end was inevitable?"

"I'm not certain it's right or wrong. It was just a fact. You did all you could for him. I'm sorry, too, that it wasn't enough."

"I don't know," she repeated, absorbing the depth of Spencer's words. "I'm sorry for him, but I think it will take time to miss him. The hurt will come later."

"I will be here," he promised, pressing her with his arm. "Whenever it comes. Whenever you need me."

She pushed thoughts of Chas, of Paulina and Silas from her mind, determined to do nothing more than enjoy her husband. Then, something occurred to her. "While we're on the subject of brothers, you haven't breathed a word about Bennet." She braced. "Is he...is everything...?"

"Bennet?" Spencer wriggled up the bed, grimacing with every bounce at a now-sleeping Miles. "He's alive, if that's what you mean. Hale and whole. Getting precisely what he deserves."

She raised a brow, waiting for him to elaborate while he settled Miles in his cradle in the corner.

When he turned and caught her look, he paused and shrugged. "I cannot claim to know the whole tale and could never do it justice, anyhow. If he makes it back to England in one piece, I've no doubt he'll utterly regale you."

He blew out his bedside candle, leaving them bathed in the warm amber glow of coals flickering in the grate, and slid beneath the quilt.

Alix settled on her back, hands folded over her belly. Spencer mimicked her posture, blinking up at the ceiling.

She sighed. He cleared his throat.

After a few silent moments, she shifted against the mattress. He followed suit, and she sighed again.

"Nervous?"

"Why is this so difficult?" she whispered back.

He chuckled, pinching her hip through her shift. "Would you be more at ease if we went out into the *garden*?"

"I would." She rolled up onto her arm and called his bluff. "And we'll pretend that you are a masked stranger."

"Here will do just fine," he grumbled, tumbling her back.

Alix relished the weight of his body against hers, his touch after so long. "I suppose." She brushed her lips to his. "It's a place to start."

The Author Wishes to Gratefully Acknowledge:

Kirstin 'Skeins' Boyd
The Waterloo Battlefield & Historical Site
Carol Achterkirchen, for her tireless efforts
The Household Cavalry Museum
J Caleb Design, for another fantastic cover
The Victoria & Albert Museum
Erica, and her love of the craft
The Miller Center & The Elizabeth Monroe Collection
Robin, who was there the whole way
Sandy Hoeft, for helping others build their dreams
The wonderful women of the Coeur du Bois RWA
And
Officer Barry Hetlet – A Hero to the End

Novels by Baird Wells

– The Hundred Days Series –

Vermillion
Viridian
Argent
Ash – Fall 2017
Indigo – Winter 2017

– Other Books –

The Glass Apple
An Unspeakable Anguish
The Last Woman in Weary Creek
Gretna Green – A novella